For Susan, my everything

EXPLANATORY NOTE

AS I explained at the start of the first two volumes of these memoirs, which were entitled *The Fun Factory* and *The Boxcar of Fun*, they came into my hands quite by chance.

When my wife and I moved into the house in Streatham where we have lived for twenty-odd years now, we became friendly with the elderly lady who lived in the ground floor flat next door, a Mrs Lander. One day we happened to be talking about my interest in comedy and comedians, and she said:

"Of course, my grandfather knew Charlie Chaplin."

"Really?" I said.

"Oh yes," Mrs Lander said. "They were really quite thick, apparently."

Eventually Mrs Lander moved to a residential care home, and then a few months later her daughter dropped round to tell us that sadly she had passed away.

"She wanted me to thank you for your kindness," the daughter said, "and asked me to make sure you had this."

The battered old trunk she left me – which was brown, reinforced by wooden ribs, and secured by what looked like an army belt – had been used as a repository for the memorabilia of a career treading the boards. There were wooden swords and shields, in the Roman style, and some old-fashioned football kit. There was also a big black cape, of the sort you might see a magician wearing, and a top hat, and a mechanical contraption with a couple of off-white feathers clinging to it.

Underneath all this, lying flat at the bottom of the trunk, were papers, including posters from old music hall and vaudeville bills, mostly featuring the sketches of the great Fred Karno. Tucked in amongst these charming relics were old black-and-white photographs of groups of dapper young men and fresh-faced women posing together in front of a railway carriage.

Who were they, I wondered, and what had they been doing?

I inspected the old photographs more closely. Surely that dapper young fellow with the toothy smile was Charlie Chaplin? And who was *that* one, standing over to one side, captured in an instant glowering at young Chaplin as though he would cheerfully throttle him till his eyes popped out?

Well, the answers were to be found in a brown leather satchel right at the bottom of the trunk, in the memoirs of the owner, one Arthur Dandoe, comedian.

The first volume of these, *The Fun Factory*, covered the period in which Dandoe worked for Fred Karno in the Edwardian music halls of Great Britain.

The second, *The Boxcar of Fun*, detailed Dandoe's time criss-crossing the North American continent playing the booming vaudeville circuits there for Karno.

Karno – who called himself 'the Guv'nor' – was the entrepreneur king of the British music hall. He created hugely popular and spectacular sketches with brilliant effects and enormous casts, and up to a dozen Karno companies would be touring the country at any one time, playing something from his massive repertoire. Each of these companies would operate on a strictly hierarchical basis, with a number one comic, the star, at the apex, but no name was bigger than Karno's.

Arthur joined Karno's organisation at the same time as another young hopeful called Charlie Chaplin, and both developed the same burning ambition – to rise to become the next number one comic of a Karno company.

Charlie, however, was not content to let the matter be resolved in a fair fight. He used sabotage and downright dirty tricks to undermine not only Arthur's chances of advancement but also his blossoming romance with a beautiful young actress called Tilly Beckett.

Their battle for supremacy in the world of comedy, and their rivalry for Tilly's hand, continued across the Atlantic into vaudeville, and lasted until Charlie was finally persuaded to take the plunge into moving pictures.

Now Arthur and his friend Stan Jefferson, Charlie's long-time understudy, were finally free to play without Chaplin, and all that remained was to decide who would be the new number one.

This is where the third volume – the one you are holding in your hands – begins. It covers the period from 1914 to the spring of 1918, when the golden era of American vaudeville was coming to an end, the flickers were taking over, and Charlie Chaplin was about to become the most famous man the world had ever known.

I have no reason to doubt that the memoirs represent a truthful account, and where Dandoe touches upon verifiable historical fact he is invariably accurate – considerably more so than his contemporary managed in his 1964 autobiography, at any rate. Readers can judge whether or not Dandoe is to be believed regarding more personal matters. In editing the papers, I have confined myself, more or less, to the addition of a few historical notes.

C. W. England
Streatham, December 2017

PART 1

1
THE ROOM

"**WHAT** am I doing here?"

The pale young man in the dark suit didn't answer, he just stared levelly at me across the table, the faintest suggestion of a smile on his lips.

I looked around at the room I had been held in for who knew how long. Four grey walls, no windows, except a grimy one above the door leading to the grey corridor outside. We could be in a basement, we could be on the twenty-fifth floor, there was no way of knowing.

"I said, what am I doing here? And while we are about it, where the hell *is* here?"

Again no answer, and the faint smile lingered.

"You know that ostrich was crazy, there was something wrong with it, there's no way anyone can say that was my fault," I blurted out, unsettled by the silent treatment. The young man gave a small shrug, but said nothing. I decided it was probably best if I didn't say anything else until I knew what the hell was going on, so I buttoned it.

We sat there for an awkward few minutes – or it might have been an awkward hour or two, I couldn't tell – until finally there were footsteps in the corridor outside. A jangling of keys, the door swung open, and the other dark-suited young man came in. He was smaller than his colleague, and a little on the chunky side, but he was definitely the one in charge. As he scraped a wooden seat over to the table and sat down opposite me I could hear the door being double – triple – locked from the outside.

Not good.

This fellow's first name was John. I was pretty sure I'd overheard that earlier on, but I didn't think we were on friendly enough terms for me to use it.

"He wants to know why he's here," the first guy said.

The one called John nodded, but said nothing. He opened his briefcase, a brown leather affair fastened with a brass buckle, and took out a brown folder tied with a ribbon. He slipped the knot, and withdrew a folded newspaper, which he slapped down on the table in front of me. The paper was the *Dodge City Daily Globe*, and the huge banner headline screamed at me.

CHARLIE CHAPLIN SLAIN!

"Oh," I said. "That."

"Yes, Mr Dandoe," said the one called John. "That."

Dandoe, that's my name. Arthur Dandoe. Although I hadn't used it for quite a while by the time these two sharp fellows caught up with me at Smoky Joe's on 43rd Street, must have been the evening of whatever day yesterday was. I was minding my own business and two fingers of bourbon when I heard a man's voice behind me sing out those two words.

"Arthur Dandoe!"

Before I could stop myself I had turned round like a fool to see who it was, and of course it wasn't some mate from the old country, or someone who owed me money or even a drink, it was this smug slicker, this John, smirking away like he'd pulled off some great fancy stroke.

Well, a moment later I had my arm halfway up my back, and I was being bundled unceremoniously into a dark motor van with no windows, eventually ending up here – wherever here was – apparently without any official processing or paperwork whatsoever.

It had put quite a scare into me, I don't mind telling you. The not knowing was the worst bit, and actually seeing the newspaper on the table and realising it was to do with what happened back in Dodge made me feel a little tiny bit better, because at least I could start to work out how to handle it.

I exhaled slowly. "I suppose he is quite definitely dead? There's no doubt about it?"

"Oh yes, he's dead. He's deader 'n vaudeville."

Which I thought was an unnecessary little dig. Let me see you do four-a-day, seven days a week, criss-crossing the continent for six years, and *then* I'll listen to you pronouncing on the good health or otherwise of Dame Vaudeville, Johnny boy, I thought (but didn't say).

"So," I said. "You are the police."

"No, Mr Dandoe, we are not the p-police, neither the state police of Montana, nor of the state in which we currently find ourselves. Neither are we the B-Bureau of Investigation, come to that."

"Who the hell are you then?"

"You don't n-need to know. All I will tell you is that our jurisdiction covers the whole of the United States of America, and that at this time of war our p-powers are more or less unlimited."

John rattled this out so fast it took me a moment to catch up, and when I did I quickly reckoned I didn't much like the sound of it. Even his stutter made him somehow more menacing not less.

"Meaning...?" I asked tentatively.

"We can hold you here indefinitely, we can ch-charge you, or we can return you to the bosom of your mother c-country at this her time of greatest need. It's up to you."

My mouth went dry. The threat was unmistakeable, because if ever I was forcibly deported back to England it would surely be a short step double-quick to the mincing machine of the Western Front.

"We even," John said, almost as an afterthought, "have the power to release you, if we so choose."

"All right," I said. "You got me. What do you want?"

John leaned back and steepled his fingers. "We want you to tell us about Ch-charlie Chaplin."

2
NUMBER ONE

THREE AND A HALF YEARS EARLIER.

1914 was going to be a great year. I could just feel it.

I was sitting in a window seat in the specially-appointed box-car that the Fred Karno comedy company used to criss-cross the United States. The 'Boxcar of Fun', we called it. We, the comedians, were in one half of the carriage, and all the set and costumes for our vaudeville turn, *A Night in an English Music Hall*, were packed into the other. The car was hooked onto the back of a locomotive riding the Atchison, Topeka and Santa Fe railroad from Kansas City up to its Chicago terminus, where we would be hitched onto another train heading for Philadelphia.

The reason for my optimism? Charlie Chaplin, our leading performer and the bane of my life, was gone. Gone! He'd left us to join the Keystone picture company in Los Angeles, left the booming world of vaudeville to hitch his star to the rickety and unpredictable wagon of the flickers, the movies, the galloping tintypes.

We all thought he was stark staring mad.

Now, Charlie and I had been rivals from the very first

moment we met, some seven years earlier, at Fred Karno's Fun Factory. We were both just starting out – I had been spotted by the Guv'nor in a show at Cambridge, where I was a college porter, while he had been taken on only after a campaign of wheedling and pleading by his elder brother Sydney, who was already a Karno number one.

And that was soon our ambition, Charlie and myself. To become a Karno number one.

We both rose through the ranks, learning the ropes, gaining good notices, and by the time the next opportunity to step up came along even Karno himself couldn't choose between us. So one night at the Oxford he got us both to play the lead role in *The Football Match*, one of his classic sketches, Charlie playing the matinee and myself the evening show, and then he would decide.

I was going well, too, until one of the ex-pro footballers in the act, a fellow named Billy Wragg, completely wrecked my knee, broke it, smashed it up there onstage right in front of everyone, leaving the way clear for Charlie to step up to the number one position unopposed.

And ever since I'd been trying to catch up again, while he'd been using his exalted status to stymie me at every turn, even getting me sacked from the American touring company for a time. What's more, he'd taken advantage of my absence to get in thick with my girl, the lovely Tilly Beckett, with whom I had fallen madly in love the first time I saw her gorgeous smile in the lamplight outside the Fun Factory. When she fell pregnant and he cruelly discarded her and drove her away just to save his own career, well, it was the final straw.

I decided Charlie had to go.

It happened that he was being courted by a certain Mack

Sennett, who wanted him to leave Karno and work for Keystone Pictures in Los Angeles, making harum-scarum slapstick kick-arse-and-fall-over comedy films. The money was good, true enough, but Charlie could see as well as any of us that it would be a kind of career suicide. Vaudeville was booming and he was beginning to make a name for himself, while the flickers were a novelty, an anonymous triviality, and the public already seemed to be getting bored of them.

So Charlie wasn't about to give up all he had worked for and take a leap into the unknown, not until I was able to play upon his superstitious nature with the help of a borrowed Chinese fortune teller costume and nudge him over the cliff edge.

And now, finally, I was free of the little bastard. I hugged myself with private glee, and felt a grin spread across my features, as I had several times a day since he'd headed out West to flickering oblivion, while the good old Karno boxcar trundled East to continued success without him.

Without him!

My scheme for a glorious 1914 would surely now progress on rails as straight and unswerving as those currently carving our route across the plains of Missouri and Illinois.

I would become the new number one of the Karno company. We would fulfil our dates for the Nixon-Nirdlinger people in Philadelphia, and then we would embark on a new tour of the Sullivan and Considine circuit, beginning in Chicago, then playing the likes of Milwaukee, Winnipeg, Butte, Vancouver, Portland, San Francisco, Los Angeles, Salt Lake City and Denver before finishing once more in Kansas City. Then, who knew, maybe New York? Broadway? The Moon?

And when we got to Seattle in just a couple of short months' time I would, thanks to my new-found clout as the company

7

leader, be able to restore Tilly to the company, and everyone would cheerfully pitch in to help out with little baby Arthur – yes, he was mine, didn't I mention that? – and everything would be tickety-boo.

However...

It had been days now, and the expected coronation had not yet occurred. I gnawed a fingernail and glanced for the umpteenth time at Alf Reeves, the company manager, at the far end of the boxcar, sitting with his elbows on his fold-out table and his head in his hands. What was he waiting for?

It had to be mine, didn't it? Didn't it?

The one serious misgiving I had was that Karno might stick his oar in, and there had been a twitchy day or two before we left KC as Alf had wired the Fun Factory for guidance and we all waited for the Guv'nor's reply.

In the event, when it came, Karno's response was simple, without making Alf's life any easier.

'UP TO YOU STOP
MY NAME BOX OFFICE STOP'

The message was crystal clear. It didn't matter who replaced Chaplin – as long as Karno's name was on the billing that was the important thing.

I wondered, as I had done on and off for days now, whether Alf was considering bringing someone in from outside. There were former Karno number ones plying their trade in America, that's for sure. Alf's own brother Billy was one, working the vaudeville theatres of New York as "the Original British Drunk". He had been the lead in the first Karno company to play A *Night in an English Music Hall* in the States, the very show we were offering now. Surely, though, he could command far more money nowadays as a solo than he ever would by going back to work for the notoriously stingy Karno, so perhaps that wasn't too likely.

Billie Ritchie too was floating around somewhere, but I had last seen the wiry little Scot fleeing from Karno's wrath through a dressing room window after the Guv'nor had halted an unauthorised burlesque of our show by stomping up onstage to beat up the producer, so he didn't really seem like a viable option either.

No, it was far more likely that Alf would promote from within. My credentials were well known, and Alf had been a good friend these past few years, so I was cautiously optimistic despite the nagging delay. I looked around the boxcar at the rest of the company, checking out the other runners and riders, as it were.

Diagonally across from me, the well-padded figure of Charles Griffiths was dozing comfortably, his feet up on the seat opposite. He was a senior Karno player, a skilful comedian with great timing, and a hearty soul who could be splendid if tiring company. A safe pair of hands, could Alf be thinking?

However, the number one role in *A Night in an English Music Hall* called for a degree of athleticism and flexibility that seemed quite beyond good old Charlie Griffiths.

Beyond him I could hear the constant murmur of the ongoing poker game. George Seaman was in charge, as usual. He and his wife Emily had been with Karno for donkey's years, reliable foot-soldiers, never looking to do more than make a steady living on the boards, fattened nicely by George's takings from the card table. I couldn't see George stepping up, nor could I see a potential number one in any of the marks he was currently milking of their weekly wage.

There was Freddie Karno Junior, with whom I often shared a room on our tours. He was the Guv'nor's son, which should have counted for something, but he'd found it mighty hard to persuade his old man to let him have his go as a performer, and the suspicion remained that Karno was just letting him stretch his legs before hauling him back to the office to chain him to a desk.

Next to him was Albert Austin, a mournful stick insect of a fellow who might have been the only one of us who was really missing Charlie Chaplin, having inexplicably shared the little man's opinion that the sun shone from his backside.

Opposite him was Billy Crackles, a young man with a fine star comic's name but an over-fondness for the bottle that surely ruled him out. Bert Williams had once had a solo act as a ventriloquist, and he'd only just been allowed to re-join the card school, having stung them all during one blackjack session by making them all twist until they bust by calling for them out of the side of his mouth.

Stout fellows all, but I couldn't see a leader there. Nor could I at the next table over, where George's wife Emily was teaching our sixteen year-old songbird, Annie Forrester, the rudiments of knitting, with the help of Amy Reeves, Alf's wife, whom I had known since she was Miss Amy Minister. The ladies were all accomplished comic performers, no doubt about it, reliable, smart and with a real twinkle about each of them, but the simple fact was that Karno had never yet produced a sketch where the number one part was female.

I looked over at Stan Jefferson, sitting by himself, gazing out at the patches of thin snow that we were beginning to rattle through now, his breath steaming up the window. He was still lost in thought, and I could just guess what it was that he was thinking about.

Stan had been Charlie Chaplin's understudy back in England

and on three circuits of America, but he had only ever got to play the number one role twice, both on the same day, in New York some three years ago. Charlie was taking advantage of Alf's absence on a recce to sneak a day off with Tilly, but he'd been unable to tear himself away completely, and dragged her in with him to watch Stan at work. Once he saw how funny Stan was – and he was funny, every bit as funny as Chaplin himself – he never let Stan have centre stage again.

That night in New York, by the way, was the night Mack Sennett came to see the show, and got the bright idea of recruiting Charlie for Keystone, not realising he'd been watching the brilliant understudy in action. I'd had the chance to put him straight on that but hadn't done it, which was a secret I supposed I'd have to let Stan in on one day.

Yes, Stan was a superb comic, and a fantastic mimic, and terrific company to boot, and I knew he could do the lead part standing on his head. However, he was junior to me, and Alf had been away on the night of his New York triumph and so had not seen how well he had taken to the limelight.

So I thought Stan was going to be disappointed.

No, the real threat was sitting behind a newspaper some ten feet away.

Edgar Hurley was a surly, superior sort of a chap, and he had clearly been thinking he was far too good for the rest of us ever since he joined the company two tours ago. He'd had burning ambitions to be a number one back in England, ambitions which had been repeatedly thwarted by the Guv'nor. We all thought this was because of his miserable disposition, and the fact that he made no effort to fit in or make himself at all popular. He himself, however, was convinced that it was because of his wife.

Wren Hurley was quite a spectacle. Full-figured, voluptuous, dark-haired and as flirty as the day is long. She had drawn me into a little fling during the last tour, and I had been like a hapless moth to a bright candle. I say a fling, it had never amounted to much more than a few heated fumbles in the dark recesses of the prop compartment of the boxcar, but it had fuelled my daydreams for quite a while, I can tell you. It fizzled away to nothing when it transpired that she had only been using me to make Ed jealous, and she had been so successful in that project that the brute had given her a black eye.

I realised with a jolt that the newspaper had lowered a little way, and over the top edge of it Hurley's dark eyes were boring into mine. I looked away.

"Come on, Alf," I muttered. "Not Edgar Hurley, for Christ's sake...!"

As we pulled into Chicago's Union Station Alf Reeves suddenly jerked to life, got to his feet clapping his hands and called for our attention. The card game stopped flicking and shuffling, the knitting circle stopped clickety-clicking, and all eyes and ears turned to our company manager.

"It has not been easy," he said, massaging his temples, "but I have reached a decision regarding our new number one."

3
BAIT 'N' SWITCH

I'm sorry, Arthur, truly I am. I really thought it would be you."

"Don't mention it."

"I mean, I hoped it would be me, but I never actually thought..."

"It's all right, it's all right, Stan. You will do a fine job, I'm certain of it. And at least it's not going to be that swine Hurley."

"Eddie? Eddie's all right, you just have to get to know him."

"I try not to speak to the bastard at all. You know he beats Wren?"

"Well, I'm sure I've never seen anything to suggest that. And anyway, it's not really any of our business, is it?"

"You're going to have to pay more attention to the company's welfare, you know, now that you're the number one."

"Eddie's not like that."

"Yes, well, you always think the best of people, you always have. And that's why you will be a popular and successful number one, and I wish you all the very best."

"Thank you, Arthur, that's very gracious."

We were sitting together, Stan and me, in the Karno boxcar on the second leg of our journey to Philadelphia. I'd had a sleepless night in Chicago getting over the disappointment of not being promoted to lead the company, but if I had to miss out to anyone I was glad it was Stan, probably my best friend in the world. And deep down I would probably admit that he was better equipped to play the Drunk the way Chaplin played it than I was. In fact, his impersonation of Charlie was so perfect that I doubted anyone would be able to tell the difference.

Stan leaned over and put his hand on my knee. "I know it was your dream," he said.

"Well, the extra money would have come in handy, I'll not deny that," I said. "And I was planning to give Tilly a job, once we got to Seattle."

"Really? What about the baby?"

"The baby would've come right along."

Stan grimaced dubiously. "Really? A baby in the boxcar?"

"We could have worked him into the sketch somehow."

"Hmmm," he frowned. "Well, listen, I'll talk it over with Alf, see what can be done."

"Thanks, Stan, I appreciate that."

"I love Tilly, you know that. It'd be marvellous to have her back."

Outside the boxcar's steamed-up window a wintry sun popped out between two clouds, and I suddenly had the feeling that things were going to work out just fine. Charlie was gone, out of our lives for ever, and in just a few short weeks the little Dandoe family would be reunited.

On an impulse I suddenly climbed up onto the seat. "Hey everyone!" I shouted, bringing the card game, the knitting circle, and various reading and letter-writing to a halt. "Three cheers for our new number one. Hip, hip...!"

The cheers rang out for young Stan, who beamed and blushed

almost as red as his hair. Most of our colleagues, it seemed, were as relieved as Stan and I both were to be free of Chaplin's arrogance and egotism, to feel like a proper company once more rather than merely a support system for the self-styled genius.

In fact there were big smiles everywhere you looked, with one exception. Hurley was sitting stone-faced, arms folded, glowering at us all as we cheered. It was going to take him a little longer to get over his personal disappointment, evidently.

"Come on, Eddie," I called out. "Give us a grin!"

And if looks could have killed, well, this story would be ending right here.

━━━

We were to play at the Nixon theatre in Philadelphia for a couple of weeks. It was a fill-in booking, tiding us over until we began our next tour on the Sullivan and Considine time. That was how vaudeville turns referred to working on the various circuits, by the way. You might be on the Orpheum time, or the Pantages time, or as here in Philly, on the Nixon-Nirdlinger time. The more provincial circuits of modest theatres, based around one particular city or state, would be 'small time', while breaking into the two thousand seaters or onto Broadway, well now, that would be hitting the 'big time'.

When we'd stayed in Philly before it had been just a few minutes' walk from Broad Street station, so we were surprised to see Alf hustling to organise some cabs for us, and to find ourselves riding North for block after block away from the theatre. Eventually we arrived at a boarding house on 20th Street, tired, cold, and not really paying a lot of attention to our surroundings.

So the following morning when I threw open the curtains of the bay window in the room I was sharing with Freddie, I was interested

15

to discover that across the street there was a large flat expanse of open ground, covered in a pristine layer of crisp white snow, and to the left what looked like a red terracotta church of a rather fancy design, with arches and a tower with a cupola on top.

I asked our landlord, an Irish fellow named Flanagan, about this when I made my way down for breakfast.

"Oh yesh," he said, "It'sh a cathedral, sho it ish."

"Really?" I said, raising a sly snigger from my colleagues with a discreet pantomime of wiping spittle from my face.

"A cathedral to basheball. It'sh the home of the Philadelphia Athleticsh, winnersh of the American League pennant and the World Sheriesh jusht lasht year."

"Baseball, eh?"

"That'sh right. And we're going to win it all again thish year, jusht over the road there in Shibe Park"

By this time, I was so disorientated by his Philly shash that I didn't quite follow what he was saying.

"Sibe Park?"

"No, not Shibe, *Shibe*."

"Shibe?"

"Yesh, with an Esh. *Esh*-H-I-B-E."

"I shee – I mean, I *see*."

"When the sheashon shtartsh, the very besht view ish from our upstairsh windowsh, and we can charge folksh a couple of bucksh to shit on the roof."

The breakfast room erupted into spluttering all around. Bert Williams in particular was struggling to contain his distinctive sibilant giggle – "Sss-sss-ssss!" – but our host continued oblivious.

"Yesh, people shit on the roovesh all along the shtreet. We put bleachersh up there, wooden bleachersh, shpecially for them all to shit on."

Well, in my experience there's nothing a travelling comedy troupe likes more than a running joke, and that one kept us all chuckling away happily on the drive over to the Nixon for the band call. The merriment had just died down a little when Freddie suddenly said:

"Well, I know what I am having for breakfast tomorrow..." – a perfect pause, then – "Shaushagesh!"

And off we all went again.

We were all still in fine form when we tipped up at the Nixon, having ridden alongside the Chinese Wall that carried the elevated railway line and cut the city in two, and we made our giggly way along the side alley that led to the stage door. I saw Alf Reeves standing by himself on the sidewalk in front of the theatre, and broke away from the others to see what was holding his attention. His hat was pushed back on his head, and he was scratching his chin and grimacing seemingly from an unspecified pain.

"What ho, Alf," I said. "Everything all right?"

For answer, Alf merely nodded at the bills posted on the theatre frontage. There, in letters you could have read from a couple of blocks away, I saw this:

'NIXON VAUDEVILLE PRESENTS

CHARLIE CHAPLIN'S LONDON COMEDIANS'

"Ah."

"I was afraid something like this might happen," Alf muttered grimly.

"The Guv'nor's not going to like that," I said.

"He'll blow a blinking gasket! But at least he's back in London. These people are here, and they are expecting to see Charlie bloody Chaplin."

"What are you going to do?"

Alf clapped me on the shoulder, and said: "Arthur, my friend, I just don't know." And with that the two of us went inside.

For the last three years the Karno company had been touring the States with Charlie Chaplin as the lead comic, and more and more the local newspapers and the theatre managers were building him up as the draw, the main attraction. Chaplin's name had been getting bigger and bigger, while Karno's was getting smaller and smaller. This, though, was the very first occasion that the name Fred Karno had disappeared altogether, and ironically it was to publicise the very first occasion we were to perform without Charlie Chaplin altogether.

On our previous visits to the Nixon the manager there, a red-faced fellow by the name of Linighan, had been a real Chaplin enthusiast, so it was with some trepidation that Alf steeled himself for the conversation he needed to have about the posters outside.

I followed him into the offices where he was greeted by a lady receptionist.

"Mr Reeves! Nice to see you again!"

"Good morning – Myrtle, isn't it?" Alf said with a friendly smile. "Could I have a word with Mr Linighan?"

"Oh, he doesn't work here anymore," Myrtle said. "Didn't you hear? He has the new Palace at Yonkers now."

"But he has told me all about you," another voice cut in. Alf and I turned and saw a dapper little chap in a three-piece pin-stripe, fiddling a watch on a chain out of the pocket of his waist-coat. "I am George Wilbraham, the new manager of the Nixon, and I can't *tell* you how much I have been looking forward to your visit."

Alf introduced himself, and me, and we exchanged warm handshakes with this sunbeam.

"Oh yes, my predecessor never stopped talking about Mr Charlie Chaplin," Wilbraham went on. "Charlie Chaplin and his marvellous troupe," he added with a courteous nod in my direction, and then checked his pocket watch again. He looked like he should be in charge of a railway station, not a theatre.

"That's nice," Alf said, with a barely noticeable wince.

"I can't wait to see him for myself," Wilbraham burbled. "In fact, I'm highly tempted to sit in on your band call right now, and I never do that, do I Myrtle?"

"No, Mr Wilbraham."

An electric light bulb seemed to click on in Alf's eye just then. "Pardon me, Mr Wilbraham," he said, "but do you mean to tell me that you have never seen Charlie Chaplin?"

"Never seen, never met, but mustard keen to do so!" Wilbraham cried.

"Well, then, let us go to the band call," Alf said brightly. "After you, sir."

Wilbraham checked his watch one more time, and then headed for the stairs that led to the stage.

I grabbed Reeves by the arm. "Alf...?" I hissed, but he hushed me, and followed our host.

"Oh yes, there has been great excitement, great excitement," the dapper little theatre manager cried over his shoulder.

"I'm sure there has," Alf called back. "He's been making quite a name for himself, our boy!"

Up on the stage the company were waiting. One enterprising soul had found a stove with a kettle on it, and had brewed a big pot of tea, and most were indulging in either a late supplementary breakfast or early elevenses, depending on your point of view.

"This is Mr Wilbraham, the theatre manager," Alf said, beckoning people to gather round. "And this..." Alf guided Stan

19

Jefferson into the centre of the circle that was forming, "is our number one comic, Mr *Charlie Chaplin*."

Stan was already extending his hand halfway to Mr Wilbraham in greeting when he clocked Alf's audible wink, and his face was a picture. His eyebrows shot up, and then there was a tight grimace of pain as Alf gripped his shoulder tightly, before he gathered himself.

"Pleased to make your acquaintance, I'm sure," he said, through gritted teeth.

"The pleasure is all mine, Mr Chaplin – or may I call you Charlie?"

"Please..." Stan winced ever so slightly. "Please do."

"Well. Don't let me hold you up – you have magic to concoct, stardust to sprinkle! Welcome everyone!" Wilbraham checked his pocket watch again, and then scuttled happily back to his office.

Everyone was speechless for a moment, as Alf offered us a sheepish grin, and mopped his brow with a large hand kerchief. Next to him Edgar Hurley was using a sleeve to wipe tea from his tie, where he had spluttered it involuntarily a few moments earlier. "You surely don't think that is going to hold for long," he scoffed.

"No," Alf said. "I feel like we have had our head cut off and I have stuck a sticking plaster over the neck hole, but maybe it will buy me some time to work out what to do next."

———

The show we were performing, *A Night in an English Music Hall*, was classic Karno, probably his masterpiece. He had devised it a decade or so earlier, and it had been touring ever since in the mother country under its home title, which was *Mumming Birds*.

The idea was a simple one. A show within a show, a music hall bill within a music hall bill, if you will. A pair of boxes were set on either side of the stage and populated with cast members pretending to be part of the audience, while the rest of us took it in turns to present turns of excruciating awfulness for them to barrack. The star part, the one Chaplin had made his own, was known as the Inebriated Swell, or the Drunk for short. He would arrive late, dressed to the nines and one over the eight, popping up noisily in one of the lower boxes, from which he would then tumble out onto the stage while trying to hang up his coat. The numbers man would help scoop him back into his seat, and from then on the Swell would interrupt, argue, join in, fight, and generally disrupt proceedings to great comic effect.

Now Stan had been understudying Charlie as the Swell for the whole time we had been in the States, but he had only got a run-out in the role in front of a real life flesh and blood audience on one occasion, and had carried it off so well that Charlie had made damn'd sure not to be ill and let him have another crack at it.

The stress of now having to impersonate Chaplin onstage and off only added to the pressure, so it was a nervous Stan who readied himself in front of the dressing room mirror. We all tried to rally round with encouraging banter, but it was an impromptu knockabout crosstalk routine by George and Emily Seaman that really eased the tension. It went something like this:

EMILY: I say, have you heard, it's terribly sad.

GEORGE: What is, my dear?

EMILY: That fellow Flanagan at our boarding house is unable to keep a dog.

GEORGE: Unable to keep a dog? And why is that, pray?

EMILY: Imagine him trying to train the poor thing. 'Shit, Rover! Shit! Oh no, not again...!'

Once our sig music had played and the curtain went up for *A Night in an English Music Hall*, though, we were all a little on edge. Stan was a popular lad, and everyone was hoping he'd pull it off – well, with the possible exception of Edgar Hurley.

From the instant Stan first entered as the Swell, however, we knew we were in for quite an evening. He barrelled into the stage right lower box, tumbled over his chair, righted it, and started wrestling his way out of his coat, and if you didn't absolutely know it was him you'd have sworn it was Chaplin himself. Then he made to hang up his coat, missed the peg and swung over the edge of the box, somehow managing to get his feet even higher than his head had been. And as he sprawled onto the stage chin first we knew, each of us, that Charlie had never got quite such a big laugh as the tidal wave that now broke over us.

The place was in total uproar. We were going to be all right.

At the end of the evening we all repaired to the Irish bar around the corner – there was always an Irish bar around the corner, somehow. It was amazing there was anyone left in Ireland at all. Alf stood the company a round of drinks, and the backslapping began in earnest.

"Honestly, Stan," hearty old Charlie Griffiths said, offering a toast to our number one. "I doubt if even the Guv'nor himself has ever seen his sketch done better. Much as I try my best to avoid the old swine as far as I can, I truly wish he'd been here to witness it. To Stan!"

Mr Wilbraham popped in to pay a brief homage just then,

which prompted Alf to suddenly propose a new toast. "To Charlie!" he cried, which covered old Charlie Griffiths in blushing confusion for a moment. Fortunately the theatre manager didn't stay long before glancing at his pocket watch and scurrying away again, and then in the small hours Freddie got his hands on an early edition of the *Philadelphia Inquirer*, whose reviewer had written this glorious phrase:

"Charlie Chaplin was never better."

This took the mirth to a new level, but after a while I noticed that Stan was coming down, and was actually beginning to look a little melancholy. I put my arm around his shoulder.

"Cheer up, mate," I said. "You were a marvel."

"Thanks, Arthur," Stan said, but he didn't crack a smile.

"What's up? Tell your uncle Arthur."

"Oh, I don't know. I was so thrilled to become the number one, I thought it would be the start of something, but I still feel like I'm Charlie's understudy. More than ever, in fact, seeing as he isn't even here."

Across the table, Edgar Hurley was in a sour mood. Drinking never seemed to cheer him up. "How do you think I feel?" he growled. "I am the senior man, I should be number one..."

Wren, his lovely wife, rolled her dark eyes at me. "Oh, let it go, Ed, for God's sake," she said. I got the sense that she'd had quite an earful of this kind of talk lately.

Hurley pressed on, jabbing his finger hard into his own chest. "I should be the number one, but instead here I am playing second fiddle to the bloody understudy!"

"Third," I said.

"What's that?"

"Third fiddle. You're playing third fiddle to the bloody understudy. I think you'll find that I am the next cab off the rank."

23

"What?! What do you mean...?!" Hurley spluttered, beginning to go a satisfying purple colour. I decided to let him stew on that and went to get more drinks from the bar.

There I found myself standing next to Alf Reeves, who was leaning on the bar pressing two fingers into his forehead, as if to ease a persistent headache.

"Well, Alf," I said. "Looks like we got away with it, eh?"

"Hmm," he groaned. "Maybe, maybe. But for how much longer...?"

4
BANG TO RIGHTS

ALF was right, of course. He'd backed us into a corner, good and proper, passing Stan off as Charlie. However, if we could just make it through this fortnight at the Nixon without being rumbled, then hopefully we could embark on our Sullivan and Considine tour with Stan installed as the leader of the company in his own right.

And even though Stan had blanched somewhat at the prospect of adding a baby to the company, I was sure I would be able to talk him round. It slowly began to dawn on me that there would be responsibilities, cares, worries and duties settling on my not especially mature shoulders once Tilly and little Arthur joined us in the boxcar. In which case, *not* being number one, with all the extra pressures that went with that, might even turn out to be a positive boon.

We played *A Night in an English Music Hall* to great acclaim for the rest of that first week. The reviews were as good as we had ever seen, and we were enjoying ourselves too. Stan was a much more generous leading comic than Charlie had been. When Charlie was in charge everything was about him, directing focus onto his intricate and perfectly observed genius. Stan just wanted the show to get laughs, and he didn't much care who got them, so we suddenly had a licence to busk and embellish that we hadn't had before, and we felt like comedians again after months of mere spear-carrying.

At the start of the second week I came across Alf standing in front of the theatre, where the bills now read:

'FRED KARNO'S LONDON COMEDIANS'

"It's a step in the right direction," Alf said, although there was still a healthy-sized banner beneath that read: 'featuring the celebrated comic Charlie Chaplin', which made us feel like we were short-changing Philadelphia and were about to be caught out.

On the Tuesday of the second week a group of us were standing round enjoying a convivial smoke. Freddie, Charlie Griffiths, myself and Alf were casually shooting the breeze, when we heard shouting on the stairs.

"Mr Reeves? Mr Reeves?" Wilbraham the theatre manager was bustling towards us, brandishing a freshly-minted copy of *Variety*, the gossip rag of the entertainment industry. "Explain this, sir, if you can!" he cried, slapping the paper into Alf's chest.

While Alf read, Wilbraham breathlessly enlightened the rest of us. "It says that Mr Charlie Chaplin, the celebrated vaudeville comedian, has started work in Los Angeles making funny flickers for Mack Sennett. How is that possible, when he is topping the bill here at the Nixon? Is he able to be in two places at once? You have played me for a fool, sir, and I demand satisfaction!"

The man was quite worked up, his eyes beadily darting around looking for Charlie (which is to say, looking for Stan), but I could hardly credit that he wanted a fight, not with a brawny son of toil like Alf Reeves.

"You are suggesting, what... a duel?" I asked.

"What? No! No!" Wilbraham blustered, backing away a step or two. "You Englishmen! I demand a satisfactory explanation, that is what I mean. Come on, sir, what have you to say?"

Fortunately his expostulations had given Alf a moment to think, and he calmly handed the folded copy of *Variety* back to its owner.

"Yes, it is true, Charlie has agreed to make flickers, but not until later in the year, that is all this means. You should count yourself very fortunate, Mr Wilbraham, to have him gracing your theatre on what is his vaudeville swansong."

"Well, I... oh, really?"

Charlie G, Freddie and I merely pushed ourselves away from the wall we had been leaning against, and that was enough to startle that pocket watch out of his waistcoat, and the man himself back down the stairs to his office.

"Christ!" Alf muttered as Wilbraham disappeared.

"You should be on the stage, Alf, not behind it," Freddie grinned.

"We live to fight another day," I said.

As it turned out, though, another day was about all we had before the wheels came off altogether.

We were back in the Irish bar after the following night's show, celebrating more than a little, for it had been another good one, with Stan really hitting his stride.

Suddenly I was aware of a gentle cough at my shoulder, and a figure had seemingly ghosted alongside without my even noticing he was there. I turned, and there was my friend Mr Jobson, the tall Englishman who served as butler and general factotum to John W. Considine, the co-owner of the Sullivan and Considine circuit of vaudeville theatres, and consequently our boss.

"Well, good evening!" I cried, getting to my feet. "How nice to see you again. You are with Mr Considine, I take it?"

"Yes, indeed," Jobson replied. "He is sitting in the lounge, and would very much like you to join him, along with Mr Reeves and Mr Jefferson."

"Why, it would be our pleasure, wouldn't it lads?" I said jovially, although I rather doubted that it would be. "Lead on!"

Alf and Stan slipped out of the booth where they were sitting, and followed Jobson and myself through to the adjoining room, all of us nervously fingering our collars.

There, sitting at a table by himself with a face like thunder and his fists clenching and unclenching slowly, was John W. himself. He was a colourful character, Considine, no two ways about it. A big square block of a head on him, which he liked to top off with a large cowboy hat of a type known as The Boss o' the Plains – he'd given one to Freddie K Junior, who wore it all the time.

Considine had been desperate for Karno to hang onto Charlie Chaplin, as he needed a big draw to keep his whole enterprise going, so the little man's departure had been a huge blow.

He liked us, though, me and Stan, because we had done him a good turn back in 1912, helped him put one over on his big rival, a pushy fellow called Alexander Pantages who styled himself 'King Greek'. Something like that forms a bond, let me tell you, but even so Considine was clearly not a happy man.

"Hello, Mr Considine," I said with my most charming smile. "What a very pleasant surprise."

Considine's gaze flicked up over my shoulder, and he frowned.

Sensing interesting developments in the offing, Edgar Hurley was trying to attach himself to the group, but Considine fixed him with a glare before he could take a seat.

"Who's this?" he growled.

"This is Ed Hurley," Alf said. "One of the troupe, you know?"

"Nice to meet you, Ed," Considine said, in a tone that suggested he wasn't convinced about that either way. "Now run along, there's a good chap."

Hurley flushed, and made himself scarce.

The three of us - me, Alf and Stan - then sat down opposite the burly entrepreneur, like boys about to get a thrashing from an angry headmaster.

Alf coughed. "Charlie's gone back to the boarding house, he was feeling a little under the weather," he said. "He'll be sorry to have missed you."

"Cut it out," Considine barked. "That sort of horseshit might work on that rube Wilbraham, but I know Stan here, recognised him right away. So what are you trying to pull?"

"Pull, Mr Considine?" Alf gulped.

"I know it says Charlie Chaplin out front, and I also know that Charlie Chaplin is in Los Angeles. God knows I tried hard enough to get him to stay with you fellers. So you tell me - what are you trying to pull?"

"The fact is... um... well, the fact is..." Alf said. He was drowning, and so I waded in to fish him out.

"What Alf is trying to say, Mr Considine, is that when we got here the folks at the Nixon had got it into their heads that Charlie was coming, they'd already done all the publicity and everything, so we decided that just for this two weeks it wouldn't hurt to let Stan here pretend to be him. But when we start working for you, we will be the Fred Karno company, straight up and proud, and

Stan will be the number one. And you saw, didn't you, tonight, that he is going to be a smash."

"True enough," Considine admitted. "You were terrific, boy, and if it were up to me..."

I didn't like the sound of that, and by the look of him neither did Stan, who had started picking at the grain of the table top with his fingernails.

"Listen, fellers," Considine went on. "This is how it is. I have just been in New York meeting with Marcus Loew, trying to get him to pick up Big Tim Sullivan's half of the business. It'd be a sweet deal, too, because together we'd have big houses from East coast to West, and guaranteed work all year round for our favoured artistes." He waved a meaty paw in our direction, to let us know that we were included in that group.

"Is Loew going to go for it?" I asked.

"I don't know," Considine grimaced, shaking his big square head slowly. "I just don't know. Maybe. In the meantime I need to keep everyone happy or else the whole damn thing is going to collapse around my ears like a house of cards. You get me? So when my theatre managers are all wiring me, all of them, several times a day, asking me: 'Is Charlie at Keystone? And if so, how come he's getting rave reviews in Philly? And does this mean he is coming, or not?' Then you give me a problem, which is why I'm here now."

Considine reached into his jacket pocket and brought out a fistful of beige-coloured paper.

"I should have taken a room at the Western Union office, not the Liberty Hotel," he growled. "What I did was this. I wired all my theatre bosses and told them that Stan was taking over, that he was the one getting the raves here in Philly, that he was fantastic."

"Thanks, Mr Considine," Stan said, with a big grin on his face.

"But... the thing is this, you see. They want a name, all o' them. They've been spoiled this last couple of years with the attention old Charlie's got, and they reckon it's their due. They know you boys from your previous go-rounds, and they know Stan's the understudy, and they feel... well, I know it's not fair, not right, but they feel cheated. Now it's unfortunate, but just now I need to keep all these guys with me. The Greek is sniffing around some of my prime properties, and long story short I need to listen to them. I'm sorry, son, really I am, but..." He ended with a helpless shrug of apology.

"I understand," Stan said, and I put a consoling hand on his shoulder.

"I'll wire Karno," Alf said, "see who we can get."

"Already done it," Considine said, shuffling the telegrams in his hand looking for one in particular. "I said that we needed a new star name for the show. And he replied..."

"Wait," Alf said. "Let me guess. Something like 'Karno name sells tickets'?"

"Pretty much," Considine said. "Here we are: **"STAR NOT IMPORTANT STOP KARNO BIGGEST NAME OF ALL STOP"**

We laughed. I could just imagine the Guv'nor dictating that to someone back at the Fun Factory, feel the arrogance oozing out from between the lines.

"I could've told you," Alf said. "So what now?"

"Well, I wired again right back saying that I was going to have to insist on a new star comic as soon as possible, or else bookings would be cancelled."

Alf inhaled sharply, whistling through his teeth, and Stan

looked alarmed. We all knew how well Karno was likely to have taken to that approach.

"And he replied?" Alf said tentatively, already half-flinching as though he was about to get a slap.

"He did, thank the Lord," Considine said. Here, look. 'DAN RAYNOR ARRIVING CHICAGO 19ᵀᴴ STOP'

"Dan Raynor?" I said. A glance at Alf and Stan told me that they too were drawing a blank, but then we had been away from England for quite a while.

"That's right," Considine said. "It's a relief, I'll tell you that. So I'll let all my bosses know that they are to promote the living hell out of this Dan Raynor, the bright new comic talent from London, and we're all still on. Excellent! Let's drink to it, shall we? Jobson?"

Considine beckoned to his gentleman's gentleman, who was lurking with consummate discretion over by the hat stand, while Alf, Stan and I took the opportunity to shrug furiously at one another.

So we were to have a new number one. Dan Raynor.

And I'm sure we'd have been a lot more confident about the future if any of us had ever heard of him.

5
THE KID

WE completed our three-week stint at the Nixon without again having to confront the issue of not having Charlie Chaplin with us, although the number of times Wilbraham heard one of us say: "Hey Sta – I mean, *Charlie*...?" must have made him wonder.

On the last night we convened in the adjacent Irish drinking establishment as per, and the ale-fuelled conversation inevitably turned to the subject of the mystery new comic hot-footing it from the Fun Factory.

"Well, he must be hot stuff," Ed Hurley sneered, "if the Guv'nor is happy to shove him in ahead of the likes of me."

"I reckon he must be an old hand, an experienced Northern comic," Alf Reeves said. "Karno likes to do that from time to time, recruit someone who's made a bit of a name as a solo turn, and then start them off at the top. He did that with Harry Weldon, didn't he?"

"Oh, God, I hope he's not a Harry Weldon," I said, "that great blowhard."

"I think he's more likely the next big thing, a hot youngster who's appeared from nowhere while we've been away," Freddie said.

"What, the next Charlie Chaplin, in other words?" Charles Griffiths frowned, and a cold shiver shot down my spine.

"Ed's right, though, isn't he?" Amy Reeves said. "He must be hot stuff, or else the Guv'nor would hardly have sent him over, would he? So let's hope for the best, shall we?"

Opinion was so divided that George Seaman, ever the opportunist, decided to supplement his ongoing quest to relieve the company of all its ready cash at his poker table and opened a book. By the end of the evening Griffiths had a couple of bucks riding on 'Karno's secret lovechild', and another covering bet on 'clerical error'.

I glanced around looking for Stan to see what he thought, as he'd been uncharacteristically quiet that evening, and to my surprise found that he wasn't even there.

Once I got back to our lodgings on 20th Street I popped my head into Stan's room to see if he was sleeping but his bed was empty. I was puzzled, and a little concerned, as Stan was a gregarious creature and not prone to wandering off and brooding alone. Still, there was nothing to be done until he showed up, and so I went and lay down on my own bed, intending to stare at the ceiling and contemplate the future.

Tilly was on my mind, of course, her and the little one. My plan to persuade her to re-join the Karno company once we got to Seattle was right up in the air. As number one I could have insisted that she was hired. As number one Stan would've done what he could for us, I was sure. Now, however, it would be this Dan Raynor with the final word, and none of us knew anything about him. I hoped he would turn out to be agreeable, but in my experience the men who rose to become Fred Karno's star comedians were an unpredictable bunch at best.

Perhaps it was something that happened naturally, inevitably, once someone had been made the centre of attention twice, or sometimes three times, a night, the focus of all eyes, the source of all mirth. But these fellows, even the ones I rather liked, such as Fred Kitchen and Billie Ritchie, all came to believe the world revolved entirely around them and their needs. Maybe that would have happened to Stan, but for the latest twist. Maybe it would have happened to me...?

Just then I heard a rattling, glassy noise, such as that heard when a late-returning drunk stubs a toe on an empty milk bottle lurking in a shadowed porch. The noise trundled on, though, and I realised it was coming from overhead. Something rolled across the roof towards the front window, and then dropped, smashing half a second later on the path in front of the door-steps. Curious, I hauled the sash window up and looked out, and there was what looked like a bourbon bottle in pieces down below. Someone was on the roof!

I dressed quickly, grabbed my winter coat, and clambered up the fire escape. Stan was perched up on top of the house, over by a chimney stack, staring out over the baseball stadium opposite, flakes of white snow swirling around him as if trying to decide whether or not to actually land on someone who was so fed up already. Clearly whatever had been inside the broken bottle was already inside Stan, and he was making a start on a second one.

"It's true, you must get a terrific view from up here when there's a game on," he said as I carefully made my way along the top ridge and sat alongside him. The snow-covered ball park was smooth, pristine, perfectly white in the moonlight and perfectly level apart from a gentle bump where the pitcher's mound was buried.

"What's the deal with baseball anyway?" I said. "More grown-up than rounders, not as grown-up as cricket."

35

"That's about the size of it," Stan muttered, taking a slug and then offering the bottle by the neck to me.

"So," I said, after a warming swig of my own. "Something on your mind, Stan?"

"Mmmm," he said. "I suppose I was wondering whether I would ever get out from under the almighty shadow of Mr Charles Spencer Chaplin."

"Ah," I said. "Him." I was impressed, I have to tell you, with Stan's coherence under the influence of what I took to be a considerable amount of drink, but he seemed to be controlled by a cold fury which was keeping his syllables nice and clear.

"I understudied him for so long just waiting for a chance," he mused bitterly. "The one time he let me play the part I was so damn'd funny that it sent him into a depression, and he felt compelled to get rid of me."

"I remember," I said.

"And then when we finally get shot of the little..." he paused for another slug, "...and I am allowed the limelight at last, it is only on condition that I pass myself off as him, and the laughs I earn with my skill are somehow made to contribute to his greater glory. But I did that, I didn't make a fuss, did I?"

"No, mate, you didn't."

"Thinking that once we left Philadelphia and began the tour proper, finally it would be my turn to shine, to show people what I can do, to start to build a reputation of my own."

Stan took a long draught then from the bourbon bottle, leaning backwards as he did so, and I began to be afraid he would topple over and slide helplessly down into the back garden.

"Stan!" I cried in alarm, grabbing his coat sleeve. "Steady on, chum!"

"But oh no!" Stan went on, turning to jab a finger in my face.

"Mr Charles Spencer Chaplin has other ideas. Because everyone is so enamoured of his... genius...!" Here he leaned over and spat scornfully behind the chimney. "That the mere understudy will not do. Only a shining star comedian can replace the star himself, so I am now to become the understudy to the replacement for the genius. And somewhere over there in that dusty shitbowl they call California. Charlie bastard Chaplin is laughing his head off at me."

"As long as someone is," I said after a moment.

Stan's face slowly creased into his trademark grin. "Ha ha ha!" he guffawed suddenly. "Yes! Exactly! It doesn't matter what the laugh is, or who gets it, as long as there *is* a laugh. That's the thing! Thanks, Arthur, I needed that."

This conversation could actually have gone on all night. After all, no-one, not even Stan, had more grounds for resenting Charlie Chaplin than I, but it was cold, and I was worried that if Stan took any more liquor on board he might finally surrender to gravity before I could catch him, so I said:

"Let's go inside, shall we? I think my backside is in danger of freezing to these slates."

———

So we headed to Chicago, the first stop of our fresh tour on Considine's time. The man himself had gone ahead a few days earlier. His organisation had offices there, and he wanted to make sure everything was ready all the way around his circuit for the arrival of the bright new star, Mr Dan Raynor.

This luminary was due to arrive by train on the morning of the very day we would open at the Chicago Empress, and Freddie and I were dispatched to meet him. We found the platform that

Raynor's train would come in on and stood just beyond the ticket collector to wait.

"Should we make a little sign to hold up?" Freddie asked.

"No," I said. "We're not his servants, are we? He needs to know we're not going to be at his beck and call. Start out wrong and he'll take advantage. And anyway, I think if anyone is going to spot an English comic arriving at Chicago station, it's going to be you and me."

"Fair enough," Freddie said. "Challenge accepted."

The locomotive wheezed slowly into Union Station and gasped its last up against the buffers, and as the passengers began to stream past us I saw Freddie up on his toes, trying to beat me to the punch. I grinned and began to apply myself properly. I dismissed anyone who was travelling light. The chap we were waiting for would have a travelling trunk, and if I was lucky I might even spot the 'Lusitania' label first, and then would be able to claim that I'd instinctively recognised the new man's funny bones.

More travellers strode past, with Freddie peering at their faces as they went by, trying to discern a comic's innate charisma. The poor sap! I took a step back and looked along the platform, and suddenly there! A burly fellow, middle-aged, red-faced, was bullying a porter around whilst wearing a top coat that could hardly have looked more English if he was wearing it as a piece of costume for a pantomime, one of those hound's-tooth monstrosities that seems to have a matching cape attached to the back of it, the sort of thing that a murderer might wear whilst fleeing from Sherlock Holmes. The porter was bowing and scraping this way and that, trying to lug an enormous trunk up onto his little hand cart, while the big man barked at him, prodded him, and mopped his own brow with a white hand kerchief.

"Gotcha!" I thought, but my moment of triumph was quickly deflated by the realisation that our new number one was clearly going to be an old school theatrical monster. I sighed, my shoulders sagged a little, and I couldn't help fearing for the future.

How was such a man likely to greet my scheme to add Tilly and the baby to the company, *his* company? Capriciously? Unenthusiastically?

Perhaps he would turn out to be the type who responded to flattery, to a bit of buttering up? My imagination began to turn to the grovelling I would have to do, to the levels of unctuousness I would have to summon up from somewhere, and I began to feel faintly nauseous.

I watched as the man waddled along the platform, leaning backwards slightly to balance his protuberant belly, clearly utterly full of his own importance, as arrogant as the day was long. If I wasn't careful I was already going to hate him before he'd even had his ticket punched.

"Excuse me?" a thin reedy little voice said. "But surely you are Arthur Dandoe?"

I looked round, and then down, and standing before me was a slight young fellow clutching a carpet bag. He looked like he had barely, if ever, felt the need to shave, and his sandy hair was so fine it hardly seemed to be affected by gravity at all, flying wispily around his head in the station's through draughts.

"I am, yes," I said, surprised, and the pale youth went on.

"And surely over there, that is Fred Karno Junior?"

"That's right," I frowned, only really giving him half my attention as I tried to keep an eye on the bullish chap with the trunk. "Is there something I can help you with?"

"I am Dan Raynor," the stripling cried, thrusting out his hand eagerly. I took it in a sort of disbelieving half-trance, and it was

39

cold, unnervingly so. It was as if the boy didn't have quite enough blood in him, somehow.

Freddie had seen us shaking hands, and came over to join us, his puzzled expression betraying his own disbelief. The newcomer was all enthusiasm, though, and didn't seem to notice.

"Mr Karno, sir," he beamed. "I was with your father only just over a week ago, and I am happy to report that he is in rude health."

"Um… excellent news," Freddie mumbled.

"Well, who are we waiting for?" Raynor said, looking around at the flow of humanity.

"You," I said. "We have come to collect you."

"Really?" Raynor said, his eyebrows shooting up in astonishment. "Really? That's most awfully kind!"

"Shall we?" Freddie said, and we guided him towards the cab rank.

"Gosh!" Raynor said as we made our way out. "Imagine me in a show with Arthur Dandoe! What larks!"

Freddie and I exchanged a glance, which we were able to do over the top of this little chap's sandy head.

"Do you know me, then?" I asked.

"Well, by sight, and by reputation," Raynor replied. "Everyone remembers the *Football Match*, the night you played the Oxford, and had your knee broken."

I felt a twinge in the joint just hearing the incident mentioned. "You heard about that?" I said.

"Heard about it? Why, I was there!"

"You were there?"

"Oh yes, I was right there on the stage!"

"On the stage?"

"Yes, I was one of the supers, in the crowd of football fans, up

40

towards the back, you probably wouldn't even have seen me, but oh yes, I was there all right. Arthur Dandoe – well, well, well!"

Freddie and I stopped in our tracks, and little Dan Raynor carried on walking, shaking his head in amusement at the trick life had just played on him.

"He was a super?" Freddie whispered. "Do you remember him?"

"There were around eighty, at least, for that sketch," I whispered back. "And I don't think I knew any of them."

"He must have had a pretty meteoric rise – is that right, a meteoric rise? Or do meteors only come down?"

"They come down," I said. "And they crash and they burn."

Before we took Raynor to the theatre to meet everyone else, we stopped by our hotel to drop off his baggage. When he saw the room he had been allocated, he beamed radiantly.

"Gosh!" he said. "What comfortable lodgings. Who am I sharing with, do you know?"

"Well, no-one," I said. "This is just for you."

We had become used to the number one having his own room in recent months, as Chaplin's self-importance had blossomed, and Alf had thought it prudent to continue the arrangement for the new man, just in case he turned out to be a touchy individual. In point of fact, though, nothing could have been further from the truth.

"My own room?" Raynor exclaimed. "Golly! Whatever next?!"

Well, next was the theatre, the Empress, where young Raynor's attention was taken by the bill matter adorning the front of the building. 'Fred Karno's Comedians' it read in large blue lettering, 'featuring London's brightest comic star'.

41

"How exciting!" Raynor beamed, pointing at this line of text. "Who is that?"

"Well, that would be you, Dan," Freddie said, a puzzled frown creasing his forehead as it had done pretty much since we left the station.

"Oh my... that's a bit embarrassing, isn't it?" the kid grimaced.

Just then the theatre manager, Mr Gerrard, came bustling out through the double glass doors and over to where we were standing. Freddie and I knew this Gerrard from previous visits, of course, and as he was one of the cadre of buffoons who had refused to countenance Stan taking over from Chaplin we were being decidedly frosty towards him on this visit. He ignored us completely, however, and launched straight into an oily welcome for our companion.

"And this must be Mr Raynor," Gerrard oozed. "We are so pleased, pleased and proud, that you will be beginning your triumphant tour of our beautiful country at our humble theatre. Welcome, sir, welcome!"

Young Raynor was taken aback by this, as well he might be. "Well, that's... that's charming, isn't it?" he said, glancing to me for confirmation. "Thank you, sir."

I steered our charge inside, away from the bowing and scraping, and took him up to the stage, where I delivered him into the capable hands of Alf Reeves.

"Alf? This is Dan Raynor," I said.

"Delighted, sir," Dan said, offering his hand.

"This...?" Alf said, taking a second or two to get over his initial surprise. "Well... welcome, Dan, welcome. Let me introduce you to the company..."

Alf led young Raynor around the stage to meet his new colleagues, and almost all of them were regarding him with astonishment. Edgar Hurley, however, went for disdain, and shook hands as though distancing himself from an unpleasant smell. Behind me I heard Charlie Griffiths bemoaning the fact that his bet hadn't panned out. "I was going to have a couple of bucks on 'strange pasty child', as well," he muttered.

When the introductions were complete there was a brief hiatus as we all waited for our new number one to take charge, as was the Karno way. Dan Raynor stood in the middle of the stage, blinked a couple of times, and then said:

"So, chaps. What sketch are we playing?"

As we were standing in the middle of the set, which had been assembled for a full rehearsal, and it was the set for the most readily identifiable of Karno's routines, the classic *Mumming Birds*, the Guv'nor's trademark skit, we didn't quite know what to make of this for a moment. And surely Karno must have briefed him, mustn't he, before he left?

Then it occurred to us that he must be joking. He was a deadpan artist, that's what it was, and we started to laugh. Part of it was relief, I think, that despite his unprepossessing appearance the lad clearly had funny bones. So we laughed, and young Dan laughed along with us, and when that died down he said:

"No, but really. What sketch are we playing?"

Alf frowned. "Did Karno not tell you?"

Dan shook his head and shrugged.

"He didn't say anything about it?" Alf said, suddenly perturbed.

Dan grinned amiably. "Not a dicky bird."

"Well, we are playing *A Night in an English Music Hall*."

"Right, right, I see. And what is that?"

Alf suddenly thought he saw where the confusion was coming from. "Oh, of course, you will know it as *Mumming Birds*, that is just the title we use in America, to play up the Englishness of it all, you see?"

Dan nodded thoughtfully. "Yes, yes, good, good..." he mused. "And what is *Mumming Birds* when it's at home?"

For a moment or two there was silence, broken only by the sound of a dozen jaws dropping open in amazement.

Alf had gone very pale. "You... you've never played *Mumming Birds?*" he said in a small voice.

Dan shook his head. "You chaps know what you are doing, clearly. Just point me in the right direction and I'll try not to cock it up."

Alf began to scratch his head vigorously. I glanced at my colleagues. None of them still thought Raynor might be joking.

"Oh. One other thing" the kid said. "Who is the number one?"

You could have heard a pin drop. Then Emily Seaman dropped a cup of tea, and we definitely all heard that.

"Well... *you* are, Daniel," I said.

Now it was Dan Raynor who went pale. If anything he went a little paler than Alf, but then he was probably paler to begin with.

"Lumme!" he murmured, and sat down heavily on a chair.

6
A TRAGEDY OF ERRORS

WELL, there was no time to inquire further into the circumstances of Dan Raynor's arrival. We had two shows to do that day, with a lead comic who had never even seen the classic *Mumming Birds* before. Everyone took their places, the Eton Boy and his dotty Uncle in the stage left box, the Numbers Man centre stage, the deliberately execrable acts waiting in the wings, and Stan walked young Raynor through the role of the Inebriated Swell one step at a time.

Stan was the very soul of generosity. It was eating him up that he was being replaced by this kid, but he patiently showed him every little trick and tumble.

"Coo!" little Dan said at one point. "That is fantastic, I'll never be able to do it like that! Why aren't you playing the part, Stan?"

Stan sighed. "Now you have a go, come on."

We quickly realised that Dan was going to need all the help he could get, and everyone was encouraging, giving the kid a little applause whenever he got something right. Only Ed Hurley was unable to keep his feelings secret, tutting loudly every minute or two, and cursing when he was required to do something again because the new boy had missed a step.

Long before he was even remotely ready, it was time to strike the set so that the matinee bill could get under way, and Stan took his pale protégé down into the dressing room to teach him the Drunk's make up.

Alf Reeves remained on the stage as the hands dismantled the boxes, and I wandered over.

"Well," I said. "Here's a thing."

"I know," Alf replied. "But look here. The Guv'nor knows what he is doing, we know that, don't we?"

"None better," I said.

"So he's seen something, right? And we just haven't seen it yet. Maybe he's one of those comics who comes alive in front of an audience, you know?"

"Maybe," I said. "And actually, you couldn't have charged money to watch Chaplin rehearse, could you?"

A short while later I found myself in my top hat and cape as Dr Bunco the great *prestidigitateur*, standing in the wings, trying to work out who was playing the maracas while there was an act onstage. Was there a flamenco dancing troupe coming on after us? Someone needed to tell them to put a sock in it...

Then I realised: the noise I could hear was the chattering of poor Dan Raynor's teeth. He stood there in the Swell's finery, not a dot of colour in his cheeks, leaning against the wall for support, trembling uncontrollably.

"Dan?" I hissed. "Are you all right?"

He looked at me and his eyes were glassy, unfocused. Stage fright. I'd seen this before, of course, in six years as a performer, but this had to be the worst I'd witnessed, and by a distance.

What to do? He looked like he needed a cup of hot sweet tea

and a good lie down, but there was no time for that, and besides everyone knew that the only actual cure for stage fright was to go out onto the stage and confront the demon face to face.

Suddenly Stan was there, putting his arm around the kid, and telling him it was all going to be absolutely fine. "You're funny," he whispered, "really funny, and the sketch runs on rails, it's impossible to mess it up. So come on, let's show 'em, eh?"

Raynor brightened a little, and straightened himself up, almost as if he had suddenly discovered the presence of a backbone.

Stan pushed past me then on his way to the wings on the opposite side, and as he did so he showed me his crossed fingers.

Then all at once our signature music was playing – a little ditty called *Showtime!* – and we were under way. Freddie, the Numbers Man, stepped out to introduce the first act. Those of us waiting our turn craned around the fly curtains to get our first glimpse of the new boy in action, hoping against hope that he was going to pull something out of the hat.

The entrance of the Inebriated Swell set the tone for the whole performance. He would sway drunkenly into the fake box, noisily toppling over a chair and wriggling out of his big topcoat. Then he would attempt to hang this item on a hook, he would miss, and pitch right over the edge of the box and out onto the stage proper, sprawling at the feet of the hapless Numbers Man. We all wanted to see, all fifteen of us, how young Raynor was going to measure up – after all, our livelihood was depending on it, rather.

So, on his cue – just a moment or two after his cue, to be strictly accurate – he wobbled into the stage right box, and we all held our breath. He barged and banged around a bit, rather mechanically perhaps, lacking the fluency of Charlie and Stan, but then this was his first time. He wrestled his way out of his coat, moved uncertainly towards the hook, glanced out onto the stage, which telegraphed the fall somewhat, but as I said, it was his first time and he'd barely rehearsed at all. Then he dropped the coat, made to dive over the rail... then bent double over it and deposited what little lunch we'd managed to persuade him to eat on the stage at Freddie's feet.

Well, it was certainly a moment. Not the one we were expecting, but it certainly grabbed the audience's attention, and ours.

Dan looked up apologetically at Freddie, his face paler than his white face make-up. Then he retched again, poor chap.

After this calamitous beginning the company picked itself up by sheer will power and drove on with the routine. Dan Raynor gathered himself gamely and tried to make a contribution, but he was very quiet, his voice was too thin to carry in a large theatre, and he seemed woefully short of leading man charisma, even in his very best moments.

If we were disappointed, that was nothing to how the audience were feeling. They weren't delighted by the Drunk's antics. They wanted him to be shoved back into his box so they could listen to the acts, the deliberately poor and incompetent acts.

He did contrive one big laugh, when he accidentally slipped on his backside in his own regurgitated luncheon, but those of us used to seeing that kind of pratfall done could see that he had properly hurt himself, and he was limping badly when we finally vacated the stage to half-hearted acclaim.

Down in the green room Raynor rubbed his hip sheepishly.

"I feel I have let you all down," he said, "I'm so sorry."

"Not a bit of it," Amy Reeves cried. "Anyone can have a sticky start, don't give it a second thought."

"You've given yourself quite a bump there, young man," Emily Seaman said, and Wren Hurley trotted off with a tea towel to try and find a block of ice in the alleyway outside the stage door.

"Imagine if he'd been any good," Ed Hurley muttered as the ladies fussed around our stricken number one. "He could've had his pick of 'em..."

"Never mind," Stan said, putting an encouraging arm around the lad. "You'll be much better this evening, you'll see."

He wasn't though, more's the pity. If anything he was even quieter, and the limp he had acquired made the whole performance as painful as he was making it look to walk.

So it was a subdued and disconsolate group that gathered in the bar at the end of the evening, and sorrows were quickly being drowned. We tried our best to make Dan feel better, but now that the urgency of getting him ready for the day's performances was over, there were questions that needed to be answered, and we wanted to do it as kindly as possible.

"You've never been a number one before, then, Dan?" Alf began.

"Never have," the lad admitted.

"Not back in England, not on tour, never?"

"Believe me," Dan said. "No-one is more surprised than I am that I have been thrust into the limelight. I got the impression that the Guv'nor rather picked me at random."

"At random?" I said.

"I know, it doesn't make much sense, does it?"

"How did it come about, if you don't mind me asking?" Alf said.

"Well, I was at the Fun Factory, and there were quite a few of us, all milling about, you know, waiting for the omnibuses to come along."

We could all remember that scene only too well. Dozens of Karnos would gather every afternoon at the Guv'nor's base of operations to be distributed around the capital's music halls to play their three-a-nights.

"And Karno himself came out of his office and looked down at all of us, so there was a bit of a hush, you know, while we waited to see what he might want. Suddenly he called out: 'Who wants to go to America?', and nearly everyone's hands shot up. I mean, it's a dream, isn't it, unless you've got a family or something? See the world, all that?"

"It is that," I agreed, having felt very much the same way myself not so long ago.

"And he looked down at us, and his eyes seemed to sweep over every face, until he sort of settled on me, and he pointed. 'You'll do,' he said. 'My office, now.' Then he gave a little cough, and smiled a not altogether pleasant smile, and I trotted up after him, and he said he needed a replacement to leave right away to join the American touring company, and well, here I am. He didn't tell me which show I'd be doing, certainly didn't tell me I'd be replacing Charlie Chaplin, didn't tell me anything, just asked me my name, slapped a ticket for the *Lusitania* into my hand and I left the next morning."

"I see," said Alf, rubbing at his temple. "Well, that explains..."

"Yes," I said. "I think it does."

Dan Raynor finished the pot of beer in front of him, and winced. "Now, if you'll excuse me," he said. "My hip hurts like billy-o and I think I'll call it a night. But if you could see your way to a little more rehearsing in the morning I'd really be most awfully grateful to all of you."

"Of course," Stan said. "Good night, Dan."

Amy, our mother hen, took it upon herself to see Dan back to his lodgings, leaving the rest of us to stare into our beers and contemplate.

"You don't think, do you...?" I began, and as I looked around at my friends I saw that I was not alone in my reading of the situation.

"Hmmmph," Alf growled, nodding slowly.

"The Guv'nor has sent this youth over merely to prove a point to Considine?"

"That's exactly what I think," Alf agreed sourly. "It's an article of faith for him that his own name pulls in the punters."

"So he has sent along this innocent nobody, plucked from the ranks, just to demonstrate that it doesn't matter who is in the turn, it will still draw them in."

Stan banged his fist on the table suddenly, making us all jump. "I've only met that lad today," he said, "we all have, but can any of you imagine him ever doing a bad turn to anybody? Fancy chucking him to the wolves like this!"

"It's an insult, that's what it is," Hurley growled. "A calculated insult to me and the years I have given Karno, to send this green stripling to lord it over me."

"Oh do give it a rest, Ed," Wren cut in, and her husband looked daggers at her as her reward. "Not everything is about you, you know. Think about that poor lad, sent all this way, all by himself, to a strange country, to a strange bunch of people..."

"We're not that strange," Emily piped up.

"...only to find he's the punchline to a cruel, cruel joke. I agree with Stan, it's brutal. He's a monster, that Karno, that's all he is!"

"The lad's just not up to it, anyone can see that," Hurley snarled.

"Yes, of course, I know that. He knows that, too, doesn't he? Having had his nose rubbed in it all day long? But worst of all, Karno knows it, and he just doesn't care. He's so determined to score points off Mr Considine that he has scarred this boy, scarred him forever, I shouldn't wonder. I'll be surprised if he

51

can bring himself to step out onto the stage tomorrow!" Wren, the soft thing, pulled out a lacy handkerchief from her sleeve and dabbed away a tear or two.

Amy came back in from tucking little Dan into his bed.

"Poor lamb," she said. "I don't think he's a bloodless little cove, do you?"

"What?" I said. "Who thinks that?"

"Oh, you haven't seen this, then?" Amy produced a copy of the first edition of the morning paper, folded open to a review of our matinee, and slapped it down on the table.

It wasn't good.

Alf held up his hands for quiet. "Here's the thing," he said solemnly. "It's not ideal, far from it, but here we are, we're stuck with it, and we have to make it work. We have to make damn'd sure that Considine never gets wind of what has happened, and in the meantime we rehearse, and rehearse, until we make a proper leading comic out of that boy. Agreed?"

7
KANCELLED

THE next morning after breakfast we scooted straight round to the theatre, where the manager, Mr Gerrard, let us in early to begin rehearsing. Dan Raynor gave him a friendly greeting, but the fellow just turned his back, cut him dead. After his nauseating unctuousness of the day before, as well.

Up on the stage Alf had persuaded a couple of hands to come in and erect our set – a beery lunch for those chaps, I thought – and when we trooped up there Amy, the Seamans, Bert Williams and Annie Forrester were already waiting. There was an air of purpose, of grim determination. We had to make something of the duff hand that Karno had dealt us, or... well, we had no idea what, only that it wasn't likely to be good.

Amidst the gloom and teeth-clenching I might have been the only one who was seeing a silver lining in all this. Young Daniel seemed so affable that when we got to Seattle, and the point where I'd broach the subject of adding Tilly and little Arthur to the company, he'd more than likely be a pushover.

Alf clapped his hands.

"All right," he said. "Plenty of work to do today, bringing Dan here up to speed."

"Sorry, everyone," Dan said, looking rather sheepish and rubbing his sandy head. with a little wave. "Again, I'm so sorry for yesterday, it was all a bit much. Arriving straight off the train, meeting everyone, rehearsing, and then straight onstage in Chaplin's shoes, as it were. I'm afraid it was all a bit overwhelming. But I am determined to do better, I will do better, I won't let you down."

"I'm sure you will," Alf said, patting Dan on the back so enthusiastically that the youngster had to take half a step forwards to right himself. "Now, are we all here? Not quite! Where is...? Aha."

Wren Hurley emerged from the wings fussing with a tangle in her hair, and we all looked behind her for her husband, but she was alone.

"Where's Ed?" I said.

"Oh, he's got a bee in his bonnet," she said. "He says he knows the sketch backwards, he doesn't need to rehearse it any more."

"This isn't for him, the silly arse," I said, exasperated.

"I know, I know that, that's what I said to him, but oh no, you know Ed, he's got other ideas, he knows best."

"Well, where is he then? Still in bed?"

"No, no, he's gone to see Mr Considine."

"What?!" Alf roared, stomping over to join us.

"He's gone trotting off to Mr Considine's booking office in the centre of the city somewhere," Wren wafted a hand impatiently. "He thinks that if he tells Considine that Karno has sent a spear-carrier passing him off as a leading man – no offence, Dan..."

Raynor shrugged amiably.

"...he thinks that Considine will be so blinkin' grateful that he will ask Ed to step up and take charge, which, as the senior man, he reckons is his due."

"Oh my God!" Alf clapped two hands to his forehead, as if to stop his brain from exploding.

"The steaming goof!" I said. "Doesn't he know about Considine, about his temper? He killed a man once, you know?"

Wren's nonchalance dissipated fast. "Really?" she said.

"Oh yes, in a feud. The fellow came at him in a home-made bullet-proof vest made out of silver dollars, and Considine shot him in the neck with a gun he took off a policeman."

"Arthur, quick," Alf gasped, grabbing my arm urgently. "Maybe it's not too late. Get over there and see if you can stop the idiot. And if not, well, you know Considine, don't you, maybe there'll be something, *something* you can say, something you can do...!"

———

I ran helter-skelter for seven blocks, my feet skittering from under me on the ice, but I only actually fell once, when I decided to jump off the kerb to get a clear run in the road and stubbed my toe on a lump of horse dung that had frozen solid like a boulder.

I found the Sullivan and Considine booking offices, which were above a rather fancy-looking Italian restaurant, ran up the stairs two at a time, and found myself in a waiting room. There were chairs along the wall on either side, all occupied by whey-faced vaudevillians who had turned up on spec, as was the tradition, in their onstage garb, presumably in case they were asked to go through their paces right there and then. The gymnasts must have been absolutely freezing sitting there in their leotards and tights, and one old gentleman with a dog-related act was hugging a Jack Russell like a hot water bottle.

I strode through the room, picking my way over outstretched feet and dog leads, and made for the main offices.

"Hey!" an indignant voice piped up. "We're all waiting, you know, feller!"

"Yeah," another complained. "What are we – grilled cheese?"

Which struck me as a curious thing to say. If they actually had been grilled cheese I'd have certainly found it harder to ignore them.

I pressed on into the offices, and found myself in a large open area with several desks, each with a telephone and someone working behind it. There was no sign of Ed Hurley, and no sign of the boss himself either. As I paused to get my breath back, I took in the maps of the United States on the wall, with coloured pins stuck in many of the major cities, and lists of acts arranged into vaudeville bills stuck up alongside on a series of large cork pin boards. It was clearly quite an operation, lining up entertainment 52 weeks a year for the Considine empire of Empresses, and it brought home to me forcefully all of a sudden that perhaps old Fred Karno wasn't such a big noise out here as he imagined he was.

Now that I had my bearings I approached a receptionist, a pretty young thing with her hair curled to within an inch of its life and bright red lipstick on, who was barring the way to a closed door, leading presumably to Considine's inner sanctum. She pursed her lips disapprovingly at my barging in, and then tutted loudly.

I put my fists onto the surface of her desk and leaned over urgently.

"I need to see Mr Considine, right now," I said.

The girl glanced at the door to Considine's office, and then said: "I'm afraid he's with someone at the moment."

"I know," I said. "That someone is what I need to talk to him about."

She shook her head primly. "I couldn't possibly disturb..." she began.

Suddenly the door to the inner sanctum was flung open, banging against the side of a bookcase, and John W. Considine burst out, unmistakeably incandescent with rage.

"I'm going to the Western Union office," Considine bellowed to the room in general, grabbing his coat and his Boss o' the Plains and pushing past me, seemingly without even registering that I was there.

"They'll send a boy, sir," his receptionist called, plaintively.

"I'm not waiting for a boy!" Considine bellowed and disappeared down the stairs. As he swished his coat behind him the draught whisked a large number of vaudeville line-ups from the pin boards on the walls, swirled them all around the room, where they were retrieved by harassed-looking individuals moaning in despair.

Under cover of this activity I nipped quickly over to the promoter's office, where I found Ed Hurley still sitting where Considine had left him, a stunned expression on his face.

"You chump!" I said, and he looked up at me blankly. "You told him, didn't you? You told him that poor Dan has never been a number one. And what did you think would happen? He'd be so grateful that he'd go down on his bended knees and beg you to save the day?"

Hurley still looked dazed by the storm that had evidently just broken over him, but he had the decency to look sheepish.

"He's going to send a wire to the Guv'nor," he said in a small voice.

"Right," I said. "I'd better see if I can catch him. You stay here and try not to cock anything else up."

I ran out into the street again, skating almost the width of the sidewalk on ice that had been trodden sheer by pedestrian traffic since start of business that morning. A salt-shoveller with a bucket was inching slowly towards me but hadn't quite reached this entrance. I gathered myself, and set off down the street, hoping to catch sight of Considine's cowboy hat. After all, he was a tall fellow, and would have been quite noticeable. No such luck, however. The big man was apparently propelled by wings of fury and already well out of sight.

All I could do, then, was hustle to the cable office, and there, sure enough, I could see him through the window angrily berating the wire operator, as though this would help the man convey the strength of his feelings across the Atlantic.

I pushed inside and over to the counter where I grabbed the promoter by the arm.

"Mr Considine," I rasped, trying to haul some warmer air into my freezing lungs. "Thank goodness I have caught you. I wanted to assure you on behalf of the Karno company that we will be doing everything in our power to provide the very best performances we can for you... whew!"

Considine grunted. "Huh! With a glorified extra in the lead..."

"No, no, he's..."

"I know what he is," Considine seethed. "Plucked at random from the supporting chorus, as a calculated snub to me. Well, do you know what happened to the last man to treat John W. Considine with contempt?"

"I dread to think," I said, "but we can make this work, I promise you, sir..."

"No!" Considine held up his hands to silence me. "A star

comedian I asked for and a star comedian I will have. And if your Guv'nor does not respect me enough to honour his commitment, then by God, sir, he will find out what it means to get on the wrong side of me!"

"Please, sir, I beg you, don't do anything hasty. Let us have a talk before you send a wire to Mr Karno, and I'm sure you will see that..."

"Too late!" Considine cried triumphantly. "The message has already gone, hasn't it?" He turned to the clerk for confirmation, who nodded.

I sighed. "Saying? If you don't mind my asking?"

"Saying that if he doesn't send me a reputable star name on the next damn'd available ship, I shall cancel the entire booking. This whole country is lousy with vaudeville acts, I'll fill the slot by lunchtime, you see if I don't. Ha!"

With that he jammed his cowboy hat onto his big square head and stomped out into the street once more. There seemed little to be gained from following him, so I sighed again, seeing my breath rush out in front of my face in a thin white cloud, and made my way back to the Empress to report back.

As I walked back up the half-dozen blocks, I told myself that Karno would have to back down. After all, what else could he do? And we would be back to wondering who he could possibly send. It would be rough on Dan Raynor, for sure, to reduce him to the ranks again, but I had a sneaking suspicion that the lad would actually be relieved.

When I got to the theatre, Alf was standing in the stalls watching the end of a run-through with Dan Raynor in the lead role.

"How's he doing?" I hissed.

Alf grimaced. "If we had another fortnight we might be able to pull him up to just bad," he muttered.

I filled him in on what Hurley had said to Considine, and what Considine had sent to Karno.

Alf exhaled heavily. "We'll just have to let them bang heads for a little while," he said. "It'll all sort itself out in the end."

That end came sooner than we thought. We had just finished the matinee performance, in which young Dan had pulled off a couple of nice moments (and botched quite a few more), and were all filing down to the green room for a sit-down and a cup of tea when we came across Alf in the corridor at the bottom of the stairs. He leaned heavily against a wall, one hand to his eyes, another clutching a crumpled slip of beige paper. I put my hand on his shoulder and found he was trembling.

"Alf? Whatever is it?"

"We are cancelled," he whispered.

"Cancelled? Considine cancelled us? I don't believe it!"

Alf shook his head. "Not Considine. Karno."

"*Karno* cancelled us? What do you mean? How could he?"

Alf shoved the beige paper towards me, and I flattened it out against the wall. It was a cable, sent from the Fun Factory earlier that day, and I read this bombshell before handing it round:

'COMPANY WITHDRAWN FROM US TOUR STOP ALL TO RETURN SOONEST STOP FK'

8
THE ROOM

"I don't understand," the one called John said, slinging the folder onto the table in front of him. "I asked you about your relationship with Charlie Chaplin. What has all this got to do with that?"

"Well, think about it," I said. "This was all Chaplin's fault. He was the one who thought he was a bigger name than Karno, he was the one who got himself billed as the star comic in all Considine's theatres, and now that he'd gone we were the ones left dealing with the unrealistic expectations that he'd set up. Bloody Chaplin!"

"So you blame Chaplin for the collapse of the American tour?"

"Absolutely."

"Even though it sounds like it was childish pig-headedness on this Fred Karno's part that precipitated the breakdown."

"He took a share of the blame, yes. But it was down to Chaplin, really."

John drew a sharp breath through his teeth. "I don't know..." he said, glancing at his colleague, who shrugged.

"What? What don't you know?"

"Whether we can use you or not."

"Use me? Look here, what the devil is going on?"

"Maybe, after all, the simplest thing would be for us to hand you over to the Bureau, or ship you back to England to serve your country..."

"Don't do that," I cut in quickly. "No need to be hasty. You want to know more about my relationship with Charlie, is that it? Well, there's loads more I haven't told you yet, loads more."

"L-loads more?"

"Absolutely. Loads."

John sat back in his chair and regarded me coolly for a long moment, during which my heart felt like it was trying to climb into the back of my mouth.

Then he waved a languid hand to indicate that I should continue...

PART 2

9
THE THREE MUSKETEERS

SPRING 1914

STAN, Freddie and I sat on our bags on the platform of Chicago Union Station waiting for the great locomotive to come along and whisk us off to start the next chapter of our lives. From where we perched, shivering despite our heavy coats, we could see the old Karno boxcar, which had been our travelling headquarters for the last three years and more, standing alone and forlorn. Someone – giggling Bert Williams was my guess – had once added a stripe of paint that transformed the legend 'Private Car' on the side of the wagon so that it read 'Private Kar', which had always amused us and made it feel like it was our own. Now we could see some railroad lackey scrubbing away at this additional stripe, over there in the freight yard away to our right, and somehow this brought home to us more forcefully than anything else could have that our American adventure for Fred Karno was at an end.

The company meeting to finalise the details of our evacuation from the New World was a miserable affair. As Alf explained the arrangements he'd made – travelling by train to New York, and then a couple of nights waiting to cross on board the *Oceanic* – I bitterly contemplated the ruination of all the plans I'd had since we'd got shot of Chaplin.

I'd been looking forward to making my way, town by town, theatre by theatre, way out West to Seattle for a reunion with Tilly, lovely, blonde, green-eyed Tilly, and the son she had presented me with so unexpectedly. And then? Well, Tilly and little Arthur would have joined us, I would have swung it somehow. I'd have brought Alf round, got young Dan on side, Stan would have backed the idea, Amy would have helped...

I cursed my own foolishness for thinking things would ever fall into place so damn'd neatly, especially when Karno was involved. Now, instead of heading West with a song in my heart I was to be carted off in the opposite direction entirely. Pretty soon there would be a continent, no less, between me and Tilly, and then the Atlantic Ocean as well. And what could I do about that?

Nothing at all. I was the Guv'nor's man, wasn't I?

Wasn't I...?

"No!"

The word came so firmly and so loud that it even startled me. It was a moment or two before I was absolutely certain it was even my voice that had uttered it.

"Sorry, Arthur?" Alf said, a puzzled frown on his face. "You mean no you *don't* want to have two days off in New York to do as you please? I don't understand."

"No!" I said again, a little less forcefully perhaps, but still with enough oomph to grab everybody's attention. The company looked at me, astonished, and I looked back at their open mouths, their furrowed brows.

"I am not going to go back to the Fun Factory," I declared.

"I am not a chattel for Karno to do with as he pleases. I am not going to be tossed this way and that on his whim. I have given him six years of my life and still he treats me like the dirt on his shiny little shoes. Well, I'm not going to stand for it any longer. I want to stay in America, and that is what I am going to do!"

There was a shocked silence. My colleagues were not used to seeing anyone standing up to the Guv'nor, even if he was four and a half thousand miles away.

Alf gave a little cough, almost like Karno himself, but the withering sarcasm that would have followed had the Guv'nor been there in person was mercifully absent. "Well, that's... um... I suppose that's your choice," the burly company manager said, managing to make it clear that it was not a choice he approved of. "But where will you go? What will you do?"

"I shall try my luck in Seattle," I went on. "You've all seen how vaudeville is thriving. There are far more opportunities here than at home. I shall be fine, don't worry about me."

"Or me," Stan cut in.

"Really?" I said.

"Absolutely," Stan said, the light of enthusiasm gleaming in his eyes. "I've had a belly-full of old Karno. I'm coming with you!"

I was touched, and offered him my hand, which he took with a grin. Suddenly a third hand clasped both of ours, and Freddie K. Junior was beaming at us.

"What, Fred? You too?" I said.

"Count me in," he cried. "One for all and all for one, what?"

"Your old man will be livid," Stan said.

"Won't he though?" Freddie grinned. "But you know as well as I do that he'll just shove me into the office as soon as I get back, adding up columns of figures and paying the supers and what-not. I'm not ready to go back to that. Not yet, anyway."

"Good lad!" I said, clapping him on the back.

"In that case," Alf said, scratching his chin. "In that case... well, here..." He rummaged around in his maroon-coloured folder and brought out three tickets bearing the livery of the White Star Line. "Take these to the offices of the shipping company and you should be able to return them for cash in hand. That'll start you on your way at least."

"Alf?" I said as I took the tickets from him. "Won't you get into trouble for this?"

"What the hell," he muttered. "The old bastard has messed you around enough. He owes you this much at least, I reckon."

Stan, Freddie and I embraced him in turn. "You've always seen us right, Alf," I said.

"Make me proud, boys," Alf said. "Make me proud."

So Stan, Freddie and I sat on our bags as the New York train swept into the station, and then waved as our friends and colleagues peered out of the windows at us, chugging out of our lives, possibly for ever, we couldn't possibly know. Amy, bless her, looked quite tearful as their carriage eased by, and Wren blew us a kiss that somehow managed to cause a stirring in my loins even through the steamed-up glass.

"Listen, lads," I said. "I just want to come clean. You know the reason I am going to Seattle is to meet up with Tilly, don't you?"

"Excellent news!" Freddie cried.

"What I mean is, I have no particular notion of what to actually do once we get there."

"Apart from getting to know your little chap, of course," Stan said.

"What's this?" Freddie said.

I had only confided the secret of my fatherhood to Stan, although Amy, as Tilly's best friend, had also known. Freddie, however, had been kept in blissful ignorance. "Tilly had a baby," I said. "His name is Arthur, and I am his Dad."

"Good Heavens! Why this is marvellous news! But listen, are you sure we won't be in the way?"

"In the way? Of course not, you chump," I said. "I am delighted to have you both along. I just wanted to make sure it wasn't under false pretences."

Freddie punched me hard on the arm.

"It's not just Tilly who's living in Seattle, you know?" Stan said then. "There's Mike Asher. If he has that burlesque house back on its feet then he might have something for us. And then there's old Considine, that's where his head office is, isn't it? And that big house we visited that time? If we get something together I'm sure he'll give us a go."

"You know, you're right," I said, becoming enthused. "He owes us a turn, doesn't he? Maybe even two, considering how we came to be in our current circs."

The Pacific Coast train pulled in then, and we clambered aboard, already beginning to have ideas for a new routine. And do you know, by the time we pulled into Seattle station, travel-worn and tired from laughing, we'd come up with something pretty good.

———

Stan called it *The Nutty Burglars*, and like everything that popped out of his head it was packed full of gags, piled on top of other gags, teetering atop yet more gags bursting to get out. There were four characters. Stan and I would play the burglars of the title, breaking into a big house while the swanky owners are away. They are interrupted by a maid, who would be played by Tilly, and one of the burglars distracts her by flirting while his partner in crime gets on with cracking the safe. Freddie would play a comic dolt of a policeman, who would walk in on the robbery but be totally oblivious to what was going on. Tilly would be so taken in by Stan's charming ways that she would end up helping the burglars rob her own master's house, and the climactic bit of nonsense involved a bomb with a fuse which I had to light in order to bust the safe. It happens that the maid knows how to open it, though, so the bomb is redundant. It gets passed from hand to hand until finally we throw it out of the window, where it explodes. The punchline to the whole bit was the return of the policeman in burnt and blackened rags to furiously chase us all off as the curtain comes down.

We were all fired up and eager to start this new chapter of our lives, so while Stan and Freddie set about finding us somewhere to stay I headed straight off to break the good news to Tilly.

You know the old saying? The poet Burns came up with it. 'The best laid plans of mice and men gang aft agley'? Sounds like it's going to make perfect sense until it goes all Scottish at the end? Well, it turns out that the half-baked plans that haven't really been thought through at all, they also come to grief. Perhaps slightly less surprisingly, now that I think about it.

Anyway, the last time I'd seen Tilly had been back before Christmas, when the Karnos had last been in Seattle and led by Charlie. It had been a bit of an emotional whirlwind, that week, to be honest.

I'd not seen her for well over a year when I found her working at Mike's Place, a burlesque house run by my old Karno mate Mike Asher and his wife Lucia, a statuesque burlesque beauty. I'd discovered the truth behind Tilly's mysterious departure from the company, and that the child she'd been carrying then had been mine. My son. Little Arthur.

When I last took my leave of her and the baby it was with a promise to return as the number one of the Karno company to sweep her off her feet. It occurred to me then, as I hurried through the streets towards Mike Asher's burlesque house, that I should perhaps have sent further communications in the intervening months. However, now that the Karno company was disbanded and mostly heading back to Blighty, I'd felt that writing to Tilly about that would just muddy the water unnecessarily. Far better to turn up on the doorstep, make a big surprise out of the whole thing, and in the excitement and exhilaration of that reunion she would be bound to go along with the new plan I had put together for us.

That was what I thought. And I kept on thinking it right up to the moment I turned the corner and saw Mike's Place.

The sign was gone. The one that boldly, gaudily, announced that this was a burlesque house and open for business. The windows were boarded up, and the building looked for all the world as though it had been completely abandoned.

When we were here before, Tilly had been appearing in an unlicensed burlesque of Karno's precious *Mumming Birds* with Mike Asher and Billie Ritchie. Karno himself had shown up unexpectedly the night we were there, and had forcibly ended the performance by beating seven bells out of Mike right there on the stage, threatening all kinds of legal action as he did so.

So was that what had happened? Had Karno driven Mike out of business? And if so, where had he gone? And where was Tilly, and little Arthur?

I leaned against a wall as the enormity of this struck me. Because of course I had no other way of contacting them except care of this place, this empty hulk. What was I to do?

As I stood there I noticed a couple of figures strolling up to the door, which opened to admit them with a brief flare of light from inside. So the building was not deserted after all!

I hurried over and pushed inside, to find that what had been a thriving burlesque house just a few months ago now seemed to be a nickelodeon, and a rather seedy one at that. There was a strong smell of beer and tobacco, mingled with the atmosphere of a room where the windows had not been opened in some considerable time, and I could hear a murmur of desultory sniggering at the monochrome antics of some second-rate practitioner or other.

A woman sat behind a little table by the entrance, watching the screen with a bored expression, and she glanced at me with half a spare eye and wordlessly held out a paw for the entrance coinage.

"Excuse me, madam," I said.

"Sssh!" she hissed.

"What?" I said.

"Don't disturb the patrons, if you please, sir."

"But... there's no sound," I said. "There's not even a piano player."

"That's how they like it," she whispered. "And if folk come in here making a racket they get to thinking it might be the police."

"The police?" I frowned. "Why would the police...?"

"It's half a buck to come in, and the bar is round to the right."

"Half a buck! What sort of flickers are you showing?" I whispered, but either she didn't hear me or she ignored the question, snapping her fingers impatiently for the cash.

"I just..." I began louder, and the woman put a finger to her bright red lips. I leaned over the little table. "I just require some information," I whispered. "Do you work for Mike Asher?"

"Who?" she frowned.

"Mike Asher? Last time I was in town this was his place. Mike's Place."

"Oh yeah," she said. "I remember. His wife was...?" Here she used her hands to pantomime Lucia's impressive bosom.

"That's right," I said.

"Well, they sold up and left town, oh, months back."

"Left town?" I felt my stomach fall down to my boots. "I don't suppose you know where they went?"

"Sorry..." The woman was distracted then by something on the screen, which she could see from her perch, while I could not, having not yet stumped up the wherewithal to pull the mauve velvet curtain back and go inside.

"You don't remember, do you, a girl who was with them, Mike and his wife? She had a little baby?"

"Huh...? No, I don't. Now are you coming in or not?"

But I was already pushing my way out past another couple of fellows on their way in, out into the daylight to contemplate the ruin of my hopes.

10
A FRESH START

I passed a thoroughly miserable weekend spending far too much of my boat ticket refund on drink, cursing myself for not thinking, for presuming that Tilly and the baby would just be here waiting patiently for me. I felt guilty, too, for dragging Stan and Freddie all the way to Seattle, but they were relatively sanguine about how things were turning out, and tried to make me feel better.

"We can still go to Considine with *The Nutty Burglars* idea," Stan said with his usual cheerful enthusiasm.

"As a three-hander, you mean?" Freddie frowned.

"Maybe. But the flirting between the maid and the burglar is the main source of the comedy, so perhaps we just need to find ourselves a girl. Vaudeville actresses are not exactly in short supply. Considine might even know someone who would do, and he might enjoy making suggestions, you know, which might even help him go for the idea."

"If he's anything like my old man that'd certainly perk him up," Freddie grinned.

"So come on, Arthur, cheer up. All is not lost!"

Stan was right, of course. All was not lost.

It just felt like it.

━━━━━

First thing Monday morning we presented ourselves at Considine's head office in Seattle. Even though it was early there was already a crowd of hopefuls waiting in a reception area, as there had been back in the Chicago office. All kinds of turns, some in their onstage costumes as though they had headed here straight from last night's performances, along with a handful of fellows in mufti who I took to be agents representing them, and joining them pounding the pavements. I felt a shudder pass down my spine at this glimpse of what the future held, or perhaps it was a residual effect of the weekend's drinking.

There were no chairs left unoccupied, and Stan and Freddie began to tuck themselves into a corner by a hat stand with a very British readiness to queue for as long as it would take to be seen, but I was in no mood to hang about.

"Come on," I said, stepping over outstretched feet and ignoring grumbles of discontent, heading for the entrance to the offices themselves. "Excuse me, personal friends of Mr Considine, thank you, excuse me..."

We passed into a large open room with a receptionist sitting at a desk. Behind her there were maps pinned to the walls, as there had been in Chicago, but here at Considine's headquarters it seemed that activities were at least double those of the subsidiary office. Lists of acts were pinned up alongside the maps, and coloured strings attached to pins linked the turns to the venues they were performing at. It had the look of a military operation, somehow, as though all these West Coast cities were about to be invaded and conquered.

The receptionist blinked at us, and started to insist that we wait outside to be called, but I cut her off.

"Please tell Mr Considine that his personal friends Mr Dandoe, Mr Jefferson and Mr Karno Junior are here to see him on a matter of some urgency."

The girl blinked at us again, and then hustled to her feet. "Mr Dandy...?"

"Quick as you can, there's a good girl," I said firmly, and the receptionist crossed the office and disappeared down a corridor.

"Very assertive," Stan muttered, approvingly.

"Well," I said with a grin. "We're busy men, haven't got all day."

"Hey, look at this," Freddie suddenly said. He was peering with amazement at the pinboards covering the walls from floor to ceiling, and something had caught his eye. He reached out and unpinned an envelope, handing it to me. I took it from him, wondering why on Earth he would have done this, when I suddenly realised that it had my name written on it in a curly hand.

The receptionist returned then, preceded by a plump little chap who was rather indignantly jamming a porkpie hat onto his head, having clearly been given the bum's rush.

"This way please, gentlemen," she smiled, and led us along to Considine's lair.

The big entrepreneur was pleased to see us, and shook our hands vigorously with his own chunky items.

"Boys!" he beamed. "How great to see ya! Hey, still got the old cowboy chapeau I see!"

Freddie did indeed still have his Boss o' the Plains, a gift from our host, and he hung it on the hat stand behind the door.

"Have a seat, have a seat, and tell me what I can do for you fellas!"

Considine whisked a couple of additional chairs over to his desk and the three of us sat ourselves down.

"Now, you haven't come to beg me to change my mind about booking the Karno tour, have you? Because I have to say – and you can tell your father this – I have already made other arrangements."

"No, no," Stan said, holding his hands up. "We're no longer employed by Freddie's father. In fact the rest of the company should be on board a ship heading back to England by now. We have come to Seattle to try our luck, and as we have a little... history... do we not?"

Good old Stan, I thought, reminding Considine of the big favour he owed us after we'd sabotaged Alexander Pantages' grand opening night in Winnipeg for him.

"We thought we would offer you the opportunity to be the first to book our new act."

Considine sat back in his chair and locked his fingers behind his big square head. "I'm listening."

Stan began to explain how *The Nutty Burglars* would play, and his enthusiasm brought it to life. Indeed, it sounded as though Stan had done a lot more working out in his head than Freddie and I had managed to contribute, so we just sat back and left him to it. As he described the various bits of business he'd come up with, I fingered the envelope that had been pinned to the wall in the larger office. Finally my curiosity got the better of me and I slipped a forefinger under the flap and quietly slit it open.

"Sounds grand!" Considine cried, chuckling away. "So it's the three of you? And who? Who's the girl?"

"Well," Stan said. "We were rather wondering whether you yourself might have a sugg..."

"Tilly Beckett!" I blurted out suddenly. "She was with us in

Chaplin's Karno company, you remember her? Blonde hair, green eyes?"

"Oh, yes," Considine mused. "She was quite a catch, as I recall."

"She was," I agreed. "She is. I just need a couple of days to fetch her and we'll be ready to go."

Stan and Freddie were staring at me, questions in their eyes, as Considine leaned forward.

"All right, fellas, here's what I can do for you. I can squeeze your *Nutty Burglars* onto my bills, starting in a couple of weeks from now. It'll just be supporting, of course, in the smaller houses, and it won't be Karno money. But if it plays – and it sure as hell sounds like it should – then maybe we'll be able to move you up. Will that suit?"

We all got to our feet and pumped his hand gratefully, and shortly after that we spilled into a neighbouring bar, a newly-formed vaudeville act.

"It's amazing good fortune, really," Freddie said, still scratching his head. "He's taken us on without even seeing the sketch."

"I haven't even seen it yet," I said, "and I'm in the bloody thing."

"So you have something, some hold over Considine, is that it?"

"We did him a good turn, that's all," I said.

"But what's this about Tilly?" Stan asked. "I thought you didn't know where she was."

"I didn't," I said. "But she sent me this letter, care of Considine's office, because, well, I guess we were moving around so much she didn't know how best to get in touch with me. She says she's going to Vancouver with Mike Asher and his wife to run a burlesque house up there. I just need to go and bring her back."

"You sure she'll come?" Stan frowned. "Sounds like they might have a good thing going."

"Oh, she'll come," I said, confidently, as we clinked our glasses together. "And *The Nutty Burglars* will be the hottest thing in vaudeville in no time."

———

My bullishness dwindled somewhat as I rode the Vancouver, Yukon and Westminster railroad up into Canadian territory that afternoon. Tilly had not known what address she would be living at when she'd written, only that the burlesque house where she was to be working with Mike and Lucia was near English Bay Beach, so I'd had no way of letting her know I was coming, and I was going to have to rely on my wits and a little detective work to locate her.

I strolled out into Vancouver's downtown and headed West, occasionally asking directions to be sure I was still going the right way. Down at the far end of the long streets to my right I caught regular glimpses of the harbour, with ships' masts occasionally visible above the traffic, and away to my left I could also see some sunlit stretches of sea, so I reckoned the city was occupying a fairly narrow strip of land.

When I finally reached the English Bay Beach, I had to stop and push my hat back on my head, because it looked for all the world like I had walked all the way to Southend. A long wooden pier jutted out into the bay, and a promenade looked down onto a stretch of sand dotted here and there with hardy spring bathers. A little way out into the water, there was a slide that fun-seekers could wade or swim out to, but although it was sunny there was a nip in the air, and no-one was clambering up onto it just then.

I imagined Tilly coming across this place. How it would have reminded her of her childhood, and happy times helping her old man with his Punch and Judy stand. I'd met him once, years ago, when I went on a pilgrimage to Southend trying to find Tilly, and I remembered the old chap saying:

"She were a fearsome crocodile!"

Yes, if Tilly was in Vancouver, then she'd have certainly gravitated towards this part of it. I already felt a few butterflies fluttering by in the old stomach, as though I subconsciously knew she was near.

I strolled across a lawn, past a bandstand, and then along onto the promenade. As I went I took careful note of all the mothers or nannies with small children, all the perambulators and bassinets. How old was little Arthur now? Nine months, that sort of area, I reckoned. Now did that mean he would be walking, or not yet? I realised how very little actual knowledge I had of small children, and the butterflies became a little more active.

A bill poster caught my eye, advertising a burlesque house, and I took a little detour to seek it out, but the doors were still bolted and there was no activity yet.

I cut back to the beach, and walked out to the end of the pier. Several more ladies were keeping a close eye on tiny charges, particularly as the railings were easily far enough apart to allow an adventurous toddler to take a header into the briny. I felt my insides clench at the very thought of such a mishap befalling little Arthur.

There was no sign of Tilly there that I could see, so I leant on the railing and looked out across the bay. It dawned on me that there was no way that I would get back to Seattle that night. At the very least I was going to have to visit a burlesque or two, and by the time they opened for business the railroad would be closing down.

I started to wonder whether I could possibly save a bob or two by sleeping rough, perhaps on this very beach, or at the station. Was there a bench in that bandstand...?

"Arthur! Arthur!"

A woman's voice was calling urgently, and I turned to see a determined little Lord Fauntleroy galloping at full tilt towards the end of the pier, a lollipop in his sticky hand. I set off after the little fellow and scooped him up just before he toppled off the edge, whirling him up, round and into my arms.

"Easy there!" I said, and my reward for my heroic intervention was a smack in the eye from the lollipop. Through the eye that wasn't stuck closed with fruity syrup I could see a woman trotting along the pier towards us, still shouting: "Arthur! Arthur!"

It couldn't be, could it?

I squinted at the little brute squirming in my arms, and after a moment I fancied I caught a glimpse of the sturdy jaw of my brother Lance, and then his eyes, yes, his eyes were that green colour that had so captivated me those many moons ago, and his name, of course, his name was...!

"Ow!" I protested, wrenched from my reverie by a sudden pain in my upper arm. The woman had come right up to me and walloped me with her umbrella.

"Put him down, you brute!" she shrieked, whacking me again, and the little lad wriggled free of my grasp, coming perilously close to toppling into the bay after all.

"But I was just..." I protested.

"Stay away or I'll call a policeman!"

"Where's his mother?" I asked, taking another blow on the other arm.

"Mind your own business!" the woman cried, yanking the boy back down the pier. He had started to make a loud wailing noise, and several fishermen glared at me as though it was my fault.

"No good deed shall go unpunished, eh?" a voice behind me said.

I turned, and suddenly with a shock like a bucket of cold water to the face, there she was, as beautiful as ever, her golden curls tumbling out from under a sort of beret onto the shoulders of a dark coat, her green eyes wide, and her mouth open in amazement. Mine fell open too, but no words came out as we stared at each other for a long moment. We must have looked quite a pair.

"Arthur Dandoe! It is you, isn't it?! Whatever are you doing here?"

"Looking for you," I said as we fell into an embrace and I lost myself in her familiar perfume. "Looking for you."

11
WON'T YOU COME, DEAR?

FIRST of all," Tilly said, turning away from me and leaning over a black bassinet. "Say hello to our son."

"I thought... well, his name seemed to be Arthur, and..."

"Oh Arthur Dandoe, you are an idiot! That child was three if he was a day!"

She turned to face me again, this time with an infant in her arms. He was a red-faced little chap dressed in a bright blue sailor suit – even though he didn't seem to have his land legs yet never mind those of the sea variety – topped off with a similarly nautical sunhat. He had evidently just woken up, and had considerable quantities of drool oozing down his little red chin. And yes, I could see now, he was considerably younger than the rascal with the lollipop.

"What ho, Arthur," I said, taking one tiny hand in mine and shaking it formally. "Very pleased to see you again."

"Actually..." Tilly began. "We – that is to say, Mike, Lucia and me – have stopped calling him Arthur."

"What? Why?"

"Well... it's silly really, but I called him Arthur when he was born to remind me of you, because I thought I shouldn't see you again, but then I did, and we seemed to be making plans, and so whenever I talked about you we would have to call him 'little Arthur' and you 'big Arthur', and, well, he's not going to be little forever, is he?"

"I suppose not."

"So we have got into the habit of calling him Wallace, which is his middle name. It's Scottish, from my mother's side."

"Wallace," I said, trying it out. "I like that. Wallace. It sounds fierce." I picked the boy up and brought his face level with mine. "What do you think, Wally?"

"Not Wally," Tilly said sharply. "Wallace."

So Wallace he was from that point on. He began to wriggle in protest at being squinted at by a stranger, and I tried in vain to contain his limbs as I took him to my chest. The boy pressed his sodden chin against my neck, soaking my collar, and then began to wail with a noise that would have raised the dead. I can honestly say I'd never felt quite so awkward and frankly useless in my whole life to that point.

"Um, yes, maybe not," Tilly said, retrieving the bundle and magically cooing it back to a semblance of calm almost immediately. Then she laughed at the expression on my face, which was pitched somewhere between appalled and ashamed. "Don't worry," she said. "You'll get the hang of it. Now tell me everything. The last thing I heard from you was before Christmas, when your cable said the Karnos would be coming to Seattle with a new number one."

"Yes, well..." I began, but she was full of questions.

"So Charlie has gone off to make moving pictures? Who'd have thought it? What a turn up!"

"That's right, and then..."

"But the Karnos aren't due in Seattle for another two months, or anyway they weren't when I left there. You got my letter? The one I left at Considine's? I was going to send another nearer the time..."

"I did, and if you'll let me get a word in edgewise I'll explain."

"I'm sorry. Please."

"Thank you. So first of all..."

"In your own time," she butted in.

"I..."

"Whenever you're ready."

"It was..."

"I can't wait to hear all about it."

I held my hands up in defeat, as she was clearly able to keep that particular joke going indefinitely. She smirked like a naughty schoolgirl, and once I was sure she wasn't planning to interrupt again I brought her up to date.

"When Charlie left us the company did get a new number one," I said.

"You?" she mouthed, pointing a tentative finger.

"Actually no, it was Stan." She nodded slowly at this. "And no complaints, he deserved it. The trouble was, though, that the theatres were so stuck on Charlie bloody Chaplin that they weren't happy with a mere understudy, and Considine insisted that the Guv'nor send a new lead comic from London."

"Oh! Poor Stan," Tilly said, frowning at the unfairness of that.

"Well, you know Karno, he doesn't like being told what to do, and he sent a kid called Dan Raynor who really wasn't up to much. He and Considine fell out over it, and long story short the company got ordered home."

"Back to England? Really?"

"Yes."

Her face fell, and I could see that this was a blow. "So much for your perfect little plan then. The one where you return in triumph and sweep us off our feet and back into the fold. Oh well, it was a nice idea while it lasted."

Tilly turned to tuck little Wallace back into his baby carriage, and I could tell she was trying to hide how disappointed she was. I realised that she must have set at least some store by my scheme, and she'd had several months to mull it over.

"Well, about that," I said.

"What about it? Clearly you have left Karno or else you'd be on your way back to the Fun Factory."

"I have, yes, you're right. And so has Stan and Freddie. I came to Seattle to find you, and they came with me, and along the way we have started to put together an act, and Considine is going to give us a go."

"Really?"

"Really!" I quickly explained the idea for *The Nutty Burglars*.

Tilly looked puzzled. "So who is playing the flirty maid?"

"Well, you are, obviously!" I cried. "That's what I'm doing here! I've come to fetch you!"

"Me?!!"

"Yes, of course. Who else?"

"But…"

"Don't you see? It will be an opportunity to really show what you can do, how funny you can be. It wouldn't be like being in a Karno sketch, where the girls are basically just scenery. You'd be featured, front and centre. In fact, most of the comedy comes from you and Stan. It's just what you wanted, isn't it? A chance to shine!"

I expected her to be swept up in my excitement, but she turned without a word and began to push Wallace's baby carriage briskly along the pier towards the promenade. I trotted after her, trying to catch up.

"What? What's the matter?"

"Oh, Arthur, you are infuriating! Just that one wire in all these months. That one line to pin all my hopes to. And now you turn up out of the clear blue sky and expect me to drop everything to join you on a crackpot new scheme that I'm just hearing about now, and it must be straight away, right this very minute, no time to think, or plan."

"But I thought..."

"You haven't even asked me what I've been doing."

"Well, you said, in your letter, didn't you?"

"I've been living here with Mike and Lucia, helping run a little burlesque house. It's not much, but it's steady at least, and Wallace loves them. How am I going to bring up a child on tour?"

"I'll be there, and Stan and Freddie will help out, you know they will."

"It is a full-time job, you know, not just something you can busk as you go along. Bringing a baby onto the Karno boxcar would have been one thing. At least there would have been the other girls in the company to help me out, Amy and Wren and the others. But you want me to throw in my lot with three chumps who like nothing more than going out for a beer or five after a show, and bring a ten-month old boy along for the ride!"

"Wait... *chumps?*"

"You know, you could just as easily come and live here in Vancouver with us, work at the burlesque house."

"But... I couldn't let Stan and Freddie down."

"But I could let Mike and Lucia down, you mean? After all they've done for me?"

I stopped walking after her and let her stride ahead. Then I massaged my forehead with my knuckles. I had spent weeks, months, imagining this reunion with Tilly and the baby, and always it ended up with us embarking on a new phase of our lives together. This resistance from her, this anger, took me aback. Surely she wasn't serious about staying here, was she? In this place that was so very similar to her home town, with good friends who had stood by her through thick and thin for the last couple of years? Actually, when I put it like that it was pretty obvious what Tilly was thinking. I felt a great confusion pressing down on me all of a sudden, and I felt a pang of longing for a drink, several drinks, and then a few more, to rinse it away.

I looked up, and saw that Tilly had stopped walking too, and was standing with her back to me a little way ahead, tapping her fingers on the handle of Wallace's conveyance. I took a deep breath, and walked slowly up alongside.

"You'll come and see Mike and Lucia, of course?"

I nodded and we walked along in a silence broken only by a little squeak on one of the bassinet's wheels. And I wondered – did I have my answer?

———

Tilly took me to the white-washed clap-board house that she was living in with good old Mike Asher and Lucia, his highly-emotional Latin wife. The two of them were thrilled to see me, and clasped my hand with manly enthusiasm and clasped me suffocatingly to her ample bosom respectively.

"Good Heavens!" Mike grinned, still shaking his head with disbelief. "Arthur Dandoe! Where have you been? Tell me all! Spare no detail, however small!"

So the four of us sat on their veranda, Tilly gently bouncing the little lad on her knee, looking out over the bay. I had to admit they'd found a very pleasant spot, particularly as the sun set, lighting up the clouds orange as it boiled over the horizon, and it seemed less and less likely that Tilly would be able to tear herself away. With a somewhat heavy heart, I brought my friends up to date with the collapse of the Karno tour after the departure of Charlie Chaplin.

"Yes," Mike said. "We saw a little notice in *Variety*, didn't we, Lou? Saying that he was going to be working for someone called... what was it?"

"Mack Sennett," I filled in.

"So what will you do next?"

There was a pause then, a moment. I looked at Tilly, and she looked at me, and between us it seemed we silently agreed that she would speak.

"Stan and Freddie are in Seattle," she said. "And the boys have come up with an act, and Considine is going to give them a start."

"Well, that's excellent!" Mike beamed, and Lucia leaned over and embraced me again.

"The thing is..." Tilly became tentative. "They want me to throw in with them, and bring Wallace too, but I don't want to let you down. You have been so kind, and I owe you so much..."

"Nonsense!" Mike cried. "It is we who are in your debt. You know she has devised some terrific comedy bits for our burlesques," he said, turning to me. "She's really helped us get our new place up and running, hasn't she Lou?"

"Yes!" Lucia agreed fervently, pronouncing the word like 'chess'. "But..."

"But?" Tilly prompted, with a small frown.

"My dear, my darling!" Lucia said, reaching over and taking both of Tilly's hands in hers. "I see the look in your eye, when you see the girls and they performing on the stage. You should be there, in the centre, the brightest of all!"

"Oh, sweetheart, that's very nice of you, but the baby..."

"Exactly, the baby, the baby. You cannot perform a whole evening of burlesque late into the night with a baby. But a little sketch...?"

"Lou's right, you know," Mike said, tapping his chin with his forefinger. "If you were on the road with the boys, you'd really only need to have someone watch Wallace for twenty minutes at a go while you were on the stage. And I'm sure Stan and Fred would pitch in the rest of the time, eh Arthur?"

"Absolutely!" I said, and then held my breath.

Tilly turned to look at me. Our eyes met.

"It does sound exciting, though," she said.

And then she smiled. To be precise: she smiled the smile that had lit up my life ever since we first met back at the Fun Factory. I reached for her, and she gaily flung her arms around my neck.

"We will always be here, you can come back any time..." Mike said, chucking Wallace under the chin. "And you can bring your Mummy too if you like!"

It was too late to travel to Seattle that evening, of course, so I stayed the night at the Ashers' little clapboard home. Mike had been mustard keen for us to celebrate our new start down at the burlesque house where he and Lucia were the new management team, but of course the baby had to be bedded down, so after taking a quick look round and indulging in a swift half bottle of champers Tilly and I made our way back early. I felt a cold chill of anxiety curling round my guts as I pushed the baby carriage through the darkening streets, wondering what I was letting myself in for, but that all disappeared once Wallace had nodded off and Tilly and I realised we had the place to ourselves for at least the next few hours. We had plenty of lost time to make up, and we did our very best.

12
THE NUTTY BURGLARS

SO began one of the happiest periods of my life.

Tilly and I travelled down to Seattle with little Wallace, who loved the train, and seemed almost hypnotised by the scenery flying past the window. I sat him on my knee for some of the journey, still feeling a little awkward and apprehensive about suddenly becoming a family man. At one point the little fellow suddenly went bright purple, which alarmed me greatly, having no medical skills whatsoever to call upon. Tilly was calm, however, and within a few moments Wallace himself seemed a lot more comfortable, and, I might add, sitting about an inch and a half taller. A sudden blast of a quite desperate stench revealed exactly what had been occurring, and Tilly carted the boy off to clean him up. I was left behind to look out of the window, relieved that she was such a dab hand at that kind of thing, but becoming aware that there were skills I was going to have to learn, and jolly quick-smart too.

Stan and Freddie were thrilled to see Tilly again, and were both a lot more at ease with the baby than I was, at least to begin with. They'd both had younger brothers when they were growing up, and were happy to pitch in and become honorary uncles.

Stan had a little trick where he would pop his finger into his own mouth and puff out his cheeks, which made his hat rise up above his head. Wallace never tired of seeing this, gurgling away happily, and Stan would happily repeat it over and over again. After all, a laugh was a laugh.

The Considine organisation, all those busy little bees with their pinboard maps and their thrown-together bills, had come up with some bookings for *The Nutty Burglars* starting the following week, so we began rehearsing right away, putting together the act we had promised was ready.

Fortunately Stan was a marvel at this, as I remembered from the time the two of us assembled *The Rum 'Uns from Rome* back in London a couple of years earlier. Give Stan a set up, and gags just spilled out of him. If we laughed – which we did often and long – then the gags stayed in. He and Tilly had a great rapport as the lead burglar and the flirty maid, and Freddie and I were content to let them shine.

We began in Seattle. Not at the Empress, the vast theatre we had graced as the Karno company, but at the Alhambra, a far more modest little two-hundred-and-twenty-seater, some way out from the centre of the city. *The Nutty Burglars* was ready, that first night, or at least as ready as we could make it without finding out which bits an audience was going to laugh at, but our patron, John Considine, had promised to come and see it debut, so there were plenty of nerves as our first performance drew closer.

Our slot was midway through the second half, and the house was becoming somewhat raucous. Clearly there had been drink taken, plenty of it, and people had progressed to the point where the most fun they could derive from some of the distinctly average acts that were parading before them lay in loudly abusing them until they stopped.

As a particularly execrable banjo player departed the stage earlier than anticipated, all of a sudden it was our turn. The four of us took a deep breath, and silently placed our hands one on top of the other, the Four (now) Musketeers.

Then the lights came back up, and Stan and I tiptoed onstage, two burglars breaking into a big house. We were making a big play of being as quiet as we could, of course, and so the first sequence was all pantomime, no words. The audience piped down and began to pay attention to what we were doing, and it's far easier to heckle someone if they are trying to speak to you – or sing to you, in the case of our unfortunate banjo-mangling predecessor – than it is if they are attempting to entertain you in silence.

By the time Tilly entered as the maid, the crowd was under our spell, and she was able to show the light that had been hidden under a bushel during her whole Karno career. She was terrific. She and Stan sparked off one another as if we had been doing the act for years, and it was all I could do to keep a straight face as the third wheel.

When we finished chucking the fizzing bomb from hand to hand, and Freddie appeared with his explosion-blackened face, the cheers were long and loud. We were thrilled, and so full of adrenalin that we could have gone straight out onstage and done it all over again. The second house wasn't for a couple of hours, though, which gave us time to come down to Earth.

Which we did. We sat in the green room, waiting anxiously for John Considine to come round and deliver his verdict, hoping that he would confirm that the act had a future on the Sullivan and Considine time, but he was a no-show, which put a dent in our mood somewhat.

"He didn't like it, obviously," Freddie muttered into his cup of tea. "Can't face us."

"Nonsense," I said. "How could he not like it? We got laughs, didn't we?"

"He's management," Freddie put in gloomily. "He could like it well enough, but just not see any money in it."

Considine didn't appear after the second house either, and by the end of the evening I had been nominated to call in at the offices the next day to ask him face to face. After all, we were on friendly terms, and we needed reassurance as a group that we hadn't simply been forgotten.

So the following morning – after very little by way of sleep – I took myself over to Considine's headquarters and asked to see the boss.

"I'm sorry, Mr Considine left for New York the day before yesterday," the receptionist said. "It was terribly sudden."

Well, he hadn't been at the Alhambra then. Evidently there was an emergency of some kind elsewhere in Considine's comedy kingdom. Looking back, it may well have been a minor tremor, foreshadowing the earthquake to come.

"Hmmm, I see..." I said, thoughtfully, as I sidled over to take a sneaky look at the typed bill-sheets tacked to the walls, to see if I could pick up a hint of how things actually stood for *The Nutty Burglars*. "Mind if I...?"

"Knock yourself out," the receptionist said.

A chill crept slowly down my spine as I failed to spot a single mention anywhere...

The receptionist noticed my dismay, and gave a long-suffering sigh. "What are you looking for?"

"*The Nutty Burglars*," I said.

"The Nutty Buglers? So it's a musical turn?"

"No, not Buglers. Burglars. We do a sketch. In which we burgle. Nuttily."

"Hmmm..." she began to shake her head. "No Nutty Burglars that I can see. Are you sure that is the name of the act or is it just the sketch?"

"Oh!" That was a point. What had Stan decided we were to be called? I had it suddenly, and snapped my fingers. "The Four Comiques!"

"Are you French? You don't sound French."

"I'm not, no. We aren't. We just have a French name."

"Why?"

I had to be frank. "I... really don't know."

The receptionist gave me a long look and turned back to the pinboards, muttering under her breath. Suddenly I spotted The Four Comiques on one of the lists pinned up there. A red thread was pinned connecting our name to the city of Seattle on the map, where a cluster of pins suggested dozens of turns playing a fistful of theatres.

"There we are!" I cried. "What does this mean?"

She peered at where I was pointing and translated the pins for me. "Hmmm... Seattle for the next three weeks, then Portland for four, then Tacoma and Spokane," she said.

"Splendid!" I said. "Well, then, I shall get out of your hair, and return when Mr Considine is back in town."

"As you please," she said, easing herself back in behind her desk.

I hurried back to my friends with the good news. Bookings for weeks ahead, and not too much travelling either over the next few weeks and months. Of course, the theatres weren't exactly what we had become used to when we were working for Karno. This was small-time vaudeville, whereas before we'd been just one step down from the really big time.

The very biggest vaudeville theatres in most of the towns we played in would be the Considine Empresses, and the rival Pantages venues. In the orbit of these suns, if you will, were any number of smaller satellite theatres, offering small-time vaudeville three or four times a day, and many of these were also owned by the Considine organisation or by King Greek, or by other smaller-time entrepreneurs who had a booking arrangement with one or other of the two giants. And it was in these smaller theatres that the Four Comiques plied our trade.

Not Karno venues, and not Karno money, either, let me tell you that.

But not being billed and identified as the Karno company, nobody knew we were English, which we began to enjoy. An English accent is a fine thing to have in American vaudeville, broadly speaking, but in some of the smaller theatres, it wasn't such a boon as all that. It made us sound stuck up, like we felt we were better than our audience, even though we didn't think that, particularly, and we found that affecting a nondescript American accent onstage took the edge off, somehow, allowed us to simply be funny. So that is what we did.

And strangely what we were doing felt a little more honest, somehow. We had been used to riding into towns and topping the bills in the biggest theatres, but it wasn't a notoriety that we had earned for ourselves. No, it was the Fred Karno name that was responsible, and we were mere cogs in a machine that would trundle along just as happily without us. Now, though, with *The Nutty Burglars*, we were making a name for ourselves on our own merits, and it felt good, it felt noble, it felt... better.

Along the way, Wallace took his first steps – in a public park in Tacoma, where we were having a picnic lunch before three shows at a murky little theatre there – and ventured his first word, which was "Da-daah!" (Not, I hasten to add, a sign of affection for his father, but rather an impersonation of Stan's final flourish after the bowler hat gag).

We fell into the habit of booking ourselves into digs as a married couple, Tilly and I, which we enjoyed greatly. Partly this was because it reminded us of the first flush of our romance some years before, when Freddie had been under the impression that we were married and had booked us into married digs. That period, of course, had come to a juddering halt when Charlie found out about it and shopped us to the number one, who was his elder brother Syd. Tilly had been obliged to leave the company then, and we had not seen each other for more than a year. I still hadn't forgiven Charlie for that little shenanigan, by the way, although Tilly still refused to believe he'd meant anything malicious by it.

We enjoyed posing as married, too, because we often found ourselves in the care of landladies whose maternal instincts were very well-developed. Sometimes their own children had grown up and flown the nest, sometimes they had never been blessed themselves but had never lost the yearning. Whichever, Wallace was a charmer, and more than once we found that our hostess would be happy to sit with him in the evenings when we were working. Would even put him to bed so we could stay out for a quick beer or three afterwards, if we were really lucky.

When a doting landlady was not available as an option, we would have to take the little chap with us to the theatre. Now sometimes there would be other acts on the bill who would happily keep an eye on the little rogue for the twenty minutes or so that we needed to be onstage. A few times, however, Tilly was thrown by hearing him wail, right at the very edge of the range of her hearing, during the middle of our turn.

Then, on one occasion – in Chicago, as I recall – we'd left the lad with a couple of busty sisters, dancers, who were doting on his chubby cheeks as we made our way up to the wings. Freddie muttered as we climbed the staircase:

"He knows which side his bread is buttered, old Wallace, doesn't he?"

And indeed he did seem to enjoy the attentions lavished upon him from all sides, particularly by our female colleagues. However, just before *The Nutty Burglars* was about to start, we heard a dreadful scream, unmistakeably Dandovian in origin, and Tilly flew down the stairs again to calm the baby down.

Stan and I grimaced, shrugged at one another, and then began the routine. When the time came for Tilly to make her entrance as the maid there was a momentary pause – which felt like about five minutes but was maybe only a dozen heartbeats long – during which Stan and I both imagined how the sketch would go without her. We would just crack the safe, rob the house and leave, and that would have to be that. Functional, not especially funny, but maybe people would be intrigued. Maybe they'd learn something...

Then Tilly rushed out from the wings, flushed and breathless from her gallop up the stairs, and holding little Wallace in her arms.

Stan blinked as he took this in, and I feared that the little man was going to suddenly start bursting his lungs, but Tilly seemed determined to carry on as though this was perfectly normal, and the sketch proceeded on its merry way.

Early in the piece Tilly was supposed to introduce herself as the maid of the house.

"I'm Gertrude, the... nanny," she said. Stan simply nodded, and on we went.

As for Wallace, he was clearly utterly stage-struck. He realised that there were lots of people watching, maybe a couple of hundred, and that was absolutely fine by him. And here was Stan, who was always worth looking at, and sure enough he was being funny, so the lad laughed, which made the audience laugh, which just made him laugh even more.

The climactic sequence – as I have explained, I think – involved me lighting the fuse on a dummy bomb, and the four of us passing it backwards and forwards in increasing alarm. In the midst of this, Tilly suddenly handed me the baby – whether she meant to do it or not I couldn't say, and neither could she afterwards – and then there we were all of us, bomb circulating one way, the baby the other. He thought this was a fine old game, of course, and gurgled away happily, until Freddie ran outside, the bomb flew out of the window, and went off with the most tremendous smoky bang.

Freddie reappeared then, having quickly blackened his face with two handfuls of soot and stood his hair on end, whereupon Wallace had had enough surprises, and began to wail. This turned out to be the most perfect coda to the performance, and we could not make any of the other acts that night believe that we hadn't trained our little man to within an inch of his life to get him to react so precisely on demand.

From that night on, we could always revert to the nanny set-up if push came to shove and no-one would look after Wallace, and he actually grew quite accustomed to being on display.

Rather liked it, I think.

So the Four happy Comiques travelled all over, cheerfully slogging their way through the back alleyways of small-time vaudeville. We ended up travelling as far as the Great Lakes, and then all the way back out to the West Coast again, where we spent a blissful fortnight in Vancouver. We all stayed at the English Bay Beach, where we were able to hand Wallace over to Aunt Lucia and Uncle Mike Asher in the afternoon and retrieve him from the burlesque house later, where he would invariably start to cry.

"He's just tired," Tilly would say to the cooing burlesque girls, who would sigh sympathetically and try to tickle a smile out of the little chap with their giant feathers.

I never thought he was tired, I always thought he was complaining at being dragged away from all those sequins. To be honest, Freddie usually had a very similar expression on his face when it was time to leave.

One of those Vancouver afternoons Tilly and I strolled out along the pier together, and leaned on the railing looking out over the bay. After a minute or two of companionable silence I glanced down at her at my shoulder, and saw she was beaming from ear to ear.

"What is it?" I said, thinking she had remembered something funny.

"Oh, nothing," she said. "Just... thanks."

"Thanks? What for?"

"Nothing. Everything. For coming to get me."

"You're welcome, I'm sure," I said.

"I know it's not a big deal, like it was with Karno," she said. "And I know you must miss that."

I began to protest, and she held up a finger to my lips.

"A little, you must miss it a little. But I have to say I am having the most marvellous time."

"As am I," I said, and she hooked her arm in mine and rested her head on my shoulder.

And it felt like we'd be perfectly happy just to travel around together, getting laughs with our friends and watching Wallace grow for the next year, the next decade, and on and on into our dotage.

The world had other ideas.

13
EDGAR ENGLISH

OF course, there had to be a fly in the ointment during that sunny spring and summer of 1914.

And even then, you know, at first it seemed like a small fly, not one that would prevent you from getting at the ointment. Not a really big fat annoying fly, constantly banging its fat stupid head against the window right next to your ear all day long. Just a little, buzzy annoyance.

You see, I started to see Charlie Chaplin everywhere. Months had passed since he'd disappeared to California to make moving pictures and signed the death warrant for his comedy career, and I'd almost forgotten about the little swine.

Now, though, as we toured around with *The Nutty Burglars*, we started to run into the new comedies coming out of Keystone Pictures. They were still, as they'd always been, the cue for a large part of the vaudeville audience to get up and use the facilities, but sometimes we'd go to a nickelodeon, just to keep abreast of what was happening. Apart from anything else, the flickers used to hypnotise little Wallace, so it would be a good way to get an hour or so of relative peace and quiet.

The first time we caught a glimpse of Charlie was in a little movie theatre, which had until recently been a Pantages vaudeville hall, in Portland, Oregon. The flicker was called *Kid Auto Races at Venice*, and was filmed at a racetrack, where little motorised carts were buzzing around in front of a rambunctious crowd of onlookers. What really caught our attention was that there was a camera filming the race, and we could see it up there on the screen, which meant that there must have been two cameras there, and we'd never seen a film of something being filmed before, something in which the camera was actually a character.

Then our eyes were taken by a figure strolling out onto the track, clearly aware of the onscreen camera operator and playing up for him. The carts weaved around this chap in a frankly dangerous fashion, and people started to snigger and gasp.

"Hey Arthur!" Freddie sang out. "Look – it's you!"

"What?" I said.

"It's the Stowaway, look!"

The figure was teetering from side to side, seemingly drunk, as members of the crowd tried to pull him back to safety. His jacket was tight, a couple of sizes too small, while his trousers were baggy, a couple of sizes too large. His great over-sized shoes flapped in the dust, while he twirled a bendy cane, occasionally lifting his battered derby to a passing cart or twiddling his little toothbrush moustache.

It was Chaplin, and of course he was also, as surely as anything, the Stowaway.

The Stowaway, I should explain, was a comic creation of my own devising. I had come up with him on one of our Atlantic crossings to entertain my sea-sick companions, one of whom was, naturally, Mr Charles Spencer Chaplin. I'd grabbed the too-small jacket and the too-large trousers from the Karno costume trunk, used a cane that had been given to me by the great George Robey – who used a similar one as a staple part of his own on-stage costume, by the way – slapped a derby on my head and a little moustache on my lip, and then had cavorted around in very much the style I was now seeing up on the screen, tormenting two shipboard stewards, and evading capture in a slippery fashion, just as Chaplin was doing for the camera at the Venice race track.

"The little...!" I growled.

"What?" Freddie grinned amiably. "It's just a coincidence, surely?"

"Coincidence my arse!" I fumed. "That's Chaplin!"

"Goodness me, so it is!" Freddie beamed. "Hey Stan, look, it's Charlie!"

Stan had already recognised our erstwhile number one, and so, it appeared, had Tilly, who was chuckling along with everyone else at the little fellow's antics as he wobbled back into the traffic once again, determined to hog the camera.

I vividly remembered then the most recent occasion that I'd brought the Stowaway out for inspection. It was when Stan and I accompanied Charlie to the Keystone Studios, and I had easily thrown together a costume very similar to this one that Charlie was now sporting from bits and pieces that were lying around in the wardrobe room, in the hope of encouraging him to take the plunge by showing him just how easy it was to invent something from scratch.

And now here he was cavorting around in my borrowed weeds, as it were. It's easy to invent something good, I thought. Just wait for someone else to do it, and then pinch it.

The audience were now giggling more and more at the show-off's antics, and I glowered stonily at them. Those were *my* laughs, I thought.

There was, however, some small consolation to be had. Afterwards as we left to head over to our theatre the four of us squinted at the bill matter, and found that Chaplin was listed as 'Edgar English'.

Stan snorted at this. "So much for making a name for himself!"

"I don't know why you're getting so worked up about it," Tilly said, handing Wallace to me and taking my arm. "It was just a piece of nothing, wasn't it? And it made me laugh."

"Yes, and as I recall, the Stowaway made you laugh too," I retorted. "And did so first."

"Well," she said. "I think there was probably just as much of the *Mumming Birds* Swell in there, if you ask me."

"Hmmm..." I grunted.

"Tilly's right," Stan said. "Forget about it. Eddie English could make those little flickers for the rest of his life and not have as much fun as we're going to have tonight."

"Hear, hear!" Freddie cried, waving his Boss o' the Plains in the air.

They were right, as well. *The Nutty Burglars* had a good night, and it drove all niggling thoughts of Chaplin out of my mind.

━━━━

Over the next few weeks and months, though, we saw Charlie in more flickers, either in nickelodeons or sharing a bill with us in small-time vaudeville. Sometimes he would be a version of the character we had first seen, the one he had entirely copied from me, which came to be referred to by the newspapers and on bill matter as 'The Tramp', or sometimes 'The Little Fellow'. There he was in *Mabel's Strange Predicament*, for example, in the same tight coat and baggy trousers, twiddling his moustache, chasing sparky little Mabel Normand from bedroom to bedroom.

Then, in *A Film Johnnie*, the Tramp was hanging around outside the actual Keystone Studios, which I recognised from my visit just six months before. He wheedles his way inside and disrupts the film shoots, causing only marginally more chaos than their everyday norm.

In other flickers, though, he was playing different styles of character, which I resented slightly less. In *His Favourite Pastime*, for example, he was simply a stock drunk, getting involved in some balletic routines with a beefy fellow I recognised as Roscoe Arbuckle. The papers were still referring to him as 'Charlie Chapman', or 'Chas Chatlin', but they were beginning to fall under his spell.

Then in *Mabel at the Wheel*, he was a stock pantomime villain with a drooping moustache and a range of unfettered histrionics that our old Guv'nor would have snorted at in derision, while in an item called *Caught in a Cabaret* he was a waiter who masquerades as the Ambassador for Greece in a quite incomprehensible story. Nonetheless, some blinkered idiot at the *New York Dramatic Mirror* opined that it would be 'unwise to call this the funniest picture that has ever been produced, but it comes mighty close to it'. Not that I was actually looking for Charlie's reviews or anything.

There seemed to be a new Chaplin feature on offer every week then, as we tracked up and down the West Coast from Seattle to Frisco and back, and his progress gradually became a background irritation as Tilly and I enjoyed the experience of being a little working family. I could tell it niggled away at Stan a little, and we would keep having this conversation.

"You don't think we might have...?" Stan would begin.

"Might have what?" I'd say.

"Well... done the wrong thing? Sticking with vaudeville, I mean?"

"What? No!" I'd grin. "Let him roll around in the dust, see where it gets him."

And in truth I really believed that we had taken the superior path. Onstage Tilly was blossoming, and one night as we lay in bed together listening to the boy's snores and watching the shadows from the passers-by playing in the streetlights on the ceiling like a sort of inverted yellow kinescope, Tilly sighed happily.

"You know," she began. "When you used to speak about the sensation you referred to as 'The Power', I always used to think you were making it up. Well, not making it up, exactly, but exaggerating. But tonight, do you know, I think I felt exactly the thing you were talking about, for the first time. It was... exhilarating."

The Power was how I'd come to refer to that feeling I had when the audience is entirely under my spell, when time seems to slow down, and I can feel a crowd responding as one docile creature rather than hundreds of disparate souls. It's a heady brew, and the thing I loved the most about being onstage. I had often wondered whether Charlie Chaplin felt the same way. His approach seemed so technical, somehow, as though he would perform his routines in exactly the same way if there was no audience there at all, but I had certainly felt the Power onstage *with* him, on many great nights back in our Karno days together. If he did feel it, that intoxicating dominance, I found it hard to believe that he didn't miss it now, performing only for a camera, for an audience that would only respond to his skills weeks later. It must be taking a bit of getting used to. And now Tilly was getting a taste of the Power for herself, which I was thrilled about, even if to be honest *The Nutty Burglars* - funny though it undoubtedly was - afforded me few opportunities to exercise it myself.

"Excellent," I said.

"And, you know, I would never have got to feel that working for Karno, you know I wouldn't."

"No, he's not known for using actresses to their full potential. Not once they've been on his casting couch, anyway."

Tilly punched me on the arm and laughed. "What I'm trying to say is, I feel like I've finally found what I was meant to do."

"I'm glad," I said, drawing her close. "And especially so that you have decided to do it with me."

———

Dark clouds were gathering, though, in that summer of 1914.

In early July we read in the American papers about the assassination of an archduke in Sarajevo by some Yugoslav nationalist, and how everyone was getting agitated about the possibility of a war between Austro-Hungary and the Kingdom of Serbia. Some voices back home were apparently warning that this situation could escalate into something bigger and nastier that the whole of Europe would ultimately be drawn into.

But that's not what I'm talking about.

I still used to flick through the pages of *Variety*, even though the vaudeville venues that *The Nutty Burglars* were playing in were far too small to register even on that newspaper's copious listings pages, and around that time I stumbled onto a big article about Charlie which made him sound like just about the biggest thing in the entertainment business. I say 'stumbled' – you could hardly fail to see it. Evidently Mack Sennett was releasing all of the Chaplin pictures at once in Britain, with a massive publicity campaign, which was headlined:

ARE YOU READY FOR THE
CHAPLIN BOOM?

Never one to downplay his studio's importance, Mack went on to assert as follows:

"There has never been so instantaneous a hit as that of Chas Chaplin!"

At least this one got the name right, or near enough.

The five of us were travelling back down to California to play small-time houses in Sacramento and Los Angeles. Stan and Freddie sat opposite the little Dandoe family in the train carriage, with little Wallace sitting on Tilly's lap making a series of ultimately unsuccessful grabs for her nose. Stan saw my expression, and raised an eyebrow quizzically.

Without a word I passed the paper over, and he frowned as he read it, with Freddie peering over his shoulder.

"Well!" Stan breathed.

"I know," I said.

"Whatever does it say?" Tilly said, as Wallace made another swipe for her konk.

Stan handed the paper back to me, and Tilly swung the lad over to Freddie so that she could have a read. All of a sudden though, we were into the last sequence of our *Nutty Burglars*, which just happened to be Wallace's greatest delight. I passed the paper to Tilly, and Freddie passed the baby to Stan, who passed him to me. Naturally he wanted to go back to his mother now to complete the circuit, so she passed the paper diagonally to Stan, while I feinted to give Wallace back to her but instead crossed diagonally to Freddie, then switched seats with Stan, taking the paper from him. And on and on it went. The little fellow loved this sort of caper, so it was only when I managed to distract him by pointing out a boat outside the window that Tilly actually got to catch up with what we'd read.

"Oh, but this is... well, it's astonishing, isn't it?" she said once she'd taken it in.

"It is that," I said.

"Charlie certainly seems to be a palpable hit," Freddie said, with an amiable grin.

"Yes, but it's still only the flickers, isn't it?" I said, although the thought of Charlie having such success wasn't sitting well in the pit of my stomach.

"Imagine everyone at home being able to watch him, though. That is pretty amazing..." Stan was brooding.

"It's only the flickers," I said again. "They're a novelty, that's all. They'll never stand up against live entertainment, not really. I bet Charlie hasn't heard a laugh, a real live laugh I mean, since before Christmas."

Stan grinned. "Yes, and even then it was you cackling at him when he decided to leave Karno!"

Freddie and I laughed, and Wallace waved his arms around happily, but I suddenly noticed that Tilly wasn't joining in. In point of fact all the colour had drained from her face.

"What's the matter, love?" I said. "Does it say Charlie's to be Prime Minister?"

"Prime Minister of Mirth, you mean?" Freddie chipped in. That, you may recall, was the bill matter of the great George Robey.

"He might as well. He's stolen all Robey's clothes," Stan muttered sourly.

"Mine, you mean," I cut back. "They're the Stowaway's togs."

"Which *you* borrowed from Robey."

"Well... that's as may be."

Tilly was not joining in this bit of levity. She was still staring at a page of *Variety* with something approaching horror.

"Good Lord, Tilly, whatever have you found?" I said, reaching over and putting a consoling hand on her knee.

She showed me the paper, then, pointing at a small item in a column chirpily entitled 'Brit Tit-Bits'. Her finger, I noticed, was trembling.

THAT'S THE WAY TO DO IT!' was what I read, and then in smaller print beneath:

'Britannia pier at Great Yarmouth, England, burned to the ground last weekend...'[1]

"Burned to the ground?" I said jovially, thinking perhaps this was what I was meant to notice. "It's in the sea, isn't it? How did that happen?"

Tilly indicated with a chilly flick of her blonde curls that I should read on.

"'Local Punch-and-Judy man Gordon Beckett is in prison, hospital suspected of involvement in the conflagration. He is not expected to stand trial.'" I read. Then, like a slap across the face, it hit me. "Good gracious! Is that...?"

Tilly nodded bleakly. "It's Dad."

14
AT THE SUPERBA

I had only met Gordon Beckett once, and that was about five years before. I'd been looking for Tilly, and went to Southend-on-Sea where her old man was a Punch and Judy man down on the beach, to see if he'd had any word of her, which as it happened he hadn't.

I vividly recalled, though, his conviction that the Germans were coming. By all accounts they were building a great navy, and old Beckett was convinced that they were planning an invasion by sea that would land at Southend. The old fellow stared out to sea, a look of grim determination on his face as he said: "When they come we'll set fire to the pier, Mr Punch and me... All that wood, it'll go up like billy-o!"

Some time after that, Tilly's family had been forced to do a midnight flit after the Punch-and-Judy stand suddenly exploded. It seemed that some bright spark had flicked a cigarette end in there on the way home from the pub, probably cocking a derisory snook at the whole idea of the puppet show, and had ignited old Beckett's little stockpile of dynamite and other goodies.

I had made a promise to help Tilly find her family – father, mother, sister, nephew, niece – when we returned to Blighty, without any real clue how on Earth I would start to do that.

Now, though, it appeared they'd scuttled off to Great Yarmouth, where her father's paranoia about the Germans had apparently been fanned by recent events in the Balkans, and he'd made a bid to save the citizens of his adopted town from Teutonic rape and pillage by setting fire to the Britannia Pier for them.

"Prison," Tilly said, her eyes brimming with tears. "Hospital!"

"It says he's not expected to stand trial. That's good, isn't it?" I said, but Stan inhaled sharply through his teeth, shaking his head slowly. "Clearly they can't prove anything," I pressed on, trying to find a silver lining.

"It means they don't expect him to live long enough," Tilly said in a small voice.

"No, no, no," I said. "It means…" Then, however, I saw that it might very well mean exactly what she feared.

"We have to go back," Tilly said firmly. "I have to see him, he needs to know I'm all right, he needs to see his grandson, I have to see my Mama. We have to go back."

She sat looking out of the window with a determined look on her beautiful face. Stan, Freddie and I looked at one another, as little Wallace clambered all over his Uncle Fred, trying to twist his ear off, and none of us had any idea how we were going to make the cash appear from thin air to make this possible, much as we would all have loved to.

We arrived in Los Angeles, which was hot and sticky, and found that the Considine organisation had hived us off into a dump called The Happy Hour, a 150-seat baker's oven off Main Street. Even selling out, which the place wasn't doing, we were hardly going to break even once we'd taken care of our living expenses, and the prospect of moving up to the Considine's bigger time was uncertain. All we could do was keep plugging away, keep getting the laughs, and hope word of mouth would make its way back to Seattle.

Which didn't help us with our present pickle. Tilly, understandably, became quite fretful, and we discussed the situation over and over again until we were going round in circles.

One night that week, we were lying together in the darkness, listening to the boy's light snuffling from the adjacent crib, and she came round, as she had to, to the only sensible way of looking at it.

"You're quite right, it's impossible. Even if we could scrape together enough for a ticket for just me and the little one to go, I couldn't leave you boys in the lurch."

"I suppose… we could look for someone else…" I mused.

"Oh, you'd like that, I suppose?"

"I was thinking, maybe Freddie would enjoy the casting process. He must have picked up a tip or two from his old man about how it's done."

"Ha!" Tilly slapped my cheek (upper).

"And there are plenty of pretty girls here, all desperate to get spotted and put in front of a camera, or tied to a railway track."

"You think it'd be that easy to replace me?"

"I don't, I don't!" I protested.

"Besides, it's not like I actually want to leave The Nutty B's, I'm really enjoying work more than ever."

"And you're brilliant at it," I said, partly because it was absolutely true, and partly because nothing made Tilly more affectionate than a nice earnest compliment or two. True to form, she drew herself closer to me and laid her warm leg along mine.

"So that's that?" I said. "We're forgetting about England for now?"

"Oh, you never know," Tilly said. "Something could come up."

The next afternoon we set out for a walk to kill time before our shift began. Tilly wanted to push the boy in his baby carriage around Grand Park, in the hope that he would nod off for a while. Stan, Freddie and I were deemed too stimulating for the little man, and so we were dispatched in the other direction, strolling through the theatre district in the sunshine.

"It's no wonder the Happy Hour is struggling," Stan said.

"Why? Because it's a flea pit, you mean?" Freddie piped up.

"No, look around. It's not exactly short of competition, is it?"

Stan had a point, certainly. We sauntered past any number of rival entertainment establishments in just a few minutes – a Bijou, a Liberty, a Metropolitan, a Unique, a Gem, a Banner, another Unique, a Novelty.

Our feet seemed to lead us naturally back to the Empress, the big Considine theatre that we had played with Karno's, and we gazed a little wistfully up at the fancy frontage, and browsed the bill matter. The Buster Brown Company seemed to be filling our old slot for this particular week, the Carson Brothers offered 'posturing', whatever that entailed, and I wouldn't have fancied sharing dressing room space with Columbus the Celebrated White Horse, however well-trained he was.

"We'll be back," Stan grinned. "Just wait and see. Old Considine likes us, he won't let us wallow in small-time for too long."

"I hope you're right," I said, and we wandered on.

We passed the People's Theater, a rival vaudeville house to the Empress. Last time we were in town it had boasted a bill that matched Sullivan and Considine's. Now though it was renamed the Century, and it was showing moving pictures. The three of us glanced at one another – this was a surprise and no mistake.

A couple of blocks further on, on South Broadway, we came to a brand new theatre, a building of such spectacular luxury that we all stopped and pushed the straw boaters back on our heads to admire it.

'QUINN'S SUPERBA', the sign gleamed.

"Hell of a name," I muttered. Freddie grinned.

We couldn't resist taking a quick look, and the lobby was open and quite busy so we wandered inside for a mingle. The sumptuous main hall was finished entirely in onyx, with faux columns containing concealed electric lighting. It looked like it had cost an absolute mint.

Stan was inspecting the programme, which was attached to the wall in a gleaming frame of hammered brass. "Good God!" he said suddenly, and Freddie and I tripped across the luxurious red carpet to join him.

"What is it?" Freddie asked.

"This place. It's not a theatre. It's a nickelodeon."

"Come off it!"

"It is, look...." Stan began to read aloud from the banner advertisement. "'Showing exclusively first run offerings from the General Film Company, accompanied by a ten-piece resident orchestra, the only one in the whole of California. Admission stalls ten cents, circle fifteen cents, loges twenty cents...'"

"Well," I said. "It's not exactly a nickelodeon, then, is it? At best it's a dime-a-dodeon."

"It's not far short of a quarterodeon," Freddie chipped in. "What is a loge, anyway? It'd better have a couch and pillows for twenty cents."

"And a butler," said Stan.

I cast a quick eye over the flickers on offer in this magnificent palace. At least there were no Chaplin pictures, that was something, although there was a Keystone on the bill. There was Gilbert M. Anderson in *Broncho Billy and the Sheriff*, Victor Potel starred in *Slippery Slim's Inheritance*, there was something called *How He Lost His Trousers*, a documentary from the Kalem Company called *In Old England*, and the Hearst-Selig News Pictorial, number 39.

The place was clearly thriving, as plenty of people were walking in for the afternoon matinee. Stan, Freddie and I found ourselves wandering in without a word like lost spirits, each of us wondering what was happening to the world order we knew. We took our seats in the plush new auditorium, and the place was heaving, at least as lively as you could have hoped for on a weekday afternoon. And yet these folks were here to watch pictures? We were flabbergasted.

The programme began with a so-so effort featuring someone called William West in *The Adventures of the Absent-Minded Professor*. He bumbled around, lost things, found them again, tried to write a letter with a carrot, you get the idea. The crowd were very excited, it seemed, but only half of them really appeared to be paying attention. The rest were chattering and drinking in a good-natured hubbub. A pianist – not a ten-piece orchestra, I noted, unless they were counting his individual fingers – was gamely trying to make himself heard with his plinky-plonk accompaniments to the gentle tumbling and gesturing, but he was fighting a losing battle.

Stan and I shrugged at one another with a long-suffering sigh. We were used to seeing the moving pictures greeted with indifference, but not usually by such a big crowd, and a big crowd, moreover, who had paid specially to see them.

After a couple more similarly duff offerings had been largely ignored by the room, a production title card shone up on the screen, and the Keystone picture, entitled *Mabel's Busy Day*, was next.

The first person to appear on the screen was Mabel Normand, whose busy day this was to be. She was playing a rather forlorn hot dog seller, and in order to get inside a racetrack, she bribed a copper sporting a walrus moustache with a free hotdog, and he let her slip in through a gap in the fence.

Once inside the arena, she had a contretemps or two with some spectators, one of whom was recognisable as Mack Sennett himself. Mabel was funny enough, and nice to look at too, but around us in the theatre the crowd's attitude remained more or less unimpressed.

Suddenly, though, that changed dramatically.

The scene shifted to outside the racetrack again, where a queue of people were waiting to get in. A figure swaggered past them all, but no-one in the queue objected. In fact they were all grinning fit to bust. He turned on the spot to face the camera, and immediately a cheer went up that shook the chandeliers. There was an almighty banging of seats as people leapt to their feet and punched the air. Clearly this was what they'd all been waiting for, this was what they all wanted to see.

It was Chaplin. Of course it was.

He wasn't playing a tramp in this picture. He had on a smart suit, grey, comprising an over-large jacket with a white carnation button-hole, baggy trousers, those large shoes that enabled him to do his funny rolling walk, the endlessly versatile bendy cane, the whole ensemble topped off with a moustache and a pale grey bowler hat. He was a drunk, an inebriated swell, no less, very reminiscent of the character he had played in *Mumming Birds* for Karno, and even more painfully reminiscent of my rolling drunk Stowaway.

I knew it wasn't just me who saw it, either, as I heard Stan whistle softly beside me.

I watched agog as Charlie got into a shoving match with the walrus-moustachioed policeman, exactly as I had with the stewards on board ship. He took it further, of course. In fact he took it into some quite incredible realms of violence, kicking the cop repeatedly in the chest, before sneaking into the race venue without paying.

We caught a glimpse then of the cars racing around the track, throwing up great clouds of dust as they curved past the camera. The crowd, though, were all facing away from the track, completely ignoring the cars whizzing around, simply desperate to see what Charlie was going to get up to.

In the room where we sat – actually we were obliged to stand by the unruly excitement all around – every mean-spirited arse-kick was greeted like the very soul of wit. Men and women were howling with mirth, quite literally holding their sides. I didn't know anyone actually did this in real life until that very afternoon. One or two were rolling on the floor, completely out of control, utterly unconcerned about their dignity.

The picture's story was thinness itself. Charlie stole Mabel's hotdogs, fought a number of people – including Mabel herself, who he punched in the face – and ended up losing his jacket and shirt so that only his collar and tie remained.

Even though Mabel Normand had evidently written the piece, directed it, and got her name in the title, there was no doubt that it was Charlie who was the main attraction.

I could barely breathe now. His antics were so... familiar, and the audience's reaction all around me was so... *ecstatic*, that I found I could no longer bear to watch any more.

I needed air.

No, scratch that, I needed drink.

I staggered to my feet, pushed past half a row of cheering imbeciles with tears cascading down their stupid cheeks, and stumbled up the aisle towards the back of the auditorium. My head was spinning, and I leant against a pillar for a moment to recover my equilibrium.

"Arthur...?" a voice nearby said, tentatively, disbelieving. I only just registered it above the merry hubbub all around.

I turned to see who was addressing me, and even in the flickering gloom I recognised the distinctive purple eyes peering in astonishment over the fancy silk scarf that was modestly disguising the lower half of his celebrated face.

Charlie.

15
THE FILM JOHNNIE

found Tilly back at our digs, buttoning the little man into a fresh pair of tiny trousers. I'd seen as I approached along the corridor a line of nappies drying in the communal bathroom, and thankfully our fellow residents were an indulgent lot, so we didn't have to have them strung along the side of our bed.

"Good walk?" I said, tickling Wallace and making him giggle.

"Da-dahh!" he cried, and this time he meant me and not Stanley's showman flourish.

"I've been thinking," Tilly said, a serious expression on her face.

I sighed inwardly. "About your father, you mean?"

"How about if I were to go to New York and try to work my passage? Cleaning cabins on a liner, something like that?"

"Who is looking after the baby all this time?"

"I'll cross that bridge when I get to it."

"How are you paying for the train?"

"Well, I'm... I was thinking I could jump on a boxcar."

"With a baby? That's your plan? Get an eighteen month-old child to ride the rails like a hobo."

"No, no. Well, not exactly. You remember the Karno boxcar? There are other acts with cars like that criss-crossing the country all the time. Those Marx boys for one…"

Those Marx boys were four brothers that we had met and hit it off with the year before when we were touring the big time – well, not the big time, exactly, but certainly bigger than the dump we were currently appearing in. Julius, Arthur, Lenny and Milton had a fifteen-strong company, and did indeed travel in a boxcar very similar to ours. Schedules like theirs, though, hopped from town to town, city to city, trying to keep the travelling as civilised as possible. The chances of such an act crossing the continent West to East in one go, even if they could be persuaded to let Tilly hitch a ride with a baby in tow, were somewhere between pretty slim and none at all.

"Tilly…" I began, and I could hear my tone was discouraging.

"I just need to meet the right people, and…" She could sustain this fantasy no longer, and sat heavily on the bed, plunging her face into her hands. I sat beside her, and put an arm around her shoulders, registering the sobs that she was trying to hide from me.

"I'm sorry, love," I said. "I just can't see how to do it. If I could I would, you know that."

She nodded, little nods, and leaned against me.

"Hey," I said, trying to change the subject in a manner that was jauntier than I was feeling. "Speaking of meeting the right people – guess who we bumped into this afternoon?"

"Someone who is travelling to New York and needs some company?"

"Well, I don't know so much about that, but as it happens someone we have been to New York with, in the past…"

Tilly was drawing a blank, perhaps off her game because of worrying about her old man.

"Tell me," she said.

I held a moment for maximum impact, then said: "Charlie."

"Charlie?" Tilly didn't look surprised, she just frowned, puzzled, as though she didn't even know who I meant.

"Yes, Charlie. Charlie Chaplin."

Now her eyebrows shot up. "Charlie? He's here? Oh, of course he is, this is where he works, isn't it, Los Angeles, I was forgetting, how could I have forgotten that? Where? Where did you meet him? How? How is he? What is he doing...?"

I threw my hands up to block this sudden barrage of questioning. "Whoa, whoa, whoa!" I said. "Take a breath and I'll tell you!"

I checked my pocket watch, and saw that it was time to hotfoot it to the theatre for the first of our four-a-days. So I picked up the little lad, she grabbed the bag that went with him everywhere containing items to entertain him, feed him or clean him up, and I filled her in on the way.

───

"Charlie? Is that you?" I'd said at the back of the movie theatre.

"Whisshht! Not here!" he hissed, and took me by the arm, leading me out into the onyx-clad lobby, and then straight through and out onto South Broadway, where he trotted along the front of the building and ducked into the shadowy mouth of an alley. I was so stunned to see him that I just followed along meekly and waited for him to explain the cloak and dagger.

"Sorry about that," Charlie said. "It's just that I like to watch the crowd but I have to stay incognito, otherwise I can never get away from them."

"I knew it," I said. "You miss it, don't you? The laughter. You miss it."

Charlie frowned. "I miss it? I don't miss standing on a stage at the audience's mercy, if that's what you mean. But I do need to know from time to time if such and such a trick is going down or not. How else am I to develop my art?"

"Which particular art are we talking about," I said. "The art of kicking someone up the arse, or the art of kicking a copper in the chest?"

Charlie didn't pick up on my sarcasm. "It's actually rather irritating when they love absolutely everything," he said. "One learns nothing at all. But tell me, how do you come to be here in Los Angeles? Are the Karnos in town? I've seen no mention."

"Well, some of us are," I said. I found I didn't want to tell him that the tour had foundered principally because he had left us. His head was big enough already. "The Guv'nor called the company home, but I decided to stick around and work up a vaudeville turn with Stan and Freddie."

"How marvellous!" Charlie cried. "So Stan and Fred are here too?"

"Inside," I said, jerking a thumb back towards the Superba.

Charlie flung his scarf round his face again, and stuck his head out of the alleyway so he could keep an eye on the gilded entrance. "Look here," he said, tiring of this after a moment. "We really must catch up, but I have to dash. Duty calls, all that. But here..." He fumbled in his jacket pocket, and produced a card – embossed, very smart, very new – which he handed to me. "This is where I live, it isn't so far away, just a few blocks. Come for luncheon, tomorrow, all of you. Midday? I happen to find myself completely free, so I am at your service. Say you'll come!"

"Righto," I said with a shrug, thinking a free lunch was the very least he owed me.

"Stout fellow!" Charlie cried, grasping my hand quickly. Then he darted off and slipped into the back of a limousine which had ghosted up to the kerb a little way off without my noticing it until that very moment.

I stood there, watching him ooze away luxuriously, marvelling at the coincidence of running into him, and wondering why I hadn't mentioned Tilly. Or, for that matter, Wallace.

━━━━

"So, you are meeting him tomorrow?" Tilly said, as we burrowed down into the hot dingy dressing rooms at the Happy Hour.

"We all are, we are all invited."

"I wonder..." she said, with a frown.

"What do you wonder?" I asked.

"Whether I should go."

"Of course you should. Why ever not?"

"You know perfectly well," she said, flicking her eyes at little Wallace.

I did know why she was having misgivings of course. Back when she'd fallen pregnant with the boy, she'd allowed Charlie to believe that he was the father – she had allowed me to believe that too, for a long while – and he had hurriedly given her money, money he had borrowed from Stan, as it happens, to make herself scarce. Charlie's fear, at the time, was that having gotten a girl in the family way would be a sufficient example of moral turpitude – a phrase of the Guv'nor's, borrowed from the U.S. Bureau of Immigration – to cost him his precious place as number one of a Karno company.

Later, much later, she'd admitted to me that she'd hoodwinked him, and that really I was Wallace's dad. She did this to save me from having to make the decision whether or not to abandon my own Karno career to take care of her, because she feared that either choice might have led me to resent both her and the child for ever afterwards. We were past that point now, happily.

Seeing Charlie again would be awkward for Tilly, I could see that, especially as he must still be under the impression that she'd borne his child. However, I rather wanted to put him through that embarrassment, see the wind taken from his sails, watch him squirm a little bit. It'd be good for him, I thought, especially as our encounter the day before had forcibly reminded me of just how very full of himself Charlie could be.

So I said: "Don't be silly, of course you must come. Wallace too. It's just a social call, a little bit of lunch. It'll be fun, we can all talk about old times."

Tilly still looked dubious. "Well, if you're sure...?" she said.

───

The next day we set off on foot towards the address Charlie had given me. It was approaching midday, and the scorching sun was high in the sky.

"So Charlie's in charge of luncheon?" Freddie chirped. "Wonder what we're having."

"I'm hoping for a gas-jet fry-up," Stan said. "That's his speciality."

"What on Earth is that?" Tilly asked.

"Of course, you never had one, did you, love?" I said.

We laughed as we remembered our first weeks in New York back in 1910, when Stan and Charlie had shared a room, and to make Karno's meagre wage stretch a little further we would all contribute to a meal of sausages and bacon, which we would cook on the gas-jet lamps. Freddie and I would be detailed to waft the tell-tale smoke out of the window, while Charlie would march up and down playing the violin with wild exuberance so that the landlady would not hear the fat hissing and spitting from the corridor outside. Those were some of my favourite meals, and if that was what Charlie had in mind I for one would not be complaining.

The walk was taking longer than expected in the heat, and little Wallace was beginning to suffer. The lad was red in the face and sweating, and as we turned onto 7th Avenue he began to cry. Not a serious wail, but not a happy noise either.

Tilly picked him up to comfort him, and I pushed the empty baby carriage along the sidewalk. A little ahead of us now Stan and Freddie had stopped, and were looking up at a huge new building, in the Beaux Arts style, with gigantic arched windows above the shop fronts that occupied the ground floor. It comprised two tall blocks of apartments side by side, with a matching block between them of around half the height, so that the whole was like a giant U-shape. The American flag hung down flaccidly from a diagonal pole above the entrance, and a row of taxi cabs was waiting outside. It looked rather like an embassy.

"This is the address," Stan said. "But the sign says it is the Los Angeles Athletic Club."

A doorman in full – and rather warm-looking – livery was in attendance, and Freddie stepped over to ask his advice.

"Good morning," he said. "We are looking for the address of Mr Charles Chaplin."

The doorman acquiesced with a little bow, and swept a large glass door open for us.

"It's here?" Freddie asked, and the functionary nodded, indicating with his free hand the reception desk across the spacious lobby. Freddie turned to us, with his eyebrows raised. "We have arrived," he said.

We entered a hallway of sumptuous magnificence. Two huge chandeliers hung from the ornate white ceiling, more electric lights were set into the dark wood panelling that covered the walls and some columns too, and our feet sank into a rich diamond-patterned carpet. At the far end there were brass-fronted elevators in a smaller lobby clad in white marble, with blue stained glass windows opening onto an enclosed garden.

Stan whistled softly, and Freddie ran his palm softly over some of the panelling. I could hardly believe Charlie could afford to stay in a place like this, and was sure the doorman had made a mistake, or hadn't heard the question, or maybe was foreign and hadn't understood, and would have opened the door to us whatever we had said.

I strode over to the reception desk, with Tilly beside me, and a smartly-dressed young reception clerk smiled. "A very good morning to you, sir, and to you madam. How may I help you today?"

Wallace began to grizzle again, and Tilly gave the youth an apologetic smile. "He's very hot, I'm afraid," she said.

"Of course," he said, graciously sympathetic.

"We are looking for Mr Charles Chaplin," I said.

"Of course," the young receptionist said again. "We are expecting you. I shall call his apartment directly. But first things first..." He turned and picked up a large jug full of water, glistening with condensation and rattling with ice cubes, and he poured a glass for Tilly to share with the little boy. "Perhaps this will help?" he said with an understanding smile, and Tilly nodded gratefully. "And if you like, you can wait in our private garden. There is plenty of shade, and it is not quite so stuffy as it is in here. Just past the elevators there."

"Thank you," Tilly smiled. "You are very kind."

Tilly and Wallace set off for the garden as directed, and the youth picked up the earpiece of a telephone.

"If you gentlemen would like to take a seat, I will let Mr Chaplin know his party has arrived."

We nodded, and sank onto a luxurious leather settee, which was pleasingly cool. None of us spoke while we waited, we were just too awe-struck by our surroundings. The bell of the Otis elevator went 'Ting!' a couple of times, and spewed out a stream of affluent types who walked past us and out into the street past the doorman to step into taxi cabs.

After we had waited perhaps five or six minutes, a fresh 'Ting!' heralded the arrival of our host. Charlie sauntered over to greet us in a cream-coloured linen suit, which looked enviably cool. There was, naturally, no trace of the splay-footed walk, or indeed the over-sized shoes and bendy cane. He looked happy, confident and successful – in short, all things I suspected he had been practising in front of a mirror while he kept us waiting in the lobby.

"Stan!" Charlie cried, and gathered his erstwhile roommate into an embrace. "And Freddie! How marvellous that you are here!" Freddie too was hugged, and then it was my turn. "Arthur! Thank you, thank you for coming!"

"Quite a place you have here," I said.

"Oh!" Charlie said, slapping my arm in a way that managed to convey that he knew I was joking, but also that it was actually quite a place, even if it wasn't entirely his. "It affords me the privacy I require," he said, "and besides it is quite the place for watching the cream of Los Angeles society. They all either live here or congregate here to use the facilities. See? Look there..."

He indicated two gentlemen who were walking into a sitting room together, deep in conversation. "On the left is William Desmond Taylor, he is an actor and movie director, and a friend

129

of my colleague Mabel Normand, and the older gentleman is Mr Baum, the author of all those books about the mystic land of Oz. He organises the entertainments here, like a sort of glee club. I wonder what they are cooking up..."

Meanwhile a rangy fellow, slightly stooped but fit-looking, with little round glasses perched on a beak of a nose, marched urgently over to the reception desk and consulted with the young functionary there.

Charlie pointed him out discreetly. "That's Glenn Martin, the famous aviator. They threw a dinner for him here not long ago, and he didn't realise until the end of the evening that the dining table was one of the wings of his own biplane. Ha! His face!"

Martin had been directed towards his appointment and seemed to be on his way, until Charlie sang out: "I say? Martin?" whereupon the beanpole swivelled on the heel of his leather boot and strode over.

"Why, Mister Chaplin, how are you today?"

"I am thriving, Mr Martin, and yourself?"

"I cannot complain, sir, I cannot complain."

"These are friends of mine from England," Charlie said, and we all shook the famous flier by the hand.

"They say there will be war in Europe, gentlemen. Whadda you think?" Martin said, his face serious.

"War?" I said. "Maybe a spat between the Austro-Hungarians and some Serbs. I don't see what it has to do with us."

"Well, if the Russians come in on one side, then they set themselves against the Germans, and I do believe the Kaiser fancies a war with everyone simply because there hasn't been one in a while."

"You take a keen interest in politics, Mr Martin?" Stan said.

"I do, sir, I do, for if there is to be war then it will be the first in which fliers can play a part."

"You mean for reconnaissance?" I said. "Spotting enemy positions and the like?"

"No, sir. I tell you, the aeroplane will decide the war in Europe. Flying death will smash armies and wreck mammoth battleships." He leaned in closer. "I have an idea for a plane, sir, that can soar above the conflict so that the pilot can drop bombs on one side or the other as he pleases, like Thor the Thunder God. And the generals who realise quickest that the fight can be won with flying death will be victorious, mark my words."

The celebrated aviator[2] excused himself then, and strode off urgently about his business, which I presumed involved persuading people to invest in his flying death machines.

"I must say," Charlie said, "old Martin seems even keener than the Kaiser on starting a brouhaha."

"Do you think there will be a war?" Stan asked.

"I'll tell you this much for nothing," Charlie replied. "If there is to be a war then this is the place to be, thousands and thousands of miles away from it. You couldn't get me to go back to England just now for love or money."

All of a sudden Charlie blanched. His smile evaporated, his confident veneer fell away, and his eyes widened until I could see white all around those unmistakable violet irises.

"What is this?" he hissed.

We turned to see what had thrown him so, and saw Tilly walking across the lobby with Wallace, holding him by the hand as he walked along, clearly feeling a bit more like it.

"What? What do you mean?" Stan said.

"Are you lot trying it on?" Charlie growled. "Because if you are..."

"Whatever are you talking about?" Freddie said, with a look of baffled innocence. "That's Tilly. You remember Tilly, surely, it hasn't been that long. She's with us. Come and say hello, come on..."

Charlie shook his head quickly, then just as suddenly recovered himself. By the time he had followed Freddie across the lobby to meet Tilly he had plastered his biggest, toothiest smile all over his face.

"Tilly, my dear, how lovely to see you, and looking so well!" He took Tilly's hand and kissed it flamboyantly, making a knee like some restoration fop. "And who is this little man?" Charlie offered his hand formally to our lad, who just blinked up at him, and then buried his face in Tilly's skirts.

"This is Wallace," Tilly said. "He's a little shy."

No he isn't, I thought. He just recognises an oily untrustworthy bastard when he sees one.

"Wallace?" Charlie said. "I see. I see. Well, it's a pleasure to make your acquaintance, Wallace."

Plainly Charlie hadn't met many eighteen-month old boys.

And if I was unsettled by the opulence of Charlie's lifestyle, and could hardly help feeling a certain amount of jealousy, at least those feelings were balanced somewhat by my enjoyment of Charlie's discombobulation at seeing Tilly and the little chap.

"Well," Charlie said, clapping his hands together. "Luncheon? Shall we?"

16
BE IT EVER SO HUMBLE

"I must say," I said, as the doors closed behind us. "Judging by the façade and the lobby, I thought the actual rooms would be bigger."

"Very good," Charlie smirked. "Have you never been in an elevator before?"

We had, of course. A good number of theatres that we had played in both in the States and England had them backstage for a start. But I said:

"No, mister. Is it like a magic box? Are you going to disappear us? I'm scared!"

The doors pinged open again, after a ride that was so smooth we barely noticed it had even happened.

"This way," Charlie called out, and led the way along a wide corridor, brightly sunlit thanks to a floor-to-ceiling picture window at its far end. He came to his apartment, and opened the door with his key.

"Be it ever so humble," he sang, "there's no place like home!"

He was right about that. There was no place like his home, no place that I had seen, anyway. His apartment was stupendous, a suite of rooms of such elegant splendour that we stopped in our tracks just inside the door. A dining room, with a great long red-wood table, was ahead of us. To our left we could just see into a bedroom, immaculately tidy, with a four poster bed, while along to our right was a luxurious sitting room with handsome high-backed chairs arranged as though ready for a recital of some sort on the grand piano. As we stepped wonderingly into this palace, we could see that windows ran the whole length of the outside wall, offering a view over the rooftops of downtown Los Angeles to the shimmering blue Pacific beyond.

"It's lovely and cool up here," Tilly said.

"Do you know why that is?" Charlie said. "On the floor above us, above our heads, is a swimming pool."

"No!"

"Yes, can you believe it? One hundred and sixty-six gallons of water, weighing one and half million pounds."

I saw Stan and Freddie both flinch involuntarily at the thought of so much weight suspended above their heads.

"And a little further over there are Turkish baths, which I'm told should help to keep us snug in the winter. I don't know about that, I haven't been here long enough yet."

I noticed a glass door leading out onto a balcony and stepped towards it. As I did so, I heard a chopping noise coming from a previously-unsuspected kitchen, and I stopped.

"Ah, don't be alarmed," Charlie said. "That is only Pointon. Oh, Pointon? Show yourself, there's a good chap."

The chopping ceased, and a serious-looking young man in a bronze-and-black striped waistcoat moved into the dining room as if on castors.

"Some drinks for my guests, I think," Charlie said. "Did you chill a bottle of the bubbly?"

"Indeed, sir," the young chap said with a bow of his head.

"All right, then, chop-chop. By which I mean open it and bring us some glasses, not go back to your chopping."

"Understood, sir," the young fellow said, and disappeared back into the kitchen, from where we shortly heard a tell-tale 'pop!'

"Who was that?" Tilly mouthed.

"Pointon? He's my valet."

"Your valet?" Stan goggled. "You have a valet?"

"Yes, he's preparing our luncheon right now." Charlie sauntered over to the balcony door to open it, and from the looks that passed between my friends behind his back the valet was the final straw, the thing that really put the tin lid on it all and tied it up with a ribbon.

A little later we all sat out on Charlie's balcony sipping cool champagne in the sunshine. Tilly and I were taking it in turns to clutch onto Wallace, who was desperate to run around, because the railings were sufficient to save an adult from a fall to the death but were in no way close enough together to do the job for an infant. When Tilly wasn't looking I let the tiny man have a sip from my glass, and that coupled with the noonday warmth slowed him down for a while.

"There are three types of movie that we make at Keystone," Charlie was saying. "The first is the park movie, where we take the crew to a nearby park, which has trees, benches, a boating lake, that sort of thing, and we'll come up with something there. Then there is what we call the 'event movie', which is where we take advantage of something that is already happening, such as the motor car racing picture you saw yesterday."

"*Mabel's Busy Day*," I said

"Just so. And then we have the studio movie, which we would shoot on the lot at Keystone over in Edendale, you remember the lot, don't you?"

"I do," Stan said, lapping this stuff up.

"And we will build a set as required, with the ceiling open to the sky so that we can make use of the wonderful Californian light."

"And it's going well?" Tilly said.

Charlie leaned back and closed his eyes, the very picture of self-satisfaction. "Let's just say this: every movie studio in Los Angeles, and some in Chicago, New York and San Francisco, has approached me, or should I say my representatives, about enticing me away from Keystone. Mack – that's Mack Sennett, you remember?"

Stan and I nodded, having met the Keystone boss a few times when he was chasing Charlie the year before.

"Mack," Charlie went on, "is pestering me to make a new deal, as he only signed me up for twelve months. Wasn't sure I was going to be a hit, you see. I said to him that I would sign on for next year if he would agree to pay me $1,000 a week."

"A *thou...?!*" Freddie gasped, unable to finish the word because his jaw was on the deck.

"He said that was more than he was paying himself, and I said was it *he* whose name was on big letters outside every movie house? Is it *him* that folk are queueing around the block to see?"

I had a sudden vision of Charlie's head swelling so large that it eclipsed the sweltering midday sun.

"You have already done so many pictures," Stan said. "How long does each one take?"

"Well," Charlie said, steepling his fingers, please to have the chance to show off more expertise. "The one-reelers, maybe twelve or thirteen minutes long, they take around a week to conceive, shoot and edit together, and then we are on to the next. But just now we are working on the first ever full-length comedy feature in the history of film. A six-reeler, where we can tell a whole story."

"That sounds incredible," Tilly said. "What is the title?"

Charlie paused, and looked straight into her eyes. "It is called *Tillie's Punctured Romance*," he said softly.

Tilly gave a little gasp, and even I felt my heart pick up the pace a little.

"Tilly's...?"

"*Tillie's Punctured Romance*."

Just then the admirable Pointon appeared silently in the doorway and leaned down to speak in Charlie's ear.

"Ah!" our host cried. "Luncheon is served. Shall we?"

We all drifted into the dining room, where the table was positively groaning with a handsome buffet of cold meats, salads and fruit.

And as we tucked in that title was left hanging in the air above our heads. I could see that Tilly was seriously unsettled by it, and to be frank I was myself. Had Charlie really written a full-length film about her? That was surely what he was implying. And what did that mean? Had Charlie been... pining for her? All this time?

———

After we had all eaten our fill, and then forced a little bit more down because we had no idea when we might ever see a board groaning quite as loudly as this one again, we repaired to the balcony again, and Pointon furnished us with hot coffee.

"Oh, not for me," Tilly said. "In this heat?"

"It works," Charlie insisted. "A hot drink is sometimes just the thing on a hot day. It goes against your intuition, I know, but it does work. Why do you think cricketers drink tea all summer long?"

"Because they're English," I said.

"Ha! Yes, of course, that too."

Then Charlie began describing at great length and in great detail his motor car, a 1912 Kissell Kar Roadster.

"It is bright red, like a fire engine, and I can carry four passengers in comfort, although I much prefer to travel alone. Do you know what I like best about it? The horn. It has such a comical noise, I feel like a clown!"

Little Wallace was as bored as I was, and suddenly galloped back into the apartment, and I was grateful for the excuse to slip back inside for a while.

"All right, my laddo," I muttered as I jogged after the boy. "Let's see if we can't find some jam for you to stick your fingers into, and then you can have a go on that grand piano..."

"Oh, now, come on," Stan said as he strolled in to the room behind us. "That's only making work for poor Mr Pointon."

"Yes, I suppose you're right," I admitted. "We need to find something properly breakable for you to play with, my boy..."

"Behave yourself," Stan chided. "We're civilised people, we can have a pleasant lunch with an old friend without settling scores."

"You can, maybe," I muttered.

Stan frowned, and glanced out to the balcony, where Fred and Tilly were laughing at some fresh anecdote of Charlie's. "Listen Arthur," he said, dropping his voice somewhat. "I have been wondering. You don't think, do you, that we have missed a trick?"

"What trick?"

"Well, you know, by pushing Charlie towards Keystone just to clear the way for ourselves, we've kind of... haven't we? Shot ourselves in the foot?"

"In the feet. Strictly speaking. One foot each."

"Arthur," Stan said, a little sharply, I thought. "Will you just concentrate for a moment on what I am saying to you?"

"Sorry, go ahead."

"It's just that, well, you can see how well Charlie is doing."

"Hard not to, the way he's rubbing our noses in it."

"So perhaps we ought to think about...?" Stan left the thought hanging there.

"About...?"

"You know, about the flickers."

"You, my friend, have had too much of that bubbly."

"This might just be the perfect time to ask..." Stan tailed off again, as if he was anxious about how I would react to what he was suggesting to me.

"Ask who? Ask what?"

"You know. Ask Charlie, for some help. Point us in the right direction, you know? Tell us who we should try to get to meet?"

I sighed. "We've got a good thing going, haven't we? Eh? The four of us? *The Nutty Burglars*? It's a great little number."

"I was thinking it would make a nice little movie," Stan mused.

"I have no doubt," I said. "It'd be better than that thing of Charlie's we saw yesterday for a start off. But then, think about it, Stan, think. Then we'd never be able to do it on the stage again. It would be extinguished, whereas if we stick at it we can make a living out of it for years to come. And it's only going to pick up momentum and get bigger and bigger. Just a bit of patience, that's all we need."

"I know but... well, look at where he is and where we are. It's hard not to wonder. That's all I'm saying."

"Listen," I said. "So he's got all this, this apartment, the piano, a *valet* for Christ's sake, but is he happy? Eh?"

Just then, with perfect timing, Charlie began to laugh like a drain out on the balcony, showing all his perfect white teeth.

"You're right," Stan said. "He's suffering the very torments of Hell."

"You didn't see him, Stan, at Quinn's Superba yesterday, standing at the back watching the crowd watching his flick. He wanted the laughter, he missed it. Whatever he says, he'd a million times rather be onstage with an audience in the palm of his hand than lurking with a scarf over his face watching some bloodless shadow of himself kick Chester Conklin up the arse. Trust me."

"Maybe you're right," Stan said. "Maybe..."

"I am right," I said. "We are the ones who have got it made, not Charlie."

Stan didn't look altogether convinced. Charlie himself came in from the balcony just then, and made a bee-line for young Wallace, who was pulling magazines out of a wooden rack. I'd seen him doing it, just hadn't got round to stopping him.

"Here he is!" Charlie said. "Here's the guest I have been neglecting so. Come and say hello to your Uncle Charlie."

Wallace trotted over easily enough, always happy to be the centre of attention, and the two of them sat side by side on a couple of steps that led up to the kitchen. And Charlie played with the lad quite happily for the next few minutes, managing to enthral him without words – not that Wallace had all that many words to be going on with. He started by simply imitating everything the boy did, every gesture, every

140

facial expression. Wallace stood up, Charlie stood up. Wallace scratched his nose, Charlie scratched his nose. Pretty soon the boy realised that he had a puppet at his disposal, and started having a whale of a time making Charlie copy his every move.

Then Charlie put a hat on little Wallace's head, liked it, but then wanted it back, and that hat got passed back and forth dozens of times, with the child in fits of giggles. Wallace ended up on Charlie's knee having a seemingly interminable horsey-ride, but our host showed no signs of tiring.

Then Charlie said an odd thing. "You know, I admire you, Arthur. Taking care of this little chap can't be easy, under the circumstances."

"What circumstances do you mean?" I said.

He paused for half a moment, just long enough for me to notice it. "Well, on the road, moving from town to town, theatre to theatre, it can't be easy. That's all I meant."

"Oh, we manage well enough, don't we?" I said, and Stan grinned. "Who needs a father when he has such funny uncles?"

Finally the knee stopped bouncing, and the horsey had had enough. "Run along now," Charlie said to Wallace, patting him on the bottom as he trotted over to Tilly, who was just coming in with Freddie from the balcony.

Charlie remained sitting on the kitchen step, seemingly deep in thought, and there was an awkward silence for a moment or two until Stan gave a little cough.

"We were thinking, weren't we, Arthur...?" Stan said, shooting me a look that pleaded with me to play along, "...that while we are here in Los Angeles, we should try and meet some movie people, and see if we could make some progress. *The Nutty Burglars* would be perfect for someone to see, it shows exactly what we can all do..."

141

Charlie's face, always so expressive, suddenly took on a haunted look. "No!" he said sharply, jumping to his feet. "Don't do that!"

"What?" Stan said, juddering to a halt. "Don't...?"

Charlie relaxed and smiled. "What I mean to say is, don't go to all the trouble of looking out the studios and trying to get a meeting with some self-important twit who will only say he can't possibly see you until the week after next, or maybe the week after that, by which time you'll be in...?"

"Oakland, probably," I said, wondering what Charlie was up to. "Off the top of my head."

"Oakland, exactly. Now these guys, the guys you need to meet, these are the very same guys who are calling me all the time, morning, noon and night, trying to get me to leave Keystone, offering me this and that. So why don't I do this: I'll corral a bunch of these bigwigs together, the biggest wigs in town, I promise, and I'll bring them along with me when I come to see your... Nutty Burglings. How would that be?"

"You promise?" I said, starting to laugh.

Stan glared at me. "Thanks, Charlie, that would be excellent!" he gushed, and took Charlie by the hand.

"Oh come on!" I scoffed. "You don't really think...!"

"Arthur!" Tilly scolded. "Charlie's offering to help us."

"Yes, but you surely don't think he'll actually do what he says, do you?"

"Why ever wouldn't I?" Charlie said, a hurt expression on his face.

"Well, because..." I stopped, because the answer seemed self-evident to me. Stan, Freddie and Tilly were all glowering at me as though I had committed the most egregious faux pas.

"I assure you," Charlie said, looking hurt. "If there is anything I can do to help my old friends then I shall do it. Now, tell me, where is this extravaganza of yours to be found?"

"The place is called The Happy Hour," I said, but Charlie held up a hand.

"Pointon? Oh, Pointon?!"

The valet – he had a valet! – ghosted in from the kitchen.

"Sir?"

"Make a note of this, will you? Go on, Arthur."

Within a moment or two young Pointon had a pencil poised above a small notepad, which he'd magicked up from nowhere.

"It is called The Happy Hour," I said to him. "It is on 5th, next to a carpet store called Hannigan's."

"We shall find it," Charlie beamed.

"When will you come?" Stan said, feverish with excitement now. "Shall we look for you tonight?"

"Ah," Charlie said, tapping his fingernail on his front teeth. "Tonight I have some friends who will take me automobiling, and then we will dine on the beach. But before the end of the week, you can count on me."

17
PROMISES, PROMISES

OUR shows that afternoon and evening at the Happy Hour were not, it has to be said, the absolute apex of our careers. Maybe we'd all had a little too much champagne at lunchtime. More likely it was having to squeeze ourselves into that hot and filthy hovel of a dressing room we were sharing with three other turns, which was roughly half the size of the kitchen Chaplin's valet had had all to himself to chop cool cucumbers into precise and perfect slices.

At the end of the evening we were tired and crotchety, and Stan suddenly turned on me.

"Why did you have to antagonise him?" he demanded.

"Who?" I said. "Charlie?"

"Of course, Charlie!"

"Oh come on," I retorted. "You don't seriously think he's going to put himself out on our behalf, do you?"

"Why wouldn't he?"

"We are talking about the same chap, aren't we? The one who couldn't wait to get us sacked from Karno's simply for being too funny?"

"Well, we were all younger then, and maybe now he's doing so well he wants to make amends."

"I'll believe that when I see it," I snorted.

"I think he's going to come," Freddie said, but he hadn't had quite the range of experiences with Chaplin that the rest of us had had.

"I hope he doesn't," I said. "Because if he ever sees *The Nutty Burglars* it'll be a Charlie Chaplin film before we know what's hit us."

"You know, Arthur, I think you are a tiny bit off your rocker where Charlie is concerned," Stan said, grabbing his hat and stalking out.

━━━━

Back at our digs that night, which seemed even pokier than they had that morning, what with the drying nappies hanging, as usual, from a makeshift washing line, Tilly was subdued, preoccupied. I thought I knew why – seeing Charlie again had plainly given her plenty to think about. Well, I had a tidbit of information to offer up, gleaned from a glance at *Variety*'s movie production gossip column.

"Oh, by the way," I said. "*Tillie's Punctured Romance?* It's not about you, it's nothing to do with you. He didn't even choose the character's name."

"I'm sure I never thought that he did," she said, coolly.

"It was a play, on Broadway, called *Tillie's Nightmare*. Marie Dressler plays Tillie, a country bumpkin character, in any number of things, it's her conceit not Charlie's. It's not even spelled the same way. Just so you know."

"Thank you for that."

"I didn't want you to think..."

"...that he might still have some feelings for me, you mean?"

"Yes, actually, that is exactly what I mean."

"Understood."

"Because I believe he was trying to give you the impression that he was making a cinematic love-letter of some kind."

"You're being absurd," Tilly said, and went into the bathroom.

I stayed where I was. A frisson of something or other had happened. I wasn't sure quite how he had done it, but somehow Chaplin had interposed himself between us, and not for the first time. What could he do, though, really, I said to myself. What could he offer her... apart from a balcony overlooking the Pacific and a Turkish bath and automobiling to the beach for dinner?

I decided not to bring the matter up again.

———

There was no sign of Charlie and his movie mogul posse for the next couple of days. Every performance at the Happy Hour Stan would bound onstage full of beans, and then after a couple of minutes his shoulders would slump, which meant that he had managed to scan the crowd out of the corner of his eye and knew that once again our old friend was a no-show.

This didn't dent his optimism, or his confidence that Charlie would give us a helping hand, and on those Los Angeles mornings, he dragged Freddie out with him to scour the parks for flicker folk in action. Stan was mustard-keen to learn all he could about how things worked, and one morning they stumbled upon a Keystone crew throwing Fatty Arbuckle into a boating lake. Stan was full of the experience, chattering happily away about clapperboards and hand-cranking right up to the moment we stepped onto the stage for our first show of the afternoon, only to find that once again there was neither untrustworthy hide nor tousled hair of Mr Chaplin to be glimpsed in the unprepossessing auditorium.

———

One morning towards the end of the week I found myself alone in our digs with Wallace. Tilly had gone out on an errand and Stan and Freddie were out hunting film crews, so the boy and I were left to entertain ourselves.

Now that we had grown used to one another, little Wallace and I were great chums. Even so, I'd felt a sharp pang of jealousy watching Charlie playing with him in his swanky apartment.

"You liked him, didn't you?" I said, and the lad blinked up at me from the counterpane. "You thought he was funny."

"Funny!" Wallace sang out. He knew *that* word.

"Well," I said. "He's funny enough, if you like that sort of thing, but he's not as funny as your Dad, is he, eh?"

"Dad!" the boy shouted.

"Shall we see who's the funniest? Shall we?"

The game that drove him wild with glee was a morning game. Before I had my shave, when there was a little rough stubble on my face, I would call out: "Who wants a chin pie?"

The little lad would squeal and try to run away from me, and I would let him escape from my grasp, run between my legs, hide under the bed, but eventually I would catch him, lay him wriggling on top of the blankets, pull up his vest, and blow raspberries on his soft little tummy until he was weak with laughter.

This game had become so established by that summer that I would lead into it sideways. "What do you think...?" I would muse, with the boy sitting on my knee. "What do you think... is my favourite fruit?"

"Apple!" the tiny man would say.

"Very good," I would say. "And what do you think... is my favourite colour?"

"Blue!" he would shout.

"Very good again. And what do you think is my favourite... pie?"

"Tato!"

"No..."

"Punkin!"

"No..."

"Blue!"

"Wrong! My favourite pie is... chin pie!"

Then I would make to start in with the raspberry thing, and let him wriggle free so that the chasing could begin. He'd get a chin pie eventually, though, and we both knew it.

So it wasn't long before I had him squealing, waving his arms and legs in the air, red in the face. It was satisfying to be able to make the boy laugh, but suddenly I wanted to top it, to make him laugh so hard it would obliterate the memory of the mysterious toothy stranger and his hat routine for ever.

I nipped into the bathroom, leaving Wallace still gasping on the bed. I grabbed my badger-bristle shaving brush and the bar of lathering soap, and quickly covered my face until I looked like Father Christmas.

"Who wants... chin pie with cream?" I called out, and then burst into the bedroom again. Little Wallace's eyes were like saucers, and he screamed his head off, galloping desperately around the room as I lumbered in his wake.

Of course I faked that I was going to catch him, and then let him run off again, and when he could run no more I blew soapy raspberries on his little belly until his screams of laughter brought angry thumping on the ceiling from the rudely-awakened vaudevillians upstairs.

The door to the corridor outside flew open, and Tilly was standing there.

"What on Earth is going on here?" she cried.

I grinned, suddenly aware that there was shaving soap lather absolutely everywhere. On the walls, on the floor, on the clothes hanging over the back of a chair.

"We're just having a laugh, aren't we Arthur?" I said.

"What have you done to him?" Tilly cried, swooping down on the boy. Wallace was bright red and pouring with sweat, lying on the bed struggling for breath.

"Just... playing..." I said sheepishly.

Wallace spluttered, and then promptly threw up his breakfast.

Tilly gasped, and then rubbed his back gently, calming him down. "There, there, darling," she said. "There, there." She turned to me. "Wet a towel, go on with you!"

I did as she asked, and she laid it tenderly on the child's forehead. Happily he was back on a more even keel pretty quickly, and Tilly laid him on the bed for a breather.

"You can't get him excited like that, you'll make him unwell," she hissed. "Whatever were you *thinking*?"

I shrugged, feeling pretty foolish I must admit. Because what I'd been thinking was how very much funnier I was than Charlie Chaplin. He'd only made my son giggle – I had made him ill with laughter.

━━━━

The Saturday of our week in Los Angeles duly arrived, and Stan and Freddie were greatly excited ahead of our last four performances at the Happy Hour.

"Of course Charlie would want to come to the last show," Stan said, as we got outside a liquid lunch in a downtown Irish bar. "He'll want to come for a drink afterwards, won't he?"

"It's probably taken him a few days to dragoon these fellows he's going to bring with him, too," Freddie said.

"Exactly," Stan nodded. "These are busy men, they'll take a bit of organising."

Tilly wasn't with us. She and Wallace were lunching in the park, and in any case she had not shown a great deal of interest in the prospect of the new start that Charlie and his chums might offer.

I was still pretty sceptical about it all myself. Quite apart from not believing that Charlie would make good on his word, I still believed that the thriving vaudeville pond was the place to be, even if we currently found ourselves grubbing along the muddy bottom of it. However, the boys were fired up, and the more they talked about a future in flickers the more their enthusiasm began to rub off on me.

"The crew we saw the other day were having a lot of fun, weren't they?" Stan said.

"Oh yes," Freddie agreed. "You see, they were filming a scene where the fat boy..."

"Arbuckle," Stan put in.

"... topples into a pond, and he makes such a splash that all the rowing boats capsize. And of course no-one would make a splash that big, however fat they were, so there were fellows hiding in the pond, up to their eyebrows in the water, practically, whose job it was to pull the rowing boats over without the camera seeing."

"And they did it several ways round, to try and find the best shot, as it were, and the whole thing was very..." Stan scratched his head, looking for the word – "...*inventive*, somehow."

"It was as if they turned up at the park in the morning with just an idea but no jokes at all," Freddie said. "And the jokes just kept on coming, one on top of the other. It was quite exhilarating, really, to watch."

"Yes," said Stan. "Because you know how much we enjoy putting something together, like we did with *The Rum 'Uns from Rome* back in London, or with *The Nutty Burglars* out here? It is like *that*, but all day long."

"Right," I said, "except you never get to do it in front of an audience, which is the whole point of comedy, isn't it?"

"It's different," Stan conceded. "But it still looks fun."

"And the pay is better – well, it could hardly be worse, could it?" Freddie chipped in.

Despite myself I could feel my resistance weakening.

"And look at how Charlie is living. We could establish ourselves out here. No more travelling, no more digs. It would be better, surely, for your tiny man. More settled."

"Maybe... maybe you have a point," I said. "But what could we actually... do?"

Stan leaned forward across the table. He had clearly given this some thought. "Well," he said. "There's *The Nutty Burglars*, for a start. That would make a cracking little one-reeler."

"You have all the terminology, I'll give you that."

"And that would get us up and running. After that, we come up with something else."

"What about a flicker of your Stowaway character?" Freddie said, and that started the cogs whirring and no mistake.

"Why not?" Stan agreed.

"It could be every bit as good as that Tramp thing Charlie's been doing. After all, it's practically the same stuff, isn't it? Robey's costume and Karno's Drunk, that's all it is."

"It's a little bit more than that," I said, "but it's an interesting notion."

By the time we left for the theatre I was actually coming round to the idea, and had started daydreaming about a future in which my gloriously-funny Stowaway eclipsed the miserably-derivative Chaplin hobo, before returning in triumph to big-time vaudeville with Tilly and my friends in support.

Maybe, I thought, maybe it would just be worth a punt...

So that afternoon, when Stan and I stepped onto the stage to begin our Nutty Burgling, I found myself scouring the faces in the audience every bit as eagerly as Stan was doing, checking for Charlie and his fine flicker friends.

There was no sign of them in the first show, or the second, but we all agreed that we were relieved about that. The Happy Hour was barely half-full, and the hot Californian summer made the crowds cranky, so we wouldn't have been seen at our best. By the time of the third show, the early evening offering, the weather had cooled off somewhat, and the house was nearly full. *The Nutty Burglars* were on fine form, but there was still no Charlie.

As the last bill of the day got under way everything seemed to be in our favour. It was a cool fresh evening, for once, so the dank pit that was the Happy Hour seemed more than usually habitable. A large crowd had come along, and the place was as full as we had seen it. Best of all, though, was that some of the frankly feeble acts that preceded us were going down like Marie Lloyd at the Hippodrome. A great night was brewing.

Stan and I stood in the wings, and he gave me a great big Stan grin, practically quivering with excitement. I grinned back, knowing as surely as I knew anything that these were the nights that brought the very best out of Stan, the nights where there was just a little extra on the line and we weren't just going through the motions.

Our signature music played, and the hands quickly shoved our bits and pieces of set into position. Stan and I slipped into place, the curtain went up and were off.

The first few bits of business went off like clockwork, and the audience were with us. I even began to feel the tingle of the Power, which was a very good sign. As the cracksman, I was huddled over the safe to begin with, so not able to scan the room right away, but I was confident that we were going to do a good one. Confident, that is, right up to the point when I was expecting a line from Stan, and he completely missed the cue.

I looked up at him and he was rooted to the spot, staring ahead. His shoulders were slumped, and he looked like he could barely bring himself to continue. This probably only lasted a second or two, but long enough to start that familiar grumbling in the audience, as people nudged one another wondering if they were about to witness a failure, something they could boo, something they could really get their teeth into.

"Hey Waffles!" I called out – Waffles being Stan's Nutty Burglar name. "We'd better get a shift on, don't you think?"

Stan still stood with his arms by his side, and looked like his mind was miles away. I began to become seriously concerned.

"Waffles?!!" I said again, but there was little I could do to move the scene on without him. In fact the only thing that would work was...

"What are you doing in here?! Hey, you, I'm talking to you!"

It was Tilly, the life-saver. She'd marched on stage and slapped Stan around the chops. He started, and looked around, seemingly realising only then where he was and what he was doing.

153

We had skipped some of our business, but now that Tilly was on we could press forwards. Stan shook his head quickly, and then to my great relief he and Tilly began their flirty repartee and the laughs began to flow again.

I was so concerned about keeping the train on the rails that I didn't so much as glance out into the audience, and once we got Stan down onto the dressing room the three of us gathered around him to see what was wrong.

"Do you need anything, love?" Tilly said. "A cup of tea, would that do it?"

"I'm all right," Stan said. "I'm sorry, everyone, it was just..."

"What? What was the matter?"

"I... looked out... and he wasn't there."

"Who? Charlie, do you mean?"

Stan nodded. "And suddenly I was so... it was so... disappointing, that it threw me. I'm sorry, it won't... it won't happen again."

"But, there was a big house tonight, surely you couldn't see everyone?" Freddie said.

"That's right," I said. "And there were people standing at the back, in the shadows. He'd most likely have been there, wouldn't he? He and these contacts of his'd only have wanted to nip in to see us, after all, they wouldn't have wanted to sit in for the whole bill."

Stan brightened. "You're right, you're right, of course," he said.

"Let's go to the bar round the corner, come on," Freddie said. "Charlie will probably be there already, waiting for us. You'll see."

He wasn't though.

We stayed there until two in the morning, and Chaplin didn't show, either on his own or with bigwigs in tow.

Stan, Freddie and I stared gloomily at the bottom of our

glasses – Tilly left us to it hours before – and there was nothing for it but to contemplate moving on to another week of small-time vaudeville up in Oakland.

And suddenly these small-time dates that we had been enjoying so much stretched ahead of us like a jail sentence, with no prospect of remission for good behaviour.

18
TWO MORE COMIQUES

THE railway journey up to Oakland, which sits across the bay from San Francisco, was a quiet one. All of us were lost in our thoughts, it seemed, even Wallace, who had his face pressed to the window, captivated by the ever-changing view.

Every now and then Stan would spark into life, and say something like: "Do you think we should have tried to send him a message before we left?"

"No," I replied to that. "He should have sent us one."

"Yes, but..." Stan sighed, and slumped back into his contemplations.

Tilly, too, was staring into the distance, and I put my hand on hers.

"It's not exactly the first time," I said.

"Hmmm?"

"I said, it's not the first time that Charlie has let us down."

Tilly tutted. "You're rather enjoying this, aren't you? Everyone's disappointment? Proving you right about Charlie, giving you another chance to moan about him, blame him for all your misfortune."

"What? No!"

Tilly went quiet then, brooding, and it was a minute or two before she spoke again. "Well, in any case, I was actually thinking about my father."

"Of course," I said. "I'm sorry that we can't afford to go back to England, love, but that's just how it is."

"I know," she said, with a sad little smile.

"Have you written? Maybe we could have the lad photographed, what do you think?"

"That would be nice. But I don't have an address, do I? I thought of writing care of the Great Yarmouth police station, but there could be several of those, and I don't know that they take mail for prisoners, so how would I know he had received it? How could he write back to let me know that he had? Care of the Considine organisation in Seattle? It could be months before we get back up there, and I'd have to be wondering that whole time."

"You've clearly thought it through," I said.

"I've been doing little else," she said, and squeezed my hand.

Freddie seemed to wake up, then, and he said: "Maybe, you know, he just couldn't persuade anyone to come and see us."

"He didn't even turn up himself," I said.

"I know, I know, but maybe he meant to, and... and... other people...?"

"It's quite simple," I said. "He didn't want us to be in Los Angeles, he didn't want us to get involved in making pictures, because he didn't want the competition. He wants all the limelight for himself."

"Oh, for goodness sake...!" Tilly muttered

"No, no," Stan said, frowning. "Charlie wouldn't..."

"When you suggested we should speak to movie people, at that lunch last week, what did he say?"

"He said he'd help us."

"'No', he said, 'don't do that'. That's what he said, because he was already working out how to block our path."

"I can't believe that, not even Charlie..."

"We could have spent the whole of last week knocking on doors, trying to get on, and who knows, maybe we'd have struck lucky, but we didn't, and why not? Because Charlie, Mr Charlie Chaplin, said: 'Don't do that, *I'll* arrange everything'. And then he left us to stew in our own juices in that god-forsaken boiler-house of a theatre, knowing perfectly well that by the time we realised he wasn't going to make good on his promise, it would be too late for us to do anything about it. Because who knows when Considine will send us back to Los Angeles? Not for months, probably."

"There are film companies in other cities," Stan said. "Chicago, San Francisco, New York, Jacksonville."

"That's right, and certainly we can try our luck when we are in those places, but I think we should realise that vaudeville is our bread and butter, and buckle down, and concentrate on making something of ourselves there, put this flicker nonsense out of our heads."

After a moment Stan grinned. "You're right, Arthur," he said. "Vaudeville is our bread and butter."

Freddie looked less convinced. "If only there was some jam as well," he muttered.

━━━━

As if to taunt our new resolution, Oakland's Broadway seemed to be bursting at the seams with brand new picture houses, all ornate frontages and fancy electric signage. There were vaudeville theatres too, the list headed by another spanking new Pantages with more than its share of electric bulbs, and we had played the Bell on one of the Karno tours. This time we were at the Bijou, a small independent vaudeville venue that booked through the Considine office, and we tried not to get too down-cast by the many grander operations that surrounded us.

When we arrived we tried, as usual, to get an idea of the calibre of acts alongside us on the bill, but it turned out that the owner had surrendered all the space on his posters, programmes and (as we discovered later) the drop curtain to advertising products. So Zam-Zam, which we speculated might be a magic act, turned out in fact to be a candy laxative, 'good for what ails yer!' Similarly Clark-Gandion, an unfamiliar double act, was actually a brand of surgical truss, and La France was not a singing diva so much as it was a waist-reducing corset. The only actual reference to the nature of the entertainment on offer was in a far from prominent line at the bottom, which read merely: 'Vaudeville Thrice Nightly'.

"Oh well," Freddie said. "Better than four a night, anyway."

The week began quietly, as the theatre was not particularly well-attended, and we were all struggling to regain a bit of spark after our Los Angeles disappointment. I say 'disappointment', I was actually feeling a little more strongly than that. The more I thought about it, the more sure I was that Charlie had acted quite deliberately to sabotage us.

It was an effort of will, but gradually I managed to make myself calm down a little, telling myself that the episode was behind me, that Charlie had had his fun, had his little stab at my back, but it was over now and done with, and there was no way he could play any further part in my life.

I was wrong about that.

In the mornings that week, several days in a row, Tilly disappeared with Freddie, looking for something. They were very mysterious about it, and neither Stan nor I were quite sure what was going on.

I knew that Freddie had taken a shine to Tilly years ago, back in the Fun Factory days, but he was my friend and I had no thought that he would make a play for her. Not like Charlie did, over and over again, until even Tilly started wondering whether he was more interested in her or in putting one over on me.

It was peculiar, though, and it meant that I was left alone with my son and my speculations.

"What are they up to, eh?" I said many times to the boy as I spooned some kind of mushed-up goo into his gummy little mouth. "Your Mum and your Uncle Fred?"

On the Thursday evening, I think it was, after the evening's shows were completed, Tilly came into the dressing room we three lads were sharing with The Blinis, a juggling trio (or possibly a candy laxative) who were at that moment up on the stage, and she closed the door behind her.

"Aye aye," I said. "What's going on?"

"I have something to tell you," Tilly said. "Well, actually, Freddie and I do, don't we, Fred?"

"That's right," Freddie said. "Absolutely."

I felt a cold finger walking down my spine.

"What's up?" Stan said.

"I saw Charlie in Los Angeles, at his apartment," Tilly said.

"We all did," Stan frowned.

"Yes, but I mean a second time, a couple of days after that lunch. I went back there on my own. I told him about my father,"

160

Tilly said. "I told him how desperate I was to go back to England to see him, that it might be the last opportunity to show him his grandson, and..."

"And what?" I prompted.

"Well, you see, Charlie somehow seems to have got hold of the impression that I might want to reveal that Wallace was his son to some newspaper or other, I don't know how that could possibly have happened. And this notion made him quite... agitated."

"I should think it did," I said.

"So what he has done, is... and I suppose I shouldn't really be surprised, given what happened before."

"When he paid you to absent yourself from the Karno company, you mean?"

"Quite. He has given me money. In fact, he has most carefully calculated the amount you and I would need to travel across the country to New York and secure a passage – a one-way passage – back to England."

"He really wants to be rid of you," Stan said, shaking his head slowly at me.

"Mmm," I said, grinding my teeth. "Clearly the continent is not big enough for the both of us."

"Now," Tilly went on. "Much as I would like to do this, I am in fact quite desperate to go, I couldn't let you down, Stan, and you Freddie, and neither could I ask Arthur to do it. You have thrown your lot in with us, and I haven't the right to ask you to begin again at scratch."

"Well," Stan began. "If it is the only way..."

"Bless you, Stan, but I could not possibly ask it of you. However, we have come up with a solution."

"We?"

"Myself, and Freddie here. Haven't we, Fred?"

"We have."

"I will travel back to London with little Wallace, and Freddie will accompany us."

"*Freddie* will?" I said, sideswiped by this.

"The old man simply will not let up cabling me, pestering me," Freddie explained. "He wants me to run the old Fun Factory so he can concentrate all his energies on digging the Karsino out of a hole. It is the family business – you understand, don't you?"

"Of course, of course we do," Stan said, picking miserably at a thread on his trouser leg.

"That's not all, though, is it?" I said.

"No," Tilly said. "Once we get back to London, Freddie will get the Guv'nor to pay me back for his crossing, so I shall have the money to return, once I have seen my father and shown him his grandson, and generally seen what's what. I should be gone for a month, maybe six weeks at the most. In the meantime..." – she gave an enigmatic smirk – "... the Four Comiques will still be able to fulfil all their engagements."

"How?" I said. "There'll only be Two Comiques left."

"Aha," Freddie said. "And *that's* the big surprise. Come on!"

He led the way, grinning all the while, out of the stage door and around the corner to a bar. Stan and I followed, bemused, and watched Freddie and Tilly as they scoured the various nooks and crannies, until Tilly found what they were looking for in a booth at the back.

"To quote our son, if I may..." she said to me. "'Da daaah!'"

Stan and I looked at one another, unable to imagine what awaited us in that booth behind its dark wood and stained glass screen. We stepped tentatively forward, and peered in.

There, sitting opposite one another, raising their glasses in greeting, were Ed Hurley and his wife, the lovely Wren.

"Look who we found in San Francisco!" Tilly said.

"Well!" Stan said, scratching his head, and then grasping Ed by the hand and pumping it enthusiastically.

"Hello Arthur, how lovely to see you again," Wren said with her voice like warm velvet, setting off distant alarm bells that resonated deep in my abdominal regions.

"Two Comiques, plus Two more Comiques, equals Four Comiques!" Freddie beamed.

"That name's got to go for a start," Ed muttered.

19
THOSE LOVE PANGS

SO that was decided then. Nothing Stan and I could really do or say. It was a fait accompli. The Hurleys would take over from Freddie and Tilly in *The Nutty Burglars*, until Tilly returned from England, at which point I supposed we would have to think again. Actually it was going to work out rather nicely for Ed and Wren, as they had just found themselves stranded in San Francisco.

"We got to New York," Wren explained, "but all the way Ed was restless. He still thought Karno should have made him the number one when Charlie left, and again when the theatres balked at Stan, and yet again when Dan Raynor didn't work out."

"Poor kid," I said, shaking my head.

"And so the thought of turning up at the Fun Factory and doffing his cap to the old Guv'nor, saying 'yes sir, no sir and three bags full sir', well, it stuck in Ed's throat, so it did."

At that moment, Ed was holding forth over by the bar to Stan, very possibly going over the same ground, while Tilly and Freddie had their heads together, already making plans for their trip.

"So what did you do?" I said.

"Well, Ed was impressed – he won't tell you this himself, but he was – when you three boys took the ticket money and struck out on your own. He thought it was a brassy move, and a big raspberry to old Karno, too, so we decided to follow suit. Just before we got on the boat, it was, you should have seen Alf Reeves' face! Anyway, as luck would have it we got hooked up fairly quickly, before the money ran out, anyway, and found a slot with the Buster Brown company. You know, they do an act based on the comic strip in the papers?"

"Not really," I shrugged.

"Buster and his dog were both played by dwarves, really quite unpleasant old men who'd been doing the show for years, and they were really set in their ways. Well, you know what Ed's like, he kept suggesting changes and throwing his weight around and in the end, we had to go our separate ways."

"They fired you, you mean?"

"Don't tell Ed," Wren whispered, dropping her voice and grasping my arm. "He thinks there were no more dates, but yes, I... agreed a settlement. Which has very nearly run out now, so bumping into Tilly and Freddie the other day was quite providential."

"Indeed," I said. "For all of us."

"It will be so nice to work with you again, Arthur," she said, allowing her fingers to trail across the back of my hand in a way that made me want to rearrange my clothing.

It was agreed that the Hurleys would take over at the start of the next week, when the Four Comiques headed to Bakersfield, and Tilly, Freddie and wee Wallace began their trans-continental trek to New York and on to Olde England.

That made for some pretty frantic rehearsals in Stan and Freddie's room in the mornings, which by the way made us distinctly unpopular with the other vaudevillians who were sharing the house having rolled in during the wee small hours.

Wren looked good in the part of the maid, and Tilly passed on tips as best she could, but the real test of Wren's rapport with Stan would only come while performing in front of a live house.

"I want her to be good, of course," Tilly confided. "But not too good."

"I understand perfectly," I said.

Ed, on the other hand, bristled when he discovered that he was expected to play a supporting role. He began trying to inflate his importance right from the off, but of course it didn't make a lot of sense for a burglary scene to have a policeman in it any more than we had already, so Stan and I did have to keep slapping him down, and Freddie became so exasperated that he made himself scarce.

The rush to get the Hurleys ready and three shows a day at the Bijou meant that there was precious little time for me to spend with Tilly and Wallace before they left. In fact, I'm not sure I saw the lad awake that whole time.

So when the week was done, and we were in our room for our last night together – for a little while at least – there was still some talking to be done.

We stood in the near-dark, with the moonlight shining through a gap in the ill-fitting curtains, looking down at the sleeping form of our son and listening to his gentle snoring. I slipped my arm around Tilly's waist, and she drew closer to me.

"I've been thinking," she said.

"Me too," I said, reaching down to pat Wallace on the head and ruffle his soft fly-away hair.

"Oh?" Tilly replied. "Because my mind is made up, you know, I'm going."

"Yes, yes, I understand that," I said. I slipped my hand into my trouser pocket and found the ring that I had bought from a market that morning. Silver, with a design like the head of Mr Punch, which I'd been delighted to come across. Perfect for what I had in mind...

"I've been thinking," Tilly said again.

"All right, you first," I smiled.

"I've been thinking that going back to England for a couple of months might actually be quite a good idea."

"Really?"

"Might be good... for us."

"In what way?"

"Just a little time apart to think, that's all."

"Think? About what?"

Tilly sighed. "When you came to find me in Vancouver, you know, I nearly said no to you then. But I thought now that Charlie was out of your life that you could put this bitter, poisonous rivalry of yours behind you, and grow up out of his shadow, so I decided to take the chance, take the risk and throw in with you once again. Because I love you, Arthur, and I know you love me, but I can't cope with this anger you have for Charlie, it twists you, it eats you up, and it hurts the people around you."

"But it's not me!" I cried. "It's him! He's the one doing it, it's been him all along! Even last week! He promised to give us a helping hand and then what? Nothing!"

"He gave me money to go back to England and see my father..."

"So that he can get rid of *me* once and for all!"

"And he would have come to see the *Nutty Burglars*, but he couldn't persuade any of his contacts to come with him, and he was embarrassed to come alone because he felt he'd let us down. He was quite upset about it, actually."

"What? When was this?"

"When I went back a second time."

"Oh, he's playing you, Tilly, that's all! You've put the wind up him, he thinks you can tell the press he's some kind of morally bankrupt philanderer!"

"I'm not proud of that. I did what I had to do. But this rivalry of yours has made my life a misery for so long I thought it was about time I got something back."

"I see." I clenched my fist, crushing the ring into the flesh of my palm. Tilly looked down at it.

"What have you got there?"

I held my open palm out to her. The Mr Punch ring nestled in the middle of it, on a reddened imprint of itself. His garish smile mocked me as he rocked gently from side to side.

"What is that?"

"It's for you," I said.

"Oh...!" Tilly's mouth made a perfect 'O'.

"I thought..."

"You were never going to...!"

"I was... well. I thought we should make this little chap legitimate, you know."

Tilly gave a little laugh. "Well, God knows we've been pretending to be married long enough."

"Ha!"

"So, is that it?" Tilly said.

"What?"

"Is that all I'm getting? By way of a proposal?"

"What do you...?"

"I mean, can't you do it any better than that? On your knees, Dandoe, and ask me properly!"

I got down on one knee and took her hand, and I have to say I was mightily confused.

"Um... Matilda Jean Beckett..." Tilly smirked "...will you do me the inestimable honour of becoming my wife?"

Tilly sighed, and gave me a sad little smile. "That's so nice," she said.

"Well?" I said after a moment. "What's your answer?"

She took a deep breath. "I'll give you my answer when I return."

"When you return?"

"But I'm going to need to see a new Dandoe, one that isn't burdened by this darkness, do you understand?"

"I think so."

"I believe I deserve that, and Wallace deserves that. If we are going to make a life together, I want it to be a life built on happiness and laughter. You need to show me you've put this thing with Charlie Chaplin behind you once and for all. Otherwise I'll just take myself and Wallace back up to Vancouver and that will be that."

"I see. Righto."

She took my hands and lifted me up to my feet, and then she stood up on tiptoes and kissed me.

———

In the blink of an eye, it seemed, Tilly and I were standing together on the platform at the Oakland 16th Street Station, and the Omaha train was hissing and steaming as if the locomotive itself was impatient to be on its way.

"I'll be back before you know it," Tilly whispered as we embraced. "You be good, now. Watch out for that Wren Hurley."

"You'll be back in six weeks, what sort of trouble can I get up to in six weeks?"

"Two weeks of thinking about it, and four weeks of doing something about it," Tilly growled.

169

"Give my regards to your father," I said. "I hope he approves of his grandson."

Tilly grinned, but I could see that she was trying to hide her concern that she might not be in time. After all, we had only that small piece in *Variety* about the pier fire in Great Yarmouth to go on for information, and one way and another she could be making a long trip with only disappointment at the end of it.

The guard gave a couple of sharp blasts on his whistle, and the last passengers left on the platform began to hurry up into the carriages.

I hugged her one last time. "Soon, love," I said, and then Tilly kissed my neck and turned away, leaving a tear tracking down my cheek.

Freddie was holding Wallace, and he passed the boy up to his mother. My little family disappeared into the shadows momentarily, before finding a spot at a window from which to wave goodbye.

"I'll take care of them, don't you worry," Freddie said.

"I know you will," I said, grasping his hand. "You take care of yourself too."

"Hey," he said, beaming a big old Freddie grin at me and Stan "If the old man puts me in charge of the Fun Factory, maybe you two should come and work for me, what d'you think?"

"It's a thought," Stan grinned, shaking our friend by the hand. "It certainly is."

With that the locomotive sighed, and the carriages clinked heavily together, bouncing an inch or two back and forth, before slowly moving off.

Freddie skipped up the steps and pulled the door shut behind him, appearing alongside Tilly and Wallace at the window. The little boy was enjoying the game of waving goodbye, flapping both hands energetically. Freddie gave us a salute with a big smile, and the lad swiftly copied this new gesture, which made Tilly laugh. I could see, though, that she was trying not to cry, and not quite succeeding.

I stood watching the train until it was almost out of sight, a dark faintly smoking dot on the horizon.

"It's going to be a long six weeks," I said.

"It is that," Stan said beside me, and I saw that he was looking over at the opposite platform, where Ed Hurley and his wife were sitting on their bags, waiting for us to join them for the much shorter journey to our next engagement in Sacramento. We couldn't hear them, but it was plain that he was complaining about something, and that she was trying to tell him to let it go, whatever it was.

"I think I'll be able to stand it for six weeks," Stan said. "Any longer than that and I might just throttle him."

I was missing Tilly already, and vividly recalled our conversation from the night before, but I couldn't help it.

All I could think just then was: "Bloody Charlie Chaplin! This is all your fault!"

20
THE ROOM

SUMMER OF 1917, SOMEWHERE IN AMERICA

THE one called John sat back in his chair, assessing me coolly.

"Now we're g-getting to it," he said.

"G-getting to what?" I said, hoping that a little light-hearted mockery might lighten the mood. It didn't.

"To the nub of this thing between you and Chaplin," John said, and I could see the effort he was making to keep his stutter down, which made me feel bad all of a sudden.

"Ah."

"He was breaking through, becoming successful, becoming a star, while you and your chums were still grubbing around trying to scrape a living among vaudeville's bottom-feeders."

John's partner, the quiet one, sniggered at this.

"Jealousy, pure and simple," John went on, throwing his pencil onto his pad.

"There was more to it than that, a lot more. Have you not been paying attention?"

"I got that you felt f-foolish, having manipulated him into choosing to make a career in the flickers rather than competing with you in the world of vaudeville. That all rather b-backfired on you, didn't it?"

"Yes, but..."

John's partner sniggered again, and I started to feel that it was getting hot in that enclosed room. I glanced at the windows but it didn't look like they were used to being opened, if they opened at all.

"After all, what was Chaplin supposed to do? Deliberately fail in order to make your m-miserable life more tolerable?"

The silent one snorted through his nose at that.

"Look," I said. "You're missing the point. You're missing the point entirely."

"Oh I am? Enlighten me."

"All right then. When we met Chaplin in 1914, he was success-ful, yes, and I was a little jealous, obviously, we all were. I admit that. And it was a bit of a facer that he was only in the moving pictures because of me, that was an unforeseen consequence. But you have to remember that he was only at the start of his movie career, he hadn't yet become what he since became, and he was terribly insecure. So when he bumped into us, his first thought was... no wait, his *very* first thought was to swank around and lord it over us, rub our noses in his fancy apartment and his valet and his automobile. His *next* first thought was to make sure that he got rid of us."

"Got rid of you? His friends and former colleagues?"

"Exactly. Got rid of the competition. He knew, don't you see, that Stan and I were every bit as good as him, we'd shown it often enough. I told you, didn't I, about the night Stan pretended to be him in New York, which was the very night that Mack Sennett saw the Karno show? So really it was Stan that had so impressed Sennett, not Charlie at all?"

"You mentioned that," John said.

"Well, we never spoke about it, but Charlie will have put two and two together. Even the telegram that Sennett sent asking to meet him asked for 'Mr Chaffin'. It could have been either of them. Chaplin or Jefferson."

"So?"

"So when Stan started to show an interest in trying to get a start in the flickers – and yes, I admit I was getting interested myself, too – Charlie went into a panic. He promised to arrange for these top movie guys to come and see us, but he had no intention of doing it. All he really wanted to do was to make sure that we wasted our week in Los Angeles by leaving things to him. He knew that we were tied to Considine, and we wouldn't be back for weeks, maybe even months, so he stuck a huge spanner in our works. He sabotaged us. Who knows what we might have been able to set up if he had just let us get on with it?"

"Hmmm," John said, picking up his pencil again and tapping his teeth with it.

"And then there was the business with Tilly, don't forget," I said, beginning to get cross.

"Ah yes, when your lover let Chaplin believe he was the f-father of your son in order to extort money from him," John drawled.

"It wasn't like that," I snapped.

"Oh?"

"He assumed it, she just didn't ever... disabuse him of his misapprehension." I tailed off, feeling that I was not being quite convincing, not even being convinced myself. "But that is beside the point," I said, picking up again.

"And what then *is* the point, Mr Dandoe?"

"Do you really not see? Don't you see what he did?"

"Chaplin?"

"Of course, Chaplin. He paid her off. He gave her money."

"He gave her the money to go see her father for maybe the last time. Some might call that an act of considerable g-generosity."

John's partner nodded in agreement. It was exasperating.

"But don't you *see*? He gave her just exactly enough money for the two of us – the three of us counting the boy – to go back to England..."

"That's right."

"To go back to England and stay there. Not enough money to come back to America. Just enough to get me out of his hair for good. Just enough to make sure that I was as far away from him as possible."

"Still seems like a remarkably noble gesture to me."

"Just enough to split up the Four Comiques, just enough to ruin *The Nutty Burglars*..."

"Well..."

"Just enough to dump Stan in the shit, too, in other words!" I cried, warming to my theme. "And what was *I* supposed to do for a living, what was Tilly supposed to do, stuck in England without the wherewithal to get back?"

"I'm not sure I quite..." John began.

"But that's not the worst of it," I said, thumping my fist on the table. "He knew, he knew what was coming. He said as much. He knew that the safest place to be if there was a war was right here in America. He said it, in so many words!"

"I'm not sure anyone knew for certain what was going to happen that summer," John frowned.

"Oh, he knew! That aviator friend of his knew," I said. "He knew that there was a good chance that England would go to war, he knew that England was about to become a really dangerous place to be, he knew that, and so that's where he wanted *me* to be."

175

"Come on, now, *really*?" John said, with an infuriatingly patronising sneer.

"He tried to kill me!" I shouted. "The little bastard tried to kill me, and he tried to get the Kaiser to do his dirty work for him!"

I was standing now, leaning across the table on my fists, panting. John regarded me evenly, and took a white hand kerchief from an inside pocket, with which he carefully wiped my spittle from his face.

"Well," he said. "I'm beginning to wonder whether you can help us at all, Mr Dandoe. To be perfectly frank, you are beginning to sound a little unhinged."

Unhinged? Suddenly I felt extremely self-conscious. I was painfully aware that this man held my future in the palm of his hand, and I sat back down, not looking him in the eye. As I tried to calm myself, my gaze drifted down to his ankle, where the elegantly nonchalant crossing of his legs had caused his trouser to ride up above his sock. With a start I thought I caught a glimpse of an inch or two of lady's silk stocking encasing his calf before he saw where I was looking and gave his trouser leg a quick downward tweak. Maybe I was losing it...

"I'm sorry," I said, with effortful calmness. "But if you will permit me to continue I am sure I can demonstrate that I have grounds for complaint that are perfectly well-founded and... rational."

With a gracious waft of a pale, languid hand, John invited me to do just that.

PART 3

21
OVER BY CHRISTMAS

IT was all going to be over by Christmas. That's what everyone said, that's what everyone thought, on both sides, apparently. The Germans thought that if they pushed quickly through Belgium and took Paris, then that would pretty much be that. So they surrounded Liège, a well-fortified little garrison town just across the border that Stan and I had played when we were on our uppers back in the summer of 1912. The piece we were in was an incomprehensible nonsense entitled *Fun on the Tyrol*, and even then the town had seemed to be on standby, waiting for something even more awful to happen. Apparently it had.

Evidently we had some kind of treaty with Belgium which obliged us to step in to preserve their independence, and so that was that. We were in.

In America there was much interest in the war. To begin with it seemed impossible that America could take sides, being a nation made up almost entirely of immigrants. As well as the numbers who could trace their heritage back to the Pilgrim Fathers, there were many more who had come from Germany, from Russia, from France, from Ireland, from the Balkan countries, all mixed together in that melting pot, all of which meant the American view was that of an interested, but detached, observer.

There was even smug talk of how the war could be good for business, as America was ideally placed to trade with both sides at once. So men on both sides could be killed, virtually simultaneously, with American bullets.

This even-handed neutrality didn't last all that long, though. Before long the newspapers were filled with salacious stories of atrocities committed by brutal German soldiers as they struggled to take plucky Belgium, of the rape and murder of women and children by the monstrous Kaiser's cohorts. There were incidents in America, beginning to creep into conversations here and there, of German shop windows being trashed, of people with German-sounding names being spat at in the street.

The fond hopes of a boom in trade were quickly dashed too, as the Atlantic became a battlefield. German submarines threatened to sink any shipping attempting to cross between America and England, and the numbers of ships prepared to risk it was dramatically reduced.

This meant that my hopes of seeing Tilly and Wallace again any time soon rested on an early resolution of the conflict, and so I scoured the papers daily for any indication that a decisive moment was in the offing, but as Christmas approached it became clear that the war in Flanders, where the British Expeditionary Force had halted the Germans, was going to drag on well into 1915.

So Tilly would not be able to keep her promise to return to us within a couple of months, and I would not, realistically, be able to make my way over to reunite with her and Wallace. Crossings were just impossible – you could not get a ticket for love nor money, and it wasn't as if I had either. Syd Chaplin made it over, though, somehow, in November, and benefitted from the sort of leg-up that Charlie was so anxious not to afford to me or Stan. He started working at Keystone developing a pear-drop shaped screen character called 'Gussle', which I am pleased to say never took.

Those of us without Chaplin's connections were rather stuck, and even the post was problematical. Quite apart from the fact that you never knew for certain if your letter would actually make it without being sent to the bottom of the briny by one of the Kaiser's U-boats – really, you might have been better off sticking it in a bottle and chucking it off a cliff – I simply hadn't a clue where to write to.

You see, when Tilly left we'd been so confident that it would be easy to meet up again, that she had taken a list of our engagements for the upcoming eight weeks, believing it would just be a question of aiming for one and pitching up at the stage door. Or failing that, the inevitable Irish pub around the corner. We hadn't even considered the possibility of writing to one another. I did try writing to her care of the police station in Great Yarmouth, sending her a list of our engagements as far into the future as I could manage, but I had no idea if that had got through to her.

It didn't stop my heart from thumping with anticipation whenever I approached a new stage door, but there was never any word from her, let alone the surprise appearance of her and Wallace that I day-dreamed about constantly.

The Four Comiques – now myself, Stan, Ed and Wren – continued to play *The Nutty Burglars* in John W. Considine's smaller theatres for the next few months. The word from the theatre managers in almost every place we played was that they were going to recommend to Considine that he put us into more substantial venues, as we certainly had the chops for a step up.

So slowly, but surely we began to find ourselves in ever-so-slightly more impressive theatres, and our wage packets became ever-so-slightly more agreeable too.

I barely noticed, though, as it just meant there was a little more money for me to drink away after the evening's performances, wherever we were, moping about Tilly and Wallace, wondering how I was ever going to see them again, and cursing the blasted Germans and Charlie bloody Chaplin.

Charlie himself continued to churn out his two-reelers, and we ignored them as best we could, still simmering with resentment for the way he had stymied us back in Los Angeles. I was, anyway. Stan always came away subdued and thoughtful after seeing a new Chaplin flicker. There was one called *Dough and Dynamite*, I remember, that autumn that did particularly well, and another entitled *His Musical Career*, which Stan was very taken with. It featured an attempt to get a piano up a long staircase that he seemed to think a very promising scenario.

As it happened, I was not the only one of the Comiques who was dissatisfied with life's rich tapestry as that much-vaunted Christmas approached. Ed Hurley had been chafing at the bit ever since he joined us, unhappy at being employed, effectively, by myself and Stan, whom he regarded as belonging at least a couple of rungs beneath him on the great ladder of show-business. One evening he joined us in the bar – which was by no means his regular habit, I might add – and decided to push the matter.

We sat in a booth, partitioned off from the rest of the place by a screen with stained glass panels, and he prodded the table with his forefinger to emphasize his points.

"The thing is," he said. "When we started on this tour with you, it was only supposed to be for a couple of months at the most."

"That's true," Stan said. "But events..."

"I know, I know, exactly," Ed butted in. "But the fact is there is no telling when Tilly will come back, if she ever does..."

"Ed, for goodness sake!" Wren cried, glancing at me solicitously.

"Listen, there's no point in beating about the bush. She's gone, and she's not coming back. There, I've said it. So Wren and I are no longer filling in, are we? We are no longer the second best option. We are it. We are both part of the act, equal parts with the two of you, and that is how we should be proceeding into the foreseeable future."

I glowered at him, thinking that the foreseeable future looked pretty grim if I was to be spending it with Edgar Hurley, but Stan was more conciliatory.

"Well, we are already splitting the take four ways," he said.

"Even though the three of us have more to do than you do," I put in, feeling provocative. Ed's gaze was icy.

"I'm not talking about the money," Ed said, and the effort he was making to keep his temper under control showed in the twitch at his jaw hinge. "What I mean is we should all have an equal say in all the decisions that are made regarding the future of The Four Comiques."

"What do you have in mind?" Stan asked, a mildly puzzled expression on his face.

"Well," Ed said. "I have been thinking that perhaps it would be a good notion to come up with a different piece."

Wren covered her eyes with her hands. I imagined she'd been privy to what was coming next.

"A different piece?" Stan said.

"One that makes more profitable use of the talents of the individual members of the team," Ed said, and sat back in the manner of a man who has just made an unanswerable point.

"Meaning yourself," I said, cutting to it. Ed said nothing, merely inclining his head to acknowledge that of course this was obvious.

"Oh," Stan said. "I see."

"Nice try," I said. "But if you think, in your wildest dreams, that..."

Stan put a hand on my arm, and I realised I was getting up out of my seat. "Now look," Stan said, and even though the four of us were nominally equal partners in this venture, there was an unspoken agreement that Stan was the leader. "*The Nutty Burglars* is doing better and better. We are getting better bookings, and there's every chance that finally, *finally*, it's going to start paying off for us. So where's the sense in ditching it and starting again from scratch, trying to establish another act? Even though," he added, kindly – too kindly, I thought – "there's no doubt you could shoulder a heavier burden, and should the opportunity arise for you and Wren to move on to something bigger and better, then I'm sure Arthur and I would not wish to stand in your way. I can't say fairer than that, can I?"

Ed, thwarted, seemed to have frozen in his seat for a moment, but then he nodded brusquely, got to his feet, wished us all a good night and went back to our lodgings. Without his wife.

"That was fair, wasn't it?" Stan asked.

"More than fair," I said. Wren smiled, and Stan went to the bar for some refills.

Wren put her hand on my arm. "Now then," she said, turning her big brown eyes on me.

"I'm sorry, Wren," I said. "There's just something about Ed that rubs me up the wrong way."

"He was right about one thing, though, wasn't he?" she

replied. "You might as well get used to the idea. Tilly might not be able to return for months, years even. This horrible, horrible war. She's going to have to make a life for herself over there, for you and your little boy, and it would only be human for you to do the same."

"What are you saying?" I frowned. "Maybe I've had a couple of beers too many, but..."

"I'm just saying. We had feelings for one another once, didn't we? And feelings like that never entirely disappear, now do they?"

I noticed – I could hardly fail to notice – that she was sitting closer to me than she had been a moment or two earlier, and her always spectacular bosom was pressing against my arm. It felt oddly familiar, and at one time, maybe a year and a half before, it would have been the preamble to a snatched liaison in the props and costumes compartment of the Karno boxcar, but we'd both moved on from that.

Hadn't we?

"Feelings?" I said, my mouth suddenly dry. Where was Stan with those drinks?

"You know what I mean," Wren breathed.

"Now look here," I said thickly. "What I remember is you using me, using me quite shamelessly just to make old Ed jealous."

"Is that all you remember?" she said, coyly, suggestively.

"I remember him giving you a black eye," I said, "and everything between you being tickety-boo thereafter."

"Is that what you think?"

"And even though you are married, back then I was single, but now I am spoken for."

"By a girl who is thousands of miles away for who knows how long."

"It was a bit of a kiss and a fumble, that's all. You know perfectly well that we never... you know."

"Maybe if we had," she whispered in my ear, "it would be easier now to forget about it and put the whole chapter behind us. But since we didn't...?"

Stan was walking across the room with our drinks now, and I thought with some relief that this would be a good opportunity to pass the baton, as it were, and visit the facilities to compose and rearrange myself. Before I could move, though, I felt the warm tip of Wren's tongue slip slowly, warmly, wetly into my ear. I felt my eyeballs rolling involuntarily up into my head, and all thoughts of standing up were banished for the next few minutes. Then she pulled away quickly, and Stan plonked the three glasses down with a grin, entirely ignorant of what had just occurred.

"Actually," he said cheerfully. "You know what? I have a good feeling about the New Year."

———

As it turned out, Stan's optimism soon seemed more like prescience, as we received a message that our first engagement of January 1915 would be at the Milwaukee Empress. Not one of Considine's biggest or most prestigious, not by any means, but still a considerable step up from the fleapits we had been playing. An Empress, by God! It felt like the start of something bigger, something better, and the four of us passed a very jovial Christmas together in our lodgings as a result. I even managed not to get into any kind of argument with Hurley.

Our landlady for that week in Cedar Rapids, Iowa, whipped up a memorable Christmas luncheon with, if not all the trimmings, then at least a goodly proportion of them. We were joined at the table by a couple of acts who were appearing at the Majestic along with the cowboy Will Rogers. One was called

Lennett and Wilson, who styled themselves 'Comedy Horizontal Bar Experts', and I said at one point that I considered myself an expert at standing at the bar until I finally became horizontal, and they laughed as though they had never heard that one before. The other was an aerial acrobatic double act called Frobel and Ruge. Billy Ruge dressed as a Chinaman onstage, but off it he was a rather grumpy little New Yorker.

"Fancy spending Christmas in this part of da woild," he grumbled.

"Da what?" I said.

"Woild, da woild."

"Oh, world, yes, I see."

Their party trick, which they showed us in the landlady's parlour that afternoon, was for strongman Bill Frobel to roll Ruge up like a medicine ball and then roll him around, bounce him off walls, throw him in the air and catch him.

All in all it was a very convivial occasion, although as it happened Cedar Rapids audiences had the reputation of being the coldest in the Mid-West. We'd all seen a sign backstage in one of the theatres we'd played in back in the Bronx which read: "You think you're good? Try playing Cedar Rapids!" As if to complement this, we found a sign by the stage door of the theatre right there in Cedar Rapids warning: "Don't send out your laundry until we have seen your act." However, we four had played Glasgow for Fred Karno, and nothing much was likely to put a scare into us after that.

I thought a lot about Tilly and Wallace that day, and wondered what sort of Christmas they were having. I hoped she had found her father in Great Yarmouth, and that he had been both well and innocent, but I had no way of knowing. I'd sent I don't know how many letters into the void, and Tilly might well have tried writing to me – I just couldn't tell.

After that Christmas lunch was over and we were recovering, Wren suddenly noticed that our landlady had pinned some mistletoe over the door to her parlour. She pulled her husband to his feet, and he groaned under the newly-acquired weight of a mass of plum duff to oblige her. Wren insisted on a Christmas kiss from Stan, and from Lennett and Wilson, and then she turned to me.

"Come on then, Arthur," she whispered playfully. "Let's see if this brings back any memories, shall we?"

She pressed her soft lips to mine, and wrapped her arms around my neck, and after a moment I felt the tip of her warm wet little tongue worming past my defences and exploring my teeth and beyond.

The kiss went on and on, and I was uncomfortably aware that Edgar was only a few feet away, but Wren kept her lips locked to mine, and her eyes were shut, and her belly pressed firmly against me. It was a kind of exquisitely delicious agony, that I wished would end but could do nothing to stop.

Finally she broke away and I looked around guiltily, but Edgar had succumbed to the meal and had closed his eyes. Lennett and Wilson were politely complimenting our landlady, but Stan gave me a long quizzical look.

Which meant that as the New Year turned I found myself guiltily thinking more about Wren and her evident availability than I did about Tilly, lovely yet faraway Tilly, the love of my life.

So imagine my state of mind when we four hapless Comiques stepped from our cab in front of the Milwaukee Empress in the first week of January, anticipating the first of a new run of proper-sized theatres, a significant step back up towards the big time at last, only to find ourselves faced with a sign on the front doors reading 'Under New Management', and a pair of workmen in overalls changing the large sign above the main lobby from 'Vaudeville Nightly' to, of all things in the wide world, 'Tillie's Punctured Romance'.

It was almost too much to take in.

A long-established vaudeville theatre turned overnight into a flicker hall.

Our main chance trampled mercilessly by Charlie Chaplin's first full-length feature release.

And a title, moreover, that made it feel like the cold hand of fate was pointing an accusing finger down at the top of my head.

It was like the very crack of doom itself.

I stood on the icy pavement, and even though I had my big winter coat on and was not at all cold, I was trembling.

22
THE DOMINOES
TOPPLE

IT was a huge blow, and no mistake.

Quite apart from the fact that we had set such store by clambering back onto the Empress circuit, we now had no work for the week, and there was no-one left working at the theatre with any links to the Considine organisation and the network of local theatrical landladies so we were effectively out on the street. It was, though, only the morning, so there was the rest of that Monday to find a roof at least, if not a replacement engagement. We convened in the warmth of a coffee shop with an open fire, where Stan and I had sometimes breakfasted when we were at the Empress with the Karnos a couple of years before, to discuss our next move.

"I wonder what's happened," Stan mused.

"Well, clearly something pretty dramatic," Ed said. "The pity of it is that no-one saw fit to tell us, or even leave a message for us advising us what to do next."

"They probably had more on their plate than worrying about us," Wren said, and Ed became indignant.

"They have a duty to let us know of any changes so we do not travel unnecessarily. More than that, it is common courtesy! We should not be expected to fend for ourselves like this. I have a good mind to go and tell Considine so himself, to his face!"

"Actually," Stan said, brightening. "That is not the worst idea. Chicago is only a couple of hours away, we could be there by mid-afternoon. And if Mr Considine is not in his office, at least there will be someone who can tell us what we are supposed to be doing. What do you think, Arthur?"

"Hmmm?" I have to say I was not really fully engaged in the conversation. My mind was spinning after the latest development, and my resolution not to let Chaplin drive me mad, in order that I could be the reformed individual Tilly was hoping I could become, was being sorely tested. It was his fault though – he kept doing things that annoyed me. All right, so his movie was not just playing here in Milwaukee, it was released all over the country, and he would hardly have had any say in converting one single vaudeville house into a cinema, but still. I felt him hovering above my head like a dark cloud, further thunderbolts clutched in his perfectly manicured hands, his purple eyes flashing with malevolent mirth...

"I said, perhaps we should head for Chicago, see if we can't beard old Considine in his cave, what?"

"Yes, why not," I said. "There's not likely to be much for us here, is there?"

———

So that afternoon we rode the rails down the west side of Lake Michigan down into the Windy City, where we made our miserable way to the headquarters of the Sullivan and Considine comedy empire.

Our first inkling that all was really not well came when we reached the reception room. Normally this would be packed with hopeful performers of all kinds, typically in their gaudy stage costumes as though they never wore anything else, hoping to be granted an audience with one of the bookers inside. On this day, however, the room was deserted.

The reception desk, too, which was usually attended by a fiercely unhelpful harridan, one of a seemingly endless rotation upon whom Considine could call, but this too was unpopulated. The room beyond, which last time I had seen it had been filled with energetic young chaps and ladies scribbling lists of performers and pinning them to pinboards on the walls alongside giant maps of the continent, was also empty. A few desultory sheets of paper wafted in the breeze from the open door, and one of the maps was keeling over at the corner having popped a drawing pin onto the floor somewhere. Where once there was busy endeavour, and aspiration, and hope, now there was only echoing silence.

We looked at one another, bemused.

"Where is everyone?" Wren said in a little voice, as though speaking louder might actually have raised the ghosts of the departed.

"Hello?" Stan called out, not wanting to step beyond the receptionist's desk without invitation.

Suddenly there was a crash from one of the offices away to our right, as though a great pile of papers had been swept from a desk and thrown to the floor. Evidently there was still someone in residence.

Stan, Wren and I were a little wary of intruding, but Hurley was fired up by indignation at having been left high and dry in Milwaukee without any kind of explanation, and he was determined to let somebody know about it. He strode around

192

the receptionist's unoccupied station and went in search of the source of the noise. As he blew through, the half-hanging map sighed to the floor in his wake.

Arriving at the office door, Hurley rapped firmly. The door was wrenched open in front of him and a figure stood there, his broad shoulders blocking out the light from the windows behind.

"Who are you?" the silhouette demanded.

"Well, who are you?" Hurley said, drawing himself up to his full height to try and match the imposing fellow before him.

"Who wants to know?" the fellow growled, and I recognised the voice then.

"First tell me to whom I am speaking," Ed demanded, not wanting to back down.

They could have gone on like that for some time, I think, if I hadn't stepped forward.

"Mr Considine?" I said.

"Good grief..." Stan whispered. "So it is."

We hardly recognised the man who had been our champion. His hair, normally slicked down to his big square head and oiled to within an inch of its life, was jutting out in all directions. He had not shaved for several days, that much was clear. His collar had sprung free from his shirt at one side and was waving up around his ear. His shirt was hanging out of his trousers, and his tie hung loose around his neck.

"Arthur? Stan? Is that you?" Considine said, peering at us over Ed's shoulder. "Good to see you, fellas. I'll be with you in a minute. I just need to see what this jumped-up chimpanzee wants from me. It'll be money, if I know anything!"

"Well!" Hurley spluttered, going a sort of beetroot colour.

"He's with us, Mr Considine," I said. "Don't you remember Edgar? From the Karno company?"

"Can't say I do," Considine frowned. "I remember this lovely creature though," the burly entrepreneur went on, pushing past Hurley to take his wife's hand up to his bristly lips.

"What has happened here?" Stan asked.

Considine slumped, and went back to pull his office door shut before we got a close look at the chaos within.

"I need a drink," he said. "Let's go round to Joe's and I'll tell you all about it."

———

"My troubles really began just over a year back," Considine said a little while later, clutching a large glass of bourbon in one big paw. "Big Tim Sullivan and I had built up the premier vaudeville circuit in the country, the first to offer venues coast to coast. I could offer a turn seventy weeks' straight work with no doubling-up. I could bring acts over from Europe – well, you know, I had the Fred Karno company tour the biggest theatres on my circuit five times in three years. I made Charlie Chaplin, you know?"

"You did, sir," I said, happy to see someone else taking the credit for that.

"Well, Sullivan, God rest his soul, he wasn't really what you'd call an active partner, he was more of a money man. Most of the organisation fell to me, but we were expanding all the time. I was buying theatres in cities across the land, and where there wasn't a theatre big enough or grand enough for our purpose, well by God we'd build one. Yes sir. No-one could hold a candle to us, not even that weasel King Greek."

Ed and Wren were lost at this, so I leaned over and filled them in.

"King Greek is the name Alexander Pantages goes by," I

explained. "He and Mr Considine have a big rivalry, isn't that right, sir?"

"You could say that," Considine growled, emptying his glass and waving at the barman for another. "If you call sabotage, cheating and theft 'a big rivalry' then yes, that is what we had."

"You remember how Pantages had our props and costumes sent to the Yukon? It was before you joined Karno, but we told you of it, I'm sure," Stan said to Ed and Wren, and they nodded.

"So in the fall of 1913," Considine began again, with a big sigh. "Big Tim Sullivan went crazy, crazy as a damned loon. It was the syphilis, they reckon, eating away at his mind. Whatever it was, they locked him in the booby hatch and he got worse and worse until, they say, he escaped, and next thing they knew, his body was found on the railroad tracks. No-one knows how it got there. God knows he had his fingers in enough pies. He was involved in most of the protection rackets on the Lower West Side for years, so maybe someone had it in for him. It's just as likely, though, judging by the state of his mind the last time I visited him, that he thought he was a locomotive."

"Good heavens!" Wren gasped.

"So that was my backing gone, overnight. The Greek got wind of it, however I tried to keep it quiet, and he started sniffing around some of my prize houses, seeing if he couldn't shake a couple loose. Well, I'm not a man to just step aside. I saw off Wyatt Earp, you know, when he tried to move in on my gambling houses in Seattle. So I proposed a partnership with Marcus Loew. He owns nearly as many theatres as me, and he was always looking for the chance to poke the Greek in the eye, just like I am. We were all set to go into business together, but then this damned war kicked off in Europe, and suddenly the value of all Loew's holdings was less certain. Not to mention that we weren't going to get any acts over from England, not with the U-boats trying to sink all the damn ships. So Loew got cold feet, and he held off, and he held off, until finally the loan I'd had to take out to buy my latest venture got called in, and I hadn't the money to pay. And since every theatre I have bought has been financed by loans taken out against the one before, the whole circuit is collapsing around my ears like a ring of goddamn dominoes."

"The whole circuit?" Stan breathed.

"The whole damn thing, and the booking organisation that fed it. And who do you think is carving it up between them? Why, King Greek, of course, and that son of a bitch Marcus Loew. I swear they were plotting together all along, and Loew just strung me along until I could no longer support the business I'd built over two decades of blood, sweat and tears."

What could we say to that? We sat in silence, contemplating the ruin of the man who had been our chief hope of building a career in vaudeville.

"When we got to Milwaukee," Ed said, breaking the moment. "The theatre was under new management, and no-one was there to tell us, and there was no word."

"Ed!" Wren hissed. Clearly our erstwhile boss had more problems to deal with than our embarrassment.

"Ed?" Considine said. "It is Ed, right?"

"Edgar. Edgar Hurley."

"Edgar. You're right, it was not good enough, and I will see that someone is fired, first thing in the morning."

"Thank you," Ed said, primly.

"Of course, I shall have to hire somebody first, so that I will have somebody to fire, but rest assured you can leave the matter in my capable hands."

Ed sat tight-lipped, once again going red in the face. Considine turned to me and Stan.

"In short, boys, I am out of the entertainment business as of now. Don't hitch your flag to my wagon, for I'm surrounded by injuns, cut-throat injuns! But I wish you all the best."

The big man stood and drained another glass, which he smacked down onto the table, before stomping out to wallow some more in the ruins of his once-mighty empire.

After he had gone we sat there for a while, just staring at the wet rings our glasses had made on the wooden table. The zeroes stared back at us, eloquently summing up the balance sheet of our careers at that moment. Even Ed's selfish bullishness was subdued to silent contemplation.

"Same again?" The barman had wandered over to break into our miserable reverie. We looked up, and it suddenly struck us that Considine had left us with the tab. We scrabbled the change from our pockets together to pay it off, and hardly dared risk another drink, much as we wanted one, until we knew where the next dime was coming from.

━━━━━

On the corner, a street stand was selling the Chicago Tribune. I hadn't seen a newspaper for several days, and I wondered if there had been any changes in the war situation. Any hint, however small, that Tilly might soon be able to join me on this side of the Atlantic would have given me a much-needed lift just then, which would make it worth the single coin it cost.

The war in Europe was, however, relegated below the fold by a far more important turn of events, neatly summed up by the screaming banner headline:

197

CHARLIE CHAPLIN IN CHICAGO!

As if things were not bad enough! I threw the newspaper back at the poor fellow who had just handed it to me, and stormed off down the street in a blind fury. Behind me I was dimly aware of Wren apologising to the bewildered vendor, turning on her abundant charms, no doubt, to smooth things over.

A block or two away I realised that I was going nowhere, indeed had nowhere to go, and I stopped and slumped on a bench just inside a small green park. There was a light covering of snow which I thought nothing of until it started to soak into my trouser legs.

As I began to calm down I suddenly had a flash of what Tilly would have made of my reaction just then. Wasn't this exactly the sort of thing she was talking about just before she left? What a fool I was!

Stan caught up with me first. The Hurleys were hanging back.

"You... um... forgot your paper," Stan ventured, holding up the rag in question. "It says that... the Germans and the British, on Christmas Day, they all played a game of football in No Man's Land. Between the trenches. That must have been quite a thing."

"Trenches? No Man's Land? What the hell is going on over there?"

"I know, I can't really imagine it."

"My brother, you know, Lance? He fought in the Boer War. Didn't really tell me anything much about it. Actually, 'I shit meself' was pretty much all he ever said, but I'm pretty sure he was on the move all over the place, not just sat in a hole with the Boers sat in another hole fifty yards away, waiting for something to happen."

"It's incomprehensible, I agree. Hopefully it will all be over soon."

"So, go on then," I said.

"What?"

"Tell me what Charlie is doing here."

"Oh, ah, yes, right. I thought that might be... why you... ah... yes." Stan flipped the war stories out of sight and looked at the lead article. "Evidently Charlie has... um... broken with Mack Sennett and Keystone, and signed a new deal worth... oh I say! One thousand two hundred and fifty dollars."

"A year?"

"A week."

"A week!"

Stan nodded, grimacing his disbelief. "Plus a ten thousand dollar signing bonus."

"What?! But that's...! What idiots are paying him that much?"

"The company is called Essanay. They make the Broncho Billy films."

"I know, in San Francisco."

"Yes, and they have studios here, too, apparently, so Charlie is just starting work now in Chicago, hence the hullabaloo."

Stan pushed his hat back and scratched his head. I looked up at the sky, and then caught his eye. He started to giggle, and before long I had started too. There was nothing in the world more infectious than Stan laughing, and the whole ludicrous situation we found ourselves in, the sheer gulf between literally having no work at all, a benefactor going bust, no prospects, nowhere to stay, and barely enough money to feed ourselves until the end of the week, and Charlie Chaplin starting a new job at one thousand two hundred and fifty dollars a week... well.

We had to laugh.

23
THE EYES HAVE IT

"I think part of the problem is the name," Ed said, when we convened the next morning for breakfast in the cheapest hotel we'd been able to find the night before. I'm sure if we'd looked a little longer and walked a little farther we'd have found one that didn't even do breakfast, but still.

"*The Nutty Burglars?* That does the job perfectly, doesn't it?" I said.

"No, no, no. I mean the Four Comiques. I mean, what is that? We are not French. There's nothing French about us. Even the number four in the Four Comiques is not French. It doesn't make any sense at all."

"What do you have in mind?" I asked, realising that the man was not going to shut up until he'd said his piece.

"Hurley, Stan, Art and Wren," Ed pronounced, then sat back with a smug smile.

"Eh?" Stan said.

"Hurley, Stan, Art and Wren. It's got a nice rhythm to it, and that half-rhyme makes it really memorable."

I glanced over at the others, and could see that the idea was not quite sitting right. And if I knew one thing about show folk it was this: billing is everything. Even in an act that had no bookings and was on the very brink of extinction, we would be arguing about this for the rest of the morning.

"I notice that I come last," Wren grumbled, scraping a thin layer of butter onto some cold toast.

"It's for the half-rhyme," Ed said.

"Well, why not Hurley, Wren, Art and Stan?" she replied.

"It's not as..."

"Why are you called by your surname, and the rest of us by our first names?" Stan frowned.

"So that he gets two syllables," I muttered.

"No, it's just better," Ed protested.

"When did I become Art?" I asked. "At least the rest of you get a whole one of your names in the title. I just get half of mine. Art, Art, Art. I'm not an Art."

Ed was becoming exasperated now. "All right, do better if you think you can!"

I knew exactly what would wind him up the tightest, and I was in a mischievous mood, so I pretended to give it some serious thought, and then said: "How about The Stan Jefferson Quartet?"

"What?"

"Oh, no... " Stan waved a hand modestly.

"Stan's the lead, he's the main part, he's the star. Who needs to know who we three are? It's all about Stan."

I could see that Ed was going to reach boiling point, and glanced across at Wren. She caught my barely perceptible wink, and chipped in.

"I like it," she said. "I think it sounds classical."

"It sounds ridiculous!" Ed blustered, getting halfway up to his feet and jabbing a forefinger in my face. "And if you think I'm going to...!"

"All right, all right, let's calm down, shall we?" Stan said, putting his arm round Ed's shoulders, and proving by the way that he was the leader of our little troupe. "This is a conversation for another day. Bookings first, then billing, eh?"

———

The four of us decided to split up and do the rounds of the bookers' offices. There were quite a few in Chicago, servicing a large number of small and even smaller time venues in the boondocks outside the city centre. There was a chance that we could pick up some dates filling in, if an act had to cancel because of illness or perhaps a unicycling mishap. I saw one of those, once, by the way. The fellow's seat flew off without him realising, and he sat down heavily on the unprotected central pole, at which every male member of the audience involuntarily clutched himself.

So I spent the morning knocking on doors, and sitting in waiting rooms with other under-employed vaudevillians of various description. I discovered, by the way, that not wearing a gaudy onstage outfit was actually an advantage, as I was frequently taken for a tradesman of some sort and thus spoken to immediately, which saved time. The pickings, however were somewhere between slim and none. The only sniff I got would have required us to stand in for a sick monologist, and split his money four ways. We'd have done better sitting outside the theatre with a cup, frankly.

I was leaving one of these offices, which was reached via a staircase between two shop fronts, when I stepped out onto the pavement I saw heading towards me such an extraordinary-looking fellow that I stopped in my tracks. I wasn't the only one, either – other passers-by were turning to gawk as they passed him.

He was not tall, or particularly well-built. His clothes were ordinary, if a little on the baggy side. His hair jutted out in tufts under his derby hat, and he had a great soup-strainer of a moustache which almost perfectly concealed his mouth. The truly distinctive feature, though, the one that was drawing so much attention, was that he seemed completely cross-eyed. He cut such an odd figure that I didn't even spare a glance to the fellow he was walking along with, until that one tapped me on the arm and said:

"Arthur Dandoe?"

Of course, who should it be but Chaplin? He was almost as flabbergasted to see me as I was to see him, and I'd taken a step back in amazement and banged the back of my head on the door frame behind me.

"Good Lord! Charlie! Fancy seeing you!"

"I thought you were in England!" he cried, his face a kaleidoscope of puzzlement, fake pleasure and alarm.

"No," I said. "Tilly went back, and Freddie went with her, but Stan and I stayed."

"*Freddie* went with her," Charlie said, wonderingly. "Well, well, well. And so what are you and Stan up to now?"

"We are... well, we are still... um..." I mumbled as I wondered what to tell him, and my eyes flicked back to the extraordinarily ill-appointed ones of Charlie's companion.

"Oh, I beg your pardon!" Charlie said. "How rude of me! This is my colleague Mr Ben Turpin, comedy film actor. Ben, meet Mr Arthur Dandoe, vaudevillian."

"A pleasure, Mr Turpin," I said, and we shook hands.

"Vaudevillian, eh?" Turpin said in a raspy voice, looking over my shoulder. Well, looking over both of my shoulders at once.

"That's right," I said. "We do a turn called *The Nutty Burglars*."

"Without Tilly and Freddie?" Charlie asked.

"You remember the Hurleys, Wren and Edgar?"

Charlie frowned, as if trying to force his memory back to a time of utter insignificance to him. It made me want to punch him in the face. Finally he ventured:

"Gorgeous, and a bit of a prig?"

"That's them, although I wouldn't call Edgar gorgeous myself."

Turpin laughed, and then asked: "And where y'at wi' dat?"

I'd had a moment or two to think by then, and managed to come up with: "This week we are booked into the Milwaukee Empress."

"Well, well!" Charlie said. "Back in the old Empresses, eh? Good for you, good for you!"

I smiled as he patronised me, neglecting to mention, of course, that we had been cancelled and summarily replaced by a Chaplin film.

"I did my time in vaudeville an' I liked it well enough. That's how I ended up wi' dese..." Turpin pointed at his crossed eyes, redundantly, since I hadn't been able to look at anything else since our conversation began. "Playing Happy Hooligan for years, and they just stuck. But I'd rather make my fifty bucks a week in da flickers. Work during the daytime, an' the evenings are my own."

"Wait a moment," I said. "You are working for fifty bucks a week?"

"That's right," Turpin replied. "Why y'ax?"

"Only because, according to the *Chicago Herald*..." I began, but suddenly Charlie started coughing.

"Ahem! Oh my, a glass of water! Would you, Ben?"

204

"Sure thing," Turpin said, and trotted over to a nearby soda stand.

"Arthur!" Charlie hissed urgently. "There's no need to draw Ben's attention to how much I am being paid."

"It was in the newspaper," I said.

"I know, but somehow that passed him by, and there's no need to cause any more awkwardness than we absolutely need, is there? Since he and I have to work together?"

"As you wish," I replied, and Charlie patted my arm gratefully. Turpin came back then with some water, which Charlie took and sipped at.

"Because Charlie is being paid one thousand two hundred and fifty dollars a week," I said to Turpin then. His criss-cross eyes widened, and he juddered, as though an electric shock had passed through his body. Chaplin, meanwhile, spluttered water all down his shirt front.

"You don't say?"

"And a bonus of ten thousand," I said. "It was ten thousand, wasn't it, Charlie?"

Chaplin composed himself and tried to re-join the side of us, the workers, against the side of them, the management. "I shan't see any of that," he muttered grimly. "They promise you the world when they want you to sign but then they try and back out once they've got you."

Turpin was looking at Chaplin quizzically[3]. At least I think he was.

"Well, we should be on our way," Charlie said.

"I'll walk with you," I said, enjoying the little man's discomfort. "So I have been thinking about heading out to California. You recall we spoke about getting into the movies? Me and Stan?"

Charlie shot me a look then, and I saw that he got my drift.

"Listen," he said, "about that. I tried to get some fellows to come along, really I did, but no-one of any account was free until the following week, and you'd've been gone by then. But I told them all about you and they'll be looking out, I'm sure, any time you go back."

"Well," I went on. "I thought I might go and see Mack at Keystone."

I wasn't really thinking of doing that. I could hardly afford the train ticket, but I just wanted to give Chaplin something to chew on. He grinned mirthlessly, showing all his pearly whites. He knew he had no influence at his old studio any more, and I knew it too.

"Syd is there, you know?" he said.

"I heard that," I said. The thought of Syd coming all the way over from England, a crossing that must have been fraught with terrifying uncertainty and fantastic expense, to piggy-back on Charlie's success, only for Charlie to up sticks and leave had given me a pleasurable frisson of *schadenfreude* – not that I would have used that word at that time, for fear of being beaten up in whatever bar I happened to be holed up.

"Ah, here we are, look Ben," Charlie said then, clearly itching to get away. We were passing a shoe store, and Charlie made for the entrance. "Arthur? What an astonishing coincidence to bump into you here, but we really must dash. I'd come and see your show, but..."

"But it will take you some time to round up all your important movie people, by which time we'll have moved on, I understand, I understand perfectly," I said, enjoying riding him. What poor old Ben Turpin must have made of it I don't know.

"But Milwaukee is just a little too far, I was going to say."

"So, it's shoes you are looking for, is it?"

Charlie sighed. "Yes, I need some for my character, to wear

onscreen. I had to leave the ones I have been using back at Keystone."

"Because you left under a cloud, rather?"

"Well," he said. "That's as may be."

"You want some used second hand shoes, though, don't you? Big battered ones?"

"If I find any big enough then I shall pay someone to batter them."

"Well, when I put together that exact same costume, when I did the Stowaway, remember? I found the shoes in the Karno trunk, they were just stock funny big shoes, like everyone uses. Robey, Billie Ritchie, everyone. And then again in the wardrobe room at Keystone, remember? That time we visited, you me and Stan? And Mack offered us all a job? Remember that?"

From his tight lips I gathered that he did remember that, and also no doubt recalled that he had made it a condition of signing with Keystone a year ago that Stan and I were not to be employed along with him.

"The costume department here is more limited," he said, and turned to his companion. "We should go."

"Pleasure to meet you, young feller," Turpin said to me. "And listen, if you'd like a day or two as an extra on da lot, while you're in town, just pitch up at Essanay and mention ma name."

"That's very kind, Ben, thank you," I said.

"Don't mention it. Anything for an old vaudevillian. This business is hard enough wid'out folks helping one another out if we can. Am I right?

———

The Four Comiques reconvened as arranged to discuss how each of us had fared with the various bookers we had approached that day.

"No joy, I'm afraid," Stan sighed. "No-one's cried off sick, or got stranded in another city, or suddenly retired from the business for ever."

"I have a similar tale of woe to relate," Ed said, although in fairness I was not really expecting him to be the one who struck gold, as that would have required him to be personable.

"Well, I bumped into an old friend," I said.

"Someone from the Karno days?" Stan asked.

"Indeed."

"Male or female?"

"I don't want you to guess," I said. "It was Charlie. I met him in the street."

Stan, Wren and Ed looked at me as though this was the most fantastical proposition they had ever heard.

"Yes, that's right," I said, as none of them seemed about to speak. "Charlie Chaplin."

"What did you say?" Stan asked quietly. "When he asked what we were all up to, what did you tell him?"

"Um... ah... well, as it happens I told him we were booked to play the Milwaukee Empress this week."

"And that it was cancelled?"

"That detail may have slipped my mind at that moment."

Stan and Ed both heaved a sigh of relief. "Good," Stan said. "Good, well done."

"The last thing we want is for anyone to know we are on our uppers," Ed said. "Especially the one man we know who is quite obscenely successful."

"Yes," I said. "Anyway I might have got us some work, if we want it, as extras on the Essanay movie lot."

"Wait," Stan said, shocked. "Charlie offered to get you some work? *Charlie* did?"

"Well, no, the man he was with, actually. The most extraordinary crossed-eyes you ever saw."

"You're sure he was talking to you?"

"Pretty sure."

"Hmmm," Stan said. "We are going to have to think about this one."

"Is nobody going to ask me how I got on?" Wren said then.

"I'm sorry, Wren," I said. "Did you have any luck?"

"I didn't get us any bookings, no," Wren said.

"Oh well," Stan said. "Perhaps we should try again tomorrow..."

"*But*," Wren went on. "I did have one interesting conversation. I met Kalma. You remember Kalma, Ed? We shared a bill with him in New York, when we were with the Buster Brown company?"

"That popinjay," Ed snorted. "He's an illusionist, but the only thing that is illusory about him is his talent. Ha!"

"He was always perfectly charming to me."

"Yes, my dear, because he was hoping to make your husband disappear, and then, unless I am wildly mistaken, your clothing."

"Well, isn't that nice?" Wren said. "What the lovely Kalma told me, if you are interested..."

"Yes, of course, go on Wren," Stan said.

"Is that he happened to be discussing *The Nutty Burglars* only last week with the agent Claude Bostock, and Gordon Bostock, his brother, who is also an agent."

"Discussing...?"

"They caught us in Cedar Rapids over Christmas, apparently, and thought we were aces, so Kalma said we should certainly go and see them, see if they could do anything for us."

"Oh? How do we...? I mean, where...?" Stan stuttered, suddenly as excited as I had seen him for quite a while.

"Their office is right here in Chicago, and I have already arranged for us all to go and see them on Wednesday. You may now thank me and buy me a drink."

24
HIS NEW JOB

THE Essanay film studio in Chicago was very different from the only other one I had visited, which was of course the Keystone lot in Edendale. There the various stages were open to the elements, and the Californian sunlight was diffused by great swathes of white linen draped overhead. Conditions in a Chicago January were far from Californian. There was ice on the roads, and a light snowfall during the night had dusted the trees and the windowsills, while the temperature felt barely above freezing, so I was glad to find that all the filming was to take place indoors under electric lighting.

Wren was pleased too, as she had accompanied me for this little adventure. Stan and Ed had decided against, for reasons of their own. Stan was afraid Charlie would be uncomfortable if we turned up at his place of work, particularly as he was starting anew.

"That," I said, "is precisely why I want to go. He deserves a little discomfort after the way he spiked us back in Los Angeles."

"Well, I think I shall do another round of the bookers, and try and get a sense of how the Bostocks are regarded in the business before we meet them."

"Admirably professional," I said. "We shall see you this evening, when Mr Chaplin will be paying for the drinks."

Ed also felt that it would be inappropriate to tag along. He claimed to feel awkward as he had not himself met Ben Turpin, but I am sure he felt that being a mere extra was beneath an artiste of his stature.

Wren, though, was nothing if not game, and we strolled up to the door arm-in-arm to present ourselves. "If nothing else," she said, "it will get me away from Ed for a few hours."

The Essanay studio was a converted warehouse in an industrial part of the city, as befitted the organisation's full designation: The Essanay Film Manufacturing Company.

Once inside the building we found ourselves directed to a waiting room, which was depressingly full of would-be stars of the flickers, coughing, and eyeing one another up with barely-concealed hostility. My heart sank at the thought of joining this rabble, and so I led Wren straight up to the young secretary at the desk.

"Excuse me?" I said, as a little ripple of 'Who do they think they are?' murmured around the waiting room.

The young girl looked up. She was pretty, with light brown hair, and a very nice smile, and she looked like she should certainly be in pictures before anyone else in that waiting room.

"Take a seat, please," she said.

"We were invited to come along by Mr Ben Turpin," I said.

"Oh!" This little name-drop had the desired effect and more, as Wren and I were quickly whisked through a swinging door into an inner office, where a slim dark-haired chap was consulting a page of typed script with lots of odd notations jotted upon it, arrows and the like.

"Mr Robbins? Here's some friends of Ben's. How many more do you need?"

"One of each should do it, thanks Edna. These two will do fine."

This Robbins wafted a hand carelessly at another door behind him, and went back to his studies.

Through this further door we discovered a wardrobe room, and I was given a rather fancy military uniform to wear, blue, with black straps across the chest, and a fur collar, and a fur hat, as well as cavalry pants and high boots. A dark moustache was glued to my face, a sabre in a scabbard was hung from my belt, and the effect was Eastern European and historical without being particularly specific.

When I saw Wren some half an hour later, she had been transformed into a noblewoman with a long gown, an abundance of costume jewellery, and most eye-catchingly of all, a wig of blonde ringlets covering her own lush dark brown locks. My breath caught in my throat momentarily, because as the light caught her and her necklaces sparkled, she tossed those blonde ringlets and just for an instant I was looking at the very image of Tilly.

It threw me, I don't mind admitting. I'd been having a hard time of it, missing Tilly and contemplating an uncertain future, having heard nothing from her for months. I don't say that it excuses what happened a little later, but it might have been part of it.

The first thing that struck me when we were shown through to the stage itself was that there was none of the chaos that had characterised the Keystone lot, where three films were being made on adjacent sets while further constructions were noisily hammered into being just feet away.

There was a good deal of hanging around, actually. Fellows in similar garb to mine loafed on a staircase smoking, while sundry other ladies in gowns like Wren's leaned on the wall complaining that the dresses would not permit them to sit. There was a table to one side where cups of coffee were available, and so we took advantage. I had high hopes that there might be lunch at some point, too, which would make the whole day worthwhile.

I spotted Ben Turpin then and took Wren over to meet him.

"Ben?" I said. "Remember me? Charlie's friend from yesterday?"

My voice barely caught on the word 'friend', but then I was an actor. Ben swivelled sharply, and I saw him unable quite to conceal a hip flask which he had been using to top up his coffee.

"Oh! Hey!" he cried, his eyes darting left and right, but not necessarily both together. "There y'are! You made it, eh?"

"Yes, thanks to you," I said. "This is Wren."

Wren offered her hand, and then stopped, as if not quite certain that Ben would be able to locate it. He did, however, taking it genteelly in one hand while shoving his flask away with the other.

"Say," he said to me with a sly nudge. "*You*'ve done all right for yourself!"

"That's not..." I began, but Ben winked, and it was such an extraordinary sight that my protests tailed away.

"Want some?" Ben said then, allowing his flask to peek cheekily out of his jacket pocket.

Wren and I both received a generous splash of Ben's bourbon in our coffees. Again, I don't offer this as an excuse for what happened, but who knows? It may have been a factor.

Charlie appeared then, dressed as his Tramp character – he had evidently found some big shoes to batter – and all work and conversation stopped to observe this moment, the start of Chaplin's Essanay film-making career.

Charlie looked slowly at everyone, without speaking, and then gave a little smile. Suddenly, without explanation or preamble, he launched into a clog-dancing routine that he had performed as a boy with the Eight Lancashire Lads. The stage crew, the actors and we uniformed extras watched in amazement until the dance reached its big finish, and then there was a moment of stunned silence until someone realised that applause was expected and began a round.

"I am ready," Chaplin pronounced, to a good deal of eye-rolling and barely-concealed smirking.

Anti-climactically, Charlie spent the next long while deep in conversation with the man Robbins[4]. They were discussing some technical issue, and I could see that Charlie was unhappy with some detail of what was planned. I saw him glance in our direction, but my moustache and fur hat and Wren's blonde wig caused his eye to scoot over us without recognition.

I felt mischievous, gate-crashing his work in disguise, as it were, but also a little foolish. As we waited for something, anything, to happen, I couldn't help remembering that Charlie and I had started in the same place, on the same rung of the ladder, when we both joined Karno back in ought seven. And yet here he was, lording it over everyone for twelve hundred and fifty bucks a week while I was wearing an itchy false moustache for beer money and a free luncheon.

Finally a young fellow who was the assistant to the director – Charlie himself was directing – clapped his hands and began arranging us around the staircase. It seemed that we were merely to decorate the place as the main female character arrived, and we were told to bow and scrape as she did so, because she was the duchess of something or other. We couldn't grasp what the overall story was, but it turned out that there simply wasn't one, at least not where this scene was concerned.

The whole scenario was merely a film-within-a-film. The idea was that the Tramp had come along to some fictional studios – named Lockstone as a sly dig back at Mack Sennett – for a job and a free lunch, much as Wren and I had done, and he then disrupts the shooting with anarchic interventions. This explained why there were two cameras – one was merely a prop – and why Charlie's costume was incongruously contemporary.

So we filmed this duchess parading in front of our various grovelling, and as she began to have a dramatic confrontation with the other main actor the Tramp would barrel in and mess things up. Several times there was confusion as the actor playing the director of the film-within-a-film would shout "Cut!" and remonstrate with Charlie, and the extras would wander off and light up, not realising that the real camera was still cranking until the real director shouted "Cut!" in his turn.

I also enjoyed, hidden in the ranks as I was, watching Charlie attempting to direct the actors, which he would invariably do by acting out their part in front of them and then saying: "There, do it like that!" The eye-rolling resentment that ensued the moment his back was turned was greatly heart-warming, somehow.

Lunch was, as anticipated, the highlight of the day, a help-yourself spread of cold meats and pies the like of which Wren and I hadn't seen for an age, perhaps not since we were in the copper mining town of Butte, visiting Irish Mike's Orpheum bar. No actor ever turns his nose up at a lunch like that – one never knows when the next chance will come along – so we troughed like trenchermen.

Ben Turpin waddled over and topped up our drinks from his flask again, which made the whole meal go down even easier. The result, however, was that Wren and I were both over-full and more than a little tipsy by the time the bell went to summon us back to the stage.

It seemed we had come to the sequence that Charlie and Mr Robbins, who was directing the real camera team, had disagreed about, and they were still going at it. Meanwhile we all waited, and waited, a little uncomfortable now under the lights in our fur-lined costumes, and I frankly began to feel like I could do with forty winks.

Charlie was now dressed as a soldier, similar to we extras. He had an over-large sword strapped to him which kept catching on the floor, and the flimsy story was that the main actor in the film-within-a-film had not turned up, and the Tramp had taken his place.

Now to one side of this main set a curtain hid an area that was being used to film the backstage scenes, and to the other side there was a swinging door leading off to another room. What Charlie wanted to do was a sequence in which he travelled left-to-right, barrelling through all three of these rooms through the curtain, across the main set, and then out through the swinging door into the third set. Robbins, the producer, was insisting that this could be filmed in three separate shots, but Charlie was insisting he wanted to do the action all in one go. This would necessitate the building of a little railroad to carry a dolly truck with the camera mounted on it, and the painstakingly careful choreography of everyone who would get in Charlie's path as he tumbled through the scenes.

Chaplin, of course, got his way, and so we were obliged to hang around while this miniature railroad was constructed, with Charlie all the while attempting to perfect the timing with which his sabre would jab the fake director in the backside as he passed by.

"I'm so bored," Wren murmured, having sidled over to me.

"I know," I said. "Me too."

"Can you imagine anyone ever laughing at any of this?" she giggled.

I grinned. "Not really, no. It's amazing how important these guys think they are. It's as if there's nothing in the world as interesting as the flickers, so let's make a flicker about the flickers."

Wren giggled some more. "If only they had another camera, they could make a flicker about the flicker about the flickers."

Maybe it was Ben Turpin's flask doing the work, but I began to find this exceedingly amusing. "My God!" I said. "Can you imagine how much Charlie would love that idea? Not only letting people see his genius, but letting them see how he does what he does?"

"They could make a whole movie about the building of this little railway," Wren whispered in my ear, and I laughed.

No one was paying us any attention, and it was clearly going to be a long while yet before the set-up was ready, so when Wren suggested that we should slip away for a few minutes, I could see no good reason not to. We slipped along a corridor behind the set, and found ourselves in a dark props room, with dusty bits and pieces strewn around from other flickers.

"Oh," Wren gasped. "Arthur, those lights! I am so hot!"

"Me too," I said, removing my fur hat and unbuckling my jacket.

"Help me, there's an angel," Wren said. "This dress is so tight, I haven't sat down since breakfast time."

I unhooked all the little hooks down the back of her gown, and she stepped out of it in her undergarments, sighing with relief like one being released from prison. Amongst the props there was a chaise longue, and she draped herself across it with a luxurious moan of release.

"Take that jacket off, you're making me hot just looking at you," she said, and I did so, placing it around the shoulders of a plaster replica of the Venus de Milo. Then Wren patted the seat beside her. "Don't be shy," she said in a low voice. I recognised the danger signals then, I think, but I was so relieved to shed the costume and relax for a little while that I stretched out on the chaise. She moved her feet out of my way, and before I knew it she had slipped right around and laid her head in my lap.

"This brings it all back, doesn't it?" she said, and I felt her voice resonating in my groin.

"What do you mean?" I said thickly.

"Well, surrounded by props and costumes, away from prying eyes. We've been here before, haven't we?"

And we had. The brief fling that we'd had back in the Karno days had mostly taken place in the props and costumes compartment of the Karno boxcar, with the rest of the company – including, of course, her husband – behind a curtain just a few feet away. And although it had turned out that she'd been principally interested in trying to provoke Edgar into jealousy, nonetheless neither of us was in any doubt that we found one another intoxicatingly attractive.

"Not quite the same, though, is it?" I said.

"No," she said then, moving again so that she could slide slowly up my body until our mouths were very close. "This time Ed is not in the picture."

"No," I said. "He didn't want to come, did he?"

"And I did," she breathed.

Well, then we were kissing, ever more passionately, and my hand was seeking her breast, and hers was on my trousers, and pretty soon one thing was leading to another. We fumbled our way out of what remained of our costumes, still kissing frantically. I hadn't felt like that for at least six months, not since Tilly left of course, and Wren was giving every impression of being similarly starved.

Her silky warm body was in my arms, and my nose was buried in a forest of blonde ringlets.

"Oh Arthur!" Wren breathed as she moved under me.

"Oh Tilly!" I gasped.

"What? What did you say?"

"Nothing," I said, catching myself, and beginning to move a little more urgently, to try and take her mind off my distracted blunder.

"Ahh!" she said. "I thought... ahhh!"

I'd closed my eyes, and behind my eyelids I was dimly aware that the room suddenly seemed much brighter. I opened my eyes again, and in the new illumination I noticed something else that I hadn't seen before. On the floor, a little way off, I saw a length of track, like a little railway, that seemed to run away into the next room. I frowned, trying to make sense of this image, but with a large part of my attention taken up with the soft, gorgeous woman squirming beneath me, the rationale remained elusive...

Until that is, there was suddenly a hubbub next door. I heard shrieks, and protest, and thumps and bangs. I heard the squealing of some little wheels that needed oiling. I heard voices shouting "Hey, mind out!" and "My ass, you chump!"

Then there was a thump, and something smacked into the door to my left, which swung flat against the wall. A figure in a blue soldier costume barrelled through and did a flying tumble into the far wall, bringing a shelf of empty tin cans crashing down onto his head.

At the same moment a little cart appeared with a camera on it and a man cranking away furiously, while the man Robbins pointed furiously and then shouted "Cut!"

I froze for a moment or two, faced with this surreal development. There was a moment of still silence, and then laughter

220

broke out. The film crew laughed fit to bust, and they were quickly joined by the extras from the next room, all crowding in at the door to look.

Wren craned her head around to see what had occurred, and shock and embarrassment flooded her features.

The two of us began scrambling to cover ourselves, grabbing our bits of costume, and hustling around behind a packing crate, where we began to wriggle into the clothes as quickly as we could. This just seemed to redouble the mirth of those watching, at which point the figure who had crashed through the door rose from under the pile of cans with a smug grin on his face.

"Good, good, excellent! See?" he said, jabbing Robbins in his chest with a smug forefinger. "See Jess? I told you this was funnier. Perhaps you'll listen to me from now on."

"Well, if you'd let me know a couple were going to be fornicating in here then perhaps I would have listened to you," Robbins said.

"A couple... what?"

Jess Robbins pointed at where Wren and I were desperately trying to dress, and Charlie's face went from incomprehension to outright fury.

"Listen, Charlie. We ain't got time to set all that up again, an' we sure as hell can't use what we just shot. Let's just do it piecemeal tomorrow like I planned, an' call it a day, OK?"

Charlie, steaming with frustration and rage, watched the crew trundle the camera away down the rails and then stomped over to us.

"Well, thanks a lot!" he shouted. "You've just ruined a whole afternoon's work, wasted everyone's time, and disgraced yourselves into the bargain. You're fired!"

I looked up at him, and saw him suddenly recognise me. His

eyes shot wide open, and he glanced over at Wren, who was keeping her back to him out of modesty as she wriggled into her gown. All Charlie could see was the curve of her back and the blonde ringlets falling around her face.

"Tilly...?" he breathed in disbelief.

"Sorry. Sorry, Charlie," I said. "We'll be... we'll be on our way."

25
THE KEYSTONE FOUR

"**SO** how much did you get paid?" Stan asked, later that evening when we got together in a saloon to discuss what we had been up to.

"We got lunch," I said.

"Just lunch?"

"It was a good lunch."

"No money at all, though? That seems odd."

"Ah, yes, well, you see, the fact is... we were fired."

"Fired?!" Ed said, and Wren stared down at her drink.

"I'm afraid so."

"Charlie *fired* you?" Stan said, boggling with disbelief. "Why?"

"You know, he's always felt threatened by me, and I think he was worried that I was just too funny."

"Ha ha ha. No, really – why?"

I glanced at Wren, who was still not looking at any of us.

"Um, we... spoiled a shot, you see. We were in one place, weren't we, and we were supposed to be in another, and the way the flickers work is... that was a problem. So we were fired."

"That arrogant son of a bitch," Ed said angrily. "I've a good mind to go down there and tell him what I think of him firing my wife!"

"Please don't," Wren blurted out. "It was embarrassing enough. Let's just forget about it, shall we?"

"Well, I...!"

"Please, Ed?"

Ed's bad-tempered bluster dissipated slowly, and Stan changed the subject. "Well," he said. "I have had no joy getting us a booking, I'm afraid. But I have asked around about the Bostock brothers, who we are meeting tomorrow, thanks to Wren, and the general consensus is that they are very good news. They are very well thought of by bookers and other acts alike, and if we could only persuade them to take over our affairs it could be a very good opportunity for us."

Our spirits were given a lift by this, and we agreed to have an early night so as to appear as bright-eyed and bushy-tailed as possible the next morning. As it happened, we could not afford to stay for another drink anyway. As I made to follow Stan and Ed outside Wren grabbed my arm.

"Arthur?"

"Wren, listen, what happened. It... I'm sorry, I got carried away..."

"I know, we both did, didn't we?"

"So... um...?"

Wren looked sheepish, guilty even. "I have something for you," she said, not meeting my eyes. She took my hand and placed an envelope on it.

"What's this?"

"I should have given it to you before, I'm sorry about that. I found it when we went to Considine's office last week. It was in a pile on a desk there, and your name caught my eye so I picked it up."

"Why didn't you give it to me?"

"I don't know, you were talking to Considine, and then you were so very cross about Charlie Chaplin being in town, I just couldn't get near you. After that it must have... slipped my mind."

"I see. Well, that's..."

Wren was flushed, and gave a little gulp. "And then you said her name, didn't you, and I realised how selfish I was being...! I'm sorry!" She put her hand to her mouth then, and rushed out. Such strange behaviour – I couldn't fathom it.

I looked at the envelope then. It looked like it had been through quite a journey, battered from pillar to post. I could make out my name on the front in a curly hand, and the address care of Considine's in Chicago. I flipped it over and found the sender's name written across the back flap, and my heart skipped a beat.

T. Beckett, Gt Yarmouth, England.

I ripped it open with trembling fingers.

'Dearest,' Tilly began, and I had to pause after that single word to compose myself.

'I will be brief, for there is no telling whether this missive will ever reach you. I have tried everything I can think of to make contact with you, but so far it seems to no avail as you have not replied. How foolish we were not to make better arrangements, but then we expected to be reunited quickly, didn't we? Oh well, that is so much spilt milk, isn't it?

'Wallace and I reached Gt Yarmouth to find my father in hospital and out of danger. He had suffered burns in the pier fire but was recovering well. He was no longer under suspicion of causing the conflagration, even though he had been stockpiling some explosives underneath the boardwalk, the silly man, which naturally hadn't helped matters. The arson was the work of suffragettes, who had been denied use of a meeting hall there. Incredibly, they were quite content to allow my father to take the blame and the consequences until they belatedly realised that doing so provided no benefit whatsoever to their cause, and so they finally came forward to claim the credit. I still sympathise with the struggle, naturally, but the people are hard to like after causing us so much trouble.

'Rest assured your son is well and growing ever so fast. Write to me if you get this, at 24 Palmer Road, Great Yarmouth, Norfolk.

'All my love, always, Tilly.'

I stared at the page for a long time, reading it over and over. No mention of any plan to return to the States, at which I was naturally relieved, on account of the deadly peril and so on, but also, I have to say, a little bit disappointed. There was a brisk tone to the letter that suggested she had written these details many times, and I wondered how many of her letters had gone astray, or had perhaps arrived at theatres in the days after I had left them. It was quite a fluke that this one had got through, when I thought about it. And she'd clearly received none of mine at the time of writing it.

But now I had an address, and I should have to give some thought to establishing a better line of communication. Things were looking up.

━━━

Ten-thirty sharp – early in the day for vaudeville business – found the Four Comiques arrayed in an optimistic row, all freshly-shaven (the three men, anyway), pink-faced, clean-shirted and at our most presentable, sitting in front of the rather grand dark-wood desk of the agent Claude Bostock. He was a genial enough chap, in his thirties, with a loud-checked jacket that gave him a decidedly vaude-villian aspect. His brother, Gordon, was dressed more soberly, and stood by the window behind. They seemed remarkably similar in every other way, and it was hard to gauge which of them was the senior.

"I could not believe it when Mrs Hurley told me that you had no representation. Could I, Gordon?" Claude said.

"No, he couldn't believe it," Gordon added, inspecting his fingernails in the sunlight.

Ed looked oddly vindicated at this, which was irritating. It was not as if he had been pushing us to get an agent, but suddenly it was Stan's fault, and mine, that we hadn't yet had one.

"Well, you see," I said, "we were booked directly into Sullivan and Considine theatres, until very recently."

"Ah yes, poor Considine," Claude said sadly. "A real pity, isn't it, Gordon?"

"It is," Gordon agreed. "He was a very fair man to deal with. Not like..."

"Now then," Claude put in. "We will have to deal with his rivals more than ever before, since they are expanding, so let's not complain."

"Quite," Gordon said, pursing his lips.

"And sometimes a personal connection such as yours with Mr Considine makes it difficult to push oneself forward as much as one might."

Ed nodded. "Exactly," he said, as though he had been trying to make that very point for weeks.

"Now then. We deal with a large number of circuits of all sizes, and I feel that an act such as yours should be able to work pretty much every week."

Stan beamed. "That's nice to hear," he said.

"Oh, that's really the minimum," Claude said. "Isn't it, Gordon?"

"We should be looking for bigger and bigger time for you, is what Claude means."

"As long as you are prepared to put in the work."

"Whatever it takes," Stan said firmly.

"Well, good. That is good news." Claude beamed at all of us, and we, I have to admit, beamed at one another. It seemed that things were looking up. If the group could acquire these two gentlemen as our agents, then we would be spared the miserable business of traipsing around trying to get ourselves booked. Of course, we would be paying them a cut, but hopefully that would be a piece of a significantly larger pie.

"Now tell me," Claude went on. "You were all in the Fred Karno company, am I right?"

"Yes, sir," Stan said. "First in England, and then here in America on the Sullivan and Considine time."

"Performing *A Night in an English Music Hall*, correct?"

"That's right, and also *The Wow Wows* and *A Night in the Club*."

"Indeed. And in all of these productions you, Stan, were understudy to Charlie Chaplin, if I am not mistaken."

"No sir, you are not," Stan said, with a little frown. For my part, I felt the cold chill of something unpleasant approaching, but I couldn't think yet what it was to be.

"So it would be fair to say that you are well-versed in Chaplin's style and techniques?"

Stan didn't say anything to this. I muttered, on his behalf: "Stan is even better than Chaplin."

"And the rest of you," Claude went on, "are equally well-versed in supporting a Chaplin performance?"

"Well," Ed bristled. "It was not like we were supporting him, we were all part of a team."

"I see, I see," Claude mused. I had a sudden suspicion that he was merely making a show of considering something he and his brother had already decided upon. The two of them glanced at one another, and Gordon gave a little nod.

"All right," Claude said. "Here's what we think. *The Nutty Burglars* is a very funny act, no doubt about it."

"Thank you, Mr Bostock," Stan said.

"We certainly are confident that we should be able to do something for you."

"Excellent."

"We would, however, like to propose a change or two."

"We think," Gordon said, taking over now, "that you have the perfect opportunity. The time is right to exploit the quite extraordinary popularity of your former colleague."

"Chaplin," I said, through gritted teeth.

"Precisely. And who better to do that than those who know him best of all?"

"Too well," I muttered.

"What do you have in mind, exactly?" Stan asked.

"Just the merest tweak, really," Gordon said, examining his nails.

"Yes," Claude said. "The scenario remains untouched. The only change, really, is that Stan's character becomes Charlie Chaplin."

"A simple impersonation for one of your skills and experience," Gordon added.

"Then, correspondingly, Arthur here will become Chester Conklin, Charlie's usual sidekick in the films."

"Which is really only adding a walrus moustache," Gordon put in, leaning forwards with his hands on Claude's desk as the two brothers double-teamed us.

"And the talented Mrs Hurley will no doubt make a marvellous Mabel Normand. There, what do you think?"

Claude and Gordon smiled at us, as though they had just proposed the most brilliant suggestion. Stan was shaken, I could see that. I was struggling for breath, such was the weight of the depression pressing down on me all of a sudden. Wren seemed intrigued, but Ed, naturally enough, was angry enough for all four of us.

"What about me?" he pouted. "You have forgotten me."

"Ah, well, you are the easiest of all. You can remain a generic cop."

"A generic cop! Is that what you think I am playing?"

"Or," Claude said. "How about this? A *Keystone* Cop."

"Brilliant!" Gordon said, snapping his fingers. "That really is the cherry on the cake!"

"I... um..." Stan said. "We... erm... that is to say..."

"And instead of The Four Comiques, you will be billed as – how's this?" Claude mimed with his hands an improbably impressive marquee billing in the air, as he offered up his suggestion. "The Keystone Four."

"The Keystone Four?" I snarled then, and Stan put his hand on my arm.

"I wonder," my friend said. "I wonder if we might have a minute or two in private. To discuss this?"

"Of course, of course!" Claude cried, affability incarnate. "Gordon and I will step outside for a cigarillo. Gordon?"

The two brothers promptly left us alone. Stan turned to the three of us, eyebrows raised.

"So?" he said. "What do we think of that?"

"No," Ed said firmly. "Absolutely not. Generic cop! Who do they think they are talking to?!"

"I think it would be fun to play Mabel Normand. Make a change from playing Tilly Beckett, anyway," Wren said, with an arch glance in my direction.

"Charlie's not even at Keystone any more. It doesn't make any sense!"

"I suppose he is still associated with the name, even so. He did make thirty-odd films there last year, and they are still showing everywhere. Arthur? What about you?"

I sighed. The thought of turning our whole working life into a four-times-a-day glorification of the genius of Charles Spencer Chaplin made my gorge rise. But what else did we have in the offing? Nothing at all. I looked at Stan, and thought I saw that he was leaning towards the idea, although not liking it much more than I did, and Wren sounded interested too, so if I were to align myself with the grumpy Edgar Hurley the Comiques would be split two and two, and there would be impasse. So I said:

"Well, you know, all it would really involve for me is slapping on a moustache. No-one knows what Chester Conklin sounds like, do they? So I shouldn't think it would take much getting away with, for my part. It's you, Stan, you who'll have to carry the bulk of the burden if we decide to do this, so I guess if you are up for it, then I am too."

"Gah!" Hurley expostulated, throwing his hands in the air.

"Arthur's right," Wren said. "It should be your choice, Stan. What do you think?"

Stan looked at each of us in turn, a serious expression clouding his thin features. Then he broke into a big Stan grin and held out his hand, palm down.

"The Keystone Four it is, then!"

Wren and I put our hands on top of his, and waited, daring

Edgar not to join in. Finally he gave up and slapped his hand angrily on top of the pile.

"The Keystone Four!"

26
WAFFLES & CO

THE Bostock brothers slipped us some cash to cover a few days of rehearsal, and managed to get us a booking for the very next week, all of which boded well for our new business partnership.

They were also happy for me to use them as a kind of *poste restante* service, so I dashed off a letter to Tilly in Great Yarmouth letting her know that all was well. I related the fall of poor old Considine, and our new attachment to the Bostocks. Naturally I told her how much I was missing her and Wallace. After that, though, I found I was skipping over much of what had been on my mind since I'd last seen her.

I didn't mention bumping into Charlie in Chicago or his big new deal, for fear of fuelling her anxiety about my supposed fixation. Neither did I mention the day I spent at Essanay, for obvious reasons. I was feeling pretty foolish about that, and so was Wren, I think.

Nor did I tell her that we were becoming a full-time Chaplin tribute act, although it did occur to me that it might go a long way towards demonstrating the increased maturity of my attitude to Chaplin if I could survive that with a reasonable amount of equanimity.

Stan threw himself enthusiastically into honing his impersonation of Charlie, and dragged us along to see all the Keystone shorts he could find on offer. Wren was eagerly watching Mabel Normand for tics and mannerisms, while I caught the odd glimpse of Chester Conklin in action, and felt pretty certain that I wouldn't really need to do much to pull that turn off. He was a pop-eyed performer with a trademark moustache covering most of the bottom half of his face, so I would really only need to invest in a second-hand hairpiece and a pot of theatrical glue.

Edgar Hurley did not accompany us on our trips to the cinemas. He reckoned that as Charlie had barely ever featured alongside the Keystone Cops he would be better occupied watching them, and whatever performance titbits he was picking up he was keeping to himself. Stan and I were both somewhat irritated by this, but Ed's part was small enough that we thought we could stand to wait and see what he was going to do, rather than get into a row with him.

At the weekend we made our way by train to Altoona in Pennsylvania, where the newly-refurbished *Nutty Burglars* were to make their bow at the Orpheum, no less. Ed stared out of the window the whole way, doubtless plotting his character's regeneration, and Wren too was remarkably subdued, which I took to be nerves.

The Hurleys were effectively incommunicado, then, and Stan was dry-running Charlie's gestures in his head, eyes closed, fingers twitching this way and that, so I was alone with my thoughts. The Pennsylvania railroad from Pittsburgh dropped down from the Allegheny Mountains into Altoona via the famous Horseshoe Curve, which arched steeply and spectacularly around a valley, running along three sides of a large reservoir. We passed another train going the other way, climbing up the gradient, of which we then got a good view on the other side of the curve. I imagined Wallace looking out at it, pressing his little nose to the window, and scribbling with his fat little finger in the patch that he had steamed up.

I picked up a newspaper and forced myself to read a little more about the progress of the war. It was so complex, and so appalling, and so downright discouraging, that I could only stomach a little at a time.

That Spring the Allies were on the offensive in Artois and Champagne, and were also attacking somewhere called the Dardanelles, which was the pet scheme of a bright spark called Churchill. The Austro-Hungarians were being driven back from Galicia by the Russians, who were on our side, I think, and there was even some sabre-rattling between the Japanese and the Chinese.

It all seemed a long long way away, until I started reading about something called a Zeppelin. This was a massive cigar-shaped airship that could fly from Germany to England and rain bombs down onto the civilian population, and it sounded very much like the 'flying death' we had heard about from Charlie's aviator acquaintance, Glenn Martin.

The Zeppelin raid I read about that morning had been an attempt to bomb the port of Hull, but the British weather had blown the silver monsters off course, and the bombs had actually fallen on King's Lynn, Sheringham and Great Yarmouth.

"Whatever is it?" Stan said from the seat opposite. "You've gone as white as a sheet."

I showed him the paragraph that had so shaken me. "Great Yarmouth. That's where Tilly is, and Wallace."

I'd thought them safe there, not giving much credence to Tilly's father and his crazy conviction that the Kaiser would launch an invasion, but this, fiery death falling from the skies onto my girl and our little lad, this was a far worse nightmare to deal with.

"I need to go," I said, suddenly, struck by a new resolve.

"My dear chap, are you sure?"

"I can go and come back," I said. "Which is to say, I can go to England, find Tilly and Wallace, and bring them back, here, to the States."

Stan put his hands on his knees and looked me in the eye. "Now listen," he said. "You know I love Tilly and little Wallace as much as I love anyone, but this is madness."

"I have to try," I said.

"Think, first," Stan said. "How will you get across? Never mind the expense for a moment. All the liners have been laid up for months for fear of mines and submarines, quite apart from the fact that hardly anyone wants to make the trip. The Kaiser has declared all the waters around the British Isles a war zone, hasn't he? Which mean the Germans are perfectly prepared to open fire on merchant ships, even passenger ships for all we know."

"Yes, but there must be something I can do!"

"And then when you get to England, it's a country at war. How will you avoid getting caught up in it?"

"The British Army is made up of volunteers, isn't it?" I said. "A few women with white feathers don't scare me, and I'll be sure to drink my beer from a tankard with a glass bottom."

"Huh?"

"So I don't accidentally take the King's shilling. You haven't heard that old one?"

"Yes, but, listen, what if you can't get back? And what if the government brings in compulsory service in the meanwhile?"

"They'll never do it," I scoffed. "Compel the British working man to defend a government they had no part in electing? It'd be pandemonium."

"Maybe, maybe..." Stan frowned.

"You don't think I should at least try?"

"I'm being selfish, I admit it," Stan said, with a grin, dropping his voice to a low whisper. "I was just thinking about being left here to deal with Edgar bloody Hurley all by myself. Of course we must look into it, see what can be done, if anything."

━━━━

The Orpheum theatre posters already billed us as The Keystone Four, promising that Stan was 'the Nation's Premier Chaplin Impersonator'. I was impressed, I must admit, by the push the Bostocks had given us. Grateful, too, as Stan was far too modest to have suggested such a line for himself. And, of course, if there was a better Chaplin than Stan, who had lived in Charlie's pocket for years, then he'd be quite a thing to see. I thought even Charlie himself would have struggled to match his Chaplin, which was a ridiculous thing to think, of course, but Stan had something, an indefinable something, that Charlie never had. It was in his rapport with the audience, his feel for how they were reacting to him, and his connection to them. Charlie always gave the impression that he would be just as happy performing to an empty room, perfecting his 'art'.

I stood in the wings that Monday afternoon waiting for our first performance as the Keystone Four, clutching my toolbag, which bore the legend 'Waffles & Co, Berglars. Merder's Dun', and twitching my Chester Conklin moustache, which I was wishing I'd trimmed a little more.

Suddenly, in the wings opposite, I saw a familiar figure, hopping from one foot to the other in over-sized boots, twirling a bendy cane, and twitching his own smaller moustache. A chill went down my spine – it was Stan, of course, and he shot me a big Stan grin, but it was so like Charlie that I was thrown, and almost missed my cue to begin.

In fact, at several points during the opening of the sketch I found myself caught out, just staring at Stan, transported back to performing old Karno routines with Chaplin as the Drunken Swell. He was able to fill the gaps, naturally, as the audience were lapping up every moment, but I caught him frowning at me once or twice, and felt an unusual belligerence rising in myself, as though it were Chaplin himself finding fault. I shook my head to clear it, to try and regain my concentration, and the Conklin trademark came loose and flew across the stage, necessitating a quick grovel and grab to cover.

Wren came on then, and her Mabel was almost as pitch perfect as Stan's Charlie, so that the sketch fairly sailed along until Edgar Hurley made his appearance as the cop to interrupt the burglary in progress. Not content with his part at the best of times, Hurley had taken the opportunity to build himself up. And how.

The cop who strode onto the stage was a very different fellow to the chump we were used to. For a start he had a big letter K painted onto his uniform, in case anyone should be in any doubt that he was a Keystone cop. Now, the most distinctive of the film cops was probably Conklin (already taken) or Fatty Arbuckle (a reach for Hurley), so he'd decided to take on the persona of their leader, Ford Sterling. This he had achieved with the addition of a little goatee beard and a manic expression, with eyes as crossed as Ben Turpin's.

Hurley hadn't stopped there, though. Now he wasn't just a

generic cop, he was the Chief of Police, which suited his ego far better, and Ford Sterling was a star. Not quite a Chaplin or a Normand, admittedly, but certainly the equal of a Conklin.

So he strutted out to join us barely managing to conceal a self-satisfied smirk.

"Hold it right there!" he shouted. "What is going on here?"

"Um..." Stan said. Our generic cop had never been this forceful.

"My Keystone Cops have this whole place surrounded!" Hurley cried, taking centre stage and calling into the wings. "You men! Some of you go round the back, the rest of you watch the street. And Fatty! You guard that cat flap, guard it with your... life!"

Stan and I were frantically trying to adapt to this different scenario, and I could see that Wren was equally perplexed. The sketch had always featured a lone policeman who was a dumb fall guy for the burglars to outsmart, with the help of the arch little maid, but now here was the leader of a whole squad of police intent on carrying out a full-scale investigation.

"My name is Sterling, and I am the Chief of Police. Nothing happens in this town without me knowing about it. So," Hurley bellowed at Stan. "Who are you? Explain yourself!"

"The... master of the house?" Stan asked, not seeing what Ed was getting at.

"And you, my dear? Who are you?"

"The maid, sir," Wren ventured.

"I see. So you can confirm that this is your master?"

"I can."

"And you can confirm that this is your maid?"

"Yes," Stan said.

"Aha," Police Chief Edgar Hurley said, beginning to pace up

and down, his comedy eyebrows pumping up and down furiously. "Now we are getting somewhere. Then perhaps you can tell me just exactly what is going on here."

Well, the sketch was grinding to a halt thanks to Hurley's new characterisation. After all, whenever Charlie was faced with an authority figure in one of his flicks he didn't stand still and answer questions, he kicked him up the backside and carefully choreographed mayhem would ensue. However, as Ed had sprung this on us, we hadn't prepared anything.

Stan shot me a look, and then suddenly pirouetted away from Ed Hurley, and delivered a neat kick up his rear end. Then as he spun past me, he hissed:

"Light the bomb!"

I quickly grabbed the prop bomb – a black ball the size of a water melon with the word 'BOMB' painted on it in white – and lit the firework fuse. I understood immediately what Stan was doing. He was cutting straight to the end of the routine, closing off any further opportunities for Ed to extemporise.

Ed saw this too, and opened his mouth to protest, but the next thing he knew he had the bomb in his hands, and the pass-the-parcel climax to the sketch was under way. Our far-from-generic cop had planned something new here, as well, though, and instead of the bomb passing between the four of us onstage, as usual, Ed threw it off into the wings. It came back then, from a stagehand who had been given more notice than we, Eds colleagues, had been given, and Ed proceeded to play out the length of the routine with the bomb passing on and off stage, and Stan, Wren and myself reduced to baffled spectators.

The offstage explosion occurred, but instead of running off-stage with the bomb and quickly blacking himself up with soot before coming back on as the visual punchline Ed remained onstage, slapped his hands to his face in shock, shouted out "Fatty!" and then ran off.

There was a moment or two then when Stan, Wren and I simply stood onstage not knowing what to do next. Robbed of our punchline, cheated of the big laugh that brought down the curtain on the piece, we gaped at one another. Then Stan simply turned on his heel and walked off, not even bothering to do Chaplin's trademark walk. Wren followed, and I grabbed the burglar's tool bag and shambled off in their wake to the sound of my own footsteps. A little applause broke out then, but nothing like what we deserved for our earlier efforts.

With Wren trotting anxiously behind, Stan and I raced down to the dressing room to confront Hurley, only to find that he was furiously waiting to tear a strip off us.

"What was that?" Ed shouted as soon as we came into the room. "You just skipped straight to the end. I was just getting going!"

"What?!" I shouted back. "What the hell were you doing?!"

"I was just adding a few touches, exactly the same as the rest of you!"

"A few touches?" Stan yelled, as angry as I had ever seen him. "You went into a whole new scene that none of us knew anything about!"

"All you had to do was play along," Ed protested. "It would've been fine!"

"What were you even supposed to be?" I said.

"I thought that was obvious. I was the leader of the Keystone Cops."

"Hence the big K you painted on your uniform?"

"Exactly."

"Just as the real Keystone Cops never, ever do, you mean?"

"It's an embellishment, that's all. Perfectly understandable."

"Perfectly rubbish!" Stan snarled.

"And why in the name of all that's holy did you make out that there were other cops surrounding the house?" I said.

"The leader of the Keystone Cops doesn't go out on his own, that's why?"

"There are lots of things the leader of the Keystone Cops doesn't do. He doesn't *talk*, for a start! He certainly doesn't conduct lengthy investigations simply to establish who the characters in the scene are!"

"All right," Stan said. "Let's all calm down a bit, shall we? Don't you see, Ed, that referring to other cops sets up an expectation of a particular kind? That these other cops are going to appear, as they do in the flickers, and chase around the place, and that's not going to happen so it's not helpful. Surely you see that, don't you?"

"I think it works," Ed said stubbornly.

"Oh, Ed!" his wife sighed, exasperated.

"And you see, don't you, that throwing the bomb offstage and having it blow up someone the audience haven't seen is not as funny as blowing up the policeman?"

"I am sick to death of doing that soot make-up quick-change," Ed said, folding his arms.

"Well, that's the joke, so...!" I said.

"I don't know what you're all getting so worked up about," Ed protested. "I'm only trying to make the thing better!"

"For yourself..." I muttered.

"Well, what about him?" Ed said, pointing at me. "Did he run all his changes past everyone? He didn't run anything past me, I can tell you that."

"Arthur only put on a moustache," Wren said.

"Yes, well, I suppose I shouldn't be surprised that you're taking *his* part," Ed said nastily, and Stan held his hands up for calm once more.

"Here is what we are going to do," he said, and there was an edge to his tone that made Ed back down. "We will rehearse the piece properly tomorrow morning. Any changes anyone wants to suggest will be discussed then, but I can tell you this. For the second show this evening, there will be no imaginary Keystone Cops offstage, there will be no additional dialogue for the policeman, who will be a lone constable and not a damn'd police chief, and the bomb will blow *you* up, Edgar, you and nobody else. If that is not acceptable, you can make alternate arrangements and I shall do likewise. Have I made myself clear?"

"Perfectly," I said, glaring at Hurley.

"Yes, thank you Stan," Wren said. "Come on Ed, let's go and find a cup of tea somewhere."

"Hrrmmph!" Ed grunted gracelessly, and giving both me and Stan a look that I imagine was supposed to wither us, he followed his wife outside.

"Unbelievable!" I said, sitting on a settee. "Absolutely unbelievable!"

Stan sighed heavily. "What on Earth was he thinking, the chump?"

"Well, you showed him who's boss, anyway," I said. "I've never seen you so masterful. It was like listening to the Guv'nor himself."

"Do you think so?" Stan laughed.

"Absolutely! I just wish Freddie had been here to see it!"

"Yes, good old Freddie," Stan said. "I wonder what he's up to. I hope he's all right."

"I'm sure," I said.

"And Tilly and little Wallace too, of course."

"Yes," I said, but a chill shadow smothered my smile, and it was Zeppelin-shaped.

27
A GENTLEMAN OF NERVE

AFTER the Keystone Cop incident, Ed brooded. He didn't care to socialise with us after the show any more, but at least he behaved himself onstage, did what we needed him to do and no more.

Wren, too, took to heading back to our lodgings rather than spending any more time than she had to in the company of me and Stan. This was not like her, she was usually game for a laugh, and one evening I pressed her to come to the saloon with us, but she simply turned and walked away. I grabbed her arm, not hard, just to keep her attention, and she flinched in pain as though I had hurt her, although she insisted it was nothing.

It seemed that a line had been drawn, and it was hard to escape the feeling that where there had once been Four Comiques, now there was two-plus-two. More accurately, by then we were the Keystone Two-plus-two, of course, and the Bostocks managed to book us in for a good stint on the Proctor time. The Proctor theatres were based in and around New York and New Jersey, and offered continuous vaudeville performances from noon to midnight. For the price of admission a patron could stay all day, and New Yorkers were well familiar with their slogan: 'After Breakfast Go to Proctor's, After Proctor's Go to Bed'.

We were able to take semi-permanent residence in an apartment on 47th Street, which was happily handy for a bar we had frequented in the Karno days. We had two bedrooms – the Hurleys had one and Stan and I shared the other – and a communal kitchen/dining room and bathroom, and we almost felt like we were proper Americans.

There was a saying in vaudeville that you could work for a year in New York without ever packing a bag, and certainly most of the venues we played that spring were within easy reach of our new home. And the rent was cheap, and we were not having to buy expensive cross-country train tickets, so I was able to start putting a bit of money aside.

As for the act itself, audiences loved it. Stan was getting very good reviews for his turn as Charlie, living up to his billing as the nation's premier Chaplin impersonator. We would occasionally cross paths with rivals in the field – including one who had changed his name by deed poll to 'Charles Aplin', for example – but none of them could hold a candle to Stan.

However, the coolness between me and Stan on the one hand and the Hurleys on the other was not the only concern that Spring. I began to wonder if I was losing my marbles.

You see, I found myself onstage every afternoon and evening playing opposite Charlie, and I was having a hard time of it. I knew it was really Stan, of course, and I knew he was putting it on, but several times during the act I felt a surge of hostility towards him that I could barely keep under control.

Stan himself didn't help matters. When Charlie had first gone to play in the flickers, Stan and I had hardly paid any attention to him, he was out of our lives. He was doing his thing, and we were doing ours. Now, though, Stan was eagerly rifling through any newspaper he could get his hands on looking for fresh titbits about Charlie.

Chaplin's Essanay films were coming out by this time, and if anything they were even more popular and acclaimed than the Keystone offerings, even though to me they seemed just as flimsy and unremarkable. *His New Job* was the first, which turned out to be the movie that Wren and I had sabotaged in Chicago. Then Charlie had moved to Niles, outside San Francisco, and had made *The Champion*, a frenetic boxing film, and *In the Park*, another quick nonsense. Stan insisted that we all attend, even though Charlie was no longer working with Chester Conklin or Mabel Normand. Or, for that matter, with any generic Keystone Cops. And when the audiences roared, he would turn to us with a big beam on his thin face.

"This is all good for us, you know!" he'd say.

I knew he was probably right, and that the Keystone Four could only profit from Chaplin's inexorable rise, but I sometimes thought I'd have been happier to hear that our careers were utterly ruined, if only it meant his calamitous downfall as well.

But no, Chaplin was on the up, and little bits of paraphernalia started appearing everywhere. It got so you could hardly go into a drugstore or a tobacconist's without being confronted by dozens of little statues of Charlie, his simpering smile, his bright white teeth, his head archly cocked to one side. And every time Stan saw one of these atrocities he would buy one and perch it on the mantelpiece at the apartment, until I could barely bring myself to venture into the main room because it had virtually turned into a shrine to the Little Feller.

I couldn't bring myself to say this to Stan, but I wasn't sure how much longer I could stomach it. My thoughts turned constantly to Tilly, to how things were not so very long ago, and to how we could possibly be reunited.

I'd had a letter from her, via the Bostocks, in which she admitted that she'd had to spend the return ticket money and so could no longer afford to return to America, and she wouldn't be happy to risk a crossing with young Wallace in any case.

Wallace, too, was on my mind a lot. Eight months was a huge chunk in the life of such a small child. I found myself wondering if he would even remember me. I looked at other children in the parks and on the streets, trying to work out which ones were the age the little lad must be now. Would he be walking by himself, confidently stepping out like that child in the rather nasty blue sailor suit, smugly licking on his red lollipop? With a bleak laugh I thought that if I didn't manage to get over there and find them, and this blasted war dragged on and on, he might be in an actual naval uniform before I saw him again.

It was clearly going to be up to me, then, to do something, but passenger crossings at that time were very few and far between, and tickets were like hen's teeth.

Then in March there was a story that the American newspapers quickly began to call The Thrasher Incident. The British steamship RMS *Falaba* was torpedoed and sunk by the German U-boat *U-28*, and 104 people were killed[5]. The reason the American press became so agitated was that one of these unfortunates was an American passenger, a mining engineer from Massachusetts called Leon Thrasher – a great vaudeville name, I thought, but that's by-the-by.

Now, at first this seemed to put the old kibosh on my plans to travel to England and search for Tilly, but in fact, the Thrasher Incident made crossings suddenly seem more viable. For one thing, the British navy began a blockade of German ports, so maybe the U-boats wouldn't be able to get out to sea any more. And for another, if the Americans made so much fuss over the death of a single citizen, who would risk sinking a ship with so many more of them on board? The Germans wanted to keep the Americans out of the war at any price, so surely the U-boats would leave passenger liners alone from now on?

That's what Cunard reckoned, anyway. Their fleet was repainted in its old black, white and red livery, having skulked across the seas a few times in a sort of plain dull grey in the hope of not being seen, and there were tickets for Atlantic crossings on sale.

Towards the end of April I'd made up my mind. First thing one morning I took Stan out for breakfast, partly to get away from his damn'd shrine to Chaplin, and outlined my plan.

"There is a large liner crossing from Liverpool now, as we speak, and I have just enough money to buy myself a berth in steerage for its return voyage."

"I see," Stan said seriously. "Well, that'd take a bit of nerve, and no mistake."

"To get back to the States," I said, "with Tilly and the boy, I'm going to need more."

Stan reached across and put his hand on my shoulder. "I gave Charlie money once to send Tilly away from you," he said. "It seems only right that I should give you the money to bring her back. I do have some cash saved up. It will clean me out, mind, but nothing would make me happier than to see you three together again."

I embraced him then, for he was the best friend a man ever had.

That same day I headed down to the shipping office to buy

myself a ticket. While I was waiting for a portly gentlemen in front of me to make his plentiful arrangements I looked over a page from the newspaper that had been pinned to the wall of the waiting room. It featured an advertisement for Cunard's crossings to Europe via Liverpool. Beneath this was a block of text in a box under the urgent headline 'NOTICE!" It went on:

'Travellers intending to embark on the Atlantic voyage are reminded that a state of war exists between Germany and her allies and Great Britain and her allies; that the zone of war includes the waters adjacent to the British Isles; that in accordance with formal notice given by the Imperial German Government, vessels flying the flag of Great Britain, or of any of her allies, are liable to destruction in those waters and that travellers sailing in the war zone do so at their own risk.'

This statement was released by the Imperial German Embassy in Washington D.C.

Once it was my turn, I said to the desk clerk: "What do you make of that?"

"It's just bluster," he said. "We have pinned it up, because it is in all the newspapers and we want the public to know that we are unconcerned."

"Bluster, you say?"

"Yeah, they just want to try and put people off, see? Hit Cunard in the pocket, because they wouldn't really dare to attack one of our ships."

"Has anyone been put off, do you think?"

"Not that I know of, but then if they have been then I wouldn't see 'em, now would I?"

"I suppose not."

"Now, I have people waiting, sir. Do you want a ticket or don't ya?"

I took a deep breath. "Yes," I said. "One single passage, steerage, please."

———

The company meeting we held at the Proctor's 125th Street theatre later to break the news to the Hurleys was a bit of a bumpy ride. I explained what I had in mind, and Ed was indignant, not to say livid.

"Well how long will you be gone?" he puffed.

"I can't say. As long as it takes."

"And what are *we* supposed to do in the meantime? Sit on our hands?"

"It will just mean a few weeks, a month at the most, probably," Stan said. "We shall manage."

"Pardon me, but isn't that what Tilly said when she left in the first place? And yet here we are, eight months or more later, and still no sign of her."

"Thanks, Ed," I said. "You're really cheering me up, as usual. I'm going, and there's an end of it."

"I think it is romantic," Wren said, not catching my eye. "Tilly is a lucky girl."

"Well," Ed pronounced. "I think we are well within our rights to look for a replacement. It shouldn't be too hard."

"Charming!"

"Not to fill your boots, Arthur, I shall do that, naturally. I mean a replacement to play the cop, of course."

"I thought it would be easier just to take a short break..." Stan began.

"Nonsense! In fact, I bumped into an old Karno colleague just yesterday who would fit the bill splendidly. Ted Banks."

"Ted Banks?" Stan and I looked at one another.

"Yes, do you know him?"

"I know the name," I said. "When Stan and I left Karno in '12 he and Charles Cardon took our places, so we didn't actually get to work with either of them..."

"But he has replaced you before, and he has worked with Chaplin. See? He will be perfect."

"We are not talking about replacing Arthur, though, are we?" Stan said, looking slightly alarmed. "We'll only need Ted to stand in for a few engagements."

"Whatever it turns out to be," Ed said with a not altogether pleasant smile.

———

My departure was set for 10am on the following Saturday. Irritatingly, we were not due to be in New York City for that last week, we were playing out in Albany, which was a three hour train ride away. The Keystone Four - or Five, as we now were, since Ted Banks was coming along to learn the ropes - boarded the train on the Sunday morning. Stan and I were still a little bleary-eyed from the night before, but Ed, Wren and Ted, sitting across the centre aisle from us, were full of the joys, chattering away cheerfully. Ted Banks was a tall, lugubrious fellow, of a sort you often found in vaudeville, funnily enough. He looked like he would never make you laugh in conversation in a month of Sundays, but onstage he would do a perfectly good job for you. It turned out he and the Hurleys had toured together quite extensively in England, and the three of them were clearly pretty thick.

"You won't leave me alone with those three for too long, will you?" Stan muttered.

"It'll be fine," I said. "You've shown them who's in charge."

"Yeah..." Stan said, shooting them a sidelong glance. "Who knows how long *that* will last?"

I did feel bad, abandoning Stan to his fate, pursuing my own selfish ends, but the pull of retrieving Tilly and Wallace from a nation at war was too strong to ignore. It was simply something I had to do.

"Listen," I said, keeping my voice low. "Maybe this will work out for the best, you know? If Ted works out, then when I bring Tilly and the lad back we can keep him and dump the Hurleys, can't we?"

Stan brightened. "You're right, at that!" he said, slapping his hand on the arm of the seat. "So, you will play until Friday, and then get the railway train down to the quays early Saturday morning, whereupon Ed will play your part, and Ted will play Ed's."

"That's the plan."

"Well, all right. I hope you have a good trip. What ship is it, by the way? Is it one we know?"

"It is, actually," I said. "It's the *Lusitania*."

28
THE KNOCKOUT

THAT week at the Proctor's Theatre in Albany seemed to take an age. I was on edge, not sleeping well, filled with excitement at the thought of heading back to England to look for Tilly and my son. I hadn't seen them since the previous August, and I'd been missing them terribly.

I'd sent a wire to Tilly which simply said: 'ARRIVING 7TH ON LUSITANIA'. Cables were very expensive then, but the post office clerk assured me that there was no chance at all of a letter arriving ahead of me. I reckoned she would be able to work out for herself how long it would take me to get to Great Yarmouth, and only hoped her anticipation of our reunion would match mine.

By the Friday night of our run in Albany, I was ready to go. I was packed well in advance, and had bought a ticket for the six o'clock train in the morning.

On stage for what would be my last performance of *The Nutty Burglars* – for a short while at least – I was distracted by thoughts of leaving, and thoughts of Tilly. At one point I drifted off almost completely into a reverie, most unprofessional, and when

I snapped back to the moment, there were Charlie Chaplin and Mabel Normand looking daggers at me.

"What the...?" I said before I was quite myself, "Charlie? How the...?!"

"Pull yourself together," Charlie hissed, then louder: "There's a cop outside!"

It was Stan, of course, and I shook my head and snapped to it, turned and saw the cop, who was utterly unfamiliar. Where Ed Hurley was stocky, this chap was tall and thin with a beetling handlebar moustache. Ed's uniform didn't fit him so well, but he seemed to know what he was supposed to do, and after a few moment's confusion I saw past the facial hair and recognised Ted Banks. Of course, he and Ed would have arranged the switch as a surprise, their idea of a gag.

It was most unlike me to be thrown so badly on stage. Maybe I was leaving at the right time.

——

"Sorry, Stan," I said over a beer later. "I was off my game tonight."

"Don't worry about it," Stan grinned. "Maybe a break will do you good, eh?"

We clinked our glasses together.

"Having said that," Stan went on. "If you could see your way to making that break as short as possible I should be most grateful."

"I'll do my best," I assured him, then emptied my glass. "Now, that'll do for tonight. I need to be up and away at the crack of dawn, so I'll say goodnight."

We shook hands. "Give Tilly my love, won't you?" Stan said.

"You can do that yourself when we return," I said. "And Stan? Thanks again."

He grinned, a big Stan grin, and patted my arm. With a small lump in my throat I turned and headed outside. Once out in the open air I felt the call of nature, and realised that I wasn't going to make it back to our hotel in any comfort until I had dealt with the matter, so I strolled round the exterior of the establishment to the appropriate facility, which was an outhouse across the back yard.

Once I had made my contribution to the reeking trough I turned, and there in the doorway, silhouetted in the moonlight, was Edgar Hurley.

"Leaving without saying goodbye?" he sneered.

"Oh, you know," I said breezily. "Early start, all that." I took a step towards him, expecting him to step aside and let me pass, but he didn't do so. I stopped, wondering, through a slightly beery haze, whether I was going to have to shove my way past him.

"The thing is, though," Ed went on, in the same sneering tone. "I have a leaving present for you."

"A leaving present?"

Suddenly I was transported back to Kansas City, a year and half before. Charlie was leaving the Karno company to go and make flickers with Mack Sennett, and I had found him sitting alone on the stage at the end of his last night with us, contemplating his life. In my pocket, its unpleasant contents bumping gently against one another, there'd been a tobacco tin with a ribbon tied round it, my leaving present for him. What was inside the tin? Well, the clue came in the attached card, which was inscribed thusly:

"Some shits for a shit."

In the event I didn't give it to him. He was suddenly, unexpectedly nice to me and I couldn't go through with it. I wondered whether Ed Hurley had concocted something similar for me. At least we were standing in the proper location for such an exchange.

"Yeah," Ed said.

"Well? What is it?" I said. I should have known better.

Suddenly there was a flash of lights like a firework display, and before I knew what was happening, I was on the floor, face down in the disgusting pools of urine left by drunkards who couldn't hit a barn door, let alone a respectably ample trough.

My brain tried to focus on what had just happened? Ed... had hit me? That was it! He'd reached for his jacket pocket as though to take out a gift for me, and I, like a gullible fool, had looked down, thus positioning my chin perfectly to receive the sucker punch.

"What?" I said, spitting something nasty out of my mouth, which was beginning to hurt. "What was that for?"

"D'you think I'm a fool?" Hurley snarled.

"Yes, but that's no reason to hit a chap," I said, getting slowly to my feet and trying to dust myself off.

Smash! Hurley drove his fist into my face again, and I sat down hard, this time right in the blasted urinal trough. I felt warm liquid trickling down my lip, but was more horrified by the slightly cooler liquid seeping into the seat of my trousers.

"I shall be glad to see the back of you, Dandoe," Hurley growled. "You've been holding me back long enough, you and Jefferson."

"Holding you back? Is that what this is about, you maniac?" I said, dabbing at my nose.

"I went to see Chaplin, you know?"

"You went... what?"

"I went to see Chaplin, at the Essanay Studios, when we were in Chicago."

257

Even though I'd had a couple of beers, and had taken a couple of hard shots to the head, I suddenly saw where this was going.

"I confronted him," Hurley said, and I could just imagine him doing so. "I demanded to know how he had the temerity to sack my wife from his tinpot little film, and do you know what he told me?"

I thought perhaps I did, but said nothing.

"He told me just exactly why he had fired the pair of you, just precisely how you had contrived to ruin a whole afternoon's work with your... shenanigans!"

I decided to try a conciliatory approach. "Now look here, Ed," I said, trying to scramble up from the trough. Hurley shoved me in the chest so that I sat down again with a splash.

"No, you look here," he said, and aimed a big haymaker at the side of my head. Well, I could see he was pretty worked up, and he did have a point about my messing around with his wife. But as his huge and obvious punch came towards me, I suddenly realised something, and I slipped it. His fist whipped across my face, missing by a whisker, and clanged into a down pipe, part of the local plumbing.

"Yaargh!" Hurley roared, clutching his hand, and I clambered out of my revolting perch just as a little water tank crashed down to the floor, its supports eroded by rust and who knows what other corrosive influences.

"Wait a moment," I said. "Do you mean to tell me that you have known since Chicago? That you've kept it bottled up inside for three whole months, and you've only summoned up the courage to confront me when you know that I am leaving in the morning?"

"Aaargh!" Hurley panted, grimacing at his hand, which could well have been broken.

258

"But you haven't kept it bottled up all that time, have you, you coward?" I said then. "Now I see why Wren has been so distant. I thought she was embarrassed, as I was by the way, but no, I see it now. You've hit her, haven't you? You've punished her, and you have been damn'd careful about it. You haven't given her a black eye, because we'd have seen. You've been hitting her where it won't show."

With a roar Hurley, threw himself at me, shoving me back against the wall, driving his head into my face.

"You're out, you bastard!" he shouted. "And now Ted is in, and the three of us will manage Stan easily. I just wanted you to know that before you left, so you know there is nothing to come back for!"

Well, that gave me pause, I must say. It was as clear as could be that when I left I would be leaving old Stan in a heap of trouble, but I simply had to go, didn't I, I had to take this chance of seeing Tilly again.

I was a match for him, and he knew it, hence cold-cocking me at the start, of course, but now I was on my feet, I began to pay him back for the punishment he had meted out to Wren. No wonder she was quiet, I thought, as I pummelled her husband. No wonder she stopped coming out for a drink after the shows, and became so distant.

Hurley tried desperately to smother me in a bear hug with a view to wresting me to the ground, but I swayed out of his path and landed a good punch on his right eye.

"That'll take a tidy bit of make-up to cover it when it blackens up," I said, and the idea pleased me, so when Hurley came at me again I gave him a matching shiner on the other eye, so that he would be sure to look like a kind of grumpy panda for the next week or so.

259

He was properly angry, and he landed another couple of decent hits. I felt the teeth rattling in my jaw, but I went at him once more, and I finally put his lights out with a big smash right to the beak.

He sat slumped in the trough where he had first dumped me, although most of its contents were already soaked into my suit, and I stood over him panting.

A trickle of blood oozed slowly out of his battered ear, and suddenly I thought in a panic that the swine wasn't breathing. Christ! What if I'd killed him?

I leaned in close to check for vital signs, and he suddenly spluttered a great mist of blood and spit right in my face, and then toppled over sideways into the urine, where he lay rasping but decidedly alive.

I struggled out of there, and made my way somehow back to my bed, where I passed out.

The next thing I knew the sunlight was streaming through the curtains of the single attic room where I was lodging on an old army cot bed that week. Stan was shaking me vigorously by the arm, as the room swam slowly into focus.

"Arthur! Arthur! Wake up! What happened? And what in the name of God is that *smell*!"

"Hunh!" I said.

"You look terrible! What happened, Arthur?"

"Hurley," I mumbled. My mouth was pretty bashed up, and I began testing my teeth with my tongue.

"Oh my... I mean, look here, shouldn't you be on your way by now?"

"What time ish it?"

"It is very nearly seven. Weren't you supposed to be on the six o'clock?"

My scrambled wits finally managed to register that there was a crisis.

"Shit!" I said. "Got to go!"

I clambered off the bed, ignoring the shrieks of complaint from various parts of my aching frame. My hand hurt like the very devil.

"But you've missed the train."

"Get next one!" I mumbled, grabbing the bag that I had mercifully packed the afternoon before. "Those big boats are never on time, are they?"

"True. But at least get changed first, man. That suit stinks something rotten!"

"No time!"

I galloped down the stairs and out onto the street. There were no cabs in sight in either direction, so I pelted as fast as my battered skeleton would take me all the way to the railway station, where as fortune would have it there was a New York train steaming on the platform. I fumbled my ticket over to the ticket clerk, ignoring his screwed-up nose and disapproving expression, and he transferred me to this later train with almost indecent haste.

I leapt aboard and collapsed into a seat, panting from the exertions of the morning, and bruised and battered from those of the night before. It took me a couple of stops before I was able to collect myself sufficiently to appraise my surroundings, and I noticed then that all the seats near to me had emptied, as other passengers had moved away.

I dragged my bag along to the little bathroom cubicle, and awkwardly changed my clothes. It seemed the least I could do.

The face in the mirror looked bashed up, but I consoled myself with the thought that Ed Hurley's black eyes would be coming through back in Albany.

When I returned to my seat, I found that a tall gentleman with wire-rimmed spectacles had taken the seat opposite. I nodded to him, courteously, and he smiled in return, and we travelled in companionable silence for a little while. I was doing the mental arithmetic in my head, trying to calculate my chances of making the Lusitania.

"Excuse me," I said. "Do you happen to know when we arrive in New York?"

The tall gentleman took out his pocket watch and examined it, as though the answer was to be found there. "Ten minutes before midday, I believe," he said.

"Thank you," I replied. That would only give me a bare half hour to get to the quays...

I won't bore you with my harum-scarum chase from the railway station to the Port of New York's Pier 54, with the achingly slow cab driver, with the collision between two delivery trucks which meant taking a detour of a couple of blocks costing us precious minutes, or with the sweaty desperation as I leant out of the window for the last few hundred yards, shouting at hapless pedestrians to clear out of our way.

Let me just say that finally we rounded a corner and rattled between two giant warehouses until we burst into the sunlight onto the quay itself, and there was the mighty looming *Lusitania*, gleaming in its old magnificent livery, streamers hanging from every porthole and railing, passengers gleefully waving their hats and hand kerchiefs at friends and relatives below.

I pushed desperately through these clumps of smiling people, as a little band played a jaunty farewell song, and then I stopped, for I could see that the great liner was twenty feet from the dock-side, then twenty-five, and all the gangways had been hauled aboard, and the ropes were disappearing into their guide holes like rats' tails under a cooker.

I'd missed her.

29
THE ROOM

SUMMER OF 1917, SOMEWHERE IN AMERICA

"**AS** you can imagine," I said, "I was raging."

"With Edgar Hurley, you mean?" John said.

"Well yes, with him, the idiot, and also, by the way, with the clerk at the booking office who explained with infuriating patience that there was a company policy against granting a refund once the ship had sailed, and that it was my responsibility and mine alone to make sure that I was on it."

John began to look at his finger nails, and I felt the need to bring the conversation round to his main area of interest as soon as possible.

"Mostly, though, I raged at our old friend Charles Spencer Chaplin, for it was he, was it not, who had told that pompous cuckold Hurley information that he could easily have withheld."

"About you making m-merry with Hurley's wife?"

"Exactly, he could have kept that to himself, that would have been the... *sporting* thing to do, the friendly thing. But no, he saw the chance to spite me, d'you see? To cause trouble, to stab me in the back, and he took it knowingly and gladly, I was sure of that."

"So, because of him, you were denied the chance to cross the Atlantic towards your sweetheart and your son...?"

"And I was not happy about it."

"Until later."

"Well. Yes."

"Some might say Chaplin – and Hurley, for that matter – did you a good turn there."

"Accidentally, yes, but that was not his intention, that's my point."

"I think, Dandoe, that if I am to stick my n-neck out for you I am going to need a bit more than that."

"Oh there's more," I said. "There's plenty more."

PART 4

30
TORPEDOED

THERE was no sense waiting around in New York for the Keystone Four to return. Edgar had made it quite clear that with me out of the way he was planning to take control of the act, and so Stan needed my help. I'd gone straight back to the station and would be in Albany by seven – plenty of time to make the last performance of the evening.

The first person I encountered as I mounted the stairs from the stage door two at a time was Ted Banks, still wearing the policeman's outfit from the matinee.

"Ho! Look out! What are you doing here?" he cried.

"Shorry Ted, your shervicesh will no longer be required," I slurred through my still-sore lips and teeth, pushing past him.

"Wait, what? You can't do that!" he said plaintively, trotting up behind me.

Stan was pacing the corridor outside the dressing rooms. When he saw me his eyes widened, and he sighed as he realised immediately what had happened.

"You didn't make it! I am sorry. You must be so disappointed."

"Yesh," I said.

"But thank goodness you are here. You are a Godsend. You can do the last show."

"What? Looking like thish?" I said, indicating my battered features.

"You look a damn'd sight better than Ed," Stan said, dropping his voice.

"Really?"

"Yes," Ted said, joining our conversation. "You must have given him a right doing-over."

"He shtarted it," I growled, and Ted took a step back.

"Wren's looking after him, but I think it would be a mercy if you could take over," Stan said. "He doesn't seem quite to know what day it is."

"He probably imagines it is the middle of next week," I said, "because I'm pretty sure that's where I knocked him into."

I looked into the dressing room, to see Ed laid out on a settee there, with his wife dabbing gently at his forehead with a wet towel. She looked up at me as I came in, and I saw a triumphant half-smile flit across her lovely face.

"How is he doing?" I asked.

"He's sleeping," she said.

"Let him sleep, then. I'll do the show," I said.

"Thank you, Arthur," Wren said, and I wondered exactly what I was being thanked for.

———

Well, I stepped back behind the Chester Conklin moustache and resumed my career having only missed the afternoon performance, which meant that Ed had only had the one go at the role. He was not a tremendous success, either, as Stan confided on the train back into New York the next morning.

"He was pretty scrambled," Stan said. "I'm thinking we should keep Ted on for this next week, let Ed take a bit of time off to recover. What do you say?"

"Fine by me," I said. Privately, between me, myself and the bedpost, I was getting quite a kick out of this. Ed had given me his best shots, and I'd been up and about more or less immediately – although I'd missed the *Lusitania*, of course. In return, I'd thrashed him so badly that he could barely function. I think that showed pretty neatly where things stood between us, and he'd think twice about trying that again.

Keeping Ted with us for the week also gave me a bit more time to work out what I was going to do about getting to England.

"It is going to take me a while to save up the blasted fare again," I said. "But maybe I'll be in a position to go in a month or two, if I lay off the beer. And food."

"Well, let's do what we can to keep Ed sweet about that," Stan said. "At least we are in and around New York for the next few weeks, and if Ted finds something else to do by the time you're ready to leave, then good luck to him."

"Keep in touch with him," I said in a low voice, glancing over at where Banks was sitting with Wren and the invalid. "When I get back with Tilly and we ditch the Hurleys, we'll still need a cop."

Stan nodded, sat back.

And so that was the plan. I would continue with Stan and the Hurleys until such time as I had made enough cash to have another go at crossing the Atlantic.

That was the plan for that whole week at Proctor's 23rd Street theatre, with Ed Hurley lazing around the apartment like an invalid making a big deal of his recovery and of not talking to me.

That was the plan right up to the Saturday, when we woke to these shocking headlines on the front of the *New York Times*.

LUSITANIA SUNK BY A SUBMARINE, PROBABLY 1,260 DEAD;

TWICE TORPEDOED OFF IRISH COAST; SINKS IN FIFTEEN MINUTES;

WASHINGTON BELIEVES THAT A GRAVE CRISIS IS AT HAND.

I wandered around in a daze for the rest of that weekend, and as it happens, found sleep difficult to come by for weeks afterwards. In my mind's eye I kept seeing the moment described by one eye witness, who'd stood at the rail and watched the U-boat's conning tower break the surface, then tracked two torpedoes carving through the water towards the very liner he was standing on. The explosions sent splinters of the hull flying through the air in all directions, and the *Lusitania* began to list to one side, then slide under the waves. Some seven hundred were rescued and taken to Ireland, but I had no doubt that if I had been there I would have been among the majority that perished, and that Atlantic chill seemed to grip my very soul.

I read every detail I could get my hands on, and was just absorbing a harrowing description of friends and relatives waiting helplessly on the dock at Liverpool, waiting for news of loved ones when with a start, I suddenly remembered I'd wired Tilly that I was taking the ill-fated ship, and had completely forgotten to wire again and say I hadn't. What if she'd travelled over to Liverpool to meet the *Lusitania*? She and Wallace might be there, even now, trying to find out what had happened to me!

What could I do? I turned the options over in my over-heating mind as I raced helter-skelter around to the Western Union office.

How could I have been so stupid? It would have been bad enough even if the ship hadn't been sunk, she could have been waiting there, watching all the passengers disembarking, not understanding why I wasn't there. I couldn't see how to get word to her except by sending a wire to the Great Yarmouth address, which would mean she could not possibly hear I was alive until she had given up all hope and gone home again. Or maybe that's where she was now, waiting, and weeping...

I sent a simple message: NOT ON LUSITANIA STOP SAFE IN NY

Then I rushed back to the apartment and wrote a grovelling letter, begging her forgiveness for being so thoughtless, but assuring her that I was safe and well and would come up with another way for us to be together again, though what that might be was, at that point, beyond my powers of imagination. I could only hope that by the time it arrived she would have calmed down.

Over the next days the grave crisis developed. The fact that more than a hundred of the dead were American citizens meant that the American government came under great pressure to declare war on Germany, and we wondered what this would mean for us. President Wilson seemed determined not to take the final step, however, contenting himself with demanding assurances from the Germans that nothing like this would ever happen again.

The Germans, for their part, insisted that the *Lusitania* was carrying contraband munitions which had contributed to the ship's destruction and rapid sinking. Maybe they had a point, or maybe the 90 tons of unrefrigerated lard and butter listed on board as destined for the Royal Navy Weapons Testing Establishment in Essex really had been heading to the canteen for making cakes. The thought that someone, somewhere, might not be above using civilian passengers as a kind of human shield sent shivers down my spine.

We were booked for a week at the Proctor's in Newark, New Jersey, which was just about close enough for us to get back to our Manhattan flat, with its Chaplin memorabilia mantelpiece, at night. One morning in the middle of that week, Stan came in from an early morning walk just as I was surfacing for the day, and he wordlessly thrust a copy of the *New York Times* into my hand, indicating a small item at the bottom of an inside page.

I squinted at it, but my eyes were not yet focusing.

"What is it?" I said. "Just read it out."

Stan took the paper back. "'English comedian Arthur Dandoe...'" he read.

"What?"

"'...formerly of the Fred Karno troupe...'"

"What?!"

"Let me finish, for goodness' sake. 'English comedian Arthur Dandoe, formerly of the Fred Karno troupe, is believed to be among those whose bodies have not been recovered after the *Lusitania* tragedy.'"

"Christ above!" I swore. "It doesn't say that!"

I snatched the newspaper from him and forced my eyes to concentrate. "Good God! I say, do you think this will be in the English papers?"

"Very likely, I'd say."

"What if my father sees it? My mother?!"

"I should say you have some more letters to write," Stan said. "And you'd better hope the mail boats have better luck."

I was still frantically composing, writing to my family, and again to Tilly for good measure, just in case my previous communications had foundered for some reason, when Ed Hurley came into the living room and called a company meeting. He had recovered sufficiently to return to work, and was just about ready to start throwing his weight around again.

"I think the time has come to make it absolutely clear where everyone stands," Ed began, puffing his chest out pompously.

"All right," Stan said, with a friendly smile.

"It is clear, after the terrible recent event, that Arthur will not be returning to Blighty any time soon, nor will he be bringing Tilly and their son over here to resume their former careers."

"Thanks for reminding me," I said.

"Which means, does it not, that Wren and myself should no longer regard ourselves as stand-ins for Tilly Beckett and Freddie Karno Junior, but as fully-fledged and equal shareholders in our joint enterprise. To wit, The Keystone Four."

"The Keystone Four," Stan nodded.

"And we should have an equal say in the future direction of the act, and any further decisions, either artistic or financial, should be arrived at as the result of full and frank discussions between the four members, on an absolutely equal footing."

"What's he doing here then?" I asked, looking up from my writing and jerking a thumb at Ted Banks.

"True enough, that is a side issue, but now that I am recovered from..." he glanced at me, "...we no longer have any current need for Ted here."

"Oh," Ted said. "Well. That's just... dandy."

"Sorry, Ted," Stan said, and Wren gave him a consoling pat on the hand.

"So, are we agreed?"

Stan was a fair-minded soul, and could see no good reason to quibble. "I think that sounds perfectly reasonable. Don't you, Arthur?"

I shrugged, not looking up from my letter writing.

"Don't bother to ask me what I think," Ted muttered. "I don't know why you even asked me over."

"To say thank you for helping us out," Wren said.

"That's right," Stan chipped in. "You were great, and if anything else..." he trailed off, looking to me for help.

"Yes, if any of the equal-sharing members of this collective ever decides to sandbag another equal-sharing member in the gentleman's facilities we will most definitely be in touch," I said.

"Well, if the other members can only manage to keep their damn'd hands off one another, then...!" Ed burst out.

"All right, all right, let's calm down," Stan said. "I think we can all agree that Ed and Wren are no longer standing in for Tilly and Fred, and should have a say in what we do and where we go, that's fine, absolutely fine. Isn't it, Arthur?"

I shrugged again.

"So," Stan said, guiding Ed back to his seat. "Was there something in particular that you wanted? You and Wren?"

Wren looked at Ed, and Ed pointed at the mantelpiece, where a row of little plaster-of-Paris statues of Charlie stood, their heads cocked archly to one side.

"Yes," Ed said. "I want to be Chaplin."

31
THE HARD WAY

WHENEVER we put it to the vote, it came out two to two, of course, with me backing Stan, and Wren sticking up for Ed. Ted Banks was sitting there the first time we thrashed it out, but neither side wanted him to have a casting vote, and in any case he got up and left long before we reached any kind of resolution.

Stan proposed contacting the Bostocks to see what they thought, whereupon Ed threatened to leave with Wren at once unless he was given his way. Well, that really would have dropped us in it, so in the end Stan and I had a hard choice to make.

"Perhaps we should let the bastard have a go," I said to Stan as we had our umpteenth private chat about the ridiculous situation. "Let him find out the hard way."

"And then what?" Stan said. "He'll see the light, and we'll go back to how things were before?"

"Stranger things have happened," I said.

Which was how we came to be standing in the wings at the Proctor's in Newark that weekend, myself adorned with the Chester Conklin soup strainer, Wren in her Mabel Normand outfit and wig, Stan in a Keystone Cop uniform – the enormous painted K had almost completely faded by this time – and Edgar Hurley strutting up and down in the dark, giving his cane a few last practice twirls and twitching his moustache. The clothes had been a better fit on Stan – which is to say a more accurate reflection of Chaplin himself – than they were on Hurley, who was a stockier fellow altogether. The jacket was so tight it would barely do up over his chest, while the pants seemed to be more or less the right size for him, but still, the impersonation wasn't going to stand or fall by the costume, was it?

What the next few minutes would tell us was whether Edgar Hurley had the comic chops to carry it off. And as the act before us traipsed off and our music struck up, I couldn't quite work out which would be better, Ed falling on his face, or Ed actually making a decent fist of it. A good night for Ed would be marginally more enjoyable for all of us in the short term, but a calamity might resolve the issue of who should be Chaplin once and for all, and so would probably be worth enduring a bit of misery for. The important thing, I told myself, was to do the same job I always did, so that whatever came next it wouldn't be my fault.

The lights went on low, as usual, and the Nutty Burglars tiptoed onto the stage to begin their larcenous night's work.

Ed entered, as Stan always did, with a trademark bit of Chaplin-esque business, sauntering on and bumping into a hat stand in the near-dark, then turning and apologising to it, lifting his battered derby, and then becoming annoyed that the hat stand was seemingly not accepting his apology and pushing it over. This all went down fine, with some laughs and giggles from the crowd.

Then I, as the other burglar, would remonstrate with 'Charlie', reminding him that we needed to be quiet. Stan would look a little shame-faced at this, and would manage to get the audience's sympathy, but Ed lacked the finesse for a touch of that kind, and simply shoved me aside to take centre stage.

"Well, all right then," I thought. "You want to carry the thing all by yourself, be my guest."

I set about trying to open the safe, while Ed went through his whole repertoire of Chaplin moves, things he had clearly been rehearsing in front of a mirror, or perhaps his wife, he certainly hadn't bothered to share them with me or with Stan. Where Stan had worked his pitch-perfect Charlie impression into the fabric of the sketch, Ed had simply decided to do all the things he had thought of straight out at the stalls, basically hitting them over the head with Chaplin, Chaplin, Chaplin. I glanced into the wings, and Stan was standing there, out of the audience's line of vision, with a perplexed frown on his long face.

The crowd that evening were in a reasonably good mood, but after a while Ed had simply exhausted his credit with them, and the laughter began to die down. It was all very well seeing a bloke dressed as Chaplin cavorting around for a minute or two, but then they would have liked a bit of a story as well.

Wren made her entrance then, to a nice round of applause as the audience recognised that she was meant to be Mabel. Her first interaction was usually with me, the burglar she could see attempting to open the safe, whereupon 'Charlie' would appear and try to explain the situation. However, Ed grabbed Wren by the arm and spun her to face him, thus excising my little scene altogether.

"Fair enough," I said to myself. "If you don't want my help, you shan't have it, you arrogant so-and-so."

The key point of that memorable performance came when Ed reached one of Stan's real show-stopping moments. It was a little sequence in which he managed to combine distracting 'Mabel' with all the flirty physical dexterity that Chaplin himself could possibly have employed, whilst at the same time hurrying me, his colleague, up. Stan captured not only Charlie's physicality but also the very spirit of his character, the character the audience had already so fallen in love with, and it would never fail to draw a huge laugh from every corner of the room, followed eight or nine times out of ten, I should say, by a round of applause we had grown accustomed to waiting for.

Ed managed a rough facsimile of the action, but the only thing about it that said "Chaplin" was his little moustache. There was none of the impishness, none of the grace, none of the clockwork perfection that Stan could mimic to the very life. It was like a water buffalo attempting the ballet. Even the jacket chose this moment to give up the unequal struggle, and popped its buttons, which went skittering across the apron.

Now, it was Ed's first time, of course, and maybe if he'd let Stan guide him through a little bit of rehearsal he'd have been able to do a better job of it, but he had chosen not to.

The audience tittered a little, and then sat there waiting for whatever was to happen next. They hadn't had their socks knocked off, as previous crowds had, but they weren't unhappy, and the sketch could have continued to its conclusion merrily enough. In fact, Stan as the policeman stepped out onto the stage at that very moment to begin the denouement.

Ed wasn't having it, though. Holding both his hands up in the air he strode to the front of the apron. Not a Chaplin stride, either, an angry Edgar Hurley strut. He looked like an exasperated headmaster about to tick off a naughty school assembly, where all the children had somehow bitterly disappointed him.

"No, no, no," he said, in his own voice, not the character one he had been using to flirt with 'Mabel'. "That will not do at all. At this point we always get a big laugh, and then a round of applause. Come on, let's hear you..."

He began leading his own round of applause, and the audience, bemused, slowly joined in with him to create a gentle, bewildered ovation.

"You can do better than that!" Ed bellowed, "Come on, let's give it some oomph!"

"Jesus!" Stan breathed.

The applause slowly built up to what Ed, in full pantomime mode now, finally regarded as acceptable, and then he waved the audience quiet again.

"All right, "he said. "Now I'm going to do that bit over again, and you know what you have to do."

"No...!" Stan said, loud enough for me to hear. "Stop him, for God's sake!"

"Um... Waffles?!" I shouted, trying to attract Hurley's attention.

"Just a minute, you!" Ed said, returning to his wife. She, too, realised – anyone would! – that demanding that an audience watch a gag be performed a second time, with applause required of them afterwards, was going to be uncomfortable.

"Listen to your friend," Wren said urgently. "Look, there's a policeman!"

Ed had gone to a peculiar place. Having once begun a dialogue with the audience as himself, he felt liberated to continue it.

"Aha!" he cried. "Here's the fellow, look, look at this chap. He thinks he should be the funny man in this little vignette. What do you think of *that*, eh? Look at him!"

The audience did look at Stan, and they looked at Ed, and they clearly didn't know what to make of the question. They'd seen Ed, and they hadn't seen Stan do anything except walk on stage, so how could they possibly compare?

There was a shout from the stalls: "Get on with it!"

This was followed by a murmuring, the noise any comic performer worth his salt could identify as "Time's up!"

And Stan's instincts were as good as anyone's. "The bomb!" he hissed at me, but I was ahead of him, already grabbing the black ball and lighting the firework on top. I threw it to Stan, who lobbed it to Wren, who handed it to her husband.

"Not yet!" he said, crossly, but then realised that he had to go along with us or this last effect would be ruined. He gave a great "Harrumph!" and passed the parcel on.

Ed wasn't finished, though, with his reworking of our routine. Just at the point when he was due to chuck the bomb out of the window at the policeman, instead he suddenly ran offstage with it. The explosion duly occurred in the wings, as per, but it wasn't Stan the policeman who returned with his face blackened and hair on end, it was Ed as Chaplin, who had appropriated the climactic joke for himself. Then he strode forwards to take a curtain call, before some enterprising soul doused the lights on him.

———

"See?" Ed cried triumphantly as soon as we were down in the dressing room.

"Ed..." Wren said, but her husband was not to be halted.

"There's no great mystery to playing Chaplin," Ed went on. "Just slap on a toothbrush moustache and do a silly walk and the suckers lap it up!"

"Is that what you think was happening?" I said, marvelling at his capacity for self-delusion.

"Of course! It helps to have funny bones, of course, you can get a little bit extra out of it."

"Like Stan, you mean?"

"Oh, Stan does well enough, but his performance is such a slavish copy. It needed something else, a bit of... I don't know... *balls*!"

Stan was standing quietly, looking at the floor. His natural desire to avoid confrontation was struggling with his desire to knock Edgar's block off, and it was clearly an epic battle.

"Balls! Is that what you think?" I said, laughing.

"Yes I do," Ed pouted. "I have always thought that Chaplin was somewhat... effete. And he'd be better served by a more masculine approach."

"Ed," Wren began again. "Just let's all go for a nice quiet drink, shall we, and then we can..."

"So I think I have demonstrated to everyone's satisfaction that I can play the part every bit as well as Mr Jefferson here, and so I propose that from now on..."

"No."

"Huh?" Ed looked round to see who had spoken.

There, standing in the doorway, each wearing an expression of stone-cold fury, were Claude Bostock and his brother Gordon. Our agents.

"Good heavens!" Stan cried. "Claude! Gordon!"

"Oh I see!" Ed said, putting his hands on his hips. "You wired them."

"Wired them?" Stan said. "Of course not." He turned to our agents. "Come in, welcome, sit down. How lovely to see you!"

"Would that we could say the same," Claude said. "But we went to some considerable trouble to bring representatives of the Orpheum circuit with us this evening, in the belief that you were ready to step up to bigger time. But we were wrong, were we not, Gordon?"

"Oh, we were way off the mark," Gordon said, inspecting his fingernails.

"Whatever possessed you?" Claude said. "What evil, stupid spirit persuaded you to make the changes that you have made? Stan, you are the premier Chaplin impersonator currently working, and there are hundreds of 'em, believe me. All the theatre managers we have spoken to say the same, that you are a marvel, that you are the Little Fellow to the life, and yet what do we see when we come along to see for ourselves? You are playing a walk-on, and this lumpen oaf is hogging the act!"

"Ha ha!" I laughed. "Lumpen oaf!"

"How dare you?" Ed cried, going red in the face. "How *dare* you?"

Gordon stepped forwards. "I'll tell you how he dares," he said coldly. "We have invested in you, our time, our energy, our contacts, our reputations. Which entitles us to tell you when you have made a catastrophic error of judgement."

"I don't have to stand here and take this," Ed blustered.

"Oh, do be quiet," Gordon said.

"Yes, Ed, be quiet," Wren said, her patience finally snapping.

"The Orpheum circuit," Stan said, closing his eyes.

"Yes, I'm afraid they were not sold," Claude said. "But all may not be altogether lost. First of all, though, we must restore Stan to the Chaplin role, that much is absolutely certain."

"Wait a minute," Ed said. "We all have to agree."

"I agree," I said quickly.

"Me too," Stan nodded.

"And me," Wren said.

"Oh! Oh! I see!" Ed shouted, his face turning puce. "I see how the land lies! Well, I won't hold you up any longer! I quit!"

Hurley grabbed his coat and stormed out of the dressing room.

284

Wren watched him go, and then with a little apologetic shrug to us all she picked up her own coat and hat and followed.

"Don't worry," Stan said. "I'll talk him round. When he's calmed down a bit. I'll get him to come back."

Gordon Bostock looked at his fingernails, as if finally pleased with how they looked.

"Don't," he said.

32
HAVE YOU GOT THE CHAPLINOIA?

THE press couldn't agree. Some called the craze 'Chaplinitis', others called it 'Chaplinoia'. Which one was I suffering from? Well, I'm pretty sure my Chaplin wasn't inflamed, although as far as I was concerned he was a more or less constant itch.

No, I reckon I had the Chaplinoia. I was seeing him literally everywhere.

Every main street, it seemed, of every town everywhere, had a movie palace, which was showing Chaplin's films, and every one had a life-size saw-cut figure of the little man standing on the pavement outside to beckon people in, a speech bubble suspended above his head crying out: "I'm here!"

You couldn't open a newspaper without stumbling upon the new cartoon strip, *Charlie's Comic Capers*, or a story about how the French had dubbed him 'Charlot' as if to claim a direct lineage back to the Pierrot figure of *commedia dell'arte*, or else some other wild assertion that the only English word known by the Fanti savages of Ashanti-land was 'Charlee!'

You couldn't walk into a shop without dodging a balloon-seller with a likeness of Chaplin stretched into a ghastly gurn on some garish yellow monstrosity. You couldn't buy cigarettes without first reaching over Charlie Chaplin candy, or a table of plaster statuettes of Charlie Chaplin, or a prominent pile of *The Charlie Chaplin Scream Book*.

You couldn't stroll into a music shop to browse, without first wading through snowdrifts of sheets with titles like *The Chaplin Waddle, Those Charlie Chaplin Feet,* and – most gallingly – *Charlie Chaplin, the Funniest of Them All.*

Charlie Chaplin's Life Story – evidently he arrived as a penniless immigrant, and not a well-established Karno comedian earning three times as much as the other members of the company.

Charlie Chaplin dolls, Charlie Chaplin toys, Chaplin derby hats, which had gone out of fashion, but were now available pre-battered and artfully dusty, Chaplin ties and Chaplin socks – what imbecile would buy such a thing, let alone wear them?

Charlie Chaplin playing cards, Charlie Chaplin lapel pins, Charlie Chaplin lucky charms, and Charlie Chaplin coins for use in slot machines.

It was madness.

Meanwhile, Stan and I were at a loose end.

When we got back to the apartment after the Ed Hurley-as-Chaplin debacle, he and Wren had already packed up and shipped out, without saying goodbye or leaving a note or, I might add, any cash to cover their outstanding portion of the rent.

The only parting gesture they'd made – and I strongly suspect that this was Edgar rather than Wren – was to smash all the little Chaplin statues that Stan had accumulated over the preceding weeks into plaster dust.

Of all the Chaplin memorabilia that was one the bursting market, the statuettes were the ones I minded the least, funnily enough. This was because they were being pirated, and were the subject of a bitter and messy lawsuit by Chaplin and Essanay, his film company, and the thought of all the trouble they were having to go to gave me a little thrill of pleasure. Just a little one.

Claude and Gordon Bostock took charge of our affairs. They cancelled all our upcoming engagements, which amounted to about four weeks of work, and advanced the two of us some spending money to tide us over until they'd had time to come up with a new plan for us. We were summoned to a meeting with the Bostocks at the end of the following week, in Cleveland, Ohio, and we were more than happy to leave things in their hands until then. I was looking forward to seeing them again, hoping that a letter from Tilly might have arrived at their office.

We paid off our landlord, and made our way in leisurely fashion to Cleveland by train, with a few days to kill on the banks of Lake Erie.

Of course, we had barely walked a block from the railway station before we were greeted by a grinning cut-out of Charlie Chaplin outside a picture palace. In case it didn't attract your attention at first glance, a little clockwork mechanism rocked his head from side to side, along with its "I'm here!" speech balloon. Stan stopped and looked at this, shaking his own head from side to side.

"Incredible, isn't it?" he said.

"Hmm," I scowled.

"Look, they're showing a couple of new Essanay films. I haven't seen these – let's go inside, come on."

"Do we have to?" I groaned, but Stan was already pushing through the big glass doors and heading into the lobby.

I sat through *The Tramp* and *A Jitney Elopement*, with Stan eagerly lapping it up beside me. There was a healthy mid-afternoon attendance, chuckling and sighing at the Little Fellow's antics. The biggest laugh of all came during a sequence in *A Jitney Elopement*, and there was a noticeable shift in Stan's mood afterwards.

We strolled along a wide boulevard, out in the sunlight once again, but Stan was under a dark cloud.

"You saw?" he said. "Of course you did!"

"Well, yes," I said.

Back in 1910 when we were with Karno. The Guv'nor proposed a new sketch in which the main character was a dreamy boy who fell asleep and found his dreams coming to life around him. Charlie didn't think much of it and refused to play the main part, whereupon Karno suddenly promoted Stan from the ranks to play *Jimmy the Fearless*. My friend had made a huge hit of the new skit, devising all sorts of business which made it sing, including a little routine which was actually born out of his own nervousness the first time we performed it. Jimmy would absent-mindedly cut himself a slice of bread, whilst dreaming of pirates, and when he came to himself he would find that he had cut the loaf into a concertina, which he would then pretend to get a little tune out of. It always brought the house down.

As it just had when Charlie did it in *The Jitney Elopement*.

Remembering how Charlie had sat in the middle of the front row every night, and gone to Karno and offered to play the part after all, reducing Stan to the supporting cast, didn't make it any better. We soothed the ache with liberal amounts of anaesthetic, by which I mean best bourbon, and then finding ourselves in the unfamiliar position of having no show to fill our evening with, we sank some more.

The next day, a little headachy, truth to tell, we decided to ride the streetcar out to Luna Park, which was an attraction of a kind known as a trolley park. The streetcar companies built these at the end of their trolley lines, and there'd be picnic areas, trees, lawns, and often some rides and other attractions, the idea being that people would have a reason to use the cars at the weekends.

Anyway, we were rattling along through the wide sunlit main streets of Cleveland, and I was lost in my own thoughts, thinking of Tilly, of the boy, and of what next. Maybe the Bostocks would have a letter for me...?

I glanced absent-mindedly up towards the other end of the streetcar, and there, like an apparition from a nightmare, was Charlie Chaplin. He was dressed in his distinctive onscreen get-up, and making his way with that oh-so familiar gait up the car towards me, tipping his hat at the ladies, and pretending to trip over gentlemen's outstretched legs, and people were laughing, of course they were.

I felt seriously unsettled, then, and gripped the arms of the seat before risking a glance at Stan, anxiously, hoping he was seeing this too. To my relief he was, and he was amused.

Charlie reached the centre platform of the streetcar, where those passengers standing gave him a little room. He gave a little cough, and began to sing:

"You are my honey, honeysuckle, I am the bee...!"

The hairs on my arms stood on end, and I felt suddenly chilled to the bone. I had heard Chaplin singing this very song to a girl called Hetty Kelly, his first love (for all I knew), in London's Trocadero, while I myself was walking out for the very first time with Tilly, back in '08. What was happening? Was I losing my grip?

But no, everyone else seemed to be hearing what I was hearing, and enjoying the song, and slowly, gradually, I came to myself again and recognised that the voice was not Charlie's, that the singer was a young boy of about twelve, and this was not Chaplin at all.

I let out a sigh, I was so relieved. When the boy busker came to our end of the car, holding out his derby, I gave the kid a dime, which he flicked up with his thumb, caught, bit between his teeth and then slipped into his pants pocket.

"Thanks, mister," he said, with a cheeky wink.

"Whyever are you dressed as Chaplin?" I said.

"Whyever not?" the kid said.

"Well, he's completely silent, he's known for it. Isn't it a bit strange for people when he starts singing? Why not dress as an actual singer, like an Al Jolson?"

"I'll tell ya, mister. The tramp clothes are a lot easier to put together, for a start. Then there's the walk. Once you get the walk off, it's a piece of cake, people are already laughing. Then the song is kind of a bonus, see?"

"Smart kid," Stan grinned.

"Say, you fellas are from England, ain't ya?" We acknowledged this with a nod, and the kid beamed. "Me too! My folks came over from London a few years back. My old man's a stonecutter from Eltham, do you know it?"

"We do," Stan said with a smile. "How about that?"

"I'm Les," the kid said, tipping coins into his hand and then popping his derby back on his head. "See y'around!"

"Good luck to you," Stan called.

At the end of the line we hopped off the trolley and made our way up to the entrance. As we did so, a slight Chaplin-esque figure stepped off as well, and I thought nothing of it for a moment, thinking it would be young Les, but no, there was the kid over there, already striking up a song for the pleasure-seekers by the gates. This was another one.

Stan and I strolled into the park, which was pleasantly verdant, and there on one of the paths a few yards ahead of us, Chaplin was twiddling his cane and strutting his splay-footed way.

And there, off to my left, another Chaplin raised his hat to a lady, and two more strolled along arm-in-arm, and another waited in a line for an ice-cream.

I shook my head to clear it. I had the Chaplinoia all right.

"Hey!" Stan said, seemingly oblivious to the Charlies everywhere I looked. "Let's give that a go, shall we?"

He led the way over to an attraction called 'Shoot the Chute' and we took our place in the queue to have a ride. A boat-shaped car on rails filled up with about twenty people in front of us, and then began to climb up to the top of its run. The course was oval-shaped, beginning with this uphill section of track, then it would swing round and the car would plunge thrillingly into the lake, drenching passengers and passers-by alike, finally floating round again to return to its start position.

I watched from the front of the roped-off queue as the little carriage swung around the raised curve at the far end. As it rolled towards the vertiginous drop I suddenly noticed that the three people in the front row were all Charlie Chaplin. I gripped the rope tightly in disbelief as the contraption shot down into the lake amid delighted squeals and the three Chaplins were soaked, as was I, and, when I looked round, two more Chaplins queueing behind Stan.

The empty car stopped in front of us and we stepped aboard to take our seats, unable to avoid sitting in the puddles from all its previous rides. I was in the middle of the front row, Stan was to my right, and then, hopping in to sit at my left, was Charlie Chaplin. I blinked, beginning to feel like I needed a serious lie down and perhaps some kind of tonic.

Up we went, and then round, inching towards the plunge. I

couldn't look at the person to my left, so I trained my gaze on the trees at the far end of the lake. At the very last second a gap between them seemed to open, and I saw what looked like a large open meadow beyond. In that sea of green, dozens of Chaplins cavorted backwards and forwards, like it was an enclosure in a zoo, and they'd been breeding them for years. Chaplin after Chaplin raced this way and that, and – no, I wasn't mistaken – several were playing leap-frog.

I raised a quivering hand to point this ghastly apparition out to Stan, and opened my mouth to speak, and at that precise instant the car dropped down into the water, leaving my stomach and most of its accompanying internal organs back at the top of the slope.

I reckon I swallowed about half of that lake, coughing and spluttering, and as we reached the end of the ride a solicitous face looked down at me.

"You OK?" said Charlie Chaplin, water dripping from the brim of his hat and the ends of his moustache.

Stan hauled me to my feet, laughing his head off. "So?" he said, as we stood dripping on the path.

"So what?"

"So did you see? Over there?" He pointed towards the trees.

"What? All the Chaplins? Did you see them too?"

"Of course!"

"Thank God! I thought I was going mad!"

Stan strode off towards the field, and I splished and sploshed along in his wake, although I'd rather have gone almost anywhere else.

"It's a Charlie Chaplin look-a-like contest!" Stan cried, as a raised stage hove into view, decorated with posters and signs indicating that there was, indeed, a rational explanation for what I had been seeing. "Let's enter it, come on!"

It appeared that while dozens of Chaplins had come along in their own meticulously appointed costumes there was a trestle table round the back of the stage with spare jackets, trousers, battered derbies, shoes and canes for those who wanted to join in on a more impromptu basis.

Stan paid the entrance fee for both of us before I could stop him, and he began burrowing in the piles, making a serious effort to put on a good show, while I sifted somewhat less enthusiastically, suffering a strong sense of déjà vu, having similarly thrown together the outfit for the Stowaway back at Keystone just to show Chaplin how simply it could be done. He'd learnt that lesson well, I reflected, since the Stowaway's costume could now be seen on every second person walking around Luna Park.

Anyway, long story short, the contest got under way in front of a good-natured throng, most of whom seemed to have a relative in the running. Every Chaplin – and there were dozens upon dozens of them – got about half a minute to demonstrate their mastery or otherwise of the Chaplin Waddle, or Those Chaplin Feet. It rapidly got more than a little samey, in all honesty, and those who had the good fortune to go early had a distinct advantage.

Finally the judges went into a little huddle, and shortly after that the Master of Ceremonies called for hush, and read from a piece of paper.

"What tremendous fun! Thank you to everyone for taking part. Our winning Charlie Chaplin is... number 41, Leslie Hope![6]"

Well, blow me down if it wasn't young Les from the street-car who bowled out to collect his prize. He was a cocky little so-and-so, and seized the opportunity to show off a little more.

"I guess it's because I'm from London England, just like Charlie," he said. "But I reckon everyone did just fine!"

He got a handsome round of applause for that, and reprised his Chaplin as he waddled from the stage. It wasn't bad – the lad had funny bones.

As for me, I guessed the judges simply weren't ready to appreciate my own effort, in which I had concentrated less on the funny walk and more on trying to depict the darkness of Chaplin's soul.

And the nation's premier Chaplin impersonator? He placed third.

"Don't tell the Bostocks," he grinned. "Don't want them to change that billing, do we?"

33
ALICE AND BALDY

CLAUDE and Gordon Bostock were waiting for us in the dining room of the Hollenden Hotel, a lavish wood-panelled establishment in which the dark redwood and mahogany fittings were offset by a large crystal chandelier. If their intention was to impress us then it most certainly worked. At other tables with their perfectly white tablecloths and silver service the city's bigwigs were holding meetings of their own, and there was a constant low rumble of masculine voices coming from the collection of bulging waistcoats with their gleaming gold watch chains.

"Boys!" Claude beamed. "Great to see you! Come and have some tea, why don't you?"

A waiter was in attendance before the seats of our pants had touched the seats of our chairs, and we nodded for tea. I could see that Stan was a little uncomfortable, as I was, feeling distinctly under-dressed, but Claude was in his element.

"Excuse me, Claude," I said, "but before we begin I hope you don't mind my asking – has anything arrived for me? From England?"

"I'm afraid not," Claude frowned. "Gordon?"

Gordon shook his head. I bit down my disappointment and smiled.

"That's all right, never mind," I said, and Stan placed a consoling hand on my arm.

Claude gave this a moment, and then got straight down to business. "Now then. We feel – do we not, Gordon? – that there is great potential in you boys."

Gordon wafted a hand in languid agreement, and Claude went on.

"The more so now that you have divested yourselves of that creature Hurley. A shame about his wife, she was an asset, but *he*..." Claude permitted himself a shudder that said more than words could have done, although I would've liked to hear the words if they were uncomplimentary about Edgar Hurley.

"As you know, we are coming up to summer, which is pretty much an off-season for small and medium time vaudeville. Some of the larger venues with the big headliners can keep going all year round, now some of them have these cooling fans that blow air over large blocks of ice."

"We've seen them, haven't we, Stan? At the new Pantages in Winnipeg?"

"That's right," Stan agreed. We neglected to mention that we had seen the cooling system close up, whilst shoving a couple of ripe dead cats and a distinctly late skunk in there to sabotage Alexander Pantages' big opening night on behalf of his rival John W. Considine – it might have made us sound a bit barmy.

"Just so. But for the smaller time, as I say, the theatres are mostly shutting down for the hotter months. Nobody wants to be sitting indoors in a crowd when the weather makes it so oppressive. So what we thought, Gordon and I, was that we should take advantage of this fallow period, as it were, to redesign your act and get it ready for a big new push in the fall. How would that be?"

"Thank you, Mr Bostock, Mr Bostock, that would be grand," Stan beamed.

"We shall subsidise your living expenses the while so that you will not be out of pocket."

"Very generous," I said.

"Oh, self-interest, I assure you, Mr Dandoe. We plan to make a lot of money out of you fellows! Eh, Gordon?"

Gordon gave a half-smile, and shot his cuffs.

"I think a four-hander is a fine way to showcase what you are capable of," Claude went on, "so we'd like to suggest... ah, here they are, right on cue. That's a good sign, isn't it?"

Claude got to his feet and beckoned over a couple who had just walked in.

"My dears! This way!" he called, and the newcomers came over. "Let me make some introductions. This is Stan Jefferson and Arthur Dandoe. Boys, meet Alice and Baldwin Cooke."

The Cookes, a married couple evidently, shook our hands eagerly. Alice was slender, and blonde, with bright eyes and a very open expression. Baldwin was a bundle of energy, with a great luxuriant shock of dark hair.

"Baldy!" he cried as he pumped my hand up and down.

"I beg your pardon?" I said.

"Baldy, everyone calls me Baldy. It's short for Baldwin, of course, but I've got lots of hair so it's also a gag. Geddit?"

"I surely do," I said. "It's a good 'un."

Claude made sure everyone was seated and had been furnished with a cup of tea, and then he pressed on with his proposition.

"Alice and Baldy here were also in a four which just split, weren't you? With your sister and her husband?"

"Least said about that the better, I think," Alice said, with a sidelong glance at us.

"Well, I give them the highest imaginable recommendation, and I am sure you will all get along handsomely."

"I'm sure," Stan said. "What should the act be?"

"Oh, there's no need to throw baby out with the bathwater," Claude said. "I should think a reworked version of what you were doing will do very nicely. After all," he said, turning to the Cookes, "Stan here is an absolute nonpareil as Chaplin, isn't he, Gordon?"

Gordon concurred by inclining his head.

I took a deep breath. After all, if I didn't say something right that minute the deal would be done, and I felt my mental well-being was on the line.

"Does it absolutely *have* to be a Charlie Chaplin act?" I ventured. "He's on the up now, but who knows how long it will last? And is he really as popular as all that? Really?"

Stan looked at me as though I'd gone mad. "Have you forgotten Luna Park already?" he said.

"No, but surely he's just a fad, a passing novelty. I mean, can we really set so much store by people being so very desperate to see him, him and only him?"

Claude looked at Gordon, who raised a hand and beckoned a beige-liveried page boy over. He gave the lad a dollar and a few whispered instructions, and sat back while the page trotted over to the hotel reception to collect a paddle, to which he attached a white card. He took a pen from the receptionist and wrote two words on this card, then he raised the paddle above his head, and began slowly pacing up and down the lobby.

"Paging Charlie Chaplin!" the boy called out. "Paging Mr Charlie Chaplin!"

"What the...?" I said, but Gordon held up a perfectly-manicured hand.

"Just wait a moment," he said.

We sat and watched the page boy walking up and down paging Charlie, and before very long a little crowd had gathered in the lobby to watch. It swelled, and grew, and built, until there were people hanging over the banister rails on the staircase to get a better view of the star's imminent appearance. Word had reached the street outside, and more and more people thronged in through the revolving door, until finally there was barely enough room for the page boy to walk up and down with his paddle, and he was getting jostled and bothered by those waiting.

"Paging Charlie Chaplin!" we could hear him calling plaintively, wondering how far this was going to go, but we could also hear: "Where is he?" and "Where's Charlie?" A mumbling grumbling that turned into a chant of "Char-lee! Char-lee! Char-lee!" and a stomping of feet, and a vigorous ringing of the reception bell. "Char-lee! Char-lee! Char-lee!" – and then there were policemen shouldering their way up to the desk to try and disperse the mob.

Gordon Bostock turned to me, and raised an eyebrow as if to ask: "Satisfied?"

"All right," I said. "A very fair point, well made."

———

Fortunately Stan and I hit it off with Alice and Baldy right away. We were able to rent a cottage for the summer in the Atlantic Highlands of New Jersey, a modest place with a path leading from the end of its garden down to a sandy beach, and the four of us felt like we were on holiday. Stan said he hadn't had a vacation

300

since he was a boy in Ulverston, and I couldn't remember my family ever taking more than a day trip to Southwold during the summer months.

We discovered a shared interest in drinking whisky, indeed I credit good old Baldy Cooke with being the main influence behind switching my lifelong preference from beer to the demon firewater. Perhaps not a good thing, I grant you, but I don't blame Baldy for that. Alice could take a deal more of the sauce than her husband, who was a quick and cheerful drunk, and she quickly earned the nickname 'The Bar Fly'.

Every day we would toss ideas around, and then maybe rehearse them up to see if they worked, and we would laugh and laugh until we were exhausted, and then gallop down to the sands and throw ourselves into the Atlantic breakers to wake ourselves up for the evening's drinking.

Alice would regale us with tales of her upbringing in the business. Her father, it turned out, was an entrepreneur of sorts, who had managed Buffalo Bill Cody and his world-famous Wild West Show, which she had seen many times as a child, including once on a triumphant trip to Paris.

"There seemed to be hundreds of people in it," she recalled. "Bareback-riding Indians circling covered wagons, and then soldiers riding to the rescue and massacring them all. They used to fling themselves from those horses, and you'd be sure they'd broken an arm or a leg or a neck, even, but then afterwards they'd be walking around as if nothing had occurred. It was quite a show."

Baldy, meanwhile, was an amiable fellow but seemed to have no particular comic talents. He was what we used to call 'a trier'. He'd give it everything, but he just didn't have the natural instincts of a comedian, although he desperately wanted to be one. Often in my career, when I was at my best, I would exercise what I called

The Power, a sort of serene, almost supernatural control onstage. Baldy, I thought sadly, would never have that peculiar thrill. Nonetheless, he was game for anything we asked him to do, and he was terrific company.

Then, one evening, we were throwing together a meal from some scraps and leftovers of previous evenings. Baldy was full of the joys, as usual, and suddenly began to sing, and a gorgeous baritone voice filled the cottage. Alice wandered through to listen, a proud smile on her face, and Stan came in from the garden where he had been drying off after a swim, a look of frankest astonishment on his. Then he grinned at me, and I knew exactly what he was thinking. It was: "We can use that!"

The skit we came up with during those blissful weeks was a variation on *The Nutty Burglars* scenario, which we called *Crazy Cracksmen*.

Alice played a famous singer and Baldy her accompanist and manager, which meant we could open with a song. She bemoans her inability to attract publicity, and they come up with an idea for a stunt, whereby she will be the victim of a fake burglary. Baldy goes off to hire someone to turn the place over, and meanwhile Stan and I, as Chaplin and Conklin playing 'Waffles & Co, Berglars' as before, would arrive to burgle the place for real. We would be puzzled, of course, that the owner of the place was so obliging, and we crammed in lots of gags as the three of us worked the set. There was a long sequence where we became entangled in flypaper, passing it from one to the other, and another bit where Stan would fall crazily off a high ladder, arms and legs akimbo, which brought the house down. Finally Baldy would reappear, dressed as a burglar, having failed to find anyone to play the part for him, and the piece would dissolve into a chase, and chaos, as Alice turned on us, and a cop, usually played by the stage manager, would chase us all off.

Trust me, it was an absolute riot.

The four of us, now billed as The Stan Jefferson Quartet, played a few weeks of warm-up engagements to prepare for the fall showing that the Bostocks had put us in for, at which a cluster of important bookers would run their eye over an evening's worth of aspiring turns. The act was coming together well, and we were in good shape, although it was a bit of a harum-scarum time.

Once we were crossing into Canada to play a week at St Thomas in Ontario, and we had four bottles of whisky hidden in our props trunk. This was contraband, of course, and there was a hairy moment when we reached the border, and a customs official demanded that we open up for inspection. He found the bottles quick smart, and called his colleague over.

"We are going to have to confiscate these," he said. "And there will be a fine to pay if you don't want to spend a week in jail."

We didn't want to, but the money the Bostocks were fronting us wouldn't stretch to a fine, so we were facing a pretty gloomy prospect when Baldy suddenly piped up.

"Confiscate them if you want," he said. "They're just prop bottles for a vaudeville act. They're full of cold tea."

For a long moment the customs men stared at the bottles, and it seemed certain that they would open one to check, but then they shrugged and handed them back.

"Huh, well in that case, on your way," the man said.

Afterwards we drank a happy toast to Baldy and his nerve, and he laughed: "Obviously when he said he would have to 'confiscate' the bottles what he meant was 'drink them with his pal'".

Another time, back in Troy, New York, we were out for a late snack – we couldn't afford a proper meal – at a favourite place of ours called the Hofbrau, when Stan caught sight of a familiar face across the marble-floored dining room.

"Bill!" he called. "Come and join us!"

It was Billie Ritchie, a wiry little Scotsman who had been a number one for Karno back at the Fun Factory. He'd played with Tilly in Mike Asher's burlesque of Karno's *Mumming Birds*, which had ended in tears when the Guv'nor had got wind of it and stomped onstage to take retribution with his fists.

"Hallo Stan!" Ritchie cried. "And Arthur too, how are ye doing, boys?"

"Not bad, not bad," I said. "This is Alice and Baldy Cooke. Meet our old friend Billie Ritchie."

"Baldy?" Billie said, squinting at the wavy head of hair before him.

"A joke," Baldy grinned.

"Aye, isn't it though?" Ritchie said, his hand creeping involuntarily to his own thinning thatch.

"Sit down, sit down! What'll you have?" Stan said, and the Cookes shot me a nervous glance. Until we played this fall showing for the Bostocks and picked up some decent bookings, we were living on the very edge of bankruptcy, and could hardly stretch to treating a guest. Billie didn't know this, though, and as a Scot he would never turn down a free dinner, so he briskly ordered up a club sandwich and a highball, then turned to me.

"How's that wee lass o' yours? She was quite a catch as I recall."

"Tilly?" I said. "She's in England, I'm afraid."

"Oh," Bill said, seeing he'd touched a sore point. "Bad luck, ol' son, bad luck."

Bill and Stan chattered away then, about the turn he was currently offering on the Keith time, and about Chaplin, naturally. Billie Ritchie had played the Drunken Swell in *Mumming Birds*, and he indignantly claimed that Charlie had made a fortune doing his act. He wasn't the first to think so, nor was he the last, and I was dying to put him straight by telling him how Chaplin had in fact appropriated my Stowaway when I felt Alice tugging subtly at my sleeve.

"Psst!" she said, and showed me under the table what she had in her handbag. It was a dime purse, a sort of mechanical contraption that she would put her dimes into as a way of making some small savings. The way it worked was that the mechanism wouldn't open up until there was five dollars saved up, but Alice was fretting about the upcoming bill and she whispered:

"There's more than four bucks in there if you can get it open."

I nudged Baldy, and between us we tried everything we could think of, pulling at the thing, tugging this way and that, jamming a fork into it, and then another, but it wouldn't give up the loot, until suddenly, with a great 'crack!', it finally yielded, and coins went skittering across the marble floor in every direction.

Stan realised immediately what had happened, and the four of us left Billie sitting there all by himself as his sandwich arrived, scrabbling around with our backsides in the air under tables and amongst other diners' feet, collecting up the dimes to pay for the damn'd thing.

Although we were poor we were happy, and we knew that in *Crazy Cracksmen* we had a hit.

We just needed the fall showing to go well to make it so.

34
THE FALL

OUR first inkling that there was trouble ahead came when we spoke to the props man.

Crazy Cracksmen required a good number of bits and pieces to make it go off well, and they were not all things we could cart around with us, so we relied on the props men at the theatres we played in to find the necessary items for us. We'd usually send a letter ahead, to give the fellow time to locate this and that, and so often we'd get a scowl upon our arrival, or some wheedling would begin as to why we wouldn't have what we needed. Stan and Baldy were particularly good at twisting these chaps around their little fingers.

"Do you really need all this stuff?" the harassed props man would moan, and Stan would grin.

"You know, we can go out and do our act on a bare stage, but all those props make our act what it should be."

And then Baldy would kid the guy: "Don't worry about it, we'll get along."

And somehow this good-natured geniality would always strike a chord, and we'd always get everything we wanted. There was quite a list, too, it ran to a couple of pages – furniture, ladders, a working safe, a piano.

The showing that the Bostocks had put us in for was to be quite a gala evening. Ordinarily all the working turns would expect to play two, three, or even four houses in a day, but this event was just a single bill that was due to run twice as long as a normal one. In the audience, Claude said, we were expecting bookers from the Keith circuit, the Poli time, the Orpheums, from Loew and Pantages, Proctor's and the Fox, so there was plenty of work up for grabs.

We arrived at the venue, the new Loew's in the Bronx, and Stan and Baldy headed off to soften up the props guy. They returned almost immediately, wearing puzzled frowns.

"What's up?" I asked.

"The fellow said there was no problem," Stan said.

"That's good, isn't it?" I said

"Because another act sent him virtually the same list, item for item."

"What? What other act?"

"Don't know," Stan said, thoughtfully. "Don't know."

———

Claude and Gordon Bostock arrived before the evening's performances got under way, and came to the dressing room to let us know the state of play.

"All set?" Claude beamed. He was very sharply dressed, as was his brother. They looked prosperous and confident – in short, exactly the sort of fellows you wanted on your side.

We nodded and grinned.

"We are really looking forward to *Crazy Cracksmen*, aren't we, Gordon?"

"We are," Gordon agreed.

"We have secured you a good slot in the running order," Claude went on. "Leaving nothing to chance, you know? So you will be on in the second half, shortly after the interval. Everyone should be refreshed, not anxious to get a drink or use the facilities, and boredom should not have set in. Or at least, if it has, you will be able to snap them out of it, what?"

"Exactly," I said. "Thank you, Claude."

"We have been buttering up the booker from the Fox circuit," Claude said. "And, you know, he's very interested. *Very* interested!"

We looked at one another, excitement and confidence building. Gordon Bostock pushed away from the door jamb where he had been leaning nonchalantly, and Claude noticed this and began to take his leave.

"So do your stuff, and break your legs!"

"Just one thing," Stan said.

Claude turned. "Yes?"

"Is there another burglar skit on the bill, do you know?"

"Another...? Another burglar skit?" Claude looked at Gordon, who gave a small frown and shake of the head. "Well, I... um... let's see..."

The brothers began to pore over a sheet listing the various turns that were due to make an appearance.

"I can't tell... wait! What's this?" Gordon had pointed out a listing, and Claude squinted at it more closely. "The Keystone Trio?"

"The Keystone Trio? Who the hell are they?" I said.

"Take a wild guess, Dandoe," said a voice from the doorway. We all turned, and there, large as life and half again as unpleasant, was Edgar Hurley. To make matters worse, he was dressed as Charlie Chaplin.

"You?" I said, stunned by this development.

"Yes, me. Me and Ted Banks and Wren. We are going on midway through the first half, so by the time you lot come on after the interval you will look like so much old hat. Second-hand news!" Hurley chuckled gleefully.

"But...?!" Stan spluttered, looking to the Bostocks, but they were just as dumbfounded as we were.

"That's if you get to go on at all, of course."

"What do you mean?" I said.

"It all depends on whether my lawyer gets down here in time to stop you."

"What?!"

"Yes, you see, after our parting of the ways, I took the precaution of protecting my investment of several months industry by taking out a copyright on *The Nutty Burglars* - you didn't get round to doing that, did you?"

"You... copyrighted *The Nutty Burglars?*" Stan said. "How? You didn't write it? You haven't any rights to it at all."

"Interestingly," Hurley replied with exasperating smugness, "my lawyer didn't see it that way. And if you are planning to perform anything remotely resembling our copyrighted material on the stage tonight, well, he is going to take a dim view, let me tell you that."

"Can he?" Stan said to Claude. "Can he do that? It's just... well, it's theft, pure and simple!"

"I'll have to look into it," Claude said, but his face was troubled. "Come, Gordon."

The Bostocks left in a hurry, and Hurley smirked. "Whether you perform tonight or not is actually neither here nor there. I will certainly sue to prevent you from taking bookings that should by rights be mine." Having delivered his threat, he beamed and gave a little bow. "I wish you a good evening," he said, "however you choose to spend it!"

Hurley left the dressing room, and appalled silence reigned for a minute or two. Then Alice piped up.

"What does this mean?" she said.

Stan shook his head, as though trying to clear it of an unpleasant dream. "I'm not sure," he said.

"Is... *Crazy Cracksmen* very like *The Nutty Burglars?*" Baldy asked.

"It's not the same," I said.

"But close enough," Stan said, miserably. "Close enough for it to take a while to prove anything either way."

"But...!" I said, banging my fist on a table. "That miserable bastard! There must be something we can do!"

"I'm not sure there's anything," Stan said, hollowly. "At least not today."

Baldy walked over to our own props and costumes trunk and lifted the lid. "Here," he said, handing me a bottle of whisky. "Since we're not playing, how about some cold tea from Bonnie Scotland?"

I took the bottle from him and pulled the cork out with my teeth. "Good thinking," I said. "Very sound."

Just then Claude Bostock reappeared in the doorway. "Oh Arthur?" he said. "I almost forgot. This arrived for you, from England."

He handed an envelope across to me, and I grabbed it eagerly and tore it open. I blinked at the contents, momentarily taken aback, for it was not from Tilly but from my father in Cambridge. I couldn't remember him ever writing to me before, but his cursive script was familiar from numerous college notices alerting hapless students to the many ways in which they were disappointing him, the Head Porter.

310

'Dear Arthur,' he wrote.

'I am delighted to hear that you were not on board the RMS Lusitania when it sank. However, I had no thought that you might be, so your concern, while welcome, is misplaced. I am also, by the way, delighted that you are not in Flanders, or climbing Krakatoa, or juggling with explosives. Your mother and Lance send their best wishes, as do I.'

This was unusually droll stuff for my father, and made me wonder what he would have made of the climax to *The Nutty Burglars* – not that he ever visited the halls or anything as common as that.

Once I had got over my surprise and pleasure at hearing from the old fellow, I began to brood on Tilly, and why I had still not heard from her. I had sent a letter to her at the very same time, and by the very same post, as the one I had written to my father, so logically she must have received it, I thought. And yet she had not replied.

Was I being punished for my thoughtlessness? Had she simply moved on with her life? Without me...?

━━━━━

By the time the evening's entertainment got under way, Baldy and I had killed that bottle and moved onto a second one. Brooding on Tilly and the business with Hurley had sent me into a dark and dangerous mood, which the firewater was fuelling nicely.

"I suppose we should go up and see The Keystone Trio," Stan said mournfully. "See exactly what we're dealing with."

"Hurley won't have changed it," I growled. "He hasn't the wit."

Nonetheless I followed Stan up to the wings, where I found

Wren standing ready in her Mabel Normand get up. Hurley was on the other side of the stage, luckily for him.

"Hullo Arthur," Wren whispered. "This is an odd pickle, isn't it?"

"An odd pickle? Is that what you think it is?" I said, too loud, and she put her finger to my lips.

"Go back down, Arthur," she breathed. "It's not good for you to be here."

She turned to glance across at her husband, and as she did so her Mabel Normand curls whisked to one side, and I got a clear view of her profile. She had used a lot of make-up, that much was obvious. What was equally plain was that she had been trying, not altogether successfully, to conceal yet another black eye.

"Has he hit you?" I said, again too loudly. "He has, hasn't he?"

"Ssshhh!" Wren hissed, steering me to the top of the stairs. "Go down, Arthur, and mind your business!"

Just then the achingly familiar signature music for *The Nutty Burglars* struck up, and she whisked herself away with a muttered curse at me for distracting her.

I wandered back into the wings and watched as Hurley waddled his poor man's Chaplin walk out into the light. He turned and saw me standing there, looking at him, and he took the time, even as he was just beginning a routine on an important night, to shoot me a look of such insufferable smug triumph, that...

Something snapped.

A red mist descended.

I stepped out onto the stage, seeing that look wipe itself from Hurley's face as quickly as it had appeared, seeing it replaced by disbelief, by anger, and then by fear...

And the next thing I knew I was sitting in a cell in the 43rd Precinct police station, looking down at my bruised and bloodied knuckles, trying to remember what had happened.

Stan came to visit me in the morning. The cops let him into the holding cell where I was being kept, and he sat on the bed beside me. The two of us looked at the cracked concrete floor.

"I'm sorry, Stan. I let you down."

"The Bostocks say they can put us into a second showcase next month," Stan said.

"That's good."

"But..."

"But?"

"They say that the act is unbookable with you still in it. The bookers all saw what you did, they don't want any part of it. Of you."

"So, what? I'm out?"

Stan looked at the floor.

"That's it, isn't it? I'm out."

"I thought I should be the one to tell you. We've been through a lot together, you and I."

"We have that."

I sat there contemplating the end of my vaudeville career, the end of my working partnership with Stan, the end of my future. It resolutely refused to sink in.

"You'll carry on? With Alice and Baldy?"

"The Stan Jefferson Three," Stan nodded.

"Well. It's not as though Charlie ever works with Chester Conklin any more. You probably won't even miss me."

Stan sighed, shook his head sadly.

"But will you even be able to play *Crazy Cracksmen* again? With all that Hurley nonsense?"

"Yes, that all got sorted out last night."

"Oh?"

"Claude brought along a lawyer who made it clear to Ed that he had no business copyrighting something that he had had no part in creating. Actually he was breaking the law, interestingly enough."

"Ha! So, he's all right, then?"

"Well, he's not winning any beauty contests in the near future, but he's up and about, yes."

"What's going to happen to him?"

"Nothing, actually."

"Nothing?"

"The Bostocks agreed not to pursue him for passing off and fraudulent misuse of our material, in exchange for him not pressing charges against you."

"I see."

"The cops'll let you go later today, when they think you've had enough time to think about what you did. And sober up a bit, I guess."

"Hmmm."

"What will you do?"

"I don't know, yet. This has only just happened. It's still happening, technically."

"Of course."

Stan slapped his thighs and got to his feet. "I'd better go. We have a half-week upstate, sudden cancellation, you know?"

"Yes," I said. We stood facing one another for a long moment, two awkward English gentleman faced with an overload of emotional baggage. Then we hugged.

"We'll see each other again," Stan said, a lump in his throat.

"Soon," I agreed.

"Well... good luck." He turned to bang on the door to be let out.

"Stan?" I said. "There's something I've been wanting to tell you."

"Really?"

"When Mack Sennett saw Charlie playing the Drunk in New York, and decided he would offer him a job if ever he started his own comedy film company..."

"What about it?"

"The night he saw... was the night Charlie took a night off and you took his place."

"The night...?"

"It should have been you, Stan. It should have been you."

"Aha," Stan said, taking this in. "You know, I always thought you thought it should have been you."

"Well..."

"And you thought it would be a good idea to tell me this now because...?"

"I just wanted to get it off my chest."

"Thanks. Thank you very much."

"Don't mention it."

"I wish you hadn't."

A weary New York cop opened the door then and Stan walked out into the corridor.

"Good luck!" I called as the door banged shut again behind him.

I sat back down on the bed and contemplated a wholly uncertain future. Nothing to do, nowhere to go, and no-one to go there and do it with.

What on Earth was I supposed to do next?

35
WILD WEST BILLY

A bell was ringing as the train pulled into the station, and I felt a surge of excitement in the pit of my stomach.

The history of this place was made up of the vivid images imprinted in my mind by the lurid literature I enjoyed as a boy. Wagon trains, Indians, cavalry, buffalo, Texas Longhorns, and rustlers.

Where the Chisholm cattle trail up from Texas met the Atchison, Topeka and Santa Fe railroad heading East and West.

Where wild and raucous cowboys came to carouse and spend their hard-earned cash.

Where gunslingers who'd met their match lay mouldering on Boot Hill.

Dodge City.

When I'd emerged, blinking, from the 43rd Precinct police station I felt lost, adrift. Stan and I had spent the last few years living in one another's pockets, and I already missed his easy company, his infectious laugh, his generous spirit. He would get along fine with Alice and Baldy, I knew that, and I cursed myself for messing things up so badly.

I had a curse or two for blasted Edgar Hurley too, and his damnably attractive wife. And, as ever, I cursed Charlie Chaplin. Chaplin who had sent Tilly away from me, Tilly and my boy, and now it seemed they wanted no more to do with me. I had written God knows how many letters across the summer, and had not had a single reply, not a one. What more could I do?

I saw another of those damnable life-size cut-outs of Charlie waving at me across the street, and suddenly I knew I had to get out of the city, get away altogether, put New York, and Stan, and the Hurleys behind me, and Tilly and little Wallace too.

I suddenly remembered how excited I had been to come to America in the first place, stoked up by all the penny bloods I had read as a boy, and I had it, a plan of action.

I resolved to head way out West.

———

So I stepped off the train into the baking Kansas sun, strolled through the railway station, which was more substantial than I'd been expecting, and set about orienting myself. I knew that when Wyatt Earp and Bat Masterson had established law 'n' order in Dodge, guns were banned to the North side of the railway tracks, while to the South, along the notorious Front Street, anything went.

I headed South.

I was expecting to see wooden frame buildings and sod houses, boardwalks to keep the pedestrian traffic above the streets of baked mud, rails for cowboys to hang the reins of their trusty

317

steeds while they drink and gamble, wooden frontages, gun shops, ammo stores, saloons and whisky houses.

Maybe a barber's shop, too, a general merchandise store run by a man in a leather apron who has seen it all before, and seed stores for the sodbusters, despised by the ranchers because they settle the land and cut them off from the river. There should be a blacksmith's alongside the stables, with a sheriff's office and a calaboose for the town drunk to spend the night in while he dries out.

Instead I found myself confronted by rather stately stone buildings, reds and greys. A court house with ornamental pillars, a two-storey bargain store with plate glass display windows, and a wide main street with automobiles easing sedately along. The skyline was criss-crossed by telegraph wires, and everything about the place seemed to be trying to live down its colourful history. If a place could be said to be aggressively civilised, then it was Dodge City in 1915.

Of course, as soon as I saw it I felt a little foolish. It was always going to be this way, nothing stayed the same. The Old West was dead, throttled into irrelevance by progress, and good old vaudeville, I suddenly saw in a flash, was heading the same way.

Then, up ahead, I saw a name that took me back to the thrilling landscapes of my penny bloods. The Long Branch Saloon. Careful not to look at someone for too long in that place, unless'n you were 'lookin' fer ter get drilled', of course.

"Why not get myself a glass or two of ol' red eye, while I work out what in tarnation to do next?" I thought to myself, and I moseyed on down for a look-see.

Well, this was more like it. Steer horns on the front, a stretch of wooden boardwalk outside, a rail for tying up your horse – which a greengrocer's van pootled past – and an old timer sitting outside spitting chawing 'baccy into a spittoon. I pushed through the half-sized swinging saloon doors and strode up to the bar.

There wasn't a pianola playing, and it didn't stop when I walked in. There were a few solitary customers, none playing cards or calling one another lying Yankee dawgs, and none of them gave me a second glance.

"Bartender? Whisky," I growled. An old fellow in a white apron poured me a small glass, but he didn't slide it along the bar to me, nor did he offer to leave the bottle.

I downed the drink and turned to look around. "So this is the ol' Long Branch saloon, eh? Well, well, well."

"Not really," the old bartender said. "That burned down back in '85, along with most of the old wooden Front Street. The town tried to reinvent itself after that, and they don't really like it that this saloon even exists, but sometimes people come here just to get a taste of what it used to be like in this town, so we do steady business."

I nodded, as the last wisps of steam escaped from my excitement at being there, and turned to look out of the window. Just then I heard the faint tinkling of spurs as someone with a slow, deliberate gait and hard-heeled boots strolled along the boardwalk outside.

As I watched, an apparition passed slowly across the frontage. He was a cowboy from top to bottom, from his ten gallon hat to his leather chaps, from the twin gun belts slung criss-cross around his waist, to the bootlace tie with a silver steer's head clasp. He had a snow-white walrus moustache curling down from his top lip, and he was as bow-legged as you might expect a man to be after a lifetime on horseback.

"Who's that?" I hissed to the barman.

"That?" he said. "That's Wild West Billy."

319

"Wild West Billy?"

"He's lived here for fifty year, seen it all and done most of it himself, if you believe the tales he tells – which I don't, pertickerly, but still."

I slammed my shot glass down on the bar and pushed out through the swing doors, which rocked back and forward in my wake.

The elderly cowboy was walking on down Front Street, taking his own sweet time, and I followed, just to see where a man like that might be going, keeping what I thought was a respectful distance between us. He turned a corner, and then sauntered casually out into the middle of a side street, where he suddenly stopped dead in his tracks. I stopped too, wondering what he was doing.

The old geezer turned his head slowly and launched a mighty spit into the dust.

"Sump'n I can do fer you, sonny?" he said, without turning round. I saw his hands hanging loosely by his sides, ready to snatch up the pearl-handled pistols from his holsters.

"Christ!" I gasped. "No, I'm sorry, I didn't mean…!"

"Just a-lookin', is that it?"

"Yes, exactly. Just looking."

Wild West Billy turned slowly to face me, and launched another mighty spit.

"You prolly wouldn't know this, bein' from out of town, but if you want to be lookin' at me, it'll cost yer."

He took a pearl-handled revolver from its holster and pointed it at me, at my guts. The air of calculating menace was palpable, and I felt my bowels loosening as I shot my hands straight up in the air.

"Please!" I yelped. "I'm unarmed!"

"I see that," the old gunfighter drawled. Then, with a twitch

320

of his gun, he indicated that I should walk in front of him, and I saw no good reason just then to disobey.

Along the street I stumbled, my hands in the air, at this old codger's mercy. He wouldn't really shoot me in the back, would he? Just for having the temerity to watch him walking along? I didn't know, because I couldn't tell for sure whether this old codger was playing with a full deck. Why was nobody doing anything? My eyes darted from side to side, but there was not another soul in sight.

Finally I heard the oddly menacing jangling of his ancient spurs come to halt, and his rasping voice saying, "That's far enough."

I closed my eyes, wondering if the next instant would bring a sudden burning pain between my shoulder blades, and a mouthful of dirt.

"Turn around, sonny," the old man said, with another horribly fluid spit.

I turned to face him, and his gun twitched once, twice, suggesting – no, *insisting* – that I move to my right, and keep walking. This I did, looking up to find myself outside a familiar type of establishment styling itself Dodge City Varieties. I kept walking until I could go no further, finding myself at a box office window. The old cowboy came close then, and leaned in front of me to speak to the woman in attendance.

"This here son of a sodbuster would like a ticket fer tonight's performance," he drawled. "Give the lady two bits."

"Oh Billy!" the woman said, with a long-suffering sigh as she passed me a ticket in exchange for my coins. "You know Mr Makepeace told you not to bring people here at gunpoint."

Wild West Billy looked at me then, smiled an evil smile, and winked. "See you tonight, son, an' you can look at me all you want, since we've got yer money."

Once my heart stopped racing, and I was alone again on the street outside, I saw the bill matter for that evening's vaudeville, and Wild West Billy was indeed the headliner – 'Guts, Gore and Gunplay!'

I thought to myself that I might as well go along, as I had a ticket after all, but first I needed a drink.

———

As someone who has enjoyed and endured music hall and vaudeville on both sides of the Atlantic I can tell you that Dodge City Varieties was not the absolute apex. The theatre was stuffy and dilapidated, and that description would also fit the majority of the acts on the bill.

One of them, if you can believe this, was called The Musical Cow Milkers, and in fairness to them, they weren't trying to pull a fast one of any kind. A husband and wife brought a cow onto the stage, an honest-to-goodness cow, and then proceeded to milk it while singing a handful of intermittently harmonious duets together. The cow didn't deign to join in and make it a trio – like the rest of us, it looked on with a faintly glazed expression, waiting for it all to be over.

Wild West Billy sauntered out onto the stage in the prime spot, midway through the second half of proceedings. He stood at the front of the apron over to one side, stuck his thumbs into his gunbelt, and regarded us all with a cool gaze that seemed to take our measure and not be particularly impressed with it.

"I ain't much of a one fer talking," he drawled, managing to imply that all of us talked all the time, that was all we did, and he couldn't be doing with it. "I'm a man of action..."

"You're a low-down Yankee liar, that's what you are!" came

a cry, and out onto the stage from the opposite wing stepped a lethal-looking gunfighter dressed all in black, from his hat to his boots. Wild West Billy turned to face his antagonist and settled himself, his hands relaxed, hanging by his sides.

"Prove it," he said, and the whole audience held its breath.

They held the moment for agonising second after agonising second, then the black-clad gunfighter twitched his gun from its holster, and Wild West Billy responded like a rattlesnake. The two guns went off with a noise that made the whole audience flinch, and the black gunfighter was flying backwards, a mist of blood exploding from his chest.

Wild West Billy held his pose, and then with a twirl forwards and backwards, he tricked his pistol back into its holster, and all was calm. I found myself clicking my jaw from side to side, trying to ease my hearing back to normal.

Two stage hands trotted on and carted the ancient cowboy's rival off into the wings, which I thought was a nice touch. We all knew it was a trick, of course, an effect – it wasn't as if they could fire live rounds at one another every night, and he surely didn't have an inexhaustible supply of sidekicks – but it was very well done.

"That sort of scene was commonplace on Front Street when Dodge City was in its prime," Wild West Billy drawled, and curtains drew back to reveal a backdrop of the town's main drag in its cattle drive heyday. I saw the old cowboy's shoulders sag a little when he saw it, and I could tell he wasn't happy about the tatty painted cloth, which had definitely seen better days, and all of them a good number of years ago.

The old fellow ploughed on through a history of the town, from the early days when buffalo hunters would pile their hides as high as a house, to the coming of the railroad which made the town a pivotal destination for the cattle drives up from Texas.

I learned that railwaymen took their red caboose lanterns with them when visiting what you might call the town's 'soiled doves', hence the term 'red light district'. And we heard how Billy himself had helped Wyatt Earp, Bat Masterson and the posse of lawmen known as the Dodge City Peace Commission clean up the North Side. It could have been true, who could tell? He was certainly old enough.

There was an exhibition of extremely loud sharpshooting, which saw the spectacular demise of a certain amount of crockery, and a good deal of nervousness in the audience around me about the possibility of ricochets, and then a finale featuring another lightning-fast gun duel with another gunfighter who looked suspiciously like the first one, in a different hat.

All in all, not a bad act at all. If only the painted backdrops had been up to the same standard – there were six, each one shabbier than the one before it.

Later I sat in the Long Branch saloon contemplating a glass of sipping whisky, when a copious gobbet of something unpleasant pinged the spittoon near my feet. I looked around and there was Wild West Billy himself. He leaned on the bar beside me and ordered himself a drink by very slightly inclining his head in the general direction of Al the bartender.

"So?" he said. "Enjoy the show?"

"I did," I said. "You are clearly very skilled with your weapon."

The old cowboy snorted some of his drink back into his glass at that and began to laugh. "Ha! Skilled with ma weapon! I like that! You like that, Al? Ha ha!"

Just then a portly busybody in a three-piece suit came in

through the swing doors and waddled over to my ancient companion.

"Billy, there you are, I might have known!" he said, taking out his pocket watch and tapping it accusingly with his forefinger. "I told you no drinking between shows."

"An' I told *you* I needed a new cloth, so where is it?" the old man said, turning slowly to look dangerously at the newcomer.

"This again? I told you I can't afford to send it to Houston, and if you want it you can pay for it yourself! Now off with you, go on!"

Wild West Billy grumbled to himself, and then he walked off in his own good time, spurs jingle-jangling as he went. The portly gent heaved a long-suffering sigh, and checked his pocket watch once again, before beckoning the bartender over. He saw me watching him and smiled.

"Do as I do, not as I say, eh?" he said as his glass was filled.

"You're the manager of the Varieties?" I hazarded.

"Martin Makepeace, at your service, sir."

"I heard old Wild West Billy complaining about his cloth. Do I take it he's referring to the painted backdrops he uses?"

"He's always giving me grief about that. He uses half a dozen different scenes, and they are getting a bit tatty."

"I have some experience of this kind of work," I said. I had, as well, having painted backdrops for Karno's *Football Match* sketch back in England, not to mention a stint as a screever in Trafalgar Square, doing music hall scenes in chalk for pennies. I wasn't bad, if I say so myself. "Maybe I can do you a good turn."

"Oh?" Makepeace said, sensing a bargain.

Before I really even realised it, I'd been there for a couple of months. Makepeace gave me a trial job at the Varieties repainting one of Wild West Billy's backdrops, the one of old Front Street. Both he and the old gunslinger were so pleased with my handiwork that they hired me to spruce up all the others as well, splitting the cost between them.

After that Makepeace employed me to refurbish their stock of generic sheets, such as the cowshed backdrop used by the strange Musical Cow Milkers, and it seemed I had fallen headlong into a nice little bit of steady work.

I spent quite a bit of time with Wild West Billy, who called me 'Junior', and I even began to help him out onstage. His assistant lit out without warning one day, never to be seen or heard from again, and I was happy enough to don the black hat and blood bag and let him shoot me down. He was always firing blanks, of course, and when he needed to smash some plates or plug some tin cans to convince the audience he was using real bullets, there were little charges attached to these key target objects which I learned to set off to sell the illusion that he was an expert quick draw artist.

I was content there as the winter came on, living in an old-style room with a fireplace and a big brass bedstead above the Long Branch, until two things happened to darken my mood considerably.

The first was the arrival of a sight-seer from England. He stepped off the train in very much the same spirit as I had myself, hoping to find the spirit of the Old West still thriving, having given himself a few hours to look around between trains. He left with a disappointed shrug shortly after, heading for the West Coast, leaving behind a newspaper from England, a copy of *The Times* of London, no less.

Well, I snatched this up, naturally, and began to read of the horrifying carnage in Flanders, and in the Dardanelles at a place called Gallipoli. Several of the inside pages were taken up by lists of officers and men who had been killed in action, and I couldn't help reading through these. It seemed like the least I could do to pay my respects to the fallen, while I was faffing about thousands of miles away acting out old gun battles with blanks.

With a shock that chilled my blood, my eye caught on one name in particular.

Frederick Karno Junior.

Killed in Action.

Gallipoli Campaign.

I couldn't think, couldn't take it in, except to wonder crazily, irrelevantly, why he had enlisted using his stage name, rather than his own and his father's real name, which was Westcott.

Freddie. Dear, jolly, generous Freddie. Alongside Stan, my best friend in the world. Gone.

I sat in the saloon bar of the Long Branch, the newspaper spread out on the table before me, and I wept.

The line that kept echoing in my grief-stricken mind was one I had heard many times before, whenever I contemplated the different paths Chaplin and I had taken since we started out together. Just now, though, I was thinking about Charlie giving money to Tilly to go back to England, and Freddie going with her in my place, and the old, old refrain went round and round my head.

It should have been me.

It should have been *me*...

The second thing that happened to blacken my mood?

We'll come to that.

36
WITH HIS BOOTS ON

THE next few days passed in what I can only describe as an alcoholic haze. I spent all my time propping up the bar of the Long Branch, except when old Wild West Billy came to turf me out so he could take his blank pot-shots at me onstage pretending to be Doc Holliday or Wild Bill Hickok.

Memories of good old Fred churned around in my whisky-soaked brain. I remembered how he'd taken a shine to Tilly, but just too late. How she'd deflected him by telling him we were married, and how he'd arranged, all unknowing, for us to share married quarters on tour for a few blissful weeks.

I wondered if Tilly knew. She would be devastated. So would Stan. And what about the Guv'nor? I even found myself feeling sorry for that old swine. Losing a son, what a terrible, terrible thing.

Chaplin, as ever, was uppermost in my thoughts too, and I just couldn't shake the notion that poor Freddie had merely suffered the fate that Charlie had intended for me.

The one consolation, if consolation it was, was that I wasn't having my nose rubbed in Chaplin's success at every turn, as

Dodge City seemed mercifully unaffected by the Chaplinoia or the Chaplinitis, whichever it was.

Until, that is, Makepeace came to me on the Monday and said that a new act was arriving on the train from Topeka, and would I go and meet them on his behalf, bring them over to the Varieties? I think he was trying to get me out into the open air as much as anything, to separate me from the whisky for an hour or two.

I traipsed dutifully up to the railroad station, noticing only when I was startled by the horn of a delivery van that I was stumbling up the middle of the street.

The bell was clanging to announce the arrival of the westbound locomotive, and as I lurched onto the platform the passengers were already climbing down the little hinged stepladders and dodging the occasional spurt of steam.

I looked up and down, trying to spot the vaudevillians, not usually the most difficult of tasks. As a breed they were fond of drawing attention to themselves. I smirked to myself as I imagined a rival turn to the Musical Cow Milkers, helping their co-star down the little steps.

That smirk froze on my face, though, when through a cloud of piston steam I saw an all-too-familiar figure.

The derby.

The cane.

The big shoes.

The trademark splay-footed waddle.

I thought to myself that I had just had too much of the sauce. If I'd had a bottle in my hand I would have looked accusingly at it and then tossed it away. I blinked hard, once, twice, hoping the apparition would go away, but it did not, it kept coming, silhouetted tauntingly against the white steam.

"No-o-o!" I wailed. "Not you!"

The figure stopped. "No-o-o!" it echoed. "What the hell are *you* doing here?!"

"I... I...!" I spluttered, feeling like my moorings were coming loose and I was going to float away.

"Arthur? Arthur Dandoe?!" said a woman's voice, and I glanced over the tormenting figure's shoulder to see Wren Hurley, carrying two carpet bags. Behind her I then spotted Ted Banks toting a trunk. I looked back at the supposed Tramp himself, and my blurred vision cleared like the steam from the train. It was Edgar Hurley, of course. Edgar blasted Hurley!

"What?" was the only word I could manage.

"Arthur! What a lovely surprise!" Wren said, dropping her bags and embracing me.

"Are you for the Dodge City Varieties, by any chance?" I said, the full horror dawning.

"Why yes. How do you...?"

"I am to bring you there."

Without further pleasantries, I picked up Wren's bags and led the way. Edgar followed with Ted, just far enough behind that he would not have to engage in conversation.

"Wren?" I hissed. "Why is the fool dressed up as Charlie Chaplin?"

"Oh, he does that all the time now. For the publicity, you see? He thinks it brings more people into the theatre if they see him around town, and God knows we've needed it, some of the places we've been playing."

"Not going too well?"

Wren sighed. "After the gala evening, when you... well, *you* know what happened. We had bookings as The Keystone Trio, but once theatres realised we didn't have Stan, they all evaporated. Some of them got quite nasty, so we had to stop using the name."

"What are you now?"

"We go by Hurley, Ted and Wren."

"How did I miss that?!" I laughed. I presumed it was because of the drinking, and in truth I hadn't really been paying that much attention to my surroundings for a good few days. When I saw the billing later, however, they were listed as Early, Todd and Rena, which explained things.

"Now, you are going to behave, aren't you?" Wren said.

"Don't tell me," I muttered. "Tell *him*..."

There were no shows that evening, and I managed to avoid Ed Hurley and co., even though the three of them were comfortably installed in rooms at the Long Branch just along the corridor from my own, by virtue of avoiding the theatre and avoidjing the bar. My friend Al, the bartender, slipped me a bottle of sipping bourbon and I nursed it on my own, sitting at my window watching the night fall on the prairie, listening to the distant coyotes howling.

At some point in the middle of the night, I was woken by a soft tapping on my bedroom door. I uncurled myself somewhat painfully from the snoozing position I had found in the wooden rocking chair by my window and padded over to the door in my stockinged feet.

Outside in the corridor there was Wren Hurley. I should have known. She wore a long white nightdress, and her luxuriant dark brown hair was loose and tumbling around her shoulders. I peered out at her, slowed by the bourbon, and she gave me a lascivious smile that I felt in my groin and my curling toes.

"Now, when I asked if you were going to behave..." she said, placing a hand on my chest and pushing me back into the room...

The argument, when it came, flared up quickly.

We were in the saloon. I was at the bar with Wild West Billy and Makepeace. Hurley, Wren and Ted Banks were sitting at a table nearby. Wren and Ted had changed into their normal clothes, but Hurley was still sporting his Chaplin get up from the evening's performances.

I was explaining to Billy and Makepeace exactly what my beef was with Hurley – the professional part of it, anyway.

"I used to play the Chester Conklin part," I said, "and my friend Stan was Chaplin. Tilly, the best girl in the world, was Mabel, and the policeman was my pal Fred." I got a lump in my throat then and reached for a drink.

"Never mind anything he tells you, it's all above board and legit!" Hurley called out.

"What do you think you are doing, going around dressed as Charlie Chaplin the whole time, anyway?" I snarled back. "It's deranged!"

"At least I have an act," Hurley spat back. "What are *you* doing? Pretending to be shot by an aged gunslinger? Very dignified!"

"You have an act because you stole it!" I shouted, and my stool went flying as I leapt to my feet. "You copyrighted work that did not belong to you, work that we came up with. Me and Stan, and Tilly and poor Freddie, God rest his soul!"

"That point is moot," Hurley said pompously.

"Moot?" I yelled. "What does *that* mean? Just having the nerve to pass that sketch off as your own is like trampling on his grave!"

"All's fair in love and war," Hurley said.

"Oh, and this is war, then, is it? Because it certainly isn't the other thing!"

Wren fluttered her eyelashes at me then, for goodness sake, and Hurley became enraged.

"What do you know of love or anything else?" he screamed, losing his temper completely. "You're just an animal! You rut where you please and you argue with your fists!"

"Any time you like!" I said, squaring up to him. I didn't throw a punch, though, because Wild West Billy had hold of my arms from behind, and Makepeace was interposing himself between myself and Hurley.

"That's enough, boys, now come on," Makepeace was saying, and Wren too was trying to calm her husband down.

"What you fellas should do in a case like this," Wild West Billy said. "Is settle it like men."

"What?" I said. "What do you mean?"

"Settle it Dodge-style, out there on Front Street, crack o' dawn."

"What?" I said again. "With guns? Really?"

"Hey!" Makepeace called out. "That's not a bad idea, you know?"

"See?" Wild West Billy said, aiming a spit at the spittoon.

"We stage a gunfight, in the street there. I'll get the man from the *Daily Globe* to come out with a photographer, we put on a bit of a show for the folks, an' it'll be a great bit of publicity for the Varieties!"

"Long Branch saloon in the background of the pictures!" Al the bartender sang out.

"Of course, why not," Makepeace said, his eyes bright with enthusiasm for the notion.

"I don't know," I said, and I think principally because I didn't seem keen, Ed was suddenly like mustard.

"I'm up for it, sure," he said. "Let's settle our differences Dodge-style."

I'm not altogether sure how word got out all over town, but as the sun rose at the far end of Front Street, there were dozens of locals already lining the sidewalks either side of the broad thoroughfare. Any automobiles had been trundled out of sight so as not to ruin the pictures, and I fancy the proud owners were probably worried about them getting dinged. Precious little chance of that, of course, unless someone had taken it upon themselves to plant the little explosive charges we used at the Varieties to make it look like old Wild West Billy was using real live rounds.

A thought occurred to me then as the old codger buckled a gun belt around my waist.

"Hey Billy," I said. "These are just the guns from the act, right?"

"Yeah, sure," he drawled. "Sure, that's right." Then he slapped a black Stetson onto my head, the one I wore every time I lost a quick draw contest to him in his act.

"Oh," I said, "I see. I'm the bad guy?"

"You've got the bad guy's hat," Billy said laconically.

"And the bad guy always loses."

"Let's see."

"Eh?"

"Let's see how it plays out," Billy said, enigmatically, spitting into the spittoon – spit-tang!

The old cowboy then waddled a few bow-legged steps over to where Chaplin – I mean, Hurley – was rehearsing a bit of business in which the gun was preternaturally heavy and he couldn't get it into the holster on his belt, even using both hands. Billy offered my opponent a white Stetson, but Hurley waved it away impatiently, indicating the trademark derby on his head. Wild West Billy sauntered back and said out of the side of his mouth.

"I knew some boys back in the day who'd shoot a plug hat like that clean off your head soon as you stepped out'n the door!"

It occurred to me then that I had forgotten the blood bag, but I wasn't going to go back for it, and in any case I didn't want to give Hurley the satisfaction. Makepeace bustled over, excited by the turnout, and rubbing his hands together at the thought of the boost in houses this could mean for the rest of the week.

"All right, fellas!" he said. "Show time!"

Wild West Billy led the two of us out into the middle of the street, and there was a buzz of anticipation from both sides of the street. Hurley kept veering off to one side, as though forced to by the weight of his heavy gun. Then he'd lift it up and swap sides to get himself back on course. He got a few laughs, and in fairness he wasn't bad. He was certainly better at Chaplin than he had been the last time I saw him.

Billy took a silver dollar from his weskit pocket, and said to me: "Call it."

"Heads," I said.

"Bad call," the old cowboy said, and nodded to the West end of the street, while Hurley waddled his Chaplin walk away to the East.

When I judged I had gone far enough, I turned, and saw what the disadvantage was – I was staring straight into the morning sun.

A little way off I could see the shadow silhouette of Charlie Chaplin, clowning around, trying to work the crowd. He teetered this way and that, put the gun on the ground and did a few practice draws with his finger, tried to lift the gun up to the same level, but couldn't manage it, fell on his backside in the dirt, on and on and on it went.

I stood there, squinting into the bright autumn sun, obliged

335

to stand and watch a man I heartily disliked indulge in an impersonation of my bitterest rival, a man who had done me down more times than I cared to think. And as if it wasn't bad enough having his gargantuan success rubbed in my face every way I turned, now I was having to watch an inferior copy of his antics at the crack of bloody dawn.

I shaded my eyes, and there was Chaplin still cavorting madly and showing off, and I decided I'd had enough. After all, I was supposed to be the bad guy, so why was I waiting to play by the rules? Let's get on with it, and then I can go back to bed.

I drew my gun and pointed it at him, at Hurley, at Chaplin, and he made a big deal of trying to lift his gun, then dropped it and put his fingers in his ears. The crowd laughed.

I pulled the trigger, and the report echoed and cracked off the shop fronts.

Hurley fell to his knees and clutched his chest with both hands.

"That's right," I thought. "Make a big number out of it. Just pick up the gun and shoot back so I can go down and everyone can go home."

There was a moment when Hurley seemed to be trying to reach for the gun on the floor, but then he pitched face-forward into the dirt and lay still.

37
ON THE RUN

THERE was even a little ripple of applause, if you can believe it.

Of course everyone expected Hurley to get up. Well, they expected Charlie to get up, because he was indestructible, wasn't he? And he was the little guy, their hero, they were all on his side. I wasn't supposed to win, I was just some wrong 'un in a black hat. And then he didn't get up for a minute, a minute and a half, and it was too long for it to be a joke, and Wren ran over to him and rolled him over onto his back. I walked up to them, hardly believing, scarcely able to fathom...

"Oh my God. Run for it, Arthur!" Wren said, her face ashen.

I looked down at Ed. His eyes were open, and there was a trickle of blood out of the side of his mouth, and a patch spreading on his shirt. That was a nice touch, I thought, crazily, in that bewildering moment. Slip some of the fake blood in my mouth – I'd have to pinch that idea.

Then I saw it, just to the side of the button on his jacket, and my heart turned to ice.

A hole that shouldn't be there.

I looked down at the gun in my hand, and then up at Wild West Billy, who had sauntered over in his slow bow-legged way. I grabbed him by the front of his waistcoat and pulled him up onto his tiptoes.

"There were bullets in the gun!" I snarled, still not quite believing it. "Real live bullets, you lunatic!"

"I just wanted to see a real gunfight. That's all."

"What are you talking about? Weren't you here back in the day when there were boys taking pot-shots at plug hats all day long?"

"I never saw a one."

"What?"

"Never saw a real life, honest-to-goodness gunfight. Never saw one. Never saw two men put their lives on the line out here on the street in front of everyone."

"You never saw one?"

"Never did."

"And that's why you put real bullets in the guns?"

"That's why."

I looked at him. "You crazy old bastard," I said. "You sad, mad, crazy old fool. Look what you did. Look what you *did*!"

"Well," the old fellow said, his breath reeking of old tobacco. "Seems to me that you did more'n I did."

I galloped into the Long Branch and up the stairs to my room two at a time. I grabbed everything of mine and stuffed it into my carpet bag willy-nilly, then I bolted back out of the door, where I bumped right into Wren coming the other way.

"Take me with you!" she said, fastening herself to the front of my coat.

"Are you mad?" I said. "I just gunned down your husband in front of witnesses and the *Dodge City Daily Globe*. How's it going to look if I disappear over the horizon with his fresh widow in tow?"

338

I shook her off and raced over to the window, trying to conceal myself behind the drapes while I checked the street below.

A nosy chattering crowd had gathered around the fallen form of Edgar Hurley. I could see the lanky figure of Ted Banks talking to a policeman, for all I knew giving him my name and description, and as I watched he turned and pointed over at the Long Branch.

"Arthur, please!" Wren cried.

"Listen," I said. "I'm going to have to go on the run, and I can't do that with you. Stay here – well, not right here in my room, that's going to look terrible – and do what you can to tell them it was an accident."

Even as I said it I knew that it was going to be a tough sell. The history of animosity between myself and Hurley, my familiarity with the guns from my nightly shoot outs with mad old Billy. It wasn't as if it was an even draw, which used to be a defence in the olden days. I'd just fired at him while he was cavorting around like Charlie Chaplin. No-one was going to believe that I hadn't known there were bullets in the gun, and Hurley wasn't going to be around to tell anyone that he hadn't known about it either.

A distant sound brought me to my senses all of a sudden. It was the bell at the railroad station – there must be a train there right now!

I grabbed my bag and looked out of the window again. A small mob had gathered behind Ted Banks and the policeman, and seemed to be urging them in the direction of the saloon. The policeman wasn't exactly Wyatt Earp. He seemed to lack the enthusiasm for tackling a desperado single-handed, so I had a minute or two.

I skipped along the landing, leaving Wren crying on my bed – go to your own room, woman, for pity's sake! – and came to a window which opened out on the back of the building. I clambered out onto a sloping roof and slid down to the ground in the back yard, then out into an alleyway, and ran along behind all the buildings on the block between me and the station. If I was lucky I could get there without being seen.

I could see the train at the platform, hissing and steaming, and its driver gave a couple of yanks on the whistle to urge stragglers to get aboard pronto. If I dashed across the street, I could get up onto the tracks and reach the back of the train by the most direct route.

I peeked out around the corner of the end building on the block, a Bargain Store that was not yet open for business, and away down the street I could see the policeman trying to persuade as many people as possible to go into the saloon with him, while the onlookers were clearly more keen that he should go in by himself.

I darted across the wide street and cut through onto the tracks. I didn't think I had been seen, and I raced along the sleepers towards the rear end of the train.

Careful not to draw attention to myself, I stepped up onto the platform and then on into the rearmost carriage, finding myself a window seat from which I could peer anxiously back towards the Long Branch.

To my horror it seemed that the possibility that I might be on the train had occurred to the policeman, or at least if not to that slow-witted fellow then to someone in the mob with him, and a crowd of a couple of dozen souls began to stride up Front Street towards the station in the wake of the unenthusiastic flatfoot.

It seemed they must surely arrive in time to prevent the train's departure, and then I would not escape a search of the carriages. I began to wonder desperately about jumping down once my pursuers reached the station, and using the train to shield me from their sight as I made a run for it.

Here they were, now, passing up behind the guard's van, as I had done moments before, and I stood to open the window so that I could climb out, but then – hallelujah! The carriages clanked and juddered together, and the train began to move off.

Out of the opposite window, I could see the cop and his impromptu posse trotting along the platform trying to shout to the engine driver to stop, but the train picked up its pace and slowly, slowly we were leaving them behind, until finally I was out of their grasp.

I sat down again, and closed the window as the draught was displeasing the couple opposite, and then let out almost as big a draught myself as I sighed heavily. I was away! No doubt someone would have the bright idea to wire ahead to the next station stop, but I felt sure I could find a way to leap clear before that juncture and take my chances on foot.

I was on the run.

38
THE ROOM

SUMMER OF 1917, SOMEWHERE IN AMERICA

THE man John patted the newspaper on the table between us, the copy of the *Dodge City Daily Globe* with its screaming banner headline:

CHAPLIN SLAIN!

"So-o-o," he said thoughtfully. "You are saying that this was a t-tragic accident?"

"It was," I said. "That mad old fool put real bullets in the gun without telling us. It might just as well have been me that got plugged."

"The whole situation g-grew out of your dispute with this man Edgar Hurley."

"Yes," I admitted.

"P-put simply; you accused him of stealing your act, the act you had d-developed with Stanley Jefferson, to wit *The Nutty Burglars?*"

"He did steal it."

"And he accused you of seducing his wife, Ethel Hurley, also known as Wren."

"Well, if you'd met her you'd know who did the seducing."

"At any rate he accused you of sleeping with his wife."

"Once."

John frowned. "More than once, surely. At the film studio in Chicago, and then once more when your paths crossed again at the saloon in Dodge City?"

"Yes, but only once that Hurley knew about."

"Hmmm..."

John said nothing for a long few moments, tapping his teeth with his pencil. His colleague sat, half-slumped in his chair, just looking at me, waiting.

It was not long before I could stand it no longer. "What?" I said. "What are you thinking?"

"I am wondering," John said. "I am wondering whether you can really be any use to us, or whether I should just hand you over to the authorities for trial."

"What use can I be?" I said. "Just tell me."

"Well, answer me this: would you say your antipathy for Mr Ch-Charlie Chaplin was a major contributory factor in this tragedy?"

"Certainly it was," I said.

"You blamed him for the death of your friend?"

"I still do."

"And for pretty much all the ill-luck that has befallen you. The separation from your sweetheart and child?"

"Yes."

"The failure of your career as a v-vaudeville artiste?"

"Well, not failure, exactly. I had some good times."

"And your subsequent slide into p-penury?"

343

"All right," I said. "No need to lay it on too thick."

"Then there's the c-collapse of your mental health? The drinking, the experiences you describe, where you believed you were seeing Chaplin everywhere?"

"I *was* seeing him everywhere."

"How about your inability to break into the moving picture industry? You put that down to him?"

"Ah," I said. "Now that story is a little more complicated."

John raised an eyebrow, and I felt a little surge of hope. There was still a chance, a chance I could wriggle out of their grasp and avoid being sent back to England and who knows what ghastly fate.

"I need to tell you what happened next..."

PART 5

39
THE TRAMP

JACKSONVILLE, Florida, was an exotic sort of a place. For a start, every second face I passed on the sidewalk there seemed to be black, from the swankiest swells strolling along right down to the street corner tramps like myself. I shambled along bustling Bay Street, past extraordinary shops selling alligator tooth whistles, heron plumes and palmetto hats. When I got to the docks I almost tripped over a docile alligator tethered to a post.

Steamers from the harbour nosed out of the mouth of the St John's River into the Atlantic, and then turned to hug the coastline all the way up to New York, ferrying wealthy passengers back and forth, honeymooners, dignitaries, celebrities, nobs of all kinds, all looking for sunshine, warmth and entertainment, all of which Jacksonville provided in spades.

Something else in plentiful supply in Jacksonville was tramps. Deadbeats, down-and-outs, hobos and bums. My now-practised eye spotted several of them shuffling up the bank of the wide river towards a little wood, and I began to follow them, hoping to pick up a few handy tips on how to get by in the city.

And you know how I knew beyond any shadow of a doubt that they were tramps? They looked like Charlie Chaplin, that's how.

For months I had been living rough, painfully aware that there were very likely 'WANTED!' posters of me on every sheriff's noticeboard from Dodge to dinner time. Sleeping rough, too, which was... well, it was rough. There you go – clue's in the name. I was tormented by visions of the bullet from Wild West Billy's gun striking down Edgar Hurley, and even though I never liked the man, I fervently wished I could call that bullet back. The only way to drive those nightmares from my mind was to think about Tilly and Wallace, who had acquired the status of a far-off and impossibly unattainable dream, and that didn't make sleep any easier.

And I discovered, much to my chagrin, that if you wanted people to give you some change, or maybe even a bit of food, then the surest way to get them to cough up was to remind them of Charlie Chaplin.

There was hardly a hobo or a bum anywhere in the continental United States at that time who hadn't rooted around in the trash or the charitable donations to some benevolent church in some small town somewhere and found himself a too-small jacket, baggy pants, over-sized shoes, a little bow tie. Derby hats and canes were at a premium, and if you had one or other of these, you guarded them jealously. And even the most filthily unshaven scoundrel would have the remnants of a crowd-pleasing little toothbrush moustache nestling amongst the stubble on his upper lip.

There was no better get-up for a bum just then, and equally there was no better disguise for a wanted man. Nobody gave you a second glance. They gave you a first glance, the one that told them there was someone who looked a bit like Charlie Chaplin,

348

but a second would have left them feeling obliged to give you some coin or a sandwich.

In short, if you wanted to survive hand-to-mouth in the early months of 1916, it wasn't enough to just be a tramp. You had to be *the* Tramp.

You'll be thinking that this must have been hard for me to take, must have fuelled my Chaplinoia, if you like, and you'd be right. It wasn't just the tramps I saw every day, though, on every street corner, or my reflection every time I glimpsed it in a shop window or a puddle. Whatever I did, wherever I went, I just couldn't get away from him.

I first hopped the train on which I'd escaped from Dodge at a little place called Las Vegas, a one-horse town where the nag in question had given up the ghost long ago.

It was late autumn, winter was coming, the weather was getting cold and raw, especially if you were reduced to sleeping outdoors, and with not much of a plan except the instinct shared by swallows and bums, I decided to head South.

In Amarillo, Texas, I was mooching along minding my business when I realised there were crowds of people in the street all heading in the same direction. I followed, and found an event of some sort being set up outside the railway station, a reception. There was a dais, and the mayor, and tables bearing food and drink for the important local dignitaries.

━━━━━

A train pulled in, and a little oompah band struck up a song of greeting, while a mob of citizens like excited children swarmed all over the train until they found their prey in a bathroom halfway through shaving himself and hauled him out of the window.

———

It was Charlie, of course, and he looked thoroughly bewildered by all the fuss. The mayor put his arm around his shoulders and said: "Mr Chaplin, your friends of Amarillo, Texas, want to show their appreciation for all the happiness you have given them by asking you to join us in a sandwich and a Coca-Cola!"

And the childish delight those grown people took in watching a small British man from Kennington nibbling a sandwich, well, it was a thing to see.

———

After that I reached St Louis and got a job as a hand loading bales of something or other onto a Mississippi barge, and was able to ride this down as far as Memphis, mostly sitting on my backside sharing a bottle of sipping whisky with my new colleagues as the big fancy steamboats paddled by with the swells leaning on the rails.

In Memphis I came across some children playing on the steps in front of a townhouse. As I drew closer I began to catch the words of the little rhyme they were all singing as they played out their little hand-slapping routine, and it went like this:

> Charlie Chaplin meek and mild
> Took a sausage from a child
> When the child began to cry
> Charlie slapped him in the eye.

Sounds about right, I thought. That 'meek and mild' felt fantastically sarcastic.

Then I made my way to the city of Atlanta, where early one Sunday morning I wandered into the First Baptist Church of Atlanta, no less, in a part of town called Peachtree. My present Chaplin Tramp outfit was nearing the end of its useful life, and I had in mind looking out a new – well, newer – pair of trousers and also some shoes, as I had walked very nearly through the soles of my own.

Before I really knew what was happening, the preacher there had fastened onto me and was using me as a prop for his sermon, which was about the iniquity of the obscene new contract Charlie had signed with the Mutual Film Corporation. Six hundred and seventy thousand dollars a year it would bring him, which was, as this fellow pointed out in a cloud of spittle:

"Four dollars and twenty six cents per minute! And for what?" he raged. "For mocking the needy, for ridiculing those least able to speak for themselves, those who have fallen on hard times, those in thrall to the demon drink!"

"Amen!" came the answering cry from the faithful.

I must have looked suitably downcast whilst taking in this staggering new landmark in Chaplin's inexorable progress, because I had offers of lunch from several charitable individuals, three of which I was able to take up before my aching stomach cried 'No more!'

And then I came here, to Florida, to Jacksonville, where I found myself trailing a little knot of indigent Chaplins until I came upon a whole little community gathered around a campfire, all of them, black and white, dressed in as close an approximation as they could manage to the outfit that Charlie had made so popular.

I shuffled close to the fire, and two chaps made a space for me. I too was an ersatz Chaplin, as close to the real thing as ground raspberry leaves and catnip were to real tea, so they probably figured I belonged.

Just to begin a conversation, I remarked upon the rash of Chaplin hobos to my neighbour, a dark-skinned fellow name of Ron, and he spent several minutes explaining that he was not a hobo, a hobo is someone who travels looking for work. A tramp is someone who only works when he has to, and tries to avoid travelling, and a bum is someone who doesn't work at all.

"I'm a tramp, you see? Like Charlie is a tramp."

"And like all these fellas," I said.

"Yeah, sure, we love Charlie. He's the patron saint of tramps."

I recalled the sermon I'd heard in Atlanta, where the preacher had been so scornful of Chaplin for mocking boys just like these, but I could see nothing but affection for him in this little group.

"You see what Charlie did for us lately? Look at this," Ron said. He took from his pocket a coin with a hole drilled through the middle so it could be threaded on a piece of elastic. "It's just a little gimmick, it's called the Charlie Chaplin coin. You hold it in your hand, and when you let it go it disappears up your sleeve."

"What's that go to do with Chaplin?"

"Lord only knows, but it's a gag, see, so..." Ron shrugged. "Anyway, the point is this. Say you find a cent. Well, then you go in the pharmacy or the drugstore or the tobacconist and you buy yourself a Charlie Chaplin coin wid it. Then you takes the elastic off it, you finds yourself a vending machine, and this coin is the same size and weight as a nickel, so you can get five cents worth o' chocolate or fruit or whatever for your penny. I tell you, it's Charlie lookin' out for the brothers, that's what it is. Ain't that right, boys?"

All around me the little group of tramps pulled these novelty coins from their pockets and dangled them from their fingers, saying; "Amen!"

Reaching the Atlantic coast brought me to my senses. I could not go on like this. Wandering from town to town like a bum, like a tramp, like *the* Tramp.

As far as being a wanted man was concerned, no-one had paid me too much mind as far as I could tell, and Jacksonville was a long way from Dodge. It was time to get myself on my feet again, get myself a job.

I had no skills, except in the comedy line. I had some experience of service, making beds and cleaning rooms back when I was a college porter, and I wondered about whether I might be able to work in a hotel. I'd need to clean myself up a bit first. The English accent would surely be an absolute boon. I could probably parley that into working as a receptionist before too long, or maybe head waiter...?

During the day I began staking out the big swanky hotels like the Mason and the Davies, trying to work out how to get in there.

If I could find a back way in, I reasoned, I could make my way up to the rooms, maybe find someone of a similar build, borrow his clothes – perhaps on a permanent basis – and then present myself as a prospective employee.

I'd have no references, of course, but I worked on a story to cover that in my head. I'd worked at the Dorchester, why not? I'd been in service as a valet. I modelled my demeanour on Jobson, Considine's English butler, treated it like a character acting job. I had been stranded in New York by the outbreak of war – it was almost the truth, after all.

The gentleman I worked for had hurried back home to enlist as an officer, and I was to follow shortly afterwards after closing up our New York apartment. He was lost on the *Lusitania*. He was a friend of the Vanderbilts. It was a tragedy, personally and professionally. But now I was ready to return to the world of work, without employment, available.

Thus it was that one evening I found myself lurking by the fancy Burbidge Hotel, considering a back way in. There was an alleyway behind that ran past the kitchen entrances, and I was watching for a quiet moment to sneak in.

Suddenly I noticed, to my astonishment and concern about my own mental equilibrium, that around half a dozen Charlie Chaplins had mustered there for some unknown reason. I felt my moorings loosening, just as I had at Cleveland's Luna Park when it seemed to be overrun with inexplicable simulacra of my nemesis. Was this real, or just my Chaplinoia...?

As if I wasn't unnerved enough, my new acquaintance Ron the tramp suddenly appeared out of the shadows right at my shoulder. He, too, was the living image of Charlie Chaplin, albeit a dark-skinned version.

"You spotted 'em, huh?" he said, with a wink.

"You can see them too?" I said, with a surge of relief.

"Yeah, but keep it under your hat. If everyone knew about it the whole hustle'd be ruined."

"What are you talking about, Ron?"

"I told you, didn't I, that Charlie was the patron saint of us tramps?"

"I don't think I'll forget that in a hurry."

"Well, tonight at the Burbidge, the mayor of Jacksonville is holding a reception for all the movie people. He loves them, you see, thinks they will be the making of the town. Now his idea of a gag, so they think he's one of 'em, is to have all the waiters dress up as Charlie Chaplin."

"Those guys there?"

"Exackerly. Now a pair of enterprising fellas such as we could mosey on over there once the shindig is under way, and no-one would bat an eyelid. There's food, food like you wouldn't believe, and drink. You wid me?"

"I'm wid you," I said.

"Thank the good Lord above for Charlie Chaplin!" Ron said.

"Huh," I grunted.

"Can I hear an 'Amen!'?"

"Yeah, yeah. Amen," I said, grudgingly, then the two of us sauntered as casually as we could over to the kitchen entrance of the Burbidge, and followed the Chaplin waiters inside.

40
BABE

IT was a good plan, the plan to blend in with all the Charlie Chaplin waiters, but it was a much better plan for me than it was for Ron. It wasn't his fault - Mother Nature had given him one crucial disadvantage.

We made it into the Burbidge by the back entrance straight into the kitchens, where mountains of food was being prepared - crab, lobster, cooked meat platters, a side of pork - and our mouths began to water. We were a little bit too canny to just tuck in right then and there, and we went through the kitchen to check out the lie of the land beyond, nudging one another in anticipation of the treats to come.

Up the stairs we could hear the murmur of conversation at the reception itself, and we got as far as the foyer outside the ballroom, where pairs of local dignitaries were still sauntering in, dressed in their finery. One or two of the ladies smiled at us as they passed by, and one said:

"Oh, isn't that simply *adorable*?!"

I gave her my best Chaplin simper, and she melted, practically had to be carried into the function by her beau.

Ron tiptoed over to get a squint into the room, and he turned back to me with an expression of pure glee on his features.

"See the big tables at the back wid the white tablecloths on 'em? That'll be the banquet, buffet-style. This is going to be a cinch!"

My stomach gave a rumble – it had been a good long while since I'd filled it up properly.

"We should go in and start collecting up empties," Ron whispered. "That way we fit right in, see?"

I nodded, and we stepped through the double doors. The room was packed with Jacksonville society, mingling with what I took to be the local movie-making community, while Chaplins moved amongst them whisking food and drinks in and out, some of them essaying drunk-Chaplin footwork, nearly dropping their trays, getting appreciative smiles.

This was going to be easy. I turned to Ron to suggest we split up, when suddenly a fellow in a tuxedo and black tie strode over to us. He wasn't a guest, I figured, as he was carrying a tray of canapes – delicious-looking little puff pastry confections that I could hardly tear my eyes away from – but he wasn't a Chaplin, either. With a frisson of alarm I figured that he must be the head waiter, the boss.

"Who are you?" he demanded in a low hiss.

"We staff," Ron said, his eyes darting from side to side.

"Like hell you are!" the man said. "You think I know no better than to hire negro Charlie Chaplins?!"

Ron's shoulders slumped. "But sir, I can work...!"

"No, no no, out you go!" the head waiter insisted. Ron, destroyed, began to shuffle towards the double doors, and I followed in his wake, dreaming of crab and lobster.

The head waiter turned to me. "Here," he said, thrusting the tray of canapes he was carrying at me. "You mingle. I'll see this chancer off the premises."

And there it was – I was in, and Ron was out. He shot me a baleful look as he left, with his bicep trapped in an iron grip, and then he was gone.

I stood for a moment, holding the tray of canapes, until a couple came over and helped themselves, barely giving me a second glance.

Oh well, I thought, I might as well make the most of it. So I popped a vol-au-vent in my mouth when I judged no-one was looking, and began to circulate. Soon my tray was picked clean by well-heeled gannets and I tracked back to the kitchen to collect another. On the way back to the reception I ate another couple of treats – after all, otherwise I was working for nothing, wasn't I?

When I returned a man was taking the stage, red-faced and beaming with pleasure. He wore a white suit, with a white waistcoat, and a gold watch chain looped across his ample belly. He wafted himself with a white panama hat and the room quieted to a respectful hush.

"Good evening, friends," he began with a huge smile. "I want to thank y'all for coming along to this mighty fine soirée in honour of our new friends from the Vim Motion Picture Company."

A wave of his arm encompassed the people he had in mind, and a ripple of warm applause broke out. As the speech seemed to have reduced the call on canapes I retreated to the back corner to watch.

"Now for those that don't know me, an' those that do, my name is J. E. T. Bowden, an' I am proud to be the mayor of this fair city..." Some applause interrupted his remarks, and he inclined his head graciously. "Thank you kindly, friends... And I want to tell you folks gathered here tonight that it is my intention, as mayor, to make Jacksonville nothing less than the movie-making capital of the world!"

Again, this was greeted enthusiastically by all present.

"Yes, the Vim company, led by Mr Louis Burstein who I can see there and who I am proud to call a personal friend, they have moved their operation down to Jacksonville from Bayonne, New Jersey. Because they have realised what all picture makers will realise soon enough. You can't make pictures in the North. The weather is so bad that every single scene needs to be shot indoors, and if you do venture outside, there's no scenery worth a dime. Yes, Madam, I said 'dime', no need for palpitations. Now then. What about Los Angeles, I hear you say, what about Hollywood?"

Some booing began at the mention of that name.

"Well, I say yes, some film companies have set up all the way out there in the desert, five whole days' of back-breaking travel by locomotive from New York City, but all the top outfits, all the men of vision and the men of profound good sense, are coming to Jacksonville!"

Uproarious cheers greeted this rabble-rousing performance.

"Because in Jacksonville, we are just twelve hours from New York by pleasure steamer, a bracing little pick-me-up of a journey which will surely entice all the top acting talent from Broadway to try their hand at the flickers.

"In Jacksonville we have scenic locations coming out of our very ears! We have the Atlantic beaches, we have the mighty St John's River, we have forests, we have swamps, we have sunshine all day long, we have an ostrich farm, we have over a thousand miles of navigable waterways and seven miles of beach front, and we have twenty-eight wholesale groceries!"

The relevance of this last item escaped me, but that didn't stop another mighty cheer.

"Hollywood may have Charlie Chaplin and the Keystone Cops..."

More booing at this, and with a start I realised that I had started it myself.

"But we have Walter Stull and we have Bobby Burns!" I gathered from the reaction in a couple of places that those two gentlemen were in the room. "We have the lovely Valda Valkyrien!" Some raunchy wolf-whistles greeted this name-check. "We have Kalem Studios, we have Biograph and Vitagraph, we have Thanhauser and Gaumont, we have Eagle and Artcraft, we have Motoscope and the New York Motion Picture Company. Over thirty of the nation's – nay, the world's – leading film companies are already based here in Jacksonville. And now we have Vim taking up residence at the old Lubin Studios on Riverside Avenue. I tell you all, friends, and I give you my word on this, a new Golden Age for Jacksonville is just around the corner.

"The good people of Jacksonville want the movies here, don't let anyone tell you different. Or did I imagine the mile-long queue of debutantes on Riverside Avenue only the other afternoon, all of them desperate to get their pretty young faces in the flickers? Eh? So welcome, a hearty Southern welcome to you all!

"I am going to conclude my remarks now, and hand over the stage to Vim's biggest star – an' I mean, biggest. We love him here in Jacksonville, and Cutie Pearce's roadhouse hasn't been the same without him. But now he's back, a glorious homecoming indeed, so please put your hands together in appreciation for the Twentieth Century Four, and their leading vocalist, the Half Ton of Jollity his good self – Mr Babe Hardy!"

A musical group materialised on the stage, a drummer, a bass player and a saxophonist, and a lady pianist in a shimmering calf-length gown.

The singer then stepped forward to wildly enthusiastic applause. He was a big fellow indeed, tall and extremely well-upholstered, yet he moved nimbly on his feet, almost like he was filled with air. He had a face like the Moon, which was glowing with modest pleasure at his reception, and he shared this with his accompanists, offering them a generous introductory gesture each, before gliding over and kissing the lady pianist's hand.

"Mrs Hardy," he said.

"Mr Hardy," she replied, and the big fellow beamed. He was every inch – and there were plenty of those inches – the Southern gentleman, and the crowd absolutely adored him.

When he opened his mouth to sing I could tell why. He had the voice of an angel, a soaring pure tenor that seemed to wring every drop of emotion from each song, even as his big smiling face seemed to regard everyone in the room his friend.

Shine on Harvest Moon was his first, a popular number from before the war, and the room was captivated[7]. Women sighed, and their menfolk were equally entranced.

Suddenly I was aware that the head waiter chappie had reappeared, and he indicated with an impatient whisk of his hand that I should follow the other Chaplins down to the kitchen. Several were lingering by the door, hanging on every note of the song, but we were all ushered down the stairs where the buffet was ready for collection.

I grabbed a large platter of sliced meats and hurried back up to the reception to catch more of the singer's performance.

After another couple of songs the buffet was complete, and the waiters were all drawn in by the entertainment. No-one was paying any attention to what was behind them. I saw a chance to grab something to eat, and I took it. I took some slices of cold beef, shoved two in my mouth and the rest in my jacket pocket. Moving along I wolfed a chicken leg, fried southern-style, and spent about half a minute wondering if I could stick a lobster inside my coat for later, before settling for a couple of stuffed crabs, jamming them together belly-to-belly to keep the insides in.

Up on stage, the big singer was introducing his finale, and thanking everyone most graciously for their kind attention, as I stuck some smaller items in my trouser pockets, trying not to think about the fluff the stickier ones would inevitably accrue and how long it had been there.

The band struck up *You Are the Ideal of my Dreams*, which Hardy delivered beautifully, clasping his hands to his heart. Knowing somehow that this was the last number, one or two hungry souls began to slip over to the buffet in order to beat the rush, so I was obliged to terminate my raid and retreat to behind a pillar at the side of the room.

Tumultuous applause greeted the close of the song, and of the act, with Hardy and his wife and their bandmates taking numerous bows, Hardy himself managing to look particularly genteel. Then with one mind a tidal wave of well-heeled jewellery-jangling Jacksonville society descended upon the groaning boards and commenced to strip it bare like it was they who had been living rough for the last six months.

I stayed out of the way, occasionally slipping a pastry from my pocket to my mouth, and tried not to attract anyone's attention. After all, I had got what I came for, and didn't want to do any more unnecessary unpaid work than I had to.

As it happened, though, I hadn't entirely escaped everyone's notice.

"Good evening to you, sir," a melodious voice said, and there beside me was the big singer, looking me up and down with a friendly smile. I had a mouthful, so I just gave him what I hoped was a cheery nod.

"Now here's the thing," the big man went on. "I figure that

362

you are not a genu-wine member of the waiting staff. Reason one: I work here at the Burbidge every night, I organise the cabaret here, and I do not recognise you. Reason two, I could see you from on the stage whilst I was singing, and you were stuffing your face like there was no tomorrow. So, friend, do you mind telling me your story?"

"I assure you, sir," I began.

Hardy pointed a delicate finger in the direction of my shirt-front. "You have crab claws poking out from the lapel of your jacket" he said discreetly, and I hurriedly poked them back out of sight. "You were saying?"

I sighed. Something about the big fellow's open and friendly demeanour made me want to tell him everything, but I could hardly afford to be taken to a police station after all the time I had been on the run – they'd've had my picture, and would send me back to Dodge. "You're right, sir," I said. "I have fallen on hard times, and took advantage of the fact that the hotel was using waiters dressed as tramps."

"No!" the big man chuckled. "That is astonishing! What nerve! I applaud you, sir, I really do."

"Actually, the idea belonged to a companion of mine who was not as fortunate as I. I was going to take these crabs to him later."

"A fine-spirited gesture indeed," the singer said. "Now tell me this. Your accent, suh. English?"

"That's right, you have a good ear," I said. "And a remarkably fine voice, if you don't mind my saying so."

The big man flushed with pleasure, and even preened a little. "Do you know, when I was a boy in Milledgeville, Georgia, I made a pilgrimage to Atlanta to hear Enrico Caruso. It was like a religious experience. I decided then and there to dedicate my life to music."

"I think he would be proud to hear you say so," I said.

"You are very kind, suh, very kind indeed. Come and join us at our table, and tell me how you came to fall so low."

"Really?" I said.

"Why certainly. This way."

He led me to a table where a number of his friends were congregated, including the members of the band, and when we arrived he introduced himself most formally. "My name is Norvell Hardy," he said, "but as you doubtless heard I am known to my friends as Babe. This is Madelyn, Mrs Hardy, and this is Bert Tracey. And you are...?"

"Arthur," I said. "Arthur Smith." I had barely had cause to use any name, let alone my own, for a good few months, but since that business in Dodge I'd thought it best to use an alias, and I stuck with one that I had used once before when trying to keep Karno from knowing that Alf Reeves had re-hired me.

"Move over, Bert," Hardy said, and his friend, a wiry little chap who, I later discovered, had once been a jockey in Australia.

"Oh Babe, not another hard luck case, mate!" this Bert sighed, giving me the gimlet eye.

"So, Mr Smith, we are all ears."

Well, he was so kind and so friendly and so... interested, that I ended up telling him a potted version of my whole story. All the while people were coming up to him, shaking him by the hand, praising his singing, but after every interruption he would turn back to me and say: "Pray continue, Mr Smith."

I glossed over the gunfight in Dodge City, skipped the fact that I was wanted for murder, but otherwise I told him all about the Karno years, touring music halls and vaudeville, the big spectacular shows, and the smaller, funnier ones with Stan. I told him about Tilly and Wallace, and our unfortunate separation due to

364

the war – I may have laid it on a bit thick – whereupon Babe Hardy pulled out a big white hand kerchief to dab at his cheeks. And naturally I told him about Chaplin, how I had started out with him, how we'd become rivals, and how Fate had driven us to opposite extremes.

"The irony," Hardy declared. "Misfortune obliges you to masquerade as Charlie Chaplin to beg, all the while knowing that you could have been every bit the success that he has become."

I agreed with him, naturally, but suddenly began to worry that pitching things as strongly as that would not seem believable to these people I had just met. Bert Tracey, in particular, was sniffing dismissively at parts of my tale, so I decided to play it down a little.

"Oh, I don't know about that, but Charlie has certainly made the most of his talents."

Hardy's moon-like face took on a look of determination. "You know what we should do?" he said, and his wife sighed, knowing perfectly well what was coming. "We should take Arthur here under our wing. Louis?!"

Louis Burstein, the head of Vim Pictures, trotted over at Hardy's beckoning finger.

"Allow me to present to you Mr Arthur Smith, a comedian from England. He has many years of vaudeville behind him, and worked with Charlie Chaplin. I think he would be an asset, and we should certainly take him on."

Burstein shrugged. "Anything you say, Babe," he said. "Anything you say."

And just like that I was in the flickers.

Babe Hardy's generosity did not end there. He insisted on installing me in a room at the Atlantic Hotel, where most of the Vim gang were staying, and advanced me fifty dollars. I was quite overcome with gratitude, and promised to pay him back.

"There is only one way in the world you can repay me," Hardy said, putting a big hand on my shoulder. "When, some day, as you most likely will, you find someone who is worse off than you, just help him out. Or her. That will be ample repayment for me."

And at the end of the evening, he arranged for all the leftover food from the reception to be placed in the luggage compartment of his old model T banger, and obliged me to direct him to the campsite by the St John's River, saying that he simply must see this community of ragged Charlie Chaplins for himself.

The flivver's headlights swept over the clearing where I had sat around this very campfire only the night before. The tramps looked at the motor, puzzled and poised to scatter, their eyes illuminated and shining oddly in the beams.

I leaned out of the motor car and beckoned to a familiar figure. "Hey, Ron!" I shouted. "Over here!"

Ron got to his feet, bewildered, and shuffled over to see who I was and what I wanted. When he saw me his face creased in surprise, but then I opened the trunk with a flourish and showed him the bounty from the reception, he caught a glorious whiff of seafood and his face lit up.

"Hey boys!" he called. "Grub's up!"

Between us we hauled the food over to the campfire, where the tramps, disbelieving, fell on it and began to destroy it, and I could hear grunts of pleasure and audible lip-smacking in the darkness all around me. Babe Hardy leaned back against his automobile and beamed almost as brightly as his headlamps.

"Didn't I tell you?" Ron said, turning to the others with his arm around my shoulders. "Charlie Chaplin - he the patron saint of tramps!"

41
AN AERIAL JOYRIDE

I believe that first night at the Atlantic Hotel – actually not so much a hotel, more a modestly comfortable set of apartment buildings – might just have been the best night's sleep of my life. I had forgotten what it felt like to lie between clean white sheets, and to doze comfortably on beyond sunrise. And then – glory be! – a hot bath!

I was just contemplating my only set of clothes – my tramp's uniform, of course – when there was a knock on the door of my new room. Hardy's Australian friend Bert Tracey was standing in the corridor outside, and when I opened the door wrapped only in a towel, he walked straight in without the niceties of a greeting.

"Morning," I said.

"Listen mate," Tracey said, directly. "A word. Babe is a generous man, generous to a fault."

"He certainly is," I began. "I can't tell you how much..."

"Yes, yes, I've heard it all before," Tracey said impatiently. "He's my friend. And if you start taking liberties, or let him down in any way, you will have me to answer to, is that clear?"

"Um, yes, of course," I said. "But I have no intention of..."

"I can't tell you how many deadbeats and strays I've had to see off, so watch it, yeah? Mate?"

"I... will," I said, my eyes fixed on the finger he was pointing right into my face.

"Now, you need to come down for breakfast, we're going to be off soon."

I was a little embarrassed to present myself in my stale shabbiness, but I had no choice, so I hurried downstairs. Babe had saved me a chair at his table, and I sat down opposite Madelyn, Mrs Hardy, who was feeding scraps of bacon rind to a small white dog.

"This is Babe Junior," she said. "Say hello to Arthur, baby," and she helped the creature wave its front paw. "Babe III doesn't come down to breakfast."

"Babe III?" I asked.

"We have a capuchin monkey, as well," Madelyn explained.

"We are going to have to smarten you up a little, aren't we?" Hardy said, scratching his chin. "Unfortunately nothing of mine is going to fit you, clearly. Bert? You're more his size? Do you have anything you might lend to our friend to tide him over?"

"Sure, why not?" Tracey grinned with gritted teeth, shooting me another narrow-eyed look.

And so, after breakfast when we piled into Hardy's old flivver, I was wearing a fresh suit, hat and shoes, and when we stopped outside a barber's shop I was overjoyed. The barber, a flamboyant Italian chap, threw both hands in the air with pleasure when he clapped eyes on Hardy, and he showed us both to adjacent reclining chairs to be shaved and generally spruced.

"Can I ask you something?" I said.

"Why certainly," Hardy said.

"How did you acquire the nickname 'Babe'?"

369

Hardy gave me a knowing smile. "Funny you should ask that right now," he said. "Tell you what. Let me answer that shortly, if indeed I still need to."

The Italian barber began to lather Hardy's face, whistling merrily as he did so.

"Now, while we have this little quiet time together," the big man said, "let me fill you in on what we do at Vim. The studios are just up the road, and they used to belong to Lubin, who are now our landlords. Mr Louis Burstein, whom you met..."

"Briefly," I said.

"He has an arrangement with the General Film Company to provide one new comedy a week, which is known as the Friday Vim. Usually – but not always – these will feature two characters called Pokes and Jabbs, played by my good colleagues Mr Walter Stull and Mr Bobby Burns. There are a number of supporting characters, including one habitually called either 'Fatty' or 'Plump' – ahem, yours truly – and another called 'Runt', played by Mr Billy Ruge."

I frowned. "That name rings a bell..." I said.

"Now, there is no filming scheduled for today, after the mayor's reception last night, but there is a meeting for the whole company, and as you are to join the company I shall bring you along."

"Once again," I said. "I can't thank you enough..."

"Oh, pish and tush!" Hardy said.

Just then the barber completed his work, towelling Hardy's face and then pinching and patting his plump cheeks between his fingers.

"Nice-a-bab-ee!" he cooed. "Nice-a-bab-ee!"

Babe Hardy leaned over to me and winked. "That's how," he said.

A little later, feeling like a new man, I accompanied Babe into the Vim Studio, where something like fifty people were gathered, far too many to meet all in one go. I did get introduced, though, to one particular player.

"This is Billy Ruge – he's from vaudeville, just like you."

"Except I was doing it before any of youse guys were even thought of," Ruge growled. Seeing him and hearing his rather surly New York accent I remembered our previous meeting. He was the wiry little acrobat and aerialist who'd dressed like a Chinaman, and I wondered if he might perhaps remember our conversation over Christmas dinner, so I said:

"Fancy seeing you in this part of da woild."

"What?"

Clearly not. I felt myself going red with embarrassment. "This part of the world, I meant."

"Oh," Ruge said. "Da woild."

"We met once," I said. "Cedar Rapids. I saw your act, too. Frobel and Ruge. Your partner threw you around like a medicine ball."

"Well, youse are one step ahead of every one of dese kids," Ruge said. "None of *dese* ever took da trouble to go see me."

"What happened to that act?" I asked.

"We fell out," the surly little acrobat muttered. Imagine dat.

The chief, Louis Burstein, arrived then, accompanied by a serious little man with a perfectly bald billiard ball of a head, decorated with a moustache uncannily like the one you would see in pictures of the Kaiser.

"Morning all," Burstein said, and the Vimites – for this was how they styled themselves collectively, I would soon discover – all responded cheerfully:

371

"Morning, boss!"

"Now," Burstein went on. "Mr Dintenfass here, our business partner from New York..."

"Yaarrhh!" said Billy Ruge at this mention of his home town, managing to combine a cheer with what sounded like the offer of a fight.

"Thanks Billy. Mr Dintenfass brings good news, gang. As you know, we have a contract to supply one comedy a week for the General Film Company to run in all their theatres across the country, the so-called Friday Vim. Well, from now on, we will be providing two comedies per week for General. There will now be a Thursday Vim as well as a Friday Vim, which means we are going to create a whole new series!"

Whoops and cheers all round greeted this announcement.

"Time for our good friends Plump and Runt to come to the fore, I think – don't you?"

"Yeah!" the Vimites chorused.

"About damn time," Billy Ruge muttered.

━━━━━

So began a period of frenzied activity. The Vim company split into two, and I joined Babe in the Plump and Runt team. We were going to have to churn out a one-reeler every single week, so ideas were at a premium, and I became a gag man, often thrashing out scenarios with Bert Tracey. He and I hit it off pretty well once we got to know each other a little better. He'd lost friends at Gallipoli, it turned out, just as I had.

I was particularly proud of one little sequence that emerged at my suggestion, where Plump and Runt were plundering the henhouse of a farm, and there were so many eggs that they decided to use them as golf balls. The yolk-spattering mayhem was a high point of the early Plump and Runts, even though Billy Ruge was not much of a golfer. Babe on the other hand would have played the links all day and then sung all night if he could.

"That was a great gag," he confided afterwards, "but it was funnier when it was you showing Billy what to do."

I'm afraid I really got off on the wrong foot with old Billy Ruge. One night at the Burbidge I was telling the story of the landlord we'd had back in Philadelphia, at the lodging house overlooking the baseball ground, and his comical Irish lisp. I'd worked it up into quite a turn by this time, and it had always gone down well, particularly when I got to the part where he went on about how baseball fans liked to "shit on my roof, sho they do...!"

Babe got a good old laugh out of it, I remember, and so did Bert, and Billy Bletcher and his wife Arline, and Willard Louis the director, but when I looked around the grinning group, old Billy was giving me the evil eye.

"My mudder was Irish," he said, "an' I'll not sit here to listen to any more of this." He got up and left, to much eyebrow-raising, and at the time I didn't think too much of it. He was a miserable presence at the best of times, and the evening was a lot more cheerful after he had departed.

Shortly after this, though, we heard the news of the rising in Dublin, the Irish bid for independence, and the last stand at the Post Office. Then, in the days that followed, about the executions, too. For the Americans it was difficult to digest, because the English were historically both allies and villains, and so they were sympathetic with the Irish, whilst also unsettled by rumours that the rebels had attempted to make a deal with the Germans[8].

There was absolutely no doubt where Billy Ruge's sympathies lay, however, and as the only Englishman within sneering range,

I began to bear the brunt of his resentment. Those few delicious occasions when I actually made it onscreen as a supporting comedian began to dry up, and I was sure it was down to Ruge having a sly word in the director's shell-like.

Ruge apart, the Vim company were a close-knit bunch, and we would make our flickers by day, then all pile along to the Burbidge or to Cutie Pearce's roadhouse after dark to hear Babe sing and drink the night away. At the weekends we would all go to the beach and just muck around together like a bunch of big kids.

Whenever we went out to the coast, my eye would invariably be drawn to the horizon, and my mind's eye beyond it towards England, towards Tilly and Wallace. It had been so long, but there was still a dull ache around my heart when I thought of them. However, a young girl called Ray Godfrey was much closer to what was now my home, and looked spectacular in a bathing suit to boot, and I found her a most welcome distraction.

Meanwhile the Plump and Runt films became a popular hit. Babe was a marvel. His face was so expressive, and his huge frame so unexpectedly nimble, and somehow his sheer likeability shone out of the screen, even when he was playing a rogue or a villain. Ruge, on the other hand, was a mechanical performer with an acrobat's precision, but without Babe's funny bones. The flickers were a success despite Ruge rather than because of him, as there was no sort of rapport between the two leads, they weren't really a team. Often they would go for almost a whole film without sharing the screen, as Ruge preferred to do his own meticulous thing rather than engaging in scenes with Babe, and you could see what was behind this thinking – when the two of them were together, everyone was looking at the other guy.

Still, the Thursday Vim was well-publicised outside cinemas and in the papers, with Babe described as '350 pounds of plumpness' and Ruge as '115 pounds of runtness'. People loved them, and the production line rolled on smoothly enough.

Until, that is, we got to *An Aerial Joyride*.

The reviews for the Plump and Runt series had been pretty complimentary, but more and more they were describing the movies as though Babe were the star and Billy Ruge was merely the supporting artist. Sometimes Billy didn't rate a mention at all. So he decided to push for a Plump and Runt film which centred more around his character, and Babe was sufficiently affable that it quickly came to pass.

The story of this one was that Runt was trying to impress his girlfriend, played by lovely Ray Godfrey, who changed her name shortly after because it kept being mistaken for a man's. Runt can't afford much, though, and has to settle for an old flivver, a topless Model T Ford – in point of fact, Babe's very own automobile. Runt is unable to drive, and so he hires Plump as his chauffeur and heads around to pick up his date. However, because the car is so narrow and the driver so wide, there is no room for poor Runt to sit beside his girl. He is obliged to balance perilously on the axle, and once the car gathers some speed Runt is thrown high into the air, and Babe is so taken with the girlfriend that he doesn't even notice.

The rest of the film would be taken up with Runt's attempts to catch the car, with the help of the police, but he is thwarted when it unexpectedly launches into the skies and begins to fly around, in the aerial joyride of the title.

Billy Ruge was doing his own stunts, of course, and proud of it. He was an acrobat, don't worry about a thing, he knew how to take a fall, he'd never broken a bone in twenty-five years, blah, blah, blah.

Babe and Ray started driving the flivver along, with Ruge

perched on the back. As they came alongside the camera they'd picked up a fair bit of speed, maybe just a touch more than they'd practised, and the car bounced on its springs as it hit a pothole. Ruge stepped onto the spinning axle and was catapulted up like a ragdoll on an aerial joyride of his own, in what looked like an absolutely spectacular stunt. Director Willard Louis clapped his hands with glee, Babe turned the motor car and rolled back cheerfully, and everybody was very excited until they looked over at Billy Ruge, who hadn't moved from where he had landed in a heap.

I was amongst the group who ran over to see if he was all right, and it was plain to see that the acrobat had broken his duck.

And both his legs.

42
PLUMP AND RUNT

THE Vim crew stood around morosely, kicking pebbles against the kerb, as two ambulance men lifted poor Billy Ruge onto a stretcher and began to cart him over to their vehicle. He had come round by this time, but wished he hadn't, and he was groaning and moaning something terrible.

The two bearers raised the stretcher up to slide it onto the back of the ambulance, and Billy let out a roar, which was matched, suddenly, by a great shout from Willard Louis, the director, who had been chewing his lip and fingering his moustache, clearly in the throes of devising some plan of action.

"Wait!" he yelled. "Put him down!"

"Aaaargh!" went Billy Ruge as the ambulance men put him back down on the floor with a little bump and looked at our leader with an inquiring expression on their faces.

"We need his clothes," Louis said.

"Whaaat?" Ruge bellowed.

"We need his clothes, we need to strip him before you take him away."

"For the love of...!" Babe said.

"I'm serious," Louis insisted. "We can get this one in the can today."

So while the veteran acrobat gasped, complained, and cursed our esteemed director (and for a brief merciful period passed out) Bert Tracey and Emory Hampton, the prop guy, wrestled him out of his top clothes and left him slumped on the stretcher in his combinations.

And as the ambulance bounced off up the road, Willard Louis looked around at those of us that were left. "Right," he said. "Who wants to be Runt?"

As it happened, I was the only member of the company who had not already appeared in a shot, thanks to Ruge's poisonous anti-British prejudice, and moreover did not need to be excused in order to carry out another job. Besides which, I was a decent match for Billy Ruge's build, especially as I had been more or less starving for the previous six months and was the runtiest I had ever been in my life, so I found myself nominated, seconded, and cast. It wasn't exactly stepping into dead man's shoes, because Billy wasn't actually dead, but he wasn't going to be needing his shoes for a while, that was for sure.

"We just need to pick up a few shots and this one is done," Louis explained, as I tried not to pay too much attention to the damp warmth of the unfortunate Ruge's trouser legs. "I'll keep you in a fairly long shot, pull your cap down to shade your handsome features, and it'll be a cinch."

For the rest of that afternoon, and the whole of the next day, I played Runt opposite Babe Hardy's Plump – or, more accurately, I played Billy Ruge playing Runt opposite Babe Hardy's Plump. After a little while, we both managed to forget the painful circumstances that had brought us together in this way, and we began to have fun.

In fact, we began to have a lot of fun.

Babe was, as I said, a naturally brilliant physical comedian, and we came up with some prime gags for that little flick. There was one sequence left to shoot, for example, early on in the story, where Babe was nervous and taking a drink to calm himself down. He was too wound up to wait for the glass to even reach his lips, he just tossed the drink up into the air and caught it in his mouth. There was no actual liquid, of course, it was all just pantomime, but Babe sold it perfectly (as Fred Kitchen had done for Karno when I saw it performed first, but I didn't let on about *that* when I suggested it).

We assembled, a little anxiously, a couple of days later to watch the finished item before it was copied and shipped out for the upcoming Thursday. Willard Louis was smirking confidently, and all eyes were on Lou Burstein, the chief.

"Well," he said when the end card came up, "you have all done a marvellous job. Another winner. How lucky that all Billy's scenes were done before his accident. Which looks sensational, by the way, well done managing to keep that in."

"Actually," Will Louis said, "Billy's scenes weren't all done. Some of that was Arthur here."

"What? You're kidding!"

"No, we finished the flick with Arthur as Runt. And you didn't even notice."

"I didn't, you're right, it didn't even occur to me. Well! How about that?"

Babe patted me on the back, and the chief turned to me.

"Thanks Arthur, you sure got us out of a tight scrape there."

"Happy to help," I said.

"So, gang. We need to turn our minds to what to do for next Thursday's Thursday Vim."

Babe put his hand up. "Well, what about another Plump and Runt?"

"I'm afraid the news on Billy is he's going to be on his back for at least a couple of months."

"I sure am sorry to hear that," Babe said. "And I only wish him well, I truly do. But what I meant was: what about a Plump and Runt with me and Arthur?"

The rest of the gang all looked at one another, and I felt a flutter of butterflies in my stomach.

"You think...?" Burstein said.

"Sure. We only played it for a day and a half, but I reckon there was more chemistry between me and Arthur than I've had in half a dozen pictures with Billy."

"Who is not going to like it one bit, by the way," Bert Tracey warned.

"We could... I mean, it could work..." Burstein mused. "But the sticking point would be all the publicity we've already put into setting up the team. It's going to look mighty odd if we change horses midstream, kind of thing. Unless..."

"Unless what, Lou?" Babe pushed.

"Well," Burstein began, shooting me a rather sneaky look, as though anticipating a problem. "It would have to be billed as if it were still Billy, because he's the name."

"Now, come on, Lou, that's not really fair," Babe said, but I stopped his protests by putting my hand on his big arm.

"Fine by me," I said with a grin.

And it was. I had been using my alias ever since that awful morning back in Dodge City – not that anybody much had even asked me my name while I was destitute and begging – and I had no particular interest in making any kind of star out of Mr Arthur Smith. Anonymity would suit me nicely.

"Are you sure?" Burstein frowned beadily. "You're not gonna go along and then cut up rough later?"

"Lou, for goodness' sake!" Babe said. "He said it was fine by him, so shake on it, and let's get to work!"

———

The first picture I did as Billy Ruge/Runt was called *Thirty Days*, and we started work on it later that very same day. It was a nice little idea, in which the boys get busted for playing poker and get sent down for the eponymous stretch, without the option. They are scared to tell their wives, though, so they pretend they are off on a business trip. In prison there are some nice scenes, and they get entangled with a fellow prisoner, Bert Tracey, who gets released at the same time as them and follows them home. They try and explain him away as a business contact, then as a detective in disguise, but they cannot shake the fellow off until their wives chase him away wielding big knives.

It was a whole lot of fun, and we worked well as a team right away. So much so, in fact, that the ideas which bubbled up for subsequent stories all featured Plump and Runt getting involved in various scrapes together rather than as love rivals trying to kill one another, as had been the norm when Billy Ruge played the character.

Vim were not the first to hit upon the idea of a big man and little man team – it was a staple of Karno's, for a start, and one of his big men had even started to crop up in Chaplin's Mutual pictures, a vast Scotsman called Eric Campbell – and we would not be the last by any manner of means, but I think Babe and I had something special going right from the start. In any event, we celebrated as though we had created a masterpiece, with

Babe in fine voice as usual, and champagne flowing like water.

All through the long hot summer of 1916, we made Plump and Runt comedies, one a week, and I was having the time of my life. We Vimites worked hard and we played hard, and the whole of Jacksonville was our playground. We would career about the place in our ancient automobiles looking for new places to film scenes, and the citizens would fall over themselves to be extras in the background, or to rent us furniture, or just to watch our spectacular shenanigans.

On one occasion, I remember, Babe and I had to make a spectacular leap from one high building to another. I was pretty nimble, but even so the idea of it was giving me palpitations. The thought of Babe, '300 pounds of plumpness', attempting the jump was even more alarming. He was game, though, more than game, and surprisingly light on his feet – you should have seen the man dance! – and when the time came for the shot, we pinned our courage to the sticking place and launched ourselves across the divide. I sprawled in a heap on the gritty tarmac roof opposite, but Babe landed triumphantly on his twinkling toes and gave a little bow.

Down in the alleyway below we had attracted quite a little crowd, and they burst into spontaneous hooting and applause.

When we had twenty flickers in the can Louis Burstein figured we had earned a week off. Ray Godfrey and I had been spending a fair bit of what little spare time we'd had together, and she had taken to calling me 'Smithy', which was adorable. The two of us nipped down to the Everglades, where we spent a hot and steamy week together. I can honestly say I have never been bitten so many times, and I'm not just talking about mosquitoes.

I arrived back at my apartment as you do after that kind of a break, both rested and exhausted, to find that a letter had been pushed under my door by the bellhop. It was from Cambridge, in my father's studied formal cursive, like a letter from a lawyer. I tore open the envelope and pulled out a couple of sheets of paper, headed with the college address on Trumpington Street and dated a couple of weeks earlier.

'My dear son,' he began. 'I could understand changing one's name from Smith to Dandoe for the purposes of show business, but not vice versa. I do hope you are not in some kind of trouble.'

I chuckled mirthlessly. My old man had a nose for 'some kind of trouble'. Thirty years of bailing out young men who'd pinched a policeman's helmet for a lark will give you that.

'The college is a very different place these days. The main buildings have been given over to a centre for officer training, and the mood is sombre. So many bright young lads joined up, and every week it seems brings word of another college member lost. It is heart-breaking to think of a whole generation of young men cut down before they even reach their prime, or discover what they might have been capable of. There are plans to engrave a lasting memorial onto the wall of the Old Court cloister leading to the chapel. I hope to God there will be no need to take up any more space than that.

'Your brother Lance was recalled to the colours despite the service he had already given in Southern Africa. He is at the front in France, and your mother and I are proud, of course, but greatly anxious. I thank God and the good fortune you have had that you are stranded in the United States of America. At least your mother and I have a little peace of mind knowing that the madness will not spread so far.'

I was touched, I must admit, by this somewhat uncharacteristic show of affection, both for me and for Lance, and I had to pause for a minute to gather myself.

'Now I find I must chide you for your thoughtlessness, young man," my father went on. Ha, I thought, this is more like it. "Not long ago we received a visit from a quite delightful young lady and her two and a half year-old son. Imagine our shock when she informed us that this was our grandson, Wallace...'

The pages dropped from nerveless fingers onto the rug.

Tilly! Tilly had been to Cambridge!

I snatched the paper up again and devoured the news.

'He is a grand little chap, and I took the greatest pleasure in showing him the newts in the lily pond by the Master's lodge, which so captivated you when you were of a similar age.

'His mother and I spoke at cross purposes for some time before I realised that she was under the impression that you were no longer in the land of the living, and indeed had perished in the *Lusitania* tragedy. The news that you were in fact still breathing caused her to faint dead away, and it was fortunate indeed that her travelling companion, a fine gentlemen in the dashing uniform of a Scots Highlander, kilt and all, was on hand to catch her as she fell.

'Happily she was recovered by the time they took their leave of us, and now that she has your address, she will no doubt write herself in due course.

'You will let us know, won't you, of any further developments, and whether there are any other grandchildren that we are as yet unaware of. Your loving parents, etc.'

This was almost too much to take in. Tilly and Wallace had been to Cambridge and met my father and mother? She'd thought I had gone down with the *Lusitania*? No wonder she hadn't written! My heart ached for her, how she must have suffered! But how had this happened? And who the hell was this fine Scots Highlander, by the way, in his dashing uniform and kilt?

No letter from Tilly followed, and all I could do to take my mind off her was to throw myself into the hurly-burly of filming. From time to time we would discover that we had rubbed the locals up the wrong way. We came up with an idea for a bank robbery flick, and decided to film it on the main street on a Sunday. The bank would be closed, and we could shoot the outside of it without inconveniencing anyone, that was our thinking, and we could make use of the deserted streets for our getaway. As in every Southern town, the Sabbath in Jacksonville was set aside for church and prayer, and churchgoers wrote irate epistles to the *Florida Tribune-Union* and *Metropolis* for days. Similarly when we needed a shot of a fire engine in action, the fire brigade were unimpressed when we called them out to a false alarm or two.

When the sun went down, Jacksonville society revolved around Babe Hardy. He was the Sun, and everyone else was just so many little planets and moons. He would sing with Madelyn at the Burbidge, and I would dance with the willowy Miss Godfrey, and then when that closed for the evening we would all move six miles upriver to the Panama Club, where the entertainment was organised by a luscious contralto called Margaret Arata with whom Babe would duet. And while he would charm audiences night after night, the rest of the Vimites would drink away the darkness until it was time to crank the camera handles once again.

Often in the small hours I would walk out on the sand with Ray and we would watch the incredible tropical storms out to sea. Sometimes it was a hell of a light show, sheets of lightning crackling back and forth across a silver screen of hot rainless clouds, and it was almost possible to believe that we were watching the flashbangs from France, all the way across the Atlantic.

And as Ray held my hand and pulled herself close to me, pretending to be scared so as to begin canoodling, I played along, little thinking that the storm clouds were gathering right above my head, and about to break.

43
STORM CLOUDS

THAT autumn we were at the Vim Studios on Riverside, working on a nicely deranged little flick called *Life Savers*. We'd all noticed – you could hardly miss it – that Ray was a real wow in a bathing suit, and so we devised an underwater adventure for Plump and Runt that would feature plenty of shots of her swimming. There was a surreal underwater sequence in which we were trying to rescue her, and in order to communicate we would write messages to one another and tie them onto passing fish.

In the midst of shooting this, pretending to walk along the sea bed past a variety of stuffed fish hanging from thin lines, Babe and I became aware of a little commotion.

A small party of smartly-suited dignitaries had arrived, escorted by Lou Burstein, and prominent amongst them was the white three-piece and panama hat combination that formed the trademark of Jacksonville's mayor, Mr J.E.T. Bowden. When this worthy realised that he had brought work to a standstill, he waved genially and said:

"Don't mind me, boys! Just showing you off to my distinguished guest."

He beckoned to me and Babe to join him, then turned to the smart chap beside him who was casting an eye over the facilities.

"Mr Plump and Mr Runt, the pride of Jacksonville, meet Mr Sydney Chaplin," the mayor said.

"A pleasure, sir, a pleasure," Babe beamed, grasping Syd by the hand. I froze, like a rabbit faced with a cobra. Syd offered his hand to me, and I took it slowly, feeling rather like a condemned man.

"And I'm very pleased to meet you both," Syd said, looking me full in the face, but showing not a hint of recognition. The mayor began to hold forth, then, and Syd moved away. I let out a long slow breath. Was it possible that he hadn't recognised me? Sometimes when you see someone you know in an unexpected context the cogs don't quite click at once, do they? Or maybe he was simply a much better actor than I gave him credit for.

I should say, just to make sure we are all on the same page, that I knew Syd Chaplin all too well. He was a number one for Karno when Charlie and I started out, indeed he had lobbied the Guv'nor hard to give his younger brother – half-brother, actually – a chance. And when Charlie had resorted to dirty tricks to get ahead of me, Syd had been an all-too-willing co-conspirator. The last I'd heard, from Charlie himself, was that Syd was managing his business affairs for him, having struck out in his attempts to make comedy films of his own for Mack Sennett at Keystone.

"Vim Studios is just one of the many film-making facilities we have he-ah in Jacksonville," the mayor was saying. "And Mr Richard Garrick, the well-respected local entreprenoo-er, is proposing to start work on a brand new studio complex on the site of the old Union Station that will be able to meet the needs of as many as twenty-five production companies of all shapes and sizes."

"Interesting," Syd said, nodding thoughtfully. "*Very* interesting. That's exactly the sort of thing we'd need."

The mayor beamed with satisfaction. "Perhaps, Mr Burstein, in the meantime you would be so kind as to show Mr Chaplin around *your* mighty fine facility?"

"This way, Syd," Burstein said gruffly, not being particularly endowed with the mayor's brand of Southern hospitality, and he and Syd moved off.

"It's the election I'm thinking of, you see?" Bowden confided in us when we were alone. "I'm up for reconsideration in the New Ye-ah, and my opponent, Mr John Martin, is standing on an anti-movie ticket. I swear to God that is the man's only policy – to kick you movie folks out of Jax once and for all. He knows that I have set myself the target of making Jacksonville the movie capital of the world, and there are plenty he-ah that stand squarely behind me on that."

"Yes indeed," Babe said heartily, and I nodded my support.

"But you see for every sweet soul that loves the movies there is another who harbours some petty resentment or other, maybe some actors crashed a car into his garden, or he fears the town will turn into Sodom or Gomorrah, so the fact is I could be run mighty close if I am not careful. Now, as luck would have it, the city council of Los Angeles are proposing a new ordinance that would ban film making in residential areas, which could just be the end of poor old Hollywood, yes suh!"

"Really?" Babe said. "Why that is extraordinary."

"So all the companies currently operating in California could just be tempted to up sticks and join our little community right he-ah. Including..." and the mayor jerked a thumb at the back of Syd Chaplin. "An' if I can persuade Mr Charlie Chaplin to hang out his shingle in our fair burg, well, I reckon it might just clinch the election for me. Yes, suh, I reckon as how it might!"

"Coo!" Ray said, pulling a towel around her shoulders. "Charlie Chaplin, coming to Jax. How's about that?"

Bowden was so pleased with this notion that he couldn't help himself, he did a little jig of glee.

"Yes, my dear, Charlie is my ace-in-the-hole!"

———

The prospect of the Chaplin brothers turning up on our doorstep did not exactly fill me with good cheer, and I began to wonder whether it might even spell the end of my time in Florida. I could hardly continue to live there under an assumed name with those two around, even if Syd had shown no sign of having recognised me just then, and continuing to work in the flickers would just be asking for trouble, as it was a small world where everyone knew everyone else's business.

What could I do, though? Where could I go?

The thought of being forced to walk away from such a good thing gave me a pain in my stomach. But several months had passed since that horrible business at Dodge, and so at least, I thought, the heat was off from that quarter.

The very next week we were making a story called *Never Again*, in which Plump and Runt are courting two sisters, played by Ray and Arline, and their stuck-up father decides to take them to Spain to separate them from the two undesirables. The boys give chase, and make a heart-stopping leap onto the steamer as it leaves the dock, but before that they rush into the ticket office to try and book their passage. It was only a quick scene so we used the booking clerk's actual premises, with Bert Tracey as the official. We rushed in, gesticulated our urgent request, he thrust the tickets in our hands, and out we went again, the work of a few minutes only.

When the camera stopped rolling, Bert was doubled up laughing at something or other, and the rest of us strolled back in to see what had tickled him so. He pointed at a poster on the wall behind him.

"Look!" he cried. "It's Runt!"

I looked where he was pointing and my heart stopped. There was a picture of me, plain as day, under the bold legend 'WANTED!', and details in smaller print of the shootout in Dodge.

"Hey Smithy!" Ray said, peering closely at the grainy photo, which I guessed had been snipped from an old Karno review. "It's you!"

For a panicky moment my life flashed before my very eyes – was my secret out? Was I finished here in Jacksonville?

Bert Tracey came out from behind the reception desk, tears streaming down his cheeks. "Great gag, mate!" he said, clapping me on the shoulder. "Great gag!"

Ray skipped over and kissed me on the cheek. "Didn't really fool me," she whispered. "Nothing like handsome enough!"

Miraculously everyone simply concluded that I had mocked the poster up and stuck it there myself, just to see if anyone would spot it, and my stock as a prankster went through the roof. My pulse did too, though, and it was a good couple of hours before I was anything like calm again.

It seemed, then, that I was still a wanted desperado.

———

I was still reeling from this body blow when Louis Burstein gathered us down at Vim for a company announcement.

"Great news, gang!" he said, standing on his desk so everyone could see him. "The Thursday Vim and the Friday Vim are both going down gangbusters, and I'm getting asked for more and more product. We are going to be expanding into a couple of new series."

Burstein raised his hands to quell a murmuring of disquiet. "Still doing Pokes and Jabbs, still doing Plump and Runts, don't worry about that. No-one's killing any golden gooses around here. But I'm delighted to say that Miss Kate Price has joined us direct from Keystone, and she is going to partner Babe in some Mr and Mrs Plumps, so give her a big welcome!"

Kate Price was a well-upholstered comedienne whom we had all seen playing opposite Fatty Arbuckle, and in fairness this did seem to be something of a coup for Vim. She emerged from Burstein's office where she had been waiting, and waved shyly as her new colleagues applauded. I was just wondering whether this meant that old Runt would be shunted to the sidelines as a result, when Burstein went on:

"Now you all know that Charlie Chaplin has only made half a dozen flickers this year, but the marketplace would be happy to see many more. So I intend to launch a new series of films to fill that gap, stories in that style, with a lead character who is as similar as we can make him to the Chaplin tramp. And who better to play this role for us than someone who grew up with Chaplin in the Fred Karno comedy company?"

Uh-oh, I thought...

"Someone with the same grounding in pantomime and possessing the self-same bag of tricks that Chaplin himself learned in music hall and vaudeville..."

My stomach was turning cartwheels now...

"Someone, moreover, who can claim to have been the

originator of the famous walk and the famous costume that Chaplin has made beloved around the world..."

My mind flashed back to my own invention of the Stowaway, and I remembered Charlie hunched on the prow of one of our trans-Atlantic boats, watching me with his violet eyes narrowed, taking in every nuance, every step, not laughing himself but noting how everyone else was cracking up.

"And as if that wasn't enough, someone who has himself lived the life of a tramp for a time..." Burstein went on.

I caught Babe glancing over at me, remembering no doubt my story when we'd first met. What did this mean? Was my secret out? My real identity known...?

"So please put your hands together...!" Burstein was saying, and I felt myself clenching, bracing for impact. "For Mister Billie Ritchie!"

There, large as life – which was never all that large – was my old Karno mate, the wiry and (it has to be said) embittered little Scotsman, striding out of Burstein's office, waving, beaming, glad-handing. Burstein steered him over to meet the Pokes and Jabbs crew first of all as the meeting broke up. I tried to keep my head down, hoping to corner him for a quiet word in private later, but as soon as he could, Ritchie made a bee-line for me.

"Arthur!" he cried out, bouncing over.

"Smith," I said quickly as we shook hands. "Arthur... *Smith*."

"Arthur... Smith. Aye, right enough," Ritchie said, his eyes flicking beadily from side to side as he cottoned on. "I thought that was you! Hey, this is a bit of all right, isn't it? It's just like the old Fun Factory!"

"It is that," I said, steering him out onto the lot by the elbow away from bothersome ears. "So you're going to make some Chaplin-style comedies, is that it?" I said as we strolled.

"An' why not, eh? After all, young Chaplin's not done too bad for himsel', has he? An we all know where he got *that* act from, do we not?"

I nodded. "He got it from me!" Ritchie and I cried, both at the same moment.

"Ach!" Ritchie laughed, punching me on the arm. "Ye knew what ah was gonna say! All right, all right, I do go on about it, but only because it's true. I did the Karno Drunk before him, an' I invented all the things he's used to make his name."

I decided not to argue the point, but there'd been Karno Drunks before Ritchie and there'd been Karno Drunks after Chaplin, and they all drew from the same gag-book.

"But tell me this," Ritchie said, giving me a narrow-eyed look. "What news o' my ol' friend Dandoe?"

I glanced around to be sure no-one was within earshot, and in point of fact, some loud hammering had begun on a new set and we were hard pushed to even hear ourselves as I brought him up to date on my adventure in Dodge, the demise of Edgar Hurley, and the reason for my alias.

"Christ!" Ritchie's eyes popped out on stalks. "Well, your secret's safe wi' me, lad, dinnae worry. I always thought Ed Hurley was a piece o' work. An' maybe now you an' I can do a bit o' work together, eh? That is, if ye can bear to see me dressed up like Chaplin wi'oot puttin' a bullet in me, eh?"

I must admit it was good to have Billie Ritchie around. He fitted in fine with the Vimites, and featured in a few Thursday and Friday Vims while he learned the ropes, ready for his first outing as a Chaplinesque lead.

He and I talked about the war late into the night. The news reports we'd read spoke of unbelievable slaughter at the Battle of the Somme, thousands mown down by machine guns on either side, and it was hard not to feel guilty, being safe here in the Florida sun while so many of my countrymen were being obliged to make the ultimate sacrifice.

Ritchie's advice, though, was always the same: "Sit it oot, man, just sit it oot. It cannae go on for ever."

He told me there were dozens of British music hall stars over in America who'd been doing just that since 1914. It was even less appealing to think of returning, now that there was conscription at home, and the war was pretty much unavoidable. So I would continue to 'sit it oot' with Billie Ritchie. However, sometimes it did feel as though it just might go on for ever, especially when the progress of the war was measured, not in miles, but in unimaginable piles of corpses.

Finally then, after weeks of uncertainty and bafflement, a letter arrived from her, from Tilly. I opened it carefully, steeling myself.

'My dearest,' Tilly began, which was almost enough to finish me off right then and there.

'Imagine my joy at hearing that you were alive and well and living in Florida! The day I heard the news that the *Lusitania* had foundered was the worst of my life, and I was lost to grief for a long while. Sadly at this time I was scarcely alone in that.

'Let me assure you at once that Wallace and I are both in the rudest of health, and he is stronger and more confident every day.

'Arthur, however did we come to such an extraordinary misunderstanding? I have thought about this a lot, and I suppose that I must take some of the responsibility.

'Your thrilling cable telling me that you would be on the *Lusitania* arrived at my family's home in Great Yarmouth just as we were making preparations for another move. I wrote a letter telling you of this, and our new address, which would have been waiting for you at Liverpool, so that you could have made your way to join us, but of course you never received that, did you, just as I never received anything you might have subsequently sent to Great Yarmouth, which we left under something of a cloud.

'My father's exoneration in respect of the pier fire apparently didn't satisfy everyone of his suitability as a children's entertainer, and life was becoming intolerable there. We resolved to move up to Skegness, which we'd heard was quite the coming resort. You will remember, I'm sure, that poster with the jolly boatman we used to see in railway stations everywhere[9].

'Now, though, it seems that the railways have been reassigned for troop movement, and this has put paid to the large numbers of day trippers who might have made my father's travails as a Punch and Judy man sustainable. The town has become a billet for the Lovat Highlanders, who are engaged in the business of fortifying the Lincolnshire coast against invasion.

'One of these, a Sgt Iain McTavish, was good enough to use one of his travel warrants to take me and Wallace on our trip to Cambridge, where I met your charming parents and received the wonderful news that you are alive.

Yes, good old Sgt Iain McTavish, I thought.

'As for my own contribution to the war effort, I have joined the nursing staff of a convalescent home here in Norfolk for soldiers returning from France, many of them I am sorry to say with severe and disabling injuries, limbs missing, or scared quite out of their wits. When I tell them I know Charlie Chaplin it brightens their lives. I am forever being asked about Charlie – I am afraid I often tell the lads that he and I were sweethearts, because they get a thrill out of that and God knows they deserve one. It is not, as you know, altogether true, but it is not an outright lie either, so I trust I am forgiven.'

I found I was grinding my teeth as I read, but I was grinding them in a forgiving way, I thought.

'There was actually one lad who was far more thrilled to discover that I knew you, as it happens. Evidently you were kind to him in Chicago, and he seemed to regard you as a kind of comedy mentor. Short, pale, wispy fair hair, I think his name was either Donald or Daniel...'

I stopped reading and closed my eyes for a moment. "Dan Raynor?" I thought. It sounded like him. I hoped he was all right. If he was convalescing in Lincolnshire at least he was out of the fighting for now, unless he got on the wrong side of a Lovat Highlander.

'As to the future, I am sure you must have moved on with your life. America seems so far away now, and so long ago. I am truly happy that you are alive, and safe.

'Think fondly of me, as I do of you, all my love, Tilly.'

I sat and looked at the letter for a long while. What was I to make of it, I wondered. The way she signed off was so distant, somehow. Affectionate enough, certainly, but not exactly encouraging me to drop everything and come and find her. It was almost as if she didn't even expect a reply.

And what of this McTavish fellow? A friend? Or something more? I could hardly blame her if it was so, could I, since she had believed me dead for a year and a half. Not to mention my own canoodling with Ray Godfrey.

As I turned it over in my hands, I noticed that there was something more enclosed in the envelope. I fished out a small photograph, the size perhaps of four postage stamps, the sort of thing a photographer might give you as a sample in the hope of persuading you to cough up for something more expansive. It was Tilly, with Wallace sitting on her knee. She was smiling, but the smile was slightly forced, as though she had been holding it for a little while. I think I only noticed because I knew her smile so well. Young Wallace, to be frank, looked a little cheesed off, but I could clearly see that he had grown quite a bit since I had seen him last. He was wearing a sailor suit with short trousers that showed off the plump little creases at the side of his knees, so he wasn't going short of a meal, that's for sure.

As for me – well, I had plenty of food for thought.

And shortly afterwards I even had dessert.

Because then Billy Ruge was arrested.

For murder.

44
THE OSTRICH

NEXT morning the little Vim community was humming with the news of Billy Ruge's arrest. He wasn't the most popular member of the company, and hadn't really been seen very much for months while he recovered from his accident. He'd been content to take the pay cheques for the Plump and Runt movies even though he was no longer actually appearing in them, and had showed no particular readiness to return to the day-to-day grind. When he did make an appearance, it was usually leaning heavily on a pair of walking sticks, and there was a strong suspicion that he might have been laying it on a bit thick, having pretty much recovered. In short, though, none of us really knew what he had been up to lately, or had any idea what he might have gotten himself mixed up in.

As for myself, I felt like my vitals were in the icy grip of some nameless fear – maybe it was the knowledge of how very close I had sailed to those rocks myself these past few months.

Anyway, there was a limit to how much we could go over and over such barren ground, and so finally we began to get on with some work. Babe and Kate Price were working on a Plumps domestic story that week which was more or less Runt-free, meaning that I was co-opted to assist Billie Ritchie on his first venture into Chaplin territory.

Burstein had given the production a free hand with the budget, reckoning that if we could kick this thing off right it would turn out to be a veritable goldmine. It was just as well, because Ritchie, so he'd assured me a couple of days earlier, didn't want to ape Chaplin, he wanted to top him.

"I want to show him, an' everyone else for that matter, who's the original and best," the little Scotsman insisted. "So we need a stunt! A stunt that tops anything he's done. Or anything Lonesome Luke has done, or Fatty Arbuckle, or any o' them fellas.[10]"

"Right-o," I said. "What do you want me to do?"

Which is how I found myself down Talleyrand Avenue shortly thereafter, attempting to procure an ostrich.

"Well, we have ostriches, a couple hundred of 'em," a smart-alec young chap in the office down at the ostrich farm said. "Which particular one do you want?"

"What?"

"What was the ostrich's name, bud?"

"They have names?"

"No, I'm just raggin' ya. What is it you want? Breast steak? Or some eggs, maybe?"

"I want a whole one."

"I see, and do you want us to kill it for you, or are you plannin' to do that your good self?"

"What? Kill it? No, I want a live one."

"Aha. You know, they don't make very good pets, ostriches. They can get very ornery if you get on the wrong side of 'em. Which isn't to say you mightn't just meet one and hit it off, just that that would be unusual. In my experience of ostriches. Which is extensive."

"I want it for a film."

"You want to put one of my ostriches in the flickers?"

"That's right, yes."

"I see, so you want one of my film star ostriches."

"You have film star ostriches?"

"No, just raggin' ya again. Our ostriches are mostly stage birds."

Fortunately he tired of making a fool of me soon after that, and an ostrich was duly delivered to the farm where Billie Ritchie's film debut was to be shot. It stood in a pen that seemed to have been used for pigs, and the fences didn't really look high enough to keep the bird in, he could have just lifted one backward-bending knee and stepped a long grey leg over it. To begin with, though, the giant creature just stood there, eyeing us warily.

The director was Pathé Lehrman, an embittered former Keystone man who, like Billie, seemed to blame Chaplin for all the ills in his world and was thus perhaps somewhat over-motivated to do something really spectacular. We'd actually met briefly, a few years ago, when Stan, Charlie and I visited Keystone.

"Hullo again," I said when he came over, but the fellow looked at me blankly, clearly didn't remember me.

Ritchie came out of the farmhouse to inspect my purchase. He was dressed exactly like Chaplin's tramp in every detail – so much for topping Charlie and not aping him, I thought.

"What's the plan, then, Bill?" I said.

"Hmm," he said, scratching his stubbly chin. "Do ye think I could ride him around?"

"Rather you than me," I said.

"Let's have a go," the little Scot said, and clambered up onto the railing. The ostrich backed away and spread its white-tipped black wings wide, making itself look big to face down what it saw as a threat. A hissing noise emitted from its sharp triangular beak, as Billie tried to entice it over.

"Come on, sweetheart," he cooed. "Come tae Daddy."

The ostrich was not in the mood to be enticed.

"Get some food," Ritchie said to me, out of the corner of his mouth.

"Food? What food? What do they eat?"

"I dunno. Did they no' send any food for the creature?"

"Not that I am aware of," I said.

"Well, what do birds eat? Worms? Bread? I think there's bread in the farm house. Run in and get it, there's a good lad."

I returned a couple of minutes later with half a crusty loaf, and Billie was still perched precariously on the fence of the pig pen, with the ostrich showing no sign of wanting to make friends. I balanced the bread on the rail and stepped back to see if the bird would show any interest, but it was far too spooked to care about bread.

"Come on, darlin'" Ritchie cooed again. "Nice bread, eh? Yum yum!"

He jumped down from the fence, thinking that if he stepped away the bird might relax a little. Just then, however, a seagull swooped down from nowhere with a screech, and flew off with the loaf, which was half as big as itself.

"Well, so much for that," Ritchie said. "Tell you what we'll go for. We'll let it oot o' the pen..."

"Right," I said, still not sure that the pen was actually holding the bird at all.

"An' get it to chase me around, film that, see what we get, eh?"

"It doesn't look like it wants to chase you," I said.

"Ach, problems, problems, you're all problems today," Ritchie complained impatiently. "All right lads, let' start the camera rollin', I'll open the gate, an Arthur, you prod it wi' a big stick until it decides tae play ball. All right?"

The crew all got into position, and I noticed a good deal of eye-rolling apprehension, but Ritchie was the one doing the stunt, so they assumed he knew what he was doing.

"Action!" Pathé Lehrman shouted, and the cranking began.

Ritchie threw open the gate of the pig pen, and stood in front of the ostrich.

"Come on, then, ye big lump!" he shouted, waving his arms up and down. "Do something! Don't just stand there, ye pop-eyed cloon!"

I'd availed myself of a stick, the longest one I could find, not wanting to be within range of that great neck and pointy beak. I poked it between the bars and jabbed the bird in its backside. It jumped up, flapping its wings in surprise, and then settled again.

"Can't catch me, you gangly great goon!" Ritchie shouted, moving in closer to taunt the baffled creature as I jabbed it again, and then again.

Suddenly it lurched into life and launched itself at Billie Ritchie, wings flapping, great wrong-looking legs pumping.

"Aha!" Ritchie cried, and bolted towards the farmhouse. "Keep rollin'!" he shouted as he barrelled past the camera with the nine-foot monster hot on his heels. "I'll lead it a merry dance!"

Ritchie jinked left, and the ostrich slipped trying to change direction, landing in a heap on one side.

"Ha ha!" Ritchie yelled, and opened up a gap between them. The camera turned and cranked, capturing every move, and the ostrich clumsily regained its footing on its mighty claws, which I suddenly noticed for the first time. They looked nasty, sharp, strong, and the ostrich was looking angry and determined as it set off after its prey once again.

"Bill!" I shouted – it was a silent movie so I wasn't disturbing the shot – "get into the farmhouse!"

Ritchie stopped in his tracks, and frowned. He looked back at the ostrich lumbering towards him, and all of a sudden he saw what I saw. An unstoppable, nine-foot tall kicking machine.

"Quick, man!" I hollered.

Ritchie shot towards the building, and the ostrich moved to cut him off. The Scotsman was driven by fear, now, and was no longer thinking about the shot, even though the camera was still whirring.

"Run!" I shouted, and the camera crew beside me all leapt to their feet, willing Ritchie to get to the door. And it seemed as though he was going to get there, his hand was reaching for the door handle and the ostrich was still a couple of yards behind. It appeared to realise that the little man was going to get away, and suddenly it reared up, with a flap of its great wings, obscuring Ritchie from our sight momentarily, and then brought its beak down with all the power contained in that great long neck, down, down, smashing down onto the top of the comic's head.

Ritchie fell on his face in the dirt, half-stunned by the blow. He staggered up to his feet, shaking his head, and reached a hand up to feel where he had been hit. He didn't seem to have the unscrambled wits left to dart for the door behind him, he just stood there.

The ostrich turned away. Its cruel beak seemed to be smiling as it looked back at us, the film crew and me, gazing in horror.

Then, lightning fast, it lashed out with one of its great long improbable legs and caught Ritchie straight in the gut. The little Scot flew backwards, crashing into the building like a child's rag doll, and then slumped to the ground, broken.

The mighty bird looked at us, as if to say "See? That's what you get!", and we froze.

Then it lifted up on its toes and shot across the farmyard in four or five enormous strides, out onto the dirt road, and disappeared over the horizon.

We rushed over to poor Billie, but it was plain to see that there was nothing to be done.

He was gone.

45
JAX BANJAXED

WITH a member of the film community to which he had pinned his hopes languishing in the town's jail, and another in the morgue, Mayor Bowden was obliged to play his ace. As he had clearly hoped, this knocked both the news of Billy Ruge's mysterious arrest and of poor Billie Ritchie's demise into a cocked hat, or, more accurately, into a small corner of the front pages of the *Tribune-Union* and the *Metropolis*.

CHARLIE CHAPLIN COMING TO JACKSONVILLE!

The headlines screamed from every news stand and from the lungs of every news boy in town, and the buzz was palpable. In the bars, on the streets, in the stores and even in the churches that were squarely backing Martin's vision of 'Gomorrah Tomorrah!' – a good slogan, we had to admit – it was all anyone in the town was talking about.

J.E.T. Bowden's slogan, by the way, was an odd play on his own initials – 'Just Easy Times, Boys!' A nice sentiment, true enough, but not one especially appealing to those hard-working citizens who thought all movie men were dangerous slackers.

Hoping to build on this coup and ram home his advantage, Mayor Bowden mobilised the movie community, and held a mammoth glittering reception at the Mason hotel, hosted by George M. Cohan, who was making pictures for Artcraft at that time. Music, naturally, was provided by The Half-Ton of Harmony himself, Babe Hardy, and his Twentieth Century Four, and the evening began with a tremendous and optimistic swing. Surely Bowden was going to win. The movies were Jacksonville, and Jacksonville was the movies.

Over at the Vim tables, however, the mood was sombre. I sat in a corner nursing a bottle of bourbon. Billie Ritchie's violent end had thrown me into a black depression, and only copious amounts of alcohol eased the pain.

It was an accident, of course, an act of God and Nature, but I couldn't help considering that if poor Billie hadn't been driven by his desire to outdo Chaplin, and lay claim to the success he believed should have been his all along, then he would still be with us, possibly sitting opposite me right at that moment.

I watched Ray Godfrey dancing with Bert, twirling lithely around the little jockey. I had been a little distant with the poor kid lately, thinking about Tilly, wondering whether she had indeed 'moved on', as she herself had put it in the letter I now knew by heart.

I looked at the photograph of Tilly and Wallace again, as I had several times a day since receiving it. Something struck me as odd, suddenly, about the shape of it. It was almost square, but not quite, and certainly not the rectangular portrait that would have been common. Then the background, particularly behind the little boy. It was patterned lower down, but plainer up above, with some unexplained dots. I puzzled away at it, moving close to a candle to squint at it more closely.

Then I saw it, the answer that made sense of it. The pattern was a tartan, specifically a kilt. The plain area with the dots? A tunic, with shiny buttons. This was McTavish, surely, standing proudly behind them, and the odd shape was because of the necessity of trimming off the man's head and feet, in the hope that I would not notice him.

Because this was not a happy snap of a single mother and her child.

It was a little family group.

I barely had time to digest the import of this before Billy Ruge turned up at the Mason, walking sticks clicking on the hard dance floor, having finally been released without charge.

All the Vimites mobbed him, pressing for details of his sensational incarceration.

"All a big misunderstanding," he said breezily. "Case of mistaken identity, that's all. Took a while to convince them, mind, seein' how the finger as was pointed at me belongs to someone *famous*, but when the incident happened I was nowhere near it and in the end they had to let me go."

"Who on Earth were you supposed to have killed?" Babe asked.

"Would you believe... Charlie Chaplin?" Ruge said, exhibiting the best timing I had seen in the year I had known him. The Vimites gasped as one. I felt as though my insides were trying to escape through my mouth.

"Charlie Chaplin's not dead, is he?" Bert asked.

"No, no, it wasn't really Charlie Chaplin," Billy replied, trying to quell the incredulity a little. "It was a feller who made his living pretendin' to be Charlie Chaplin, an' somebody shot him in an honest-to-goodness gunfight over in Dodge City. Can you believe that?"

I could.

"Well, turns out this was last autumn, and Lou showed 'em that I was here, making Pokes and Jabbs flicks with Walt and Bobby, no way I could have been in Kansas perforatin' some Chaplin-a-likey, an' so they had to spring me."

"Congratulations," Babe cried. "The mayor will be relieved that there isn't a killer in town, anyway, especially one who's gunning for his secret weapon."

Everyone cheered and patted Billy on the back, and when festivities resumed shortly afterwards, he took me to one side with a firm grip on my elbow.

"You an' me need to have a word," he said.

"What about?" I asked.

"I can tell by the way you went white when I mentioned Dodge City that you know fine well what about," he said in a low voice, moving in closer. "I'm right, aren't I?"

"I don't know what you mean," I said.

"Well, let me tell you what I was told by the gents from the Bureau of Investigation[11]," Billy said. "They told me it was Charlie Chaplin himself that contacted them, and told them the man they were after was workin' in Jacksonville, playin' the part of Runt in the Thursday Vim."

"Um..."

"An' so if I was you, son – which'd make a change, wouldn't it, seein' as you've spent most of this year bein' *me* – I'd make myself scarce."

"You didn't tell them?"

"Who, the Bureau guys? Naah, why should I do their job for 'em? Besides, I wouldn't want it to get out that the feller onscreen wasn't really Billy Ruge, when Billy Ruge is getting' all the credit and money besides. My legs are pretty much fixed now, so I'll just take over again. Get me?"

"I do," I said. "Thanks for that, anyway, Billy."

"My pleasure, son," Ruge replied. "Oh, one more thing," he said. "What da hell happened in Dodge?"

"An accident, a stupid accident," I said.

"Huh," Ruge grunted when it became clear that that was all I was going to say on the matter. He wandered off then, a self-satisfied smirk on his ugly mug, and left me to my whirling thoughts and my bourbon bottle.

Chaplin.

Charlie bloody Chaplin!

A whole continent between us, and a gulf as wide in circumstances, and yet he still couldn't resist the opportunity to reach out and ruin my life.

Clearly Syd had recognised me, even though he hadn't deigned to talk to me at all. And of course Charlie would have heard sooner or later about the Dodge City shoot-out, and the demise of Edgar Hurley. Even though there were shock reports of Chaplin's death practically every other week, thanks to a sudden unexpected disease, or a stunt gone wrong, or a cuckolded husband, *that* particular one would surely have caught his eye, and he'd have known I was the man wanted for it.

He could have left it alone, couldn't he, but no, he decided to set the Bureau of Investigation on my trail. I could hardly believe he wanted me to be caught, because it would be a hanging if I couldn't explain myself, but I thought I knew why he had done it.

It was the Vims, the Thursday Vims.

He and Syd would have sought them out and sat through a couple, maybe more, and I could just imagine his stone face, his folded arms, the silent seething, as he saw me, his greatest rival, getting laugh after laugh, and he couldn't stand it, he couldn't bear it, and so he had struck out at me, struck out again, trying to bring me down.

Well, he hadn't managed to get me incarcerated, through the merest good fortune, but he had brought an end to my Floridian idyll, that was for sure. I was going to have to leave, quick smart, and tell no-one where I was going. Not before I finished the bottle, though...

Just then the Mayor himself climbed up onto the stage, mopping his red face with a big white hand kerchief.

"Thank you, friends, for your most kind support!" he cried. "Surely we have a fair wind at our backs, the election will be ours, and Jacksonville will continue to go from strength to strength!"

As the packed room cheered to the rafters a flustered fellow, one of the mayor's personal staff, rushed in brandishing an early edition of the next morning's Florida Tribune-Union. He hopped up onto the stage and showed it to Bowden, who reeled as though he had been punched squarely in the heart. Then, helped by his underling, he left the stage, and shortly the building, without another word.

The newspaper ended up in Babe's hands, as he had been standing onstage behind the stricken mayor, and he frowned as he glanced over the lead story. From all parts of the gathering voices began to call out.

"What does it say, Babe?"

"Tell us!"

Babe stepped forward, a solemn expression on his usually jolly features. "It reads as follows," he said, and instantly there was hush. "Jacksonville has been abuzz with excitement over the prospect of Charlie Chaplin, the most popular and well-rewarded comedian on the face of the Earth, coming to town to make pictures here, as faithfully promised by Mayor J.E.T. Bowden. However..."

At this point the audience began to shift uncomfortably. Uh-oh...

"... yesterday it was announced that Mr Chaplin was terminating his association with Mutual Pictures, entering into a new agreement with First National that will net him a million dollars for just eight new pictures..."

This figure drew gasps from all parts.

"... which he will make in a brand new purpose-built facility to be constructed... in Hollywood, California."

Groans. No wonder Bowden had been so shocked – his ace-in-the-hole had turned out to be a joker. Babe read on: "The people of Jacksonville have been sold a pup!"

"Huh!" Bert Tracey grunted. "Well, that's Jax banjaxed!"

He was right, too. The voters had been promised Charlie Chaplin on their doorstep only to have this inexplicably desirable treat snatched from their eager grasp, and they took their bitter disappointment out on the mayor. Bowden had not delivered, and he was ousted. Martin came in, and film production companies didn't wait for him to make their lives intolerable, they just upped sticks and left, some for New Jersey and New York, but most headed for the Hollywood hills. Within a short month, all film production in the city had ceased, never to start again, and Jacksonville would never again rival Hollywood's supremacy.

My Jacksonville dream was over, and so, it seemed, was everyone else's. Incredibly, like so many of my dreams, it had been trampled by the Tramp.

Chaplin had done for me once again.

46
THE FOUR-MINUTE MAN

SIX months later, America was a very different place.

President Wilson had finally taken the country into the war, the final straw being a telegram apparently sent by the German Foreign Secretary, one Herr Zimmermann, to their ambassador in Mexico proposing a military alliance. He was authorised to offer the Mexicans the prospect of regaining Texas, Arizona and New Mexico if all went according to plan.

So war came to pass in April of 1917, and not every American was thrilled. Plenty of expatriate Irishmen, for example, regarded themselves as already at war with England – or, strictly speaking, already dodging a war with England by staying in the States and moaning about it – and insisted America was coming in on the wrong side. There was, though, a great swell of patriotic fervour at large. Recruitment posters popped up everywhere, on every hoarding and free wall space, with Uncle Sam pointing out at passers-by to demand that they join him, in his shiny blue jacket and star-spangled top hat.

In order to prevent food shortages citizens were encouraged to participate in 'Meatless Mondays' and then 'Wheatless Wednesdays', and to turn their back yards into 'Victory Gardens'. The President even had sheep grazing on the White House lawns to show his support.

And everywhere you turned, there were people pressuring you to enlist, or to buy Liberty Bonds to pay for the war effort. Mr George M. Cohan wrote *Over There*, which became an overnight smash[12]. He, like so many others, was no longer making movies down in Florida.

I wondered what Babe was up to, and Ray, and the others, and whether I would ever see any of them again. I felt bad about leaving without breaking properly with Ray, but I could hardly take her with me, could I, since I was on the run again?

I wondered too what Tilly and Wallace were doing, although I tried not to. Was this Lovat Highlander making my boy into a little Scotsman? He had the name for it, at least.

I'd written a reply to Tilly before I left Jacksonville, and had gone through a good number of drafts of it, I can tell you. It seemed too odd to give her my blessing to move on with her life, since I was essentially reading between the lines – and between Wallace's ear and her shoulder in that little photograph – so I simply assured her that I had no intention of attempting another crossing, and left it to her to take that as she would. What else could I do until the war ended, and when would that be? A year? Ten years? Twenty? Whenever, it would likely be too late for us. Maybe it was already. And now that I was on the move once more, I could hardly even say we were still in touch.

So I headed North with my savings, figuring that if I was going to keep a low profile, then the biggest city on the continent was probably a good place to do it. I was there when the announcement was made that President Wilson had finally been pushed to breaking point, standing stunned amongst a mass of New Yorkers as the newsboys hollered the headlines, trying to work out what this meant for me.

One consequence coming fairly hot on the heels of the war announcement was that it was once again possible to see me performing in the movie houses, many of which were formerly vaudeville theatres I had played in back in the days of my first Karno American tour. I wasn't appearing in the flickers though. I became a Four Minute Man.

We were volunteer speakers, working for the government, and we were sent out all over the country to deliver short patriotic speeches. The maximum time you were given to make an impact was four minutes, hence the job title, and this was because it took precisely four minutes for the projectionist to change the reel.

So a picture would end, and up on the screen would appear a slide, giving my name (actually not my name, the name of my alias Arthur Smith) and alerting the audience that I was to 'speak four minutes on a subject of national importance, under the authority of George Creel, chairman of the Committee on Public Information'.

It wasn't exactly paid employment, which was proving elusive, but it was possible to squeeze some small expenses out of them and two meals a day, which, with the merest hint of irony, were usually Liberty Meat (former hamburgers) with a side order of Liberty Cabbage (erstwhile sauerkraut). The best perk of all, however, was that if anyone pestered me to register for the draft myself, I could whip out my identity card and say: "I'm a Four Minute Man," and that would be the end of that. In effect I was hiding in plain sight, doing my bit.

A man called Herbert Powell ran the programme in New York. He was a balding, middle-aged bureaucrat who looked like he had never laughed in his entire life. He would give us pep talks, and choose what subjects we would speak about, which could be Universal Selective Service (the draft), the Liberty Bonds drive (or Loyalty Bonds, as we were told to call them), the Red Cross, German Spies are Everywhere, Why We Are Fighting, or The Meaning of America (available in seven languages).

They liked it that I had an English accent, and would give me speeches that were all about America coming to the aid of her oldest ally in times of need, that sort of thing.

I got wheeled out in front of a crowd several times a day, because frankly I was good at it. Not all the Four Minute Men were used to public speaking, as I was. Not all of them already knew to aim for the back row of the stalls because that meant you would hit everyone in between. Not all of them could quell murmuring and trips to the lavatory with a look, as I could, or could command the attention of the whole room for even half a minute, let alone four.

However, I was faced with a constant dilemma. I had a serious message to deliver, but I was an old vaudevillian faced with an audience of 450 or so, all of whom had just been laughing and were ready to do so again. I wanted to do it, I wanted to tickle their ribs or tap them on the funny bone.

So one night, instead of the rousing inanity that had been written for me, I said:

"Let's kick the Kaiser in the keister!"

It got a nice laugh, and meant I ended with the house cheering and was able to come off stage feeling just a tiny bit of the adrenaline rush that had once been my daily diet. It also, however, got me a telling-off from the supervisor.

"Just deliver your message without the crowd-pleasing, thank you, Mr Smith," Powell said.

"But it got a laugh," I said.

"You've got four minutes to get through to them," Powell said. "If they spend ten seconds laughing and cheering, then you only have three minutes and fifty minutes to persuade them to contribute. War is a serious business."

"I know, but..." I said.

"And if you lose ten seconds every time you speak, then every twenty-four speeches you make, you lose a whole speech, you only deliver twenty three."

"That doesn't make sense," I insisted. "If they laugh, it means they are listening."

"If they laugh it means, they are dismissing you as frivolous, and less likely to make the serious decisions that you are urging upon them. Less likely to register for the draft, less likely to buy a bond, less likely to question the motives of their German neighbours. So cut out the funnies, Mr Smith."

"But..."

"And in any case, isn't 'keister' a... *German* word?"

"Well, strictly speaking, keisters don't come any more German than the Kaiser's own," I said, but I had to give way on the jokes in the end.

Like many, I had high hopes that America's arrival might speed the end of the conflict, but even after the doughboys landed, the news from France was depressingly discouraging.

One evening I was at a movie house on 47th Street, waiting for my four minutes and looking sideways and upwards at the screen where the flicker was playing. I caught the title card, and saw that it was by a company called King Bee out of Bayonne, New Jersey, but missed the name of the star. A couple of minutes in, though, it was clearly Charlie Chaplin I was peering up the nose of, and I couldn't make head nor tail of this. Charlie had signed a huge deal with First National, and his film-making was getting ever slower as he demanded more and more time to polish his jewels, so there was no way he'd be knocking out a quick and nasty bit of slapstick such as this. Perhaps it was my Chaplinoia returning...?

I squinted up at the screen, which was distorted by my proximity, and a heavy entered the action. Surely... surely it was Babe...?!!

Babe Hardy working with Chaplin? Now that would be a real kick in the teeth. I had to know, and so I pushed through the door that led to the side aisle of the auditorium and hurried round to get a front on view.

Now I could see properly the big man was definitely Babe, and he was just getting his backside kicked by the little tramp. I started to feel acid in my stomach at the thought of my friend having been drawn into the orbit of my bitter enemy, a man who would surely destroy him once he realised how funny he was. What could I do? How could I warn him...?

The tramp on screen then executed a manoeuvre to escape his rival's clutches and pushed him over on his behind. Babe sold this completely, as he always did, with surprising grace and athleticism, but I peered again at the little man. There was something... off. There was an element missing, a fluency, a balance. Was Charlie having an off day? Was he already thrown off by being upstaged by Hardy?

The flicker reached its climax, and I stared at the end cards, hungry for information. There was no mention of Chaplin, none at all. The star was called Billy West, and his sidekick was indeed my Jacksonville playmate.

Billy West? I didn't know the name, but clearly he was a Chaplin copyist, and a good one, too. The crowd had enjoyed the comedy and were in a good mood, and it was almost as if they either didn't notice or didn't particularly care that it wasn't the real Chaplin they had just been watching. Which was... funny, wasn't it?

I started to laugh, standing there in the aisle. Not at Billy West's acting, meticulous though that had been, but at the fact that Billy West existed. I had seen Chaplin imitators onstage, of course, not least Stan and Ed Hurley – I felt a lurch in my guts at the memory – and I had even impersonated him myself more times than I cared to recall just to get a chicken leg, but an impersonator onscreen! Why, that was hilarious, wasn't it? Surely that devalued his whole currency? Why would First National, or anyone else for that matter, pay him a million dollars for eight films if they could get Billy West to make an identical flicker every week for peanuts?

I began to think I saw an ending on the horizon for Mr Charlie Chaplin, with good old Babe helping to bring him down, and actually began to rub my hands together with glee.

Suddenly I realised that the crowd were beginning to murmur and shift in their seats. I looked up at the screen and there was a slide showing. It read:

'This is to certify that Arthur Smith will speak for Four Minutes on a matter of...'

I didn't read any more, I was already running down the aisle shouting at the top of my voice:

"Ladies... ladies and gentlemen! The message I have for you is of such importance...!" – here I leapt up dramatically onto the stage – "that I have been delivering it in every movie house in town. Phew! Nearly didn't make it!"

I paused, doubling over to get my breath after that sudden burst of activity, my hands on my knees. And slowly, but building like a wave, the audience began to clap, until a tidal wave of applause broke over my head at my tireless efforts on behalf of the country, and I had to raise my hands to calm them down.

Afterwards Herbert Powell said: "That's good, I like that opening. Very mysterious, very urgent. Cost you some time, but got them on your side. Keep that, and lose the laughs. Got me, Smith?"

Later that evening I was sitting by myself in Smoky Joe's on 43rd Street, minding my own business and two fingers of bourbon.

Seeing Babe up on the screen had brought home to me how very lonely I was. I took out the little trimmed photograph of Tilly and our son in his sailor suit and gazed at it for the umpteenth time. She might have moved on, but could I honestly say that I had, in my heart?

I missed Babe and the guys at Vim too, but the Jacksonville movie boom was over, strangled by the manipulative intervention of Charlie Chaplin.

I missed my old Karno mates. Stan – whatever was Stan up to, I wondered. Still pretending to be Charlie Chaplin? Wren – what was she doing? Poor girl, left to fend for herself in the Wild West, her husband lying in the dirt dressed as Charlie Chaplin. Mike Asher – was he still running a burlesque house in Seattle, a whole continent away? And Freddie, poor Freddie, cut down in the Dardanelles two years ago now.

I felt a lump in my throat, and feared that I might break down in tears, right there in the bar.

Suddenly I heard a man's voice behind me sing out:

"Arthur Dandoe!"

Before I could stop myself, I had turned round like a fool to see who it was, and of course it wasn't some mate from the old country, or someone who owed me money or even a drink.

It was a smug-looking slicker in a sharp dark suit, with another identically-attired sidekick just behind, both of them smirking away like they'd pulled off the greatest stroke of their lives.

This was not good.

This was not good at all.

47
THE ROOM

SUMMER OF 1917, SOMEWHERE IN AMERICA

"**AND** so here we are," John said, sitting back in his chair.

"Here we are indeed," I replied. "Now are you going to tell me what the devil you want?"

John regarded me silently, thinking, which unnerved me more than somewhat.

"I don't really know what else I can tell you," I said.

He looked at his colleague, who gave a little shrug as if to say: "Up to you."

"You seem to have amassed quite a store of resentment against our friend Mr Chaplin," John mused.

"Your friend, maybe," I muttered.

"Although perhaps we should put your assertion that he deliberately destroyed the entire J-Jacksonville film industry down to your personal, shall we say... Chaplinoia?"

I didn't say anything to this. He already thought I was crackers without me adding fuel to that particular fire.

"So I wonder what you would say if I was to offer you the opportunity to, shall we say, even the score."

"I would say: 'Tell me more'."

"You are aware that our primary objective, as yours was as a Four Minute Man, is to encourage as many men as possible, indeed all the able-bodied male population aged between 21 and 31, to register for the draft, make themselves available for service, even enlist of their own volition?"

"Was?" I asked.

"I'm sorry?"

"You said that my objective 'was', when I 'was' a Four Minute Man."

"Oh yes, that's over now. Either you work for us or I ship you back to England."

I stared levelly back at him, but my heart was pumping fast. John meanwhile shrugged nonchalantly as though all this was a mere detail to him. "Or you could stay here and take your chances with the Bureau of Investigation, who are minded to hang you. The choice is yours."

"That's nice," I said. "This is the land of the free, after all."

"So it is, so it is indeed."

"I still don't see what I can do for you," I said.

John steepled his fingers, and rested his bottom lip on top of them momentarily.

"We have concluded that the single most inspirational occurrence that we could p-possibly engineer would be an announcement that Mr Charlie Chaplin had registered for the draft."

"The most popular man in the country," John's sidekick cut in.

"I know," I said coolly. "I've seen him."

"I know that you are aware of the clause in his Mutual contract which forbade him from returning to England for the duration of hostilities for fear of being m-mobilized in the armed forces."

I nodded.

"And perhaps you are also aware that this did not go down especially well in your homeland, particularly in some leading newspapers, such as the *Daily Mail*? In short, their proprietor, Lord Northcliffe, has waged a lengthy c-campaign to oblige Chaplin to do his duty."

"Really?" I smiled.

"Now Lord Northcliffe is a powerful man, as you know. His editorials did much to bring down the government of Herbert Asquith, and he was most influential in the rise of P-prime Minister David Lloyd George."

"Oh?" I said.

"And yet his scathing editorials in his many organs, which include not only your *Daily Mail* but also the *Times*, the *Daily Mirror* and the *Weekly Dispatch*, have b-barely made a dent in Chaplin's determination to shirk his duty."

John reached into his satchel and pulled out a bunch of clippings, held together by a paper clip, and he read the first example with his lip curling in obvious contempt.

"'Charles Chaplin, although slightly built, is very firm on his feet, as evidenced by his screen acrobatics. The way he is able to mount stairs suggests the alacrity with which he would go over the t-top when the whistle blew.'"

"He's certainly very fit," I said.

John flipped to another item, and read some of it out loud.

"'During the thirty-four months of the war it is estimated that Charlie has earned well over £125,000...'"

"While good men are dying!" John's sidekick was moved to chip in.

"The United States Postal Service has delivered many hundreds of white f-feathers to your erstwhile colleague..."

"Which he uses to stuff the pillows he relaxes his treacherous head upon!"

"Yes, thank you, could I just...? Without interruption?"

"Sorry."

"Did you know, Mr Dandoe, that during the Civil War, fifty years ago, rich men were able to avoid being drafted by hiring other men to take their place in the battle lines?"

"I did not know that," I said.

"Well, we as a people have moved on from those days. The rich and famous can no longer hide from their responsibilities as members of the society they p-plunder as they p-please."

"Hear, hear!" the strong, silent type muttered.

"And since the introduction of the Selective Service Act, all able-bodied men are required to register, including foreign nationals."

"I would have," I said, "but for the fact that I was unable to use my own name because of... well, you know... and so did not have any papers."

John waved this irrelevance away. "Now, Chaplin is aged between 21 and 31, is he not?"

"He is," I said.

"And he is unmarried, without dependants?"

"As far as I know."

"Then he is categorised as Class 1."

"Right."

"As you yourself would be..."

"Unless you were convicted of the murder of Edgar Hurley, of course, then you'd be Class 5," John's sidekick contributed helpfully, with a not altogether pleasant smirk. "Or dead," he added, with an illustratory pantomime of hanging himself, tongue lolling, eyes rolling.

"You must have asked him about this?" I said, trying to steer the conversation back to Charlie. "Or someone must. What does he say?"

"Well, after a long delay, he has finally p-produced a doctor's letter claiming a medical exemption because he is underweight."

"Underweight?"

"That's right."

"Is there a weight restriction? I mean, I know Yank soldiers are called 'doughboys', but does that mean you are only looking for plump chaps?"

"No, it does not."

"And even if he is underweight, can't you just stuff him full of Liberty Meat till he makes the mark?"

"If he were to register for the draft, and be drawn to serve, then the army would undertake to work on improving his physical condition, as it would with every new recruit."

I was still baffled. "So... what? How do I come into this?"

"We strongly suspect that this doctor's letter is b-bogus."

"Aha."

"And we want you to go to Los Angeles, insinuate yourself into Chaplin's c-confidence, as an old friend, and find us the evidence we need."

I exhaled slowly. I could certainly present myself at Chaplin's door, but as an old friend? I wondered how far I would get. I could hardly say no, though, could I? When the alternatives were jail and the gallows or the machine guns of the Hun?

"What is it you want to achieve, exactly?" I said, trying to buy a little thinking time.

"Once we have the evidence in our hands, we will make it clear to Mr Chaplin that we expect him to step forward and register like every other patriotic citizen."

"And if he will not?"

"We will expose him as the slacker he is in every newspaper in the land. We will make a stink that Lord Northcliffe himself will smell all the way over in London. We will finish him as a popular entertainer."

John leaned forward eagerly, and his face took on a hungry, wolfish aspect. He even seemed, temporarily, to have mastered his stutter. It struck me then just how very much he wanted this, wanted to catch Chaplin out, wanted to bring him down. And I was certainly all for that, naturally, but it suddenly occurred to me that for once I had a little leverage.

"You want me to go all the way to California and dig up dirt on Charlie?"

"That's right."

"But in the meantime I'll still be wanted?" I said, dubiously.

John shook his head impatiently. "No, no, I have taken care of that already. The Bureau of Investigation has been notified that you are a person of special interest to my office, and there is no longer a warrant out for your arrest."

He could have mentioned that earlier, I thought, fingering my collar with relief.

I nodded slowly, holding the pause for dramatic effect like the old trouper I was.

"Well in that case," I said then. "I'm your man."

PART 6

48
THE LONE STAR

A week later, the Santa Fe Sunset Flyer neared Los Angeles, and I sat in unaccustomed comfort in a Pullman carriage. It was certainly an improvement on the Karno boxcar, in which I had covered so many miles, with its tourist-class basket weave seating, and the other actual boxcars I had ridden more recently as a free-loading bum. I leaned back in the plushly-upholstered seating, gazed out at the arid miles of desert flashing by the window, and contemplated the task before me.

I'd persuaded John that I couldn't just turn up on Chaplin's doorstep expecting a hearty welcome, not with all the history between us. I needed a plausible cover story.

First of all I needed to appear affluent and successful. If I gave Charlie the remotest impression that I wanted to touch him for money, I had no doubt at all that I would get the bum's rush. So I was wearing a smart new suit, bought for me by the United States government, and my belongings were housed in a brand new suitcase.

Then I needed a reason to call, over and above the notion that we were two old friends getting together to catch up and reminisce about the old days. It might turn into that scenario, if I played my cards right, but it wouldn't wash without a plausible agenda.

We decided, John and I, that the best deceptions contained a large grain of truth. So I was to be a former Four Minute Man who'd been promoted to work on the Liberty Bond drive full time, becoming in effect a producer, recruiting the great and good to speak to large crowds and lend the weight of their fame to the cause.

I figured that would get me in, at least, and after that I'd have to play it by ear.

One aspect of my new role I was particularly happy about anyway. Arthur Dandoe was back, and Arthur Smith was finally consigned to the trash can. I'd been a little anxious as the train made its way across Kansas close to Dodge, but John had given me a letter which nestled in my inside pocket explaining that I was no longer being sought by the forces of law and order, and a card with his office's details on it in case any over-zealous lawman needed to wire for confirmation.

I couldn't help wondering what Tilly would have made of my current mission. When I'd proposed, oh so long ago now, it seemed, and given her the ring with the Mr Punch head on it, she had made it clear that I would need to put my fixation with Charlie Chaplin behind me before she would commit to spending the rest of her life with me, and what was I doing now?

Heading clear across a continent in search of revenge, that's what.

Chaplin had gone out of his way to do me down on so many occasions now. From paying one of Syd's sailor friends to heckle me, to having my leg broken, to moving in on my girl, and most recently, to trying to get me *hanged* and destroying the Jacksonville film industry just in case I should be having too good a time.

Oh yes, I still owed him one. A big one.

———

Once in Los Angeles I checked into a high class hotel, the best I could find, on the government's dime, and then the next morning I made my way over to the studios where Charlie made his films. The Lone Star Studios, they were called, and they were located in a part of the city known as Colegrave.

I presented myself at the gatehouse, where two burly gatekeepers were in attendance, and I thought I cut an imposing figure in my dapper new threads, freshly-shaved and business-like.

"Good morning, my man," I said to the closer of the two attendants. "Would you be so kind as to let Mr Chaplin know that Mr Arthur Dandoe is here to see him? I am an old friend of his from the British music hall days..."

I had barely finished the sentence when the two of them grabbed me, one at each elbow, and flung me bodily back out into the street.

Once I had got over my surprise and dusted myself down I realised that they couldn't possibly be primed to recognise my name, it must have been the reference to 'British music hall days' that had prompted the knee-jerkers.

I see, I said to myself. It's like *that*, is it?

I marched back inside and thrust my identity card in the first man's face. In point of fact, it was the card identifying me as a Four Minute Man, but I didn't let him see it long enough to focus properly on it.

"Listen to me," I said, in a much less genial tone. "I am here on important government business, and I demand you show me to Mr Chaplin at once."

This tactic rather depended on the man jumping to it quick smart, but instead he gave me a long, slow look up and down, and then drawled to his burly mate:

"Call for the studio manager, will you, Dave?", whereupon the second chap lumbered off into a side room.

"That's more like it," I said. While I was waiting, it suddenly occurred to me that it would likely be Syd Chaplin who answered that particular summons, and I was just cursing my stupidity when the door opened and a stocky fellow in shirtsleeves stepped in and gaped at me.

I, for my part, gaped back.

"Arthur Dandoe! It is you! I thought this guy must have got the name wrong!"

"Alf Reeves!" I cried, for it was indeed my old friend and company manager from the Karno tours, and we embraced one another warmly with much back-slapping. "What on Earth are you doing here?"

"Working for Charlie," he said. "Beats touring for Fred Karno, I'll tell you that. Last year I did a *Mumming Birds* tour that lasted nine months and I don't think I felt my toes in all that time, but here the Sun shines all day long!"

"Good for you," I said. "How's Amy?"

"Well, well," he smiled. "I didn't want her to risk the crossing, but she'll join me sooner or later. And Tilly?"

"She's well, too, as far as I know," I said. "But when the war started she was over there and I was over here, and well..." I shrugged, not wanting to go into it any further.

"I know," Alf said. "It took me weeks to persuade them to give me the proper visas, and then I didn't sleep a wink the whole way over thinking I heard U-boat engines. Anyway, come in, come in!"

Alf led me through the gatehouse and out into the open studio. "The largest stage currently working," he said, indicating with a sweep of his arm the hive of activity on the lot. Stage hands were carting large flats this way and that, there was a cacophony of hammering and sawing, and what looked like the main hallway of a large house was being constructed in the open air beneath an array of white linen sheets, intended to diffuse the bright Californian sunshine.

"Look at you, Alf," I said. "In the flickers!"

"I had to leave the Fun Factory," Alf said. "The Guv'nor, he's... he's not the same."

"I can imagine," I said, thinking of poor Freddie.

"Have you seen anyone else from the old days?"

"Well, I suppose the last was... Billie Ritchie."

"Ah! How's that gabby rogue?"

"Dead," I said.

"Oh my God!" Alf gasped. "I didn't hear. France?"

"Kicked to death by an ostrich," I said, gloomily.

"Good gracious!" Alf gasped. "So the Germans are using ostriches now?"

"No, no, this was in Florida," I explained. "An accident. Terrible thing."

Alf shuddered. "Well, there are a couple of old Karno-ites here with us," he said. "There's Sydney, of course, and Albert Austin."

"Ha!" I said. "He always did seem to think the sun shone out of Charlie's behind!"

"And his faith has been rewarded," Alf said drily. "Oh, and Eric Campbell, too. Did you know him?"

"I remember the name," I said, "but I never met him."

"So what brings you here? Looking for work in the pictures, is it?"

I wavered before dissembling to my old friend. "No-o-o," I said, after a moment. "I am here on government business, as it happens."

"Oh?" Alf said.

I was about to spin him the yarn about the Liberty Bond drive, when suddenly the cry went up from all parts:

"He's here!"

The banging stopped, tools were flung aside, and hands came running from all directions. Alf gave a long-suffering sigh.

"Oh," he said. "*This* nonsense."

All the stage crew and electricians were lining up across the yard and standing to attention. From the various offices and bungalows on the lot office staff were emerging and hustling over to join the lines, straightening their hair and buttoning up their jackets. Actors in costume emerged from the cabins on the far side, some pulling scraps of tissue from their collars, one portly man caught midway through a shave.

"Hullo, Dandoe," said a lean, lugubrious fellow with curly hair as he galloped past me to stand dutifully to attention with everyone else.

"Austin," I saluted.

"Come on," Alf said, and strolled to the very end of the line, where I joined him.

The gates swung open, and a sleek black sports car, polished to within an inch of its life, oozed into the lot. It drew to a halt in front of the assembled company, and I could see that the driver was a Japanese chap in some rather fancy livery. As soon as the motor car stopped, a tall gangly fellow stepped from the front door and scuttled around to open the back door on the other side for the distinguished passenger.

436

Charlie – for it was he – emerged in a black coat with an astrakhan collar, bare-headed, and strode across the studio yard affecting not to even notice the line of employees waiting there, disappearing with the tall fellow at his heels into the office block while his Japanese chauffeur drove the car away to park it out of the sunshine.

Only when the boss was out of sight did everyone relax, and the lines broke as they all hustled back to their various jobs. It was an astounding spectacle.

"Don't ask," Alf said.

"Well, I suppose I should go and speak to him before he gets busy filming."

"Oh, I shouldn't think we'll be filming much today, if anything at all."

"Oh?"

"Yes, he's supposed to be delivering a film a month, but this one's been going for two and looks like going for two more. Some days we all just hang around while he thinks about the story, and then we all go home again."

"What's up? Run out of Karno sketches to cannibalise?"

"Ha!" Alf said. "You saw *The Rink?*"

"What, Fred Karno's *Skating*, you mean?"

Alf laughed. "Or *London Suburbia*, sorry, I mean *Easy Street?*"

"So? Shall I?" I nodded towards the office, but Alf shook his head.

"Leave him for an hour or two until he gets bored with his own company and staring at the four walls. Come on, I'll make you a cup of tea and we can have a proper catch up..."

It was midday before Alf would consent to let me go, and even then he insisted on coming with me to Charlie's inner sanctum. The office block was fairly rudimentary, with the inside walls painted pale green, giving it the look of some kind of field hospital. No wonder Charlie was struggling to think of anything funny, I thought. We were greeted by the tall thin factotum I'd seen earlier.

"Can I help you, gentlemen?"

"Morning, Tom," Alf said cheerily. "I've brought a visitor."

"I'm sorry, Mr Reeves, but I'm afraid Mr Chaplin has expressly asked not to be disturbed."

"Oh, he won't mind me," Alf said, and strode up to the office door, knocking it and opening it in the same movement.

"I thought I *said*..." came a familiar voice from inside, but Alf's bonhomie rode right over the top of Charlie's irritation.

"Hey Charlie!" he sang out. "Look who's here! You'll never guess!"

I was hanging back, but Alf grabbed me by the arm and thrust me forwards into Charlie's room, which was bare, just a wooden table and a couple of chairs, one piece of blank paper and a pencil. Charlie was halfway up out of the chair when I walked in, and when he saw me his eyes widened, showing those big violet irises, and he slumped back onto the seat.

"Hallo, Charlie," I said.

"Well, well, well..." Charlie said quietly. "Well, well, well, well, well..."

"It's been a while," I said.

"It has, it has, hasn't it?"

Alf Reeves clapped his hands together. "I'll leave you two to chat," he said, turning to the door.

"No!" Charlie almost shouted. "No, Alf, stay. Stay, please."

It was clear that Chaplin thought I might have come to do him

438

harm. After all, since we had last met face to face he'd discovered that I had shot a Chaplin impersonator and he'd tried to shop me to the Bureau of Investigation. I strolled over to the other chair and sat down, thinking it might relax him, and he did seem a little easier after a moment, and let go of the pencil which I suddenly saw he had been holding like a knife.

"So," I said, and Charlie bared his teeth in a mirthless smile.

"I'm afraid we don't have anything for you," he said. "All the parts in our current film are spoken for, we've shot the opening scenes already, over at Sierra Madre, so I can't think of making a change."

"I'm not looking for work," I said.

"You're not?"

"In point of fact I have left the entertainment industry altogether."

"What? No! It can't be!"

Charlie was shocked, I could see that, but there was no mistaking an undercurrent of pure glee at this news, it twinkled in those strange violet eyes. I felt a sudden burst of enthusiasm for getting back into the game somehow, but for the moment I had another task.

"I assure you," I said.

"What then? What are you up to these days?"

"I am working for the government," I said. "It is my task to put together some large scale public appearances for our best-loved cinema personalities as part of the Liberty Bond drive. It's all part of the war effort, you know?"

"Comedy's loss is the war effort's gain."

"Well, that's gracious, thank you."

Chaplin preened, and I could almost see him relaxing by the second.

439

"Arthur is hoping that you could make some appearances across the country," Alf put in helpfully. "And perhaps encourage some others to join in as well. Douglas Fairbanks, maybe? Mary Pickford?"

Charlie's mood was changing. He understood now that I wanted something from him, and that he held the cards. A sorrowful half-smile crept across his features, and it didn't strike me as altogether sincere.

"I'm sorry," Charlie said. "I simply cannot spare the time. I am bound to make this last film for Mutual, and then I am straight into my new contract with First National."

"For a million dollars," I said.

"Is that what they are saying? You'd have to ask Syd. Of course, I'll buy some bonds, if you have them on you?"

"No, no," I said. "I'm not actually selling them myself."

"And then we are busy building the new studios on Sunset, right in among the orange groves there, it's a lovely spot, it'll be far more conducive than this..."

"I see."

"I'll tell you what," Charlie said, and the cornered animal had completely disappeared now. He was transforming, before my eyes, into the very soul of generosity. "Where are you staying?"

"Oh, the government have run to a hotel," I said, "but only for a couple of days, then they'll be expecting me back in New York."

"Come and stay with us for a few days. There are bungalows, aren't there, right here on the lot, eh Alf?"

Alf Reeves nodded, beaming.

"Take a break in California, get some sun. You can tell your bosses that you gave it everything to persuade me but I just couldn't fit it in. Come along, I won't take no for an answer."

What was going on? Was he prompted by guilt for all that he

440

had done to me over the years? Now that I was no longer a rival, did he need me to like him? Was he playing a new part now, the genial host? Acting, like he did most of the time? Did anyone know the real Charlie Chaplin? Maybe only I did, I thought.

"I'll give it some thought," I said, playing hard to get. This, however, was as promising an opportunity as I could have hoped for.

"Come to the commissary, we shall have some lunch. I think today there's sausages and bacon."

"Cooked on a gas jet by a chef standing on a chair, I hope?"

"Ha ha! Yes!" Chaplin cried. "With an assistant wafting the smoke out of the window, and another masking the sizzling noises from the landlady by playing on the violin!"

"That's what we used to do when we first came to New York," I explained to Alf. "With Stan, he was the cook, and Freddie too."

Charlie snapped his fingers as an idea struck. "And this very afternoon we are all going to see a private screening at the Hippodrome. You must come along. I think you might enjoy it."

"A comedy?"

"Oh yes."

"Who is the star? Yourself?"

"Oh no, no, no, I am merely an interested spectator. Say you'll come."

"I should be delighted."

"Excellent!" Charlie said, with a smug smirk as though he knew something I didn't know.

Well, I knew something he didn't know.

And I was in.

49
NUTS IN MAY

THAT afternoon, a little party assembled in the Lone Star Studios yard. Charlie's sports car with its Japanese chauffeur rolled around in front of the office building, followed by another slightly more practical passenger vehicle.

Charlie was taking care of some business inside, and as I waited with Alf, he introduced me to a man-mountain, six-foot five if he was an inch and almost as broad, who was engaged in some lovey-dovey smooching with a tiny pretty girl who was almost entirely hidden under the giant's great arm.

"Eric? Eric Campbell, this is Arthur Dandoe, another refugee from the Fun Factory."

"Ah, yes," Campbell said, stroking his chin. "You know, I saw that shoot-out of yours."

"You did?" I said, my heart racing suddenly as I wondered how I could have missed such an imposing figure on the streets of Dodge.

"Yes, yes, at the Oxford, back in '09, was it? When the Guv'nor couldn't choose between you and Charlie and made you both play the goalkeeper on the same day. And that footballer broke your leg." The big man winced, then shook my hand. "It's an honour, sir."

"For me too," I said.

"Meet Pearl... my wife."

I took the girl's hand, as both she and Campbell simpered at one another with the private amusement newly-weds can get from using the words 'husband' and 'wife' for the first few times.

"He married her last week," Alf murmured in a quiet aside as the Campbells moved off. "They'd only known each other five days."

"How romantic."

"Hmmph!" Alf snorted. "Yes, unless you know that she was married twice before, to the candy heir Charles Alisky – divorced him – and the millionaire Theodore Amreiter – divorced him too. Her sister Mabelle, meanwhile, was just married to William Corey, who's three times her age and owns US Steel."

"Oh," I said, beginning to see the picture.

"I give it six weeks."

Syd Chaplin stalked over to join us, and I decided to greet him cheerily despite the years of resentments I had stored up against the black-hearted villain.

"What ho, Syd!" I said, hand outstretched as he approached, affecting the posh twit greeting that was the big in-joke during our Karno time.

"Dandoe," Syd growled, not taking my hand, and not joining in the joke. "I heard you were here. You're not going to cause any trouble, are you?"

"Trouble?" I said. "Me?"

"Arthur's working for the government now," Alf said. "The war effort, you know?"

"Hmm," Syd said with a suspicious narrowing of his eyes, and then he moved off to speak to the chauffeur.

Charlie emerged then, full of bonhomie now, with an attractive young girl on his arm. She had light brown hair and a sweet innocent face, and I knew I'd seen her somewhere before. I still hadn't quite placed her, though, when the pair joined us.

"We've met, haven't we?" I said to the girl.

"Oh? I..." she said, and then I had it.

"Yes, at the studio in Chicago." She was the very pretty girl who I'd thought better suited to the movies than any of the wanna-bes in her waiting room.

"Essanay?" Charlie said, turning to his companion. "Why that's right, that's where I met you, isn't it? Arthur Dandoe, Miss Edna Purviance." He gave us the benefit of those brilliant white teeth, and then said: "Ride with us."

I squeezed in the back of the sports car after Charlie, with Edna squashed in the middle, and we rolled out of the yard and onto the road.

"I came at the invitation of Ben Turpin," I said to Edna.

"Oh yes, I remember. Fancy seeing you again," she said.

"I recall you visited with that lovely Mrs Hurley, didn't you?" Charlie said.

"Yes," I said. "We thought it would be a lark to be in one of your films."

"And her husband... what happened to him?"

I knew fine well that he was well aware of Edgar's fate, since I was sure he had identified me to the Bureau of Investigation, but I was desperately anxious to avoid a confrontation, since I had a job to do and what's more had made such a good start at infiltrating Charlie's life.

"Oh, a terrible thing, I was there. There was a gunfight, a publicity stunt, and the gun was supposed to have blanks in it, but in

444

the event the ammunition was live."

"Oh, how awful!" Edna gasped.

"I do vaguely recollect something now," Charlie mused.

"Well, he was dressed as you, and the papers declared you dead, so news might have reached you."

Chaplin waved a hand. "Oh, I have been declared dead eight or nine times now. Drowned trying to rescue a child, killed when a stunt went wrong, automobile crashes, at least two suicides, killed by jealous husband, his mangled corpse, that sort of thing. I barely even glance at them nowadays. Did you know?" he said. "Nine out of ten men who went to a costume party in the last year went as me? Ha!"

"I guess the likelihood of some of them having an accident must be quite high," I said.

"Exactly!" Charlie laughed.

"Oh, don't even joke about it," Edna said.

Charlie took her hand and patted it. "Isn't she adorable? We really are inseparable, aren't we?"

———

When we arrived at the Hippodrome on Main Street, I was surprised to discover it was actually a vaudeville theatre rather than a cinema.

"The owner, gent by the name of Adolphus Ramish, wants to get into pictures," Charlie explained as we walked in. "That's why he's invited all these luminaries along."

The lobby was crowded with people waiting, and a board placed upon an easel by the staircase announced the picture we were to be admitted to see. It read:

Stan Laurel

-in-

NUTS IN MAY

"There's Carl Laemmle from Universal," Charlie said, and made a bee-line for a diminutive chap with his thumbs stuck in the waistcoat of an expensive-looking suit. Poor Edna Purviance was suddenly left standing by herself in the middle of the room, not looking best pleased, tutting away to herself.

"Can I get you a drink?" I said, rather chivalrously I thought, but she didn't reply, or even look in my direction. After a moment's awkwardness, I decided to leave her to her quiet seething. Besides, I had seen someone else I'd much rather speak to, lurking shyly in a corner, a rather brassy woman clinging to his arm.

"Stan!" I cried out, striding over towards my friend.

"Arthur! My goodness! How marvellous!" Stan said, and we embraced. "I had no idea you would be here. This is Mae."

"I'm *Mrs* Stan Laurel," Mae said, hitting the word 'Mrs' pretty hard, as though I really ought to know who this Laurel fellow was, and I thought I caught a strong hint of an antipodean twang.

"Stan Laurel? The star of the picture, you mean?" I said, raising an eyebrow at Stan in a silent plea for assistance. "Is he here?"

"Right here," Stan said. "In fact, it's me," and as if to underline this extraordinary revelation, Mae hooked her arm possessively in his once again.

"Well!" I said. "Congratulations, old chap! I'm delighted to make your acquaintance, Mrs Laurel. And indeed yours, *Mr* Laurel."

"You see," Stan said, a little sheepishly I thought. "We couldn't be Mr and Mrs Jefferson, officially, because Mae is already married."

"Technically," Mae put in. "It's a marriage in name only. The bum lives in Australia and doesn't care whether I live or die."

"But because I changed my name, then we can be billed as 'Mr and Mrs', d'you see?"

"Oh, so it's just a stage name?"

"Yes," Stan said, at the very same moment as Mae said: "No." I blinked.

"Besides," Stan went on. "It's for luck. Stan Jefferson has thirteen letters, so…" he shrugged.

"Where did you come up with 'Laurel', for Heaven's sake?"

"Oh that was mine," Mae said, "Wasn't it, Stanley?"

"Yes, dear," Stan said quietly.

"I saw a picture of a Roman general called Scipio Africanus, y'see, in a book, an' he was wearing a laurel crown as a symbol of triumph, an' so I said: 'That's it. Stan and Mae Laurel!' Didn't I, Stan?"

"You did," my friend confirmed.

"So, you have made a movie?" I said. "Exciting."

"Yes, we're appearing here in vaudeville, and the owner wanted to make a film, so…" he shrugged.

"Appearing… in a burglar sketch, by any chance?"

"There may be a burglar involved," he said with a sly grin.

"Are Alice and Baldy with you?"

"No," Mae put in. "They were holding us back, weren't they Stan? So we dropped them, a year ago now."

"I see."

Stan gave me a sheepish grin, and just then the doors opened and the assembled throng began to shift into the auditorium, so we followed.

"You know," I said. "Stanley Laurel has thirteen letters in it."

"Ssshhhh!" Stan hissed.

447

Nuts in May, Stan's film debut, was an amiable piece of knock-about stuff. He was an escapee from a lunatic asylum in a business suit and a Napoleon hat, who seemed to believe he was the Emperor himself. This leads to various misadventures – at one point he commandeers a steam-roller and lays waste to all about him – and it was certainly a big hit with all present, judging by the laughter, and the scowl on Chaplin's face as he watched with arms tightly folded about himself. I was pleased for Stan, but my one concern was that his pale blue eyes, so striking a feature in real life, seemed to disappear somehow onscreen, so that he had two oval shapes of dark eyeliner unnervingly, almost spookily empty. I hoped that wasn't going to be a problem for him.

Afterwards in the lobby, I heard Carl Laemmle, the Universal bigwig, praising Stan's undoubted ease before the camera, which seemed to me to bode well.

Charlie and Edna swept through the crowd, most of whom were buzzing with excitement after what they had been treated to, and I followed, not wanting to miss out on my lift. Stan stood in their way, a friendly, hopeful grin on his long face. Charlie stopped and shook his hand solemnly.

"Come and see me," he said. "And we'll certainly do something."

I congratulated the beaming Stan quickly and made to follow Charlie and Edna out to the waiting motor car. He grabbed my arm.

"You're here with Charlie?" he said. "How on Earth did that happen?"

"It's complicated," I sighed.

It was, as well. I still had to make any kind of progress on discovering evidence that might help the mysterious John to bring Chaplin down, but what if he was about to help Stan launch a movie career? I had plenty to think about as we rode back to the Lone Star studios. Charlie seemed preoccupied also, staring silently out of one window as I stared out of the opposite side, with Edna squashed between us feeling neglected, judging by the periodical tuts.

———

A few days later I was installed in a bungalow on the Lone Star lot. It was fairly Spartan but comfortable enough. There was a bedstead and a bathroom, and I was pleased with it. For one thing I could let John continue to pay for my hotel room expenses and pocket the cash. And for another I was well-placed to have a snoop around after everyone had gone for the day. My best hope of finding something incriminating seemed to be in the office block, which so far had always been either occupied or locked up securely.

Whilst I pondered what to do, I stood with Alf Reeves watching Chaplin work on a little sequence on the set of a large country house. Charlie and Edna were eating ice cream, and the little fellow was trying to engineer dropping the whole scoop down the front of his trousers, and then working it down his leg so that it reappeared by his foot. Charlie's range of facial expressions was comical enough, I had to admit that, but the ice cream was not behaving itself.

"Glory be!" Alf muttered. "Finally he's getting on with something."

"Has there been some kind of problem?"

"You could say that," Alf said, in a low voice. "Listen, I shouldn't really be talking about this, but Charlie has had a bit

449

of a spat with Edna, and it's knocked him off his stride."

"What happened?" I said, always eager for details of Chaplin's unhappiness.

"Well, whenever Edna feels that Charlie is neglecting her, spending too much time with his work maybe or flirting with other ladies, she has this little what-you-might-call feminine tactic. She will pretend to faint – everyone *knows* she's pretending apart from Charlie – and then when she wakes, she asks for him and he runs gallantly to her side. The other day she fainted for real and when she woke, before she knew where she was, she asked for Tom Meighan.[13]"

"The actor?"

Alf nodded. "Good-looking chap, but married, and all of ten years older than her. She said she had just seen him in a dream, that was all, but Charlie was dreadfully jealous."

"Of a dream? Ha ha ha!"

I had laughed out loud. Too loud, as it turned out, because Charlie was striding over to us.

"See?" he was saying to the crew at large. "Arthur thinks it's funny, don't you, Arthur?"

"Ahem... yes, very," I said.

"So what can I do to make it work better? Come on, Arthur, help me out. What would Karno do?"

"Well, have you thought of not actually using ice cream?"

"Not using...?"

"What about something like mashed potato? You could shape it into scoops, and it wouldn't melt, it would keep its shape all the way down your leg, wouldn't it?"

"Mashed potato..." Charlie mused.

"After all, it doesn't matter what it tastes like, does it, as long as it looks right?"

"If you think I'm eating mashed potato all afternoon you've got another think coming," Edna sang out, but Charlie ignored her.

I was on a roll now, and I thought I knew what Babe and I would have done if this was a Plump and Runt.

"And supposing you were to be eating the ice cream on a balcony, up there, say. After all, it's a house party, isn't it? So then, look, the ice cream could slide down your leg and then out onto the floor, then it could slip through the slats and down someone's neck. The duchess over there, say, and Eric could try and get it out with a spoon, and she could slap him, the whole thing would build and build..."

Charlie was lost in a world of his own momentarily, and the whole crew had stopped work and were watching anxiously, almost holding their breath. I suddenly realised that it must be extremely unusual to see an outsider giving Charlie advice, and I wondered if I might have put my foot in it.

"Just a thought," I said.

Charlie snapped his fingers and beckoned the carpenter over. "Build me a balcony, up there," he said. "And I want it to have slats on the floor, with gaps in, understand?"

The carpenter trotted off to start work, and Edna swept past on her way to her dressing room.

"Oh, so we're doing *his* ideas, then," she said, sarcastically, "but *mine* are wasting everybody's time."

"Edna!" Charlie wheedled, but she was gone. Behind Charlie's back, Alf rolled his eyes at me.

To my great satisfaction, the suggestions I'd made played out very well. The mashed potato behaved itself much better than the ice cream had done, although Edna's face between takes suggested that it wasn't much fun to eat. And Marta Golden as

Edna's posh mother really went to town on the sequence where the ice cream went down the back of her dress, with a whole catalogue of pop-eyed gurning that had the crew in a roar. Big Eric Campbell, too, with a forked black beard glued to his chops, had an absolute ball, and for once Chaplin had allowed his supporting artistes to have the punchline to a gag.

That evening after sundown I strolled the lot, keeping in the shadows, trying to work out how I could successfully ransack the offices without getting caught. John would be getting impatient, and if I came up empty he might throw me to the wolves anyway, out of spite.

Suddenly a movement caught my eye over by the office block. Two shadowy figures scurried over to the main door and surreptitiously let themselves in. I watched, but no lights came on inside, and it looked like whoever it was didn't want to advertise their presence.

What was this, I wondered. Were there more government spies on the case? Had John grown tired of waiting to hear from me, and detailed someone else to break in?

I slunk over to the office building, keeping in the shadows and out of the line of sight from the windows. The main door was unlocked, and I opened it very slowly, very carefully, peering inside as I did so.

The reception area was dark and deserted, so I slipped inside and then stood absolutely still, listening. There was no noise at all at first, and I even began to think I might have been mistaken, but then a creak and a sigh came from one of the offices, and I tiptoed closer.

There was someone in Chaplin's office, the sparsely furnished room I had first seen him trying to write in. Nothing to steal in there, I thought, all the interesting stuff would be in the offices down the corridor. I crept closer and closer, until I could peek in through the small crack where the door was not quite pulled to.

An astonishing scene greeted my startled gaze, illuminated by the moonlight streaming in through the skylight.

A young woman lay back on Chaplin's writing table, her dress pushed up around her waist, her pale thighs gleaming above her stocking tops, her head thrown back in ecstasy. A dark-haired man, tall, broad-shouldered, loomed over her in silhouette, and his urgent thrusts were causing the table to squeak and creak alarmingly, as though it might not stand the strain of this nocturnal activity too much longer.

The girl was Edna Purviance, and the man I recognised from the film *Pudd'nhead Wilson*, in which he'd played the grown-up version of one of the swapped-at-birth babies. It was Thomas Meighan, dark and dashing, so quite clearly Edna had been doing more than merely dreaming about him.

And what was this about? On Chaplin's desk, in his inner sanctum? The girl was punishing him, punishing him for putting his work ahead of her, that's what it looked like.

I watched, fascinated, for a moment or two, wondering what they would do if they actually reduced the table to matchwood, but then I started to feel awkward and turned away. Which is when I saw the bunch of keys dangling from the keyhole. Surely these must be Charlie's keys, master keys for the whole building, that Edna had somehow borrowed for the evening in order to get her own back on him!

It was the work of a moment to slide them noiselessly into my palm, and I scuttled off up the dark corridor. I had no way of knowing how long Meighan could keep his end up, so to speak, and so I frantically fumbled for the right key for the first door until I had a brainwave.

I didn't need to hurry, did I? All I needed to do was unlock all the doors and return the keys, then once Edna and her secret lover left I could give the place a thorough going over at my leisure.

When I slipped back to Charlie's room the pyrotechnics were just reaching their climax. There was gasping and groaning, and creaking and straining, and it didn't sound like there was going to be time for me to replace the key in the hole so I placed the whole bunch gently on the floor, as though they had fallen out by themselves, and then found myself a corner at the far end of the building in which to lurk behind a small potted palm.

I was there for a while. It seemed that the performance I had stumbled across was merely the matinee, and I had to wait for the main evening event to reach its grand finale before the lovers sneaked out and left, locking me in.

I searched methodically, then, through files of production expenses, budgets, payrolls, materials, invoices and receipts, but didn't hit upon anything remotely interesting until I went into Syd Chaplin's office. He took care of all Charlie's business these days so here I found more personal items, documents, leases, correspondence, and finally – Hallelujah! – the very letter I was looking for.

To be precise, it was a carbon copy of a letter, on headed notepaper, typed and addressed to the draft board.

The writer certified and attested that Mr Charles Spencer Chaplin, currently resident at the Los Angeles Athletic Club, was, at six stone eleven pounds, significantly below the stipulated minimum weight for a man of his height, which was five feet and four inches tall, and as such should be exempted from active service.

454

It was signed Dr A. R. Binks, M.D., resident physician at the Kaspare Cohn hospital on Stephenson Avenue, East Los Angeles[14].

At first I was disappointed. I sat back in Syd's chair and looked at this document. It was brief and to the point, and exactly what I was supposed to look for, but the hope was not simply that I would find it but that I would be able to debunk it somehow.

Six stone eleven pounds? Surely the man I had seen wolfing down sausages and bacon in the commissary couldn't be quite that frail, but I couldn't see how to possibly prove such a thing, short of tricking him into stepping onto a set of scales, and even then it would be my word against this Dr Binks...

Then it struck me like a thunderbolt from a clear blue sky.

Binks.

Binks was the name we gave to the stock posh twit character in every Karno sketch in the repertoire. In *Skating*, the posh twit was Binks, the sketch devised by Syd Chaplin and the role played by both brothers at one time or another. In *A Night at the Club*, Charlie had also been a Binks. And in *The Wow Wows*, the lame skit we first brought to the States in 1910, and which nearly derailed us before we had even begun, the posh twit who seeks membership of the exclusive gentlemen's club was called Binks, Archibald Binks..

Then there was an article I had read not long before in which Charlie described how he'd invented his million-dollar walk. He could have said he'd stolen it from me, of course, or from Billie Ritchie or old Fred Kitchen or George Robey. But no, he claimed he was mimicking an old character from his childhood in old London town – he always did like to make his legend as Dickensian as possible – a rheumaticky old wheezer who occupied a local cab stand, holding the horses for a penny tip, and his name, the comedy name that Chaplin had given his self-mythologizing invention, was Binks. Rummy Binks.

Dr A. R. Binks.

Archibald Rummy Binks.

50
RUMMY BINKS

I could hardly believe it.

The arrogance of it, the contempt, or was it perhaps the lack of imagination? To use that name on that letter, it was breath-taking. Well, one thing was for sure...

I'd got him!

Back in my room, the letter tucked away in a safe hiding place, I suddenly experienced a chill, a cold flush of apprehension. What if there really *was* a Binks? What if the coincidence of the name was what had made Charlie choose him as his physician, from all those available across the city? I should have egg all over my face if I contacted John before making absolutely sure of my evidence.

So the next morning I arose, breakfasted, and then just after the absurd pomp and ceremony of Charlie's arrival I strolled towards the main gate. I could see that there was a certain amount of perplexed head-scratching when the offices were found to be unlocked – of course Edna had left with the keys so I had been unable to lock up behind myself – but the young female receptionist seemed to be bearing the brunt of the telling-off, judging by the floods of tears, and I hoped she wouldn't be sacked.

Before I could get out onto the street I was hailed, and Charlie himself was striding towards me.

"Going somewhere?" he said.

"Yes, I thought I might go and take a look at the ocean," I said, quickly picking a destination in the opposite direction to the hospital where Dr Binks was supposedly resident.

"Oh, well you can't walk, that's miles," Charlie said. "Kono will take you, I don't need him for hours. Toraichi...?!" He called to his Japanese chauffeur, who was just beginning to drive the sports car off the lot. "Take Mr Dandoe to the ocean, will you, please?"

And so my first attempt at investigation was thwarted. I didn't want to risk asking Toraichi to go straight to the hospital, for fear that he would report back to Charlie or Syd and they would smell a rat, so I let him drive me up to Santa Monica Boulevard and swing left towards the coast.

I sat in the front, not wanting to be driven around like some potentate, and this seemed to please Toraichi, who was clearly used to not being involved in any conversations that happened in the automobile.

"You like car?" he said with a big smile.

"Yes, it's very nice."

"Locomobile."

"It's certainly very grand, and you drive it very smoothly."

Toraichi looked pleased. "You drive car?"

"No, I don't know how."

"I show."

"What? Really?"

"Yes!" the chauffeur said, jabbing his thumb towards his own shirtfront. "I show!"

"Right!" I said. "Righto!"

Mr Kono drove me smoothly through a new town, with plenty of building work under way on either side, and I caught a glimpse of the splendid new Beverly Hills Hotel a little way off. The boulevard was then wide and clear for a distance, with short trees evenly spaced along the roadside, until it became built up again as we reached the sea. The sun shone dazzlingly back at me from the surface of the deep blue Pacific, and I caught sight of the pleasure pier, with the network of metal girders supporting The Whip, a shark-shaped roller coaster. I thought maybe I could hop out there and make my own way back, but Toraichi had other ideas. With a sidelong grin at me, showing all his teeth, he whipped the car away from the crowds and off up the coast, finally drawing off onto a deserted track that led inland between sand dunes and scrubby grass.

I was suddenly struck with the impression that the man wanted to kill me. That he was not a mere chauffeur, he was Charlie's hired assassin, kept on hand to tidy up any little problems that might arise for the great man. Kono stopped the motor car, and stepped out.

"You get out, please," he said.

What was going to happen? Was I about to be smacked on the head with the crank handle and dumped in the dunes? I climbed down and watched him warily, but he stepped back courteously and offered me his seat.

With a sudden rush of relief, I realised he really was going to let me drive Chaplin's car. Kono climbed in beside me, and quickly showed me the rudiments, the brake pedal, the gas, the steering wheel, and the very enjoyable horn, and before I really knew what I was doing, we were careering along the lane, parping at the odd pedestrian, the sea air in our faces, hoping to God nothing was coming the other way. Toraichi smiled encouragingly, and occasionally grabbed the wheel to stop me running off into the tufts of marram grass between the road and the sand dunes, and when I wasn't quick enough to respond to his instruction to stop, he reached his leg over mine and stamped down on my foot and the brake pedal all at once, much to the relief of the attendant at an ice cream stand whose life was flashing before his eyes. All in all, though, it was very enjoyable, and I could certainly see why people would want to do it.

Toraichi and I had bonded over this little adventure, and it was easy to persuade him to show me more of the city, and wind up innocently rolling past the Kaspare Cohn hospital on Stephenson. I managed to get him to wait outside while I dashed in, ostensibly to pick up some medicine or other for an invented ailment, and I quickly checked an embossed name board of hospital personnel by the main doors. Plenty of doctors, but no Doctor Binks. Ha!

Just to make doubly certain, I approached the reception desk, where a severe-looking lady in a white uniform that could hardly have stood to be more starched peered over her reading spectacles at me.

"I'm here to see Dr Binks," I said, politely.

"No Binks," the woman said.

"Oh? Perhaps he has moved on. Do you know where I might enquire?"

"No Binks. Never has been," she replied abruptly.

"Never has been a Dr Binks here?" I said, just making sure I had it.

"No. No Binks," she said, as definitive about it as anyone could hope for, and beginning to seem a little annoyed to boot, so I raised my hat and hustled back to the Locomobile.

That evening, thinking I would not be in Los Angeles much longer, I decided to dine at Levy's Deli, which was a rather fashionable haunt much frequented by movie folk. I was still wondering whether I had enough to contact John and set the dogs on Charlie, or whether I perhaps needed one more nail for the coffin, so I was looking forward to having a quiet meal on my own, and maybe seeing who I could spot there to divert myself.

As it happened, though, I was to be denied my thinking time, because as soon as I walked into the restaurant who should I see in full flow but Charlie himself, with the broad back of Eric Campbell towards me. I could hardly ignore them, that would look distinctly odd, so I made my way between the tables over to where the two of them were sitting.

When I got there, though, and halted the conversation mid-anecdote, I saw that the man who was holding forth was not Chaplin at all.

"Oh! I'm terribly sorry to intrude. I thought you were..."

"Charlie Chaplin," the fellow finished for me, nodding with a long-suffering expression on his face. "I get that a lot."

"Do excuse me, sir," I smiled, turning away.

"Arthur?"

It was the big man I had taken for Eric Campbell who had spoken. I glanced back, and blow me if it wasn't Babe Hardy!

"Good Heavens!" I exclaimed.

"What a pleasure! Join us, please!" Babe said, beckoning a waiter to bring me a chair. "This is my esteemed colleague, Mr Billy West."

Aha, I thought. The Chaplin impersonator.

"I thought you were working in New Jersey," I said, taking a seat.

"No, we're here now. There is still a King Bee company back in Bayonne, though."

"Raymond Hughes is their star," Billy West said. "Making copies of Billy West films."

"What? Making copies of Billy West copies of Charlie Chaplin, you mean?"

"That's it," West said with a grin. "It's a crazy old world, isn't it?"

"It sure is."

"So are you working?" Babe asked.

"I am in the government's employ," I said, deciding to stick with my cover story. "Trying to encourage the Bond drive and the draft."

"Really? Well, I'm glad to know you have found a way to serve the war effort, Arthur, "he said. "Back in New Jersey I myself was filled with what you might call patriotic fervour..."

"Was it of the sipping variety?"

Babe smiled. "I'm serious. I took myself over to a recruiting booth to offer my services to my country. I'm sorry to say they just laughed at me. The sergeant called his colleagues over and said: 'Hey, boys, look at what wants to enlist!'"

"No!"

"Like I was some sort of freak."

"Well, gosh that's... awful."

"'I know we're sending doughboys to France, but this is ridiculous!' his pal said. And: 'Even the Krauts could hardly miss a target like that.'"

"I'm so sorry."

"I left with their derision ringing in my ears. It was real hurtful. I am having to satisfy myself that making folks laugh is an honourable occupation in these straitened times."

I put a consoling hand on his big shoulder. "It is, my friend, believe me, it is."

"I thank you for saying so, and I only wish I was as convinced of it as you are."

Just then a fellow diner came past our table, peering into the corners and booths as though looking for someone in particular. I reached out and grabbed his sleeve.

"Stan?"

"Oh," Stan said. "I'm sorry, Arthur, I didn't see you there. I was looking for Charlie, apparently he is due to dine here this evening." He realised that I was sitting with friends, and turned to give them a smile of greeting, and a full-fledged double take when he saw the spitting image of Charlie Chaplin alongside me.

"I beg your pardon," I said. "Stan, this is Billy West, and my very good friend Oliver Hardy. This is my old friend Stan Jefferson – oops, I mean Stan *Laurel*, don't I?"

Babe offered his hand, and with the other he was already arranging for another chair to be brought over.

"It sure is a pleasure to make your acquaintance, Mr Laurel," he said, with a beaming smile.

"Why thank you, Mr Hardy," Stan replied with a bow, matching Babe's exaggerated courtesy.

"Stan just made his first picture, didn't you, Stan?" I said.

"Is that so?" Babe said, all friendly interest.

"I went to see it, everyone seemed very excited. What's happened about it?"

"That's just the thing," Stan said. "Carl Laemmle of Universal is interested, but Charlie said I should come and see him. I thought he would call to arrange an appointment, but Mae said I shouldn't just wait to hear from him, so I went over to the Lone Star studios, and..."

"Wait," I said. "You didn't tell the gatemen that you were an old friend from the music hall, did you?"

"As a matter of fact I did," Stan confirmed ruefully. "And they threw me right out on my arse."

"Aha."

"You are an actor, aren't you?" Stan asked Babe. "I have seen you in something, I'm sure of it."

"Oh well," Babe simpered, with a sly and modest glance at me, "perhaps a Plump and Runt comedy?"

"Of course! Those are hilarious, some really funny business. That was you?"

"Me and Arthur here."

"Wait, wait, what?" Stan said, astonished. "That was *you*?"

"Guilty," I grinned.

"I had no idea you'd been making flickers. What a dark horse you are!"

"Thirty-five of them," Babe said. "Hand-made in Jacksonville, Florida. The happiest time of my life!"

"Huh, thanks a lot!" Billy West muttered, draining his glass.

"Until now, Billy," Babe grinned. "Until now."

Just then a waiter strolled by, and Stan caught his eye. "Excuse me," he said. "But could you tell me – is Mr Chaplin dining here this evening?"

"Mr Chaplin is in a private booth with Miss Constance Collier," the waiter said, "and not to be disturbed."

"Ah. Perhaps you would be so kind as to take him a very short note?"

"Certainly, sir."

Stan scribbled a few words onto a scrap of paper and the waiter went on his way. Billy West caught sight of a friend across the dining room and excused himself, leaving me with Stan and Babe. A thought struck me.

"Hey, you know what?" I said. "I did a double act with you, Stan, didn't I, *The Rum 'Uns from Rome*, and I did a double act with you, Babe, as Plump and Runt. You two had better not do a double act together, it would cancel me out. Like God solving some kind of cosmic mathematical equation. Promise me you'll never do that. I might simply cease to exist."

"Well, now, that would never do," Babe laughed. "Would it, Stan?"

"No, no it wouldn't," Stan said, distracted by looking out for a reply from Chaplin, or even Charlie himself. A waiter seemed to be coming towards us, but in the event he was heading for the next table.

"Telephone call for you, sir," the waiter said to a self-important fellow chomping on a cigar behind us. "It's a long distance from Atlanta, Georgia."

"It sure is," Stan muttered.

Babe Hardy howled. "Ha ha ha! Oh my! It sure is!" he laughed, tears springing from his eyes and rolling down his plump cheeks. Stan started laughing too, his trademark giggle, the one that sent his eyebrows high up his forehead, and pretty soon I was joining in myself.

"Ha ha! It sure is!" Stan cried, and Babe started laughing all over again. They just kept setting one another off, and after a minute or two of this, the three of us were weak with mirth, and the whole restaurant had turned to look at us, wondering what on Earth was so damn'd funny.

Just then the waiter who had taken Stan's message returned with a reply, hurrying across the room as though the note in his hand could stop us from causing any further disturbance. As it happened he'd have been right, as one glance at its contents sobered Stan right up.

"What does he say?" I asked, seeing his disappointment.

"He says that he can't see me now as he is just tied up at the moment. But we'll get together."

"What, no time? No date? No suggestion?"

"No nothing," Stan sighed heavily. "It's just a fob-off, like I was nobody."

"Well, forget him, you know what he's like," I said.

"Yes, but... if Charlie could just... it could be so good," he said. "And Mae says that I should... oh well, never mind."

Stan was down for a little while after that, but we all got the giggles again when Babe asked for a steak and a parfait, and Stan asked them to put a parfait on his steak as well. And the rest of the evening passed as enjoyably as any I could remember, with my two friends – two funny gentlemen. Two funny, gentle men.

———

Back at the bungalow over at Lone Star, I found myself getting angry on Stan's behalf. Of course, Charlie had done this sort of thing before, when he led us all to believe he was going to help *The Nutty Burglars* into the movies, and it was all just a tactic, to prevent us from trespassing on his turf.

It motivated me, I must say, and it got the wheels ticking over and the cogs clicking as well as the teeth grinding. I had the letter, and I had discovered for myself that there was no Dr Binks at the Kaspare Cohn hospital. But was that enough?

I stared at the letter again, and suddenly something about it rang a very far distant bell.

What was nagging away at me?

The signature. That was it. The letter itself was typed, and so was the bottom line with the doctor's name on it, but the signature, that was in ink, in handwriting. I looked more closely at it.

Sincerely, Dr A. R. Binks...

It was the S of 'Sincerely' that I finally zeroed in on. It began with an upstroke that had the effect of closing both curls so that they became loops, and the whole looked like a figure eight, or perhaps an ampersand in reverse.

I'd seen this before, I was sure of it. With frantic energy, I grabbed my suitcase and tipped it out on the bed. Most of my belongings were quite new, provided by John, but some few pieces of memorabilia had survived my time as a tramp when I carried a bundle on a stick, including a notebook with postcards, letters and photographs tucked between the pages.

I found the particular item I was looking for, and my heart skipped a beat. There was no doubt about it. The capital S – in fact, the whole word 'Sincerely' – was identical.

I sat back and scrutinised the curling postcard, a smile creeping over my face. I was given this, an artiste's mass-produced autographed snap, years and years ago by a deskbound official of the Union-Castle Mail Shipping Company, when I'd been trying to track down who it was that had paid a sailor in their employ, ugly fellow with a twin-globed nose like a pair of testicles, to heckle me relentlessly while I was onstage. I'd kept it as a souvenir of my successful piece of amateur detective work on that occasion. The same fellow who'd had it in for me back then had clearly written this letter for Charlie, masquerading as the fictitious Dr Archibald Rummy Binks.

I glanced at the signature on the photograph one more time.

'Sincerely," it read.

'Sydney Chaplin'

467

51
OLD COMRADES

I awoke the next morning in an upbeat mood, ready to make my move.

Charlie Chaplin had been playing his dirty tricks on me for ten years now, with the help and connivance of his mean-spirited brother, and now it was payback time.

I stepped out into the sunshine to find some breakfast, and bumped into Alf Reeves crossing the lot.

"Morning, Alf! Busy day lined up?"

"Not today," Alf said, pretty gloomily I thought.

"Why, what's up?"

"It's Eric Campbell. You know that little wife of his, Pearl? Used to be in vaudeville, now she marries rich men and ruins 'em?"

"Uh-oh..."

"That's right. She served divorce papers on him. A month they've been married. She claims he's been getting drunk and beating her, can you imagine it? You couldn't meet a gentler giant. He's like a child behind those wild eyebrows and that devil's beard."

"Poor chap."

"Yes, well, he's in pieces, so no filming today. Charlie's not even coming in till tomorrow, he's looking at locations over in Sierra Madre. What about you?"

"Oh, I reckon I'll be out of your hair soon," I said brightly. "Heading back East."

"Shame, it's been good having you around."

"Thanks Alf, you too."

I took my time getting on the outside of some bacon and eggs in the commissary, washed down with some strong coffee, and then I strolled out into the street, full of the joys. The nearest Western Union office was only a couple of blocks away, and as I sauntered along with my hands in my pockets, I went over in my mind the message I would send to John:

C CHAPLIN DOCTORS LETTER FAKED BY S CHAPLIN STOP PROOF IN MY HANDS STOP DANDOE

That ought to do it, I reckoned, I could leave the rest to him. Of course, even Chaplin's massive popularity couldn't survive a scandal like that if it got out, as I felt sure it was about to. Shirking his duty, treating his adopted countrymen with contempt, and perpetrating a fraud to do so, well, it would be the end of him. The first Hollywood star to fall back down to Earth. Syd would probably go to jail, I thought gleefully. Maybe they both would.

I arrived at the Western Union office to find it closed until 1pm owing to staff illness. A notice taped to the door advised me that other offices could be found six blocks North, on Sunset Boulevard, or seven blocks West on Santa Monica, but it was a dry and dusty Californian day and I didn't feel like walking, so I decided to slip into a nearby saloon and have myself a little celebration of my impending victory, in the company of my friend Mr Daniels, or perhaps it would be Mr Beam.

Once installed at the bar on a tall stool, I took out Syd's letter and the photograph and looked at them once more. It was still hard to believe they would be so blasé.

I wondered what I would do next. I'd assumed I'd return to New York, where I could go back to being a Four Minute Man. Maybe John would have further work for me to do, although that didn't seem all that likely. Of course now that I was no longer being sought for murder, that shadow having been lifted, perhaps I should stay and try to get some work in the flickers. With Babe, perhaps, or with Stan...

I realised there was someone standing beside me, peering at me, rather intrusively. The barman glanced in his direction but he showed no inclination to order a drink, indeed he wasn't even facing the bar, he was standing squarely looking at me.

I gave this chap a sidelong glance, and saw that the left sleeve of his rather smart jacket was empty and pinned across his chest. He was still just standing there so I took another peek, and noticed that there was a crutch lodged in his right armpit. Who knew how he had come by his injuries, but it wouldn't do to upset a war veteran, even if he was pushing his luck.

So I said, as politely as I could manage: "Can I help you, buddy?"

"I suppose I shouldn't really be surprised at you not recognising me. After all, there's not quite as much of me as there was the last time we saw one another."

I turned to face the man, as the sound of his voice took me back, back to my teenage years as a college porter, back to the student friend who'd first got me into the business of comedy by persuading me to do an impersonation of my own father in a smoking concert while he himself dragged up for a turn as the Master's Wife.

"Good Lord!" I said. "Ralph! Ralph Luscombe! Fancy seeing you here! Fancy you even recognising me after all this time!"

"Arthur, my dear chap, it is positively glorious to see you again," Luscombe said, leaning heavily on his crutch to free his hand for shaking. "It must be... ooh... all of...?"

"Since you sneaked away from your father's export business to tour with us in *The Football Match*? That must have been '09."

"I never quite shook off the performing bug, you know?" he beamed. "They sent me to Brazil to cure me of my infatuation with the music hall, but the office out there had a Gilbert and Sullivan Society, and we did a ripping *HMS Pinafore*. I was poor little Buttercup, the rosiest, roundest and reddest beauty in all Spithead."

"You always did like a dress, as I recall," I said. "You were wearing one when I first caught you sneaking in after the gates were locked."

"Ha! So I was indeed! Now how have you been, Arthur? Tell me all."

"I've been well," I said, "but what about you, my friend?"

"Oh, this?" Luscombe said, with a dismissive tip of the head to his ruined frame. "I got the wrong end of an argument with a Boche 4.2 shell, I'm afraid. Could be worse, though. The fellow next to me copped most of it. They never found hide nor hair of him, he was just... poof, off in the wind. Along with my arm and half my leg, I might add."

I frowned. "Your leg?"

For answer, Luscombe shifted his weight onto his right foot, and then manoeuvred his crutch to give himself a swift tap on the shin, which made a deadened solid clunk.

For a moment I found I could hardly breathe. This fine, generous young man, who'd wanted nothing more than to fool around on a stage somewhere, anywhere, and make people laugh, had suffered quite unimaginable agonies, and yet here he was, as bright and cheerful as ever.

"Chin up, Arthur, I'm not for the college wall of remembrance just yet. And I always get a seat on the omnibus, what?"

"Are you travelling alone?" I managed to croak out.

"Actually, I'm not," Luscombe said with a grin. "And you will recognise my companion, too."

"I will?"

"Oh yes, I should say so."

"Who is it?"

"A surprise, a surprise, just hang onto your hat. Ah, here he is now."

I turned, and there, walking across the saloon from the washroom with a big friendly grin from ear to ear was a ghost, a walking dead man, my dear friend that I had been mourning for two long years and hadn't seen for three.

Freddie Karno junior.

Freddie.

I felt the room rapidly closing in on me and emptying of oxygen. My field of vision began to shrink, until I was gaping at Freddie as if through a porthole, which became a knothole, then a keyhole...

And then I blacked out.

―――

When I came to I was in a booth. Freddie was bringing a glass of water to my lips, and Ralph Luscombe was peering anxiously down at me.

"F-f-f-f..." I heard myself saying, blowing bubbles in the drink until he pulled back.

"Steady, old bean, you've given yourself a bit of a bump on the noggin," Luscombe said

"It was that damn'd notice in *The Times*, wasn't it?" Freddie said. "I knew it. I've seen this before."

"Not... dead?"

"No, sorry to disappoint."

"Disappoint? My dear chap!" I struggled to my feet and threw my arms around him, tears of disbelief and joy coursing down my cheeks.

Once I had regained a little composure, and overcome my embarrassment at fainting like a feeble child in front of two men who had seen so much, I pressed Freddie for an explanation.

"The Guv'nor," he said. "The war has driven him a bit cuckoo, I'm afraid. It has hit the Karsino hard, for one thing. It's just not the time for a pleasure resort on the Thames, it doesn't feel... right, somehow."

"And?" I said. "And?"

"Well, when I got back in 1914 the war started up almost immediately, as I'm sure you know. Suddenly the music halls were very different, all flag waving and patriotic songs." He closed his eyes, and then broke into song, at a woman's pitch: "'Oh we don't want to lose you, but we think you ought to go...'"

"'For your King and your country... both need you so...'" Luscombe warbled along.

"And it dripped away at one's resistance, didn't it?"

"It did, rather," Luscombe admitted.

"And one day the Guv'nor... well, he upped and volunteered me for the Engineers, and I couldn't really back out. But I'd probably have volunteered sooner or later anyway."

473

"He volunteered you?" I said, disbelieving.

"Well, yes. Anyway, I was expecting to be fighting the Huns, obviously, but in fact I got shipped out to the Gallipoli peninsula and we were fighting Turks, for some Godforsaken reason. I got shot a couple of times and shipped home."

"Shot? Where?"

"In the Dardanelles."

"Painful!" Luscombe quipped, clearly not for the first time, as Freddie smirked with pleasure at having squeezed that gag in.

"Anyway, before I got back I was listed in *The Times* obituary column as 'Killed in Action'."

"So the Army made a mistake?"

"They made many, but not that one. That was the Guv'nor's doing. He put the listing in the paper himself."

"Why, in God's name?"

"Marie – that's his sort-of-second wife," he said, turning to explain to Luscombe, "– said that he was grinning when he saw it. He said all the nobs, all the best people, are getting their boys killed out there and he thought it might be good to see the old Karno name among 'em!"

"That's... preposterous! Crackers!" I exclaimed.

"Yes," Freddie agreed fervently. "I wasn't even known as Karno in the service, I was Fred Westcott, naturally. But ever since then people look at me like I am a ghost, and grab hold of me to make sure I'm real. He didn't tell Mama what he'd done. I turned up on the doorstep and she was all in black and looked ten years older. Clara next door said she'd been crying non-stop for a fortnight. I shall never forgive the old fool, never."

"Poor Edith," I said. Freddie's mother was a good friend. "But listen, how are the two of you here together? I didn't even know you knew one another."

"We didn't," Luscombe said. "We met on the crossing, which was a little on the hairy side, wasn't it?"

"A little," Freddie agreed.

"And we discovered we had a shared objective."

"Which was?"

"To come and visit Charlie Chaplin."

"Charlie?"

"That's right. You see, we both felt he should know how much he has meant to our comrades in arms, and to ourselves. He has been the one constant beacon of light and laughter through the whole terrible nightmare, hasn't he Fred?"

"That's right," Freddie agreed. "His films are shown constantly behind the lines, and men who have seen the most ghastly horrors find that they can still laugh. It is amazing."

"Really?" I said.

Luscombe leaned forward earnestly. "In fact, he's such a presence in our lives, such a bulwark against the awfulness, that I think without him, morale would have sunk so low we should have succumbed long ago."

"Do you know," Freddie went on, "that Charlie's films are shown on the ceilings of hospital wards so that severely injured men don't miss out?"

"That's true," Luscombe confirmed. "I saw many myself while I was being patched up. One in particular, I remember, at the seaside, where Charlie was chasing a fellow's hat in the breeze, and I could actually see the fishing line that was twitching the thing this way and that, but still I laughed so hard that it took me quite a while to remember how down in the dumps I had been."

"Well," I said, struggling to quite take this in. "How about that?"

"The fellow in the next bed to me at one field hospital I was in was quite fearfully bashed up, and he would cry out at all hours of the day and night for someone to come and... you know, finish him off, put him out of his misery."

"Christ!"

"Yes, it did get a chap down, rather, I don't mind telling you, especially when I myself was more than a little preoccupied with wondering whether I would walk again. But even he, even he, when Charlie started cavorting on our ceiling, even he started chuckling away, his pain forgotten. Well, perhaps not forgotten, but at least set aside for a few blessed minutes. It was quite, quite unbelievable."

"I can believe it," Freddie said, nodding solemnly.

"I spoke to an eminent neurologist – actually, you might remember him: Broadbent? Horace Broadbent? Rooms on O staircase? Right above mine – no wait, my room was above his. Queer sort of bird. Anyway, he told me that they have the very greatest difficulty dealing with men who have experienced profound emotional and psychological trauma at the Front. Shell shock is the catch-all name they've come up with for it, but it's such a new phenomenon, they know relatively little about how to treat it. He told me that often, the first step on the road to recovery, the very first, is speaking to the patient about Charlie. Isn't that incredible? How fortunate we are to know such a man. How proud I am of the little assistance I was able to give him on his way to becoming what he has become."

"Hear, hear!" Freddie said earnestly.

"So you've come all this way on, what? A pilgrimage?"

"Precisely. To thank him, and let him know what he has done."

I was reeling. The thought that my friends would be so powerfully affected by Chaplin, so convinced he was a force for good, that they would make this long and dangerous trek just to let him know, humbly, what he meant to them and the many others who had been through such horrors, well, it took my breath away. It suddenly made me and my feelings towards Charlie, the ire that had sustained me for so many years, seem achingly small and unimportant. I felt the anchors that held me in place loosening, and my mind beginning to drift.

"Why are you here, in this saloon, though?" I spluttered, trying to get a grip of myself.

"Thought we'd meet up for a stiffener first, what?" Luscombe said, and Freddie nodded.

"After all you've seen and done, surely you're not scared of meeting *him?*"

"Well, you know," Luscombe said. "He is Charlie Chaplin."

A thought struck me. "Wait, you're going to the studio *now?*"

"Yes, we shall say that we are old friends from music hall, and..."

"Don't whatever you do, do *that,*" I said. "He's not there today anyhow. I'll take you in to see him tomorrow morning. In the meantime – luncheon, and then later dinner. I shall show you the finest haunts in town, where all the movie stars go, and we shall have steak, my treat, I absolutely insist."

"Hurrah!" said Luscombe cheerfully.

I excused myself then, and went to the washroom, where I threw cold water on my face and stared at my reflection for a long, long while.

52
PAY DAY

THE following morning I met Freddie Karno Junior and Ralph Luscombe outside the Lone Star Studio, and led them past the gate-men who might otherwise have dumped them on the sidewalk.

As they marvelled at the activity on the lot, the carpenters building yet another piece of scenery for some new gag Charlie had devised, Alf Reeves bustled over to envelop them in his arms, followed by the usually lugubrious Albert Austin, flushed and beaming for once, and Eric Campbell.

Then the cry came: "He's here!", and all present quickly assembled into the welcoming lines, standing to attention.

"What's happening?" Freddie asked.

"You'll enjoy this," I said, ushering the two visitors into formation alongside everyone else.

Toraichi Kono eased the Locomobile sleekly onto the lot, and Harrington, the valet, popped out like a jack-in-the-box to get the door for his master.

Without glancing at any of us, Chaplin stepped out in his shiny little shoes and great black coat, and swept importantly into the office building.

Once he was gone, the crowd dissolved in all directions, leaving just the ex-Karno mob behind.

"He's like a king!" Luscombe marvelled.

"Come on," I said. "I'll take you to see him."

"Perhaps we should wait," Luscombe said, anxiously. "I mean, if he's busy..."?

"Come along," I said. "You've come all this way, haven't you?"

Freddie and Ralph followed me into the reception, and I made straight for Charlie's inner sanctum.

"Oh, hey!" the young receptionist cried out. "He doesn't want to see anyone!"

"He'll see us," I said, soothingly, as if to a frightened bird. Then I gave one sharp tap on the door and walked in.

Charlie was just divesting himself of his coat, which he slung across the writing table. It creaked alarmingly, and I thought it couldn't be long before it gave up the ghost.

"Arthur?" he said. "I'm sorry, I have rather a lot to do."

"Visitors to see you," I said. "I knew you wouldn't want them to wait."

Ralph Luscombe lurched in, then, trying to walk as smartly as he could with his crutch under one armpit.

"You remember my friend Ralph Luscombe, who was a super in *The Football Match* for a time?"

Charlie was transfixed by the crutch, the limp, and the vacant sleeve. "I... of course, yes... goodness me! What a pleasure to see you again, how do you do?"

Behind the dumbstruck Luscombe, Freddie Karno Junior hove into view then. Charlie and I had spoken sorrowfully of our friend's 'Killed in Action' report so his reaction was almost as overwhelmed as mine had been. He reached forward and grasped Fred by both of his upper arms, squeezing hard.

479

"See? What did I tell you?" Freddie said to me, then: "Hullo Charlie. Long time, no see!"

"I'm delighted, my dear fellow, I can't tell you! So it was untrue!"

"It was."

"Praise be!"

Luscombe found his tongue. "I must say, it is amazing to find you all here, like Fred Karno's Army," he said. Chaplin smiled benignly, but was clearly puzzled.

"They sing this song, the boys at the Front," Freddie explained, looking to Luscombe for accompaniment, which was enthusiastically forthcoming.

> "We are Fred Karno's Army,
> A jolly lot are we,
> Fred Karno is our captain,
> Charlie Chaplin our O.C."

Charlie gave a little gasp, and the two lads launched into the rest of the verse.

> "And when we get to Berlin
> The Kaiser he will say,
> Hoch! Hoch! Mein Gott!
> What a jolly fine lot
> Are the boys of Company A![15]"

Charlie smiled and applauded enthusiastically. "Well, well!" he said. "Marvellous!"

"You have heard about the mechanised transports, tanks they are called, that roll over the trenches?"

"I... think I have..."

"They are named after Karno sketches."

"No! Really?"

"I promise you. One is 'Jail Bird', another is 'Early Bird', and I saw a 'Mumming Bird' too."

"Incredible! Incredible! What a thing!"

"Well," I said. "If you'll excuse me, I think I must leave you to it. The chaps wish to speak to you, and I heard all their stories yesterday. And besides, it doesn't really concern me, truth to tell."

"Thank you, Arthur," Charlie said, and I withdrew.

———

Two and a half hours later, I was outside on the lot, waiting for the boys to reappear, when Toraichi Kono drew the sports car up again outside the office block. Shortly after this Charlie appeared, and said to his Japanese driver: "Please take my honoured guests anywhere they would like to go," and Kono nodded once. Freddie and Ralph came out, a little subdued but looking content, and made their way over to the car.

"I'll see you this evening," I said as I strolled by. "Same place?"

"Splendid," Luscombe cried, and the motor slid towards the main gate.

Charlie stood watching them go, and then brushed away a tear. "That was extraordinary," he said. "Emotional."

"Indeed," I replied, and we stood in contemplative silence together for a moment.

"Well," he said then. "I really must..."

"I just need a quick word," I said. "Shall we go inside?"

Chaplin wasn't particularly keen, but I led the way back to his office and he acquiesced.

"What's this about?" he said, taking a seat and lighting up a cigarette.

"I wanted to thank you for your hospitality," I said. "I shall be leaving shortly."

"Ah," Charlie said. "We shall be sorry to see you go. Alf, especially."

"Yes, well," I said. "As you know, I have been engaged in work for the government in respect of the Liberty Bond drive and the draft..."

"That's right, and I regret that I am unable to spare the time to leave California and drum up support for you."

"But I know that you are anxious," I said, then paused.

Charlie frowned. "Anxious?"

"Anxious to help in any way you can, hence the use of your bungalow these past weeks."

"You're welcome, I'm sure."

"You may consider me suitably buttered up."

"Well, perhaps, but it wasn't just that. There's the history between us, naturally."

"Yes, which has not always been as cordial as it might, has it?"

"Oh, really. There's no need to go dredging up your old paranoia."

"Chaplinoia," I said.

"What?"

"That's what the newspapers are calling people's unnatural fascination with you. Chaplinoia, or Chaplinitis."

"I can't very well help that nonsense, now can I?

"I guess not," I said. But Chaplinoia or not, the fact remains, you and I have been rivals for many years. Since we first met, in fact. Back in the Karno days, when you and Syd contrived to cheat your way past me to become number one of *The Football Match* company."

"Water under a very small, old bridge," Chaplin scoffed.

"And then when you had me and Stan sacked from the American company and thrown into penury."

"Did I do that?"

"You did. And then there are the many occasions you tried to steal Tilly away from me, and then discarded her like a cheap streetwalker when she fell pregnant."

"Ah, Stan told you I borrowed money from him, I suppose…"

"Pregnant with my son," I went on.

"Yours?" Chaplin's eyebrows shot up.

"That's right."

"Are you sure?" he said slyly.

"Quite certain, thank you. Then let us not forget the times you hindered Stan, especially after you saw how funny he was when he took your place in New York that time."

"Hindered Stan?" Charlie feigned ignorance.

"Yes, you led him to believe you would help him into movies, which was just a ruse to stymie him."

"I did try to bring some people to your show, really I did," Charlie said. "It just wasn't possible in the time…"

"Yeah, yeah," I said impatiently. "And finally we come to your attempt to have me arrested, after Syd spotted me in Jacksonville."

"Arrested for shooting someone dressed up as me, you mean? You can hardly be surprised that Syd noticed that. That sort of thing does tend to make a man anxious, if you like. But he didn't tell me until after he'd done it." Charlie's eyes flicked to the door then, wondering how this conversation might end.

"And not only that, you ensured that the whole movie business in Jacksonville was destroyed, by leading that bumptious twit Bowden a merry dance."

483

"Oh, we never had any intention of moving there, we only said we might as a ploy to get more money out of First National."

He was being infuriatingly reasonable, just as he was when I was about to give him my shits-for-a-shit tobacco tin leaving present back in Kansas City. I almost wavered, but the wind was in my sails now.

"Well, I don't know that that is entirely honest, I can't really tell, but I have to tell you that I have not been completely candid with you either."

Chaplin sat silently, regarding me with his violet eyes, his nervousness betrayed by his eloquent body, one finger tapping out a rat-a-tat rhythm on his rickety writing table.

"You see, while I am engaged in government business, the department I am engaged by is principally interested in uncovering proof that you have shirked your responsibility with respect to the war effort."

"Oh, not this white feather nonsense!" Chaplin expostulated. "I have a contract which explicitly forbids me..."

"That contract would not be sufficient to exempt you from active service," I said. "It only muddies the water. To get out of the army, you would need a letter like this one."

I pulled the Binks letter from my jacket pocket, opened it out, and turned it to face him. Chaplin looked at it coldly, trying to remain calm.

"Where did you get that? How... oh, the day the offices were unlocked... Well, there's nothing untoward about that."

"What if you were required to produce this Binks?" I said. "This Dr Archibald Binks with his Fred Karno name? He doesn't seem to work at the hospital named here."

"Oh? Has he moved on?"

"If he has, and you can track him down, perhaps he will be

able to explain why his signature so closely resembles that of your brother Sydney."

Chaplin's face hardened. "What do you want?"

"What do I want? Do you propose to buy your way out of this little spot of bother? What would be an appropriate amount, do you suppose, for allowing your glittering career to continue without making you into a figure of contempt and derision the world over? How much would you be willing to pay to keep your business manager out of jail for fraudulent misrepresentation?"

"I don't know," Chaplin said, his voice flat. "Why don't you tell me?"

"It doesn't matter, though, does it, because whatever amount you stumped up to get past this, you would be able to get from your next contract in any case."

Chaplin sat very still.

"No, that's not going to wash, I'm afraid. Not because I don't want or need your money, but because when I do what I have to do next, it can't be for money."

Chaplin frowned slightly, puzzled.

"I was within an ace of doing it, you know?" I said. "The cable office was shut or I would have."

"Would have what?"

"Cabled a message to the man who desperately wants this letter, desperately wants to bring you down, to see you ruined. But then I met Freddie and Ralph, and they told me how much your work, your presence, your films have meant to the men who *have* stepped forward to serve their country."

"Unlike you yourself, of course," he sneered.

"That's true," I said, with a grin. "I have taken advantage of the accident of being over here when the whole brouhaha began, as many have, which is why I could not in all conscience look

485

a soldier in the eye if I were to be responsible for depriving the world of... well, of you."

"What do you mean?"

"Freddie and Ralph came all this way to thank you for making that hell on Earth just a little more tolerable. That means something, doesn't it? Even though I know you have only been serving yourself, your own vanity, your own legend, and you don't have a selfless bone in your body. Nonetheless it means something to people who have given more than I can begin to comprehend, something important. So, much as I wanted to do it, I couldn't send that wire."

"I see."

"I sent a different one, saying that I had found nothing, and there was nothing to find."

Chaplin nodded slowly.

"But before I go, I wanted you to know that everything you have, everything you retain, all this, all your future successes, everything you achieve from now on, you owe it all to me."

"Aha."

"And in order that my sacrifice – the sacrifice of my own revenge, that is – should not be in vain, I have some advice for you."

"Well, I'm sure I am all ears," Chaplin said, actually brightening a little now that he sensed he was going to get away with it.

"First of all, there is a man out there, a powerful young man, the man who sent me after you. His name..." I checked the letter of authority that I had been given, just to be sure, "...is John Edgar Hoover[16], and he means to shame you as a slacker, to make an example of you, because you are the most famous man in the world and you have not signed up to fight for his country. You need to do whatever you can to forestall him, so do the Liberty

486

Bond drives, make time, carve the space in your schedule to travel the country. Not for me, I don't actually give a damn, but for yourself. Make a film about the war, why don't you? Secondly, get a proper doctor to certify you properly unfit to fight, not this arrogant nonsense!" I flapped the Binks letter at him. "However did you think this would stand?"

"Syd..."

"Syd is an idiot. And lastly, do this for me. Leave Stan alone. Don't say you'll help him, don't take him under your wing, just let him be. He'll be better off standing on his own two feet without your poisonous presence. And one day, who knows, with a fair crack at it, maybe he'll even be as famous and well-loved as you inexplicably are."

Chaplin chuckled mirthlessly at that. "What will you do?"

"Oh, I'll find somewhere to hole up. It took them long enough to find me last time."

"Good luck. I appreciate..."

"I'm not doing it for you," I snapped. "A friend once did me a good turn, and all he asked for as payback was that if, one day I found myself in a position to help someone less fortunate than myself, I should do it. I can hardly conceive of more deserving cases than the men at the Front, can you? I'm doing it for Freddie and Ralph and all the other lads like them. Your work has a powerful effect on morale, apparently – God knows I can't see it myself, it just looks like arse-kicking to me – but according to them, if it was suddenly taken away we might actually lose the damn'd war."

At the door I turned back to look at him, and he was still sitting there, digesting things. Thinking, no doubt, of the great responsibility he had just learned that he bore, which wasn't going to help with his perfectionism one bit.

"Oh," I said, "and if you find yourself needing a new writing desk in the near future, I should send the bill to Mr Thomas Meighan."

"What?! What did you say?!"

Minutes later I was striding out of the Lone Star Studios with my bag in hand, never to return. I smiled to myself as I remembered Chaplin's pop-eyed reaction to my last rejoinder...

And then everything went bright.

And suddenly black, black as the deepest pit of Hell.

53
SHOULDER ARMS

"**FRITZ** is coming!" the sergeant major shouted. "This is his big push! He means to drive right through us and cut us off from the Channel, and wrap this whole bloody war up before the Americans get here! Well, we're not going to let him, are we?"

"No sir."

"I can't hear you!"

"*No sir!*"

"You blokes are going in to relieve Company D, and they've taken a bit of a beating over the last few days. Fritz has been pretty lively, with his whizz-bangs and his footballs, and we've got a real job on our hands holding this part of the line. But if we break, God help us all."

I knew better than to look around to see how my fellow Tommies were taking this, but I could tell that the atmosphere was tense, very tense, and most of the men in the barn were clenching their backsides, as I was.

I had arrived in France two months before, still reeling from the abrupt end of my American sojourn.

The moment I stepped outside the Lone Star Studios onto Lilian Avenue I was jumped, sandbagged (or possibly cold-cocked or even blackjacked) and thrown into the back of a darkened delivery van of some sort. I didn't know too much about things then, but as my journey continued by train back across the continent to the East Coast, my wits gradually cleared. I was accompanied by two brawny sons of toil in dark suits, neither of whom were particularly chatty, but I confirmed by inches over the next few days that they were underlings of friend Hoover.

Clearly John was deeply disappointed by my efforts on his behalf, and was making good on his promise to evict me from the Land of the Free, for which it seemed I no longer qualified.

I was kept under very close arrest as I was led onto a ship at the docks in New York, and I spent the entire crossing locked in a small cabin, the door of which only ever opened to admit an orderly with my meals on a tray, or else the same guy coming back for the tray later. I was not even permitted to walk on the deck, which seemed a bit much. After all, I could hardly have made a run for it, could I?

I occupied my time, roughly half and half, with fretting about submarines and making plans to bolt as soon as we docked in Southampton, but in the event, the gangway was no sooner in place than two big military police redcaps from the Black Watch – enormous actually, and wearing kilts, which somehow made them even more terrifying – were stomping aboard in double quick time to take charge of me.

I'm not sure how Hoover achieved all this, but clearly he was a resourceful and influential young man. Before I knew what was what, I was enlisted in the 9th battalion of the Royal Sussex,

490

which mysteriously seemed to be stocked mainly with Lancastrians from Burnley and Colne, and was dispatched to a training camp in Surrey. No point running away by then – I'd have been shot for desertion.

Once I had learned to tell one end of a rifle from the other, how to stick a bayonet into a scarecrow, and how to get a fitful night's sleep in a bell tent, it was straight to France, to the town of Béthune, some fifty-odd miles from Calais.

After some of the ruined villages we'd passed through on the long slow truck ride down, Béthune seemed almost miraculously unscathed as we tramped the last few miles in the hot sun with heavy packs on our backs.

The town was only six miles or so from the front trenches as the crow flies, if any crow should care to risk it. And yet the shops were doing a roaring trade – chemists offering auto-strop razors, stationers tempting us with 'Tommies' Writing Pads', and tailors flaunting new British officers' uniforms in their show windows, not to mention a tea shop serving English tea and scones that looked as though it had been transported brick by brick from the sea front at Eastbourne.

We marched through the town towards the sound of the artillery, unsure whether it was ours or theirs. As we passed along the main street of what had once been a village, a shell exploded some thirty yards ahead. All of us dived for the side of the road, throwing ourselves flat, but when we ventured a peek, we saw the local women standing in their doorways, remarkably unimpressed, and children playing in the street, and we shamefacedly brushed ourselves down and carried on.

Our billet was a farm on the way from the town to the lines. Thirty men kipped in a big barn, while our officers got to sleep in the main farm building, which was still intact, although the

491

sandbags where the windows once were suggested it was not altogether invulnerable. Turkeys, chickens, dogs, a donkey and two
goats kept us company, and to a man we were thinking 'This isn't
too bad!', especially when we were greeted with a free issue of
Glory Boys cigarettes, two packets each.

The first days were taken up with work parties, always work
parties. We would climb onto a truck marked with some mysterious painted insignia – a red shell, a green shamrock – and drive
to a bombed-out village, where we would scavenge sandbags full
of bricks which would be used to build shelters for horses or
some such. Our officers, supervising us, were difficult to take
seriously – everything seemed to be either a 'Good show!' or a
'Bad show!'

When work was done for the day, however, we would be
allowed to stroll up the chalk downs behind for a smoke, and if
you could ignore the constant sound of the guns, which of course
you couldn't, you might have been on holiday. We laid on our
backs in the late sunshine and watched the strange black crosses
in the sky, the aircraft, the Fokkers of the Luftstreitkräfte and our
Sopwith Camels. They didn't look like the 'flying death' of that
aviator Glenn Martin's imagination, swinging lazily around one
another, with occasional puffs of smoke from ground artillery
bursting around them. I think once I even saw the *dreidecker* of
the notorious Red Baron heading towards Amiens.

Our battalion was quickly in the firing line, which meant
we spent life in a constant alternation between our billets and
the trenches, six days on the farm and then four days in. These
trenches were, naturally, running parallel to the German lines
just a hundred yards or so away. There was a front trench, and
behind that support trenches, all linked by communication
trenches running perpendicular. The trenches were originally

dug by the French, but there had been so much patching up and repair work done I doubt any of those Frenchies would have recognised them, if any were still with us.

To help us find our way around, these trenches were given names such as Old Kent Road, Watling Street, Trafalgar Square – an open command area – Canterbury Avenue, Rue Albert – a hangover from the original French occupants – and then, when imagination or nostalgia failed completely, 76 Street, 78 Street. They should have called one the Thames, the amount of water there was in it, splashing over the duckboards.

We quickly learned the way of life in the trenches, perching on the firestep waiting for something to happen, passing awkwardly in the cramped and crowded passageways like straphangers on the Tube. We learned never to march around a corner without checking first. One time I blithely headed into a communication trench only to find that a rocket grenade had brought down the front parapet of the trench in front of me and I was staring straight at the enemy across a rather narrow stretch of No-Man's Land. Fritz was every bit as startled as I was, so I managed to scuttle back the way I had come before he slung his rifle, thankfully.

We learned that a sign reading 'This Trench Patrolled Only' meant that a Boche mine was suspected in the area, and we patrolled it damn'd quickly, I can tell you. Which reminds me, if you came around a corner and saw a man walking towards you, white from head to foot with a canary in a cage held before him at arm's length, this was not a ghost, it was a miner fresh from digging a chamber out of the local chalky ground.

Once darkness fell, the work parties would begin, rebuilding trench walls and firesteps that had been damaged, replacing the duckboards, or filling sandbags with white chalky soil from the miners' dumps. One strange duty required a couple of us to crouch on the firestep and hold dummy heads – such as the one I'd made of my own head when performing *The Rum 'Uns from Rome* with Stan, in another life, it felt like – up above the parapet to try and tempt a German sniper to reveal himself. One mate of mine, Bob Young, held his too high and lost a finger. He was elated at first, thinking he'd be sent home, but unfortunately for him it wasn't his trigger finger.

There wasn't much sleep to be had in the front line. There would be the occasional lull, but then a barrage would begin again from one side or the other. You had to be up at 4am to clean your rifle for a 5am rifle inspection, and by 5.05 there would be mud all over it again.

And the constant threat of sudden death kept you tightly strung, like the top string of a fiddle, always ready for a high-pitched scream. I saw a man in my company peer over the top and fall back with a bullet hole on his forehead. I saw another vaporised by a whizz-bang, while the bloke next to him stared amazed in mid-sentence, completely unhurt. Most bizarrely of all, I saw a Sergeant Major sitting by a tent, well back from the front, a pipe in his mouth still smouldering, even though he was quite dead. There was not a mark on him, but a shell had passed so closely overhead that the sudden vacuum caused by its passage had quite suffocated him where he sat.

After four days of sleepless tension, we would be rotated out again and return to our billets and work parties again, sometimes even able to stroll into town for an omelette and a beer at an estaminet as if nothing were going on at all – if only you could ignore the noise of those damn'd guns.

So that's how I ended up in that barn having the wind put up me by a burly sergeant major. We'd all heard the fighting to the North up towards Hazebrouck over the previous few days, the sound of the big German guns getting closer and closer, and like all my comrades I was seriously worried that this might just be, well, *it*.

I reckoned, though, without Charlie Chaplin, who was about to find one more way to stick his oar into my business.

Just then, a distracted-looking gent with three pips on the shoulder of his uniform popped halfway in at the door and said:

"I say. Any of you fellows know how to drive an automobile?"

Now I was new to trench warfare, but even I knew that any driving that needed doing was going to be behind the lines and not up at the sharp end where the shells and bullets were flying around, and in a split second my brain, operating at a heightened level of self-preservation, had calculated that this was definitely something I should be volunteering for.

"Yes sir," I said, snapping to attention.

"Name?"

"Dandoe, sir."

"All right Dandoe, you're with me. Thank you Sar'nt Major, carry on."

"Sir."

I had, of course, only once been behind the wheel of a vehicle, when Toraichi Kono was letting me drive Chaplin's limousine for fun, and I was going to need some good fortune to pass myself off as a driver of any kind. I followed the captain outside, and tried to look confident as he climbed into the back of a mud-spattered staff car. I got in the front passenger seat, which was a good start. The steering wheel, alarmingly, was on the right side where Toraichi's had been on the left, so everything

495

was reversed. I quickly shuffled myself across, as though this was how I always entered a motor car that I was about to drive.

Luckily it had the same self-starter as Chaplin's motor car, and so I got the engine going, which was when I discovered that the pedals were not reversed but were actually the same way round as on my previous solitary driving adventure. I stalled the thing, apologised, re-started, stalled, apologised, and then bumped off down the lane with the merest hint of an exasperated tut from my passenger. Also fortunately, we bumped past a sign reading 'LORRIES 6MPH' – the road was so pitted one could hardly have gone much faster in any case. The slow traffic meant I barely had to shift gears at all – not one of my special skills – and before long I was reasonably confident that I could handle the machine well enough.

My passenger, Captain Davies his name was, stared out of the window with his chin on his fist, frowning and distracted. I decided that it would be good to make myself useful to him, if only to avoid being sent back into the front line of trenches with the Germans about to make a big push, so I tried to engage him in cheery conversation.

"Cheer up, sir," I said. "It might never 'appen."

"It has 'appened, Dandoe," the captain said glumly.

"Why, sir, what's the matter?"

"I have been given an impossible task, that's what."

"Can I 'elp, sir?" I felt a slight Cockney accent gave me a more optimistic tone, so I stuck with it.

"I have to arrange a divisional concert," the captain explained. "But it must not be just any old shindig, with chaps volunteering to play the accordion and such. It must be a proper profession-al-looking show. It seems Harry Lauder is coming to Artois and Picardy to play a series of concerts for the troops, bringing his own mini-piano to play, and Command wish me to produce from thin air, right here in France if you please, a supporting bill of the highest possible calibre. I tell you frankly I have no idea where to begin. I suppose I could try and put the word out, but of course then every Tom, Dick and Harry will step forward claiming to be this or that, and I shall have absolutely no way of knowing who will do and who is merely trying to get out of the fighting."

My cogs were whirring at this, naturally. "I... have some experience in this area, sir," I said.

"Have you?" Davies said wearily. "Have you *really*?"

"I have, sir. I worked for Fred Karno for many years, performing with..." and I gulped down my own unwillingness to play this card, but needs must, "Charlie Chaplin, among others."

"You know Charlie Chaplin?"

"I do, sir. As a matter of fact I was at his studios in Los Angeles only a few months ago."

"Really?" Captain Davies sat forward on the back seat, intrigued. "What's he like?"

"What's he *like*?" I snorted.

"What's he like... *Sir*," Davies insisted.

"Sorry, sir. Charlie is... a complicated fellow."

"But you know him well?"

"I do, sir."

"So could you, if the need arose... *do* Charlie Chaplin? Impersonate him, I mean?"

Why not, I thought. He's been impersonating *me* for years. But I said: "I think so, yes, sir."

"Well, this is most fortuitous. You know Mr Lauder is a good friend of Chaplin's?"

"I am not surprised, sir."

"Marvellous. Marvellous! Yes, I think this is most handy.

All right, from now on, Dandoe, you are not merely my driver – watch that tree, there!" – I was not, it appeared, sufficiently skilled to steer the vehicle and receive surprising developments via the rear view mirror at the same time – "You are also my assistant. Understood?"

"Sir, yes sir."

———

I asked around the soup kitchen and the estaminets, and one old trouper led me to the rumour of another, and another, until gradually I built up a not inconsiderable bill. I found a notable solo act renowned on both sides of the Atlantic manning an observation 'sausage' high above the trenches, looking out for Fokkers. I found a small, but perfectly-formed male voice choir amongst the lads of the Welsh regiment, just longing for a chance to sing for an audience. I even found a couple of ex-Karnos kicking their heels not far from where I was billeted, Harry Bunn and Bobby Sayers, who were delighted to get a pass out of sandbag duty. With them, I knocked together a sketch with a military setting that had, I freely admit, some strong similarities to *The Nutty Burglars*, except that now I was the one playing the Chaplin part.

In the meantime, Company C had been rotated into the front trenches and were getting, as promised, a fearful battering. I tried not to think about it, or feel guilty for having been handed a pass of my own. Instead I threw myself into arranging the divisional concert, taking responsibility for all the staging and arranging the few portable lights I was able to commandeer, leaving Captain Davies to sit at the back of the large hall, puffing away at a pipeful of Golden Flake with a contented half-smile, waiting to take all the credit from the up-aboves.

On the day the great Harry Lauder arrived in Béthune, Davies greeted him officially, but it was I who arranged for his mini-piano to be installed on the stage, and who talked him through the evening ahead. He looked tired, this wiry little Scot, but his eyes were bright and he was a man on a mission. He had played many concerts on his trip through Picardy, sometimes as many as six a day, and often without any support, so he smiled gratefully when I told him there were other acts to help share the burden on this particular occasion.

Lauder had thrown himself into the war effort at home, devising a West End show with a cast of 300 positively demanding that the male members of the audience should leave the theatre and immeidately join the fight for King and country. He established Harry Lauder's Million Pound Fund to help the war injured, and his efforts had redoubled when his only son, a captain, was killed at the Somme. The concert tour that he was embarked upon behind the lines had taken the shape of a pilgrimage to visit his son's grave at the military cemetery in Pozières, and he was now working his way back to Calais, one army camp at a time.

I brought him an enamel mug of tea, and some Champion for his pipe, and we sat together on a low wall out the back of the hall. He nodded at my Charlie-in-the-army costume, and said:

"I see young Chaplin has stirred himsel' at last."

"I beg your pardon, sir?"

"He's finally seen the light, and started contributin' to the effort."

"Has he now?"

"Aye, here look..." Lauder reached into his knapsack and pulled out a Paris edition of the *Daily Mail* to point out a piece. The article was grudging, as Northcliffe's enmity for my erstwhile colleague still burned brightly, but it described Charlie's rousing appearances at Liberty Bond drives in many major American cities. One time he stood on the shoulders of Douglas Fairbanks to deliver an impassioned speech, and in Philadelphia he became so enthused that he fell clean off the stage into the lap of the Secretary for War, a Mr Franklin Roosevelt. Well, well, how about that, I thought.

I handed the paper back to Lauder. "I was very sorry to hear of your loss," I said.

A shadow crossed the great man's features, and he suddenly looked older than his forty-seven years.

"A terrible thing to lose a son," he said softly. "Do ye have bairns y'rself?"

"A son," I said. "I haven't seen him for a long while."

Lauder nodded. "I laid down on his grave," he said. "That cold brown mound, and I thought of all that he had been, and all that he had meant to me. I remembered that wee laddie beginning to run around and talk to us, and thought of the friends we had been, he and I. Such chums we were, always!"

He paused with a wan smile as the memories flooded over him, and I waited.

"And as I lay there, I tell ye, all I wanted was to reach my arms down, down into that dark grave, and clasp my boy tightly to my breast, and kiss him. And I wanted to thank him for what he had done for his country, and his mother, and for me."

I had a lump in my throat at that, and was overcome with a desperate desire to see my own son again. Three years it had been and more.

The soldiers arrived in motorbuses and packed the hall out three times that day. Each time Harry Lauder packed his grief away and bounced onto the stage with his kilt and his tam o'shanter and his cromach to sing his many well-known favourites – *I Love a Lassie, Roamin' in the Gloamin'* – and songs that had become standards during the war such as *Pack Up Your Troubles in Your Old Kit Bag.*

My turn as Chaplin was very well-received, if I say so myself. In adapting our old sketch I had made the Chaplin character into a private, as he might have appeared had he ever signed up, with a too-small tunic, baggy trousers, and an incongruous derby hat that I had found on the head of a local café owner some days earlier, while the haul of swag he hoped to sneak off with was not jewellery but a stack of tins of bully beef.

I got a great cheer as soon as I appeared, which was *his* cheer, of course, but some of the laughs I got were mine, and it felt good to be onstage in front of a packed hall once again, exercising The Power.

During our third and last house, I was just getting into my stride, that million-dollar walk I had first devised for my Stowaway turn, when I heard a stir in the audience, a disturbance in my hold over them.

I glanced out over the officers with their polished boots in the front rows of seats to the benches beyond. Someone was standing up, a nurse, a VAD, with the distinctive white nun-style headdress over a blue dress, and a red cross on her white apron. She stood staring right at me, her mouth open with disbelief.

I stopped in mid-step and peered right back at her. What was the matter, I wondered? The lights were right in my eyes, as I'd had to mount them on stands at the back of the hall rather than drilling into the beams overhead, out of respect to the local residents. I shielded my eyes with my hand, but the nurse's face was in shadow.

She reached up and slowly removed the headdress, then fiddled behind her head, suddenly releasing her hair to cascade down onto her shoulders, a shining waterfall of backlit golden ringlets that stopped my heart.

All around her, men began to murmur, and some whistles echoed around the hall, but I barely heard them. Because I knew, just as well as I knew anything, who this was, who was standing before me.

It was like a miracle.

Tilly.

I forgot what I was supposed to be doing then, it didn't matter, didn't matter at all. All that mattered was getting to her. I jumped down from the stage, causing Captain Davies to hurriedly withdraw his shiny toecaps, and I pushed and stumbled on through the tangled undergrowth of khaki knees and puttees towards her. There was a cacophony of hoots and whistling, cheering and shouting from all quarters as we met, and she was reaching, fumbling for something at her neck. She winkled a small silver chain out from beneath her nurse's uniform and showed me something there on the palm of her hand right under her chin.

A ring, a silver ring, with the head of Mr Punch.

The ring I had given her when I asked her to be my wife.

I held it in my fingertips and it was as warm as her heart. Then I took her in my arms and kissed her.

"Hoo hoo! Go on, Charlie!" came the cries from all around us.

When we finally broke off, she touched my face with her fingers, wonderingly.

"It is you, isn't it?"

For reply I kissed her again, and we held one another so tightly

I feared I might hurt her. The hooting and whistling went on, but I sensed there was some impatience creeping into it, just an undertone, and maybe a little jealousy too.

"The show must go on," I said, softly.

"Go on," she said. "I'm not going anywhere."

EPILOGUE

SHORTLY after that memorable evening the German Spring Offensive reached Béthune, which was pretty much flattened by their artillery. Fortunately I had moved on by that time, as Harry Lauder was so taken with my Chaplin routine that he took me with him all the way to Calais, and back to England too. It shouldn't really have been possible, but such was Lauder's superhuman contribution to the war effort that the army would refuse him nothing.

Fortunately, too, the 33rd Casualty Clearing Station withdrew from Béthune ahead of the worst of the shelling, and Tilly found herself back in England shortly after that.

Such a reunion we had then, and I finally saw again my little lad, my Wallace, five years old now and bright as a button. I had been such a small part of his young life, and it was hardly surprising that he looked a little bewildered at the hugs he was getting from the strange man who had come to call.

Then I had a moment's inspiration, and said: "Who wants a chin pie?" and from somewhere in the recesses of his young memory he suddenly recalled the game he had once loved so much and ran away screaming in delighted terror.

It seemed the Lovat Highlander, McTavish, was no longer on the scene, indeed Tilly told me she'd broken with him as soon as they returned from Cambridge to Skegness, the very day she'd learned that I had survived the *Lusitania* disaster. He sounded a decent enough sort, and had understood. The peculiar tone of her letter to me she explained later. She had been feeling such guilt for a year and a half thinking that I had perished while travelling to reach her that she wanted to be sure to give me no encouragement to try again.

I supposed that I could hardly have devised a more complete demonstration of my having outgrown my rivalry with Chaplin than allowing him to continue unmolested whilst I myself was carted off to the Western Front, but such was the unfettered joy of our reunion that Tilly never even mentioned that concern again.

By the time of the Armistice, the three of us had set up house in London, close to Elephant and Castle, and had begun to forge ourselves a new career back in the halls. Wallace was a stage-struck little imp, and it wasn't long before we were billed as 'The Dandoes, featuring Little Dandoe'.

Fatherhood and the war combined to put things into a different perspective for me. How could I have let Chaplin's success get to me so much?

I read of his unhappy marital adventures with much younger women, looked over at Tilly, and thought there was no way I would ever swap my life for his.

Ultimately I came to view that whole period with a kind of mellow detachment, and felt sure that that near-insanity, that Chaplinoia, was a thing of the past.

Mind you, if Stan and Babe were ever to become massively successful, then I just might lose it altogether...

ENDNOTES

1   Britannia Pier, Great Yarmouth, was destroyed by fire in 1914. This was allegedly started by suffragettes, who had been refused permission to hold a meeting there. It was rebuilt within three months.

2   Glenn Martin was an aviation pioneer who not only held records for over-water flight, but also starred (as a dashing aviator) in *A Girl of Yesterday* opposite Mary Pickford. His company built bombers for the military in both world wars.

3   Later in his film career Ben Turpin would introduce himself thus: "I'm Ben Turpin, I make three thousand dollars a week."

4   Jess Robbins, producer of Chaplin's first Essanay film, was subsequently the first director to direct Stan Laurel and Oliver Hardy in the same picture – *Lucky Dog* (1921)

5   This seemed to be nothing more or less than a massacre of innocents, and the presence of an American citizen amongst the casualties led to loud calls for America to join the war at once. The outrage only subsided a little when it emerged that

the U-boat captain had given the captain of the *Falaba* time to offload his passengers, but instead he had radioed his position to a nearby warship. And then when the submarine fired, the destructive effect of its torpedo was exacerbated by thirteen tons of contraband high explosives in the *Falaba*'s hold.

6   Leslie Hope, the twelve year-old winner of the Luna Park Chaplin lookalike contest, would later find fame as a comedian after changing his first name to Bob.

7   Oliver Hardy would sing this 1908 song in the 1939 Laurel and Hardy film *Flying Deuces*, while Stan danced.

8   The Easter Rising of 1916 was an armed insurrection launched by Irish republicans to end British rule and establish an independent Irish Republic. It lasted for six days before it was suppressed by the British Army, with most of its leaders executed after courts martial.

9   The famous 'Skegness is so Bracing!' poster was commissioned by the Great Northern Railway to advertise excursions in 1908.

10   Lonesome Luke was the creation of comedian Harold Lloyd. In 1916 he released 34 Lonesome Luke films, while Chaplin managed just eight that year.

11   The Bureau of Investigation was founded in 1908, and became the F.B.I. in 1935.

12   *Over There* was a hugely popular song with military and public alike. The chorus went as follows:

Over there, over there,
Send the word, send the word over there
That the Yanks are coming, the Yanks are coming
The drums rum-tumming everywhere.
So prepare, say a prayer,
Send the word, send the word to beware -
We'll be over, we're coming over,
And we won't come back till it's over, over there.

The song was again ubiquitous during the Second World War, which the United States similarly entered late and arguably decisively on the side of the Allies. In recent times the tune has been used by GoCompare for those adverts with the curly-moustachioed tenor, and by Donald Trump during his 2016 presidential campaign.

13 Thomas Meighan was a dashing leading actor of the silent era, b.1879. His best years were still to come, in the nine-teen-twenties.

14 The Kaspare Cohn hospital was a precursor of the now-celebrated Cedars-Sinai Medical Centre, now on a different site.

15 Several versions of this were sung by soldiers in the trenches, usually to the tune of the hymn *The Church's One Foundation*.

16 J .Edgar Hoover went on to become the most famous Director of the F.B.I. During the First World War he worked for the Justice Department in the War Emergency Division, with a wide-ranging brief and the authority to arrest and jail

disloyal foreigners without trial. In the nineteen-fifties Hoover was instrumental in revoking Chaplin's re-entry visa because of his suspected Communist sympathies, and Chaplin returned to America only once thereafter, to receive his honorary Oscar in 1972.

ACKNOWLEDGEMENTS

I would especially like to thank Ben Yarde-Buller of Old Street for taking a punt, and for his enthusiastic support and insightful input over the whole Arthur Dandoe project.

I would also like to thank Matt Baylis for some great editing and many good suggestions, and James Nunn for the splendid covers he has contributed.

Thanks to those descendants of the real Arthur Dandoe who got in touch both before and after the first and second books came out, and furnished interesting titbits from their families' collective memories – June Russell, Sandra Stickler and Linda Barber. With this third volume I have deviated further than ever from the real Arthur's story, but I hope they like the adventure I have given him.

Also thanks to Charles Walker, Jo Unwin, Rob Dinsdale, Jo Brand, David Baddiel, Mark Billingham and David Tyler.

And lastly my appreciation to Peter, John and Michael for being prepared to live on gruel, bread and water while I get all this out of my system, and to Susan without whom neither this book, the ones that preceded it, nor Peter, John and Michael would have been possible.